THE DEAD LINE

HOLLY WATT

RAVEN BOOKS
LONDON • OXFORD • NEW YORK • NEW DELHI • SYDNEY

RAVEN BOOKS
Bloomsbury Publishing Plc
50 Bedford Square, London, WC1B 3DP, UK

BLOOMSBURY, RAVEN BOOKS and the Raven Books logo are trademarks of Bloomsbury Publishing Plc

First published in Great Britain 2020

A catalogue record for this book is available from the British Library

ISBN: HB: 978-1-5266-0294-7; TPB: 978-1-5266-0293-0; eBook: 978-1-5266-0291-6

2 4 6 8 10 9 7 5 3 1

Typeset by Integra Software Services Pvt. Ltd.
Printed and bound in Great Britain by CPI Group (UK) Ltd, Croydon CR0 4YY

To Jonny

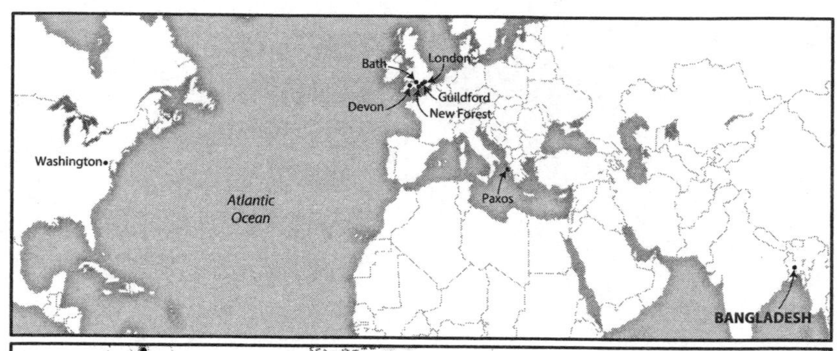
Bath
London
Devon
Guildford
New Forest
Washington
Atlantic Ocean
Paxos
BANGLADESH

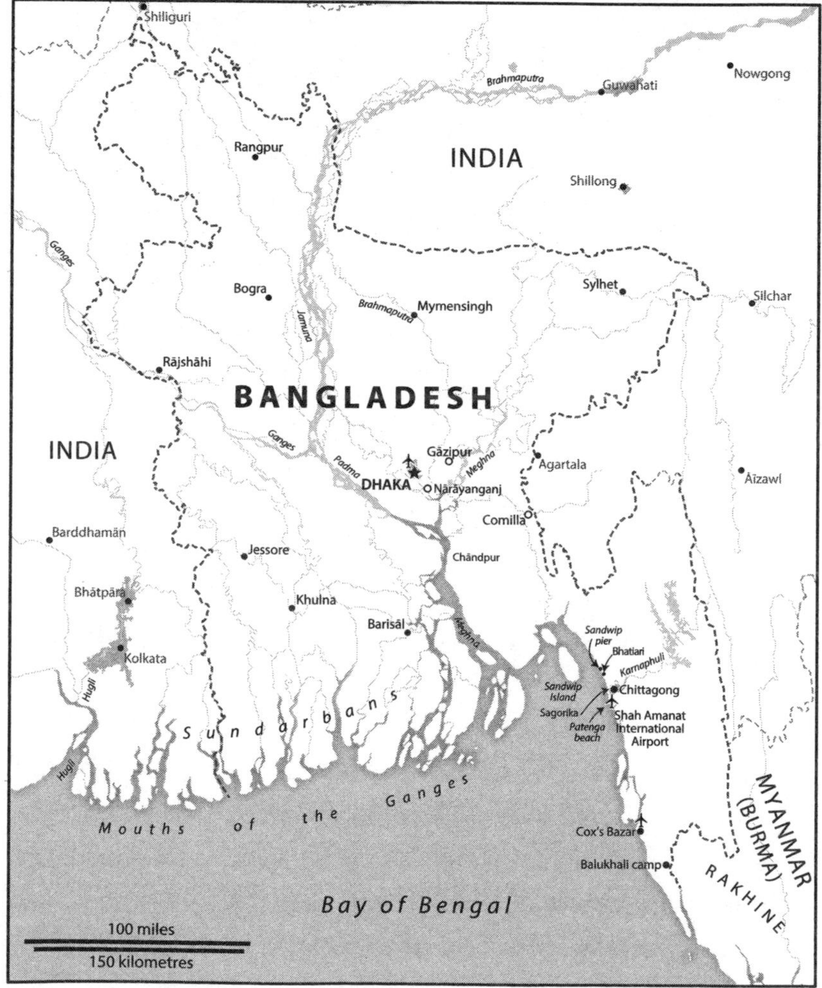
Shiliguri
Brahmaputra
Guwahati
Nowgong
Rangpur
INDIA
Shillong
Ganges
Sylhet
Silchar
Bogra
Jamuna
Brahmaputra
Mymensingh
Rājshāhi
BANGLADESH
Ganges
Gāzipur
Meghna
Agartala
Āīzawl
INDIA
Padma
DHAKA
Nārāyanganj
Comilla
Barddhamān
Jessore
Chāndpur
Bhātpāra
Khulna
Barisāl
Meghna
Sandwip pier
Bhatiari
Kolkata
Karnaphuli
Sandwip Island
Chittagong
Hugli
Sagorika
Shah Amanat International Airport
Patenga beach
Sundarbans
Hugli
Ganges
Mouths of the
MYANMAR (BURMA)
Cox's Bazar
Baluskhali camp
RAKHINE
Bay of Bengal
100 miles
150 kilometres

1

The junior reporter was losing the battle with the news editor.

'But Ross,' Tillie was shouting as Casey walked past the newsdesk, 'it might actually kill you.'

A couple of desks away, the home affairs editor looked up. 'How?' he asked hopefully.

'You know how Ross takes his coffee?' Tillie was holding the newsdesk phone, finger on the mute button.

'Half and half.' Casey paused. 'Granules and hot water. It'll kill him one day.'

'With any luck' – a mutter from the home affairs editor.

Ross was ignoring them all, head down over his newslist.

'Ross's wife is on the line.' Tillie turned to Casey.

'A brave woman,' the home affairs editor said thoughtfully.

'I do not,' Ross snarled, 'have time to speak to anyone right now.'

'Mrs Warman says' – unconsciously, Tillie put on a perfect imitation of Ross's wife – '"I put descaler in the kettle overnight, Tillie, and he's boiled it up and made coffee this morning. I think he might actually die."'

'Didn't he notice when he was drinking it?'

'Apparently, no.'

'Will the descaler finish him off altogether?' Casey asked. She couldn't remember the home affairs editor smiling before.

'I had to look it up,' said Tillie. 'Quite possibly, yes. I've told Ross he has to go to A&E.'

'Ross.' Casey tried to sound firm.

The news editor looked up. 'Listen.' Ross spoke with unusual patience. 'If I'm dead in an hour, I'll go to the doctor.'

Over Ross's head, Casey was distracted by most of the fashion team clattering down the glass staircase in the middle of the *Post*'s open-plan office. For a moment, they reminded Casey of racehorses – long legs, glossy manes, jewel silks.

Casey sighed at her jeans. But that might mean …

She left Ross and Tillie to it and headed up the stairs.

'Hello, Casey.' Cressida, the fashion editor, blocked her path, sunny and knowing all at once. 'What are you after?'

Casey's eyes flickered. 'I saw a navy top in the fashion spread this morning. It would be perfect for …'

'The Juniper one? No.'

'I just want to borrow it.'

'And put a few holes in it for your secret cameras? Absolutely not.'

Week after week, the fashion team called in outfits from designers, photographed them in unlikely scenarios and couriered them back. Occasionally, Casey, the *Post*'s investigations reporter, diverted them.

'Please.' Casey extended the syllable. 'I have to be a suave businesswoman.'

'And that' – Cressida looked her up and down – 'is going to be quite the stretch, is it?'

'How come you're not out with the rest of your team?' Casey tried distraction. 'I just saw them all leaving.'

'I'm following them. Running late. We're off to do a feature on that big new shopping centre out in west London. Each member of the team is trying to track down a certain look in . . . Oh,' Cressida flicked her hand. 'I know you're not really interested, Casey. Just take the wretched top.'

A quick smile. 'You're a star.'

'I'll tell Juniper that I must be buried in it, or something.' Cressida smiled beatifically. 'Now, do bugger off, Casey. I simply must go and shop.'

Casey sauntered back to the little investigations room, chucking the navy top on the sofa and throwing herself into her chair.

'Here.' She passed one coffee to Miranda and another to Hessa, and stared unenthusiastically at her own computer screen. 'Has it ever occurred to you that shopping professionally might be more fun than this?'

'You'd get bored.' Miranda glanced up.

Miranda was Casey's boss, technically, but they had forgotten about that a long time ago.

'Bet I wouldn't.'

Hessa passed Casey some notes. 'I got what you wanted on that Manchester project. And I'll drop that navy top off with Sagah in a bit.'

Sagah – a grumbling genius – would bury an unnoticeable camera in the folds of that beautiful navy top. A tiny microphone would be sewn into place close to the collar.

'Thanks, Hessa,' Casey grinned at her, taking an unenthusiastic sip of her coffee. 'This actually does taste like descaler.'

'What?' Hessa glanced up.

'Nothing.' Casey waved the words away, and they all turned back to their work; three investigative journalists: a quiet conspiracy.

A few years earlier, Miranda had been poached from the *Argus*, the *Post*'s deadly rival.

'You can set up your own team at the *Post*,' Dash, the head of news, had promised. 'Hand-picked. Whoever you want. And we'll give you a free rein on whatever you want to investigate.'

'But I'm in a good place at the *Argus*,' Miranda had said. And she was: running their investigations team with a ruthless efficiency. She had just brought down a cabinet minister, for having both his wife and his mistress on the public payroll. The public was indifferent to the infidelity, but furious about the waste-of-taxpayers'-money. It was the cartoonists who destroyed him, in the end.

'We'll make you even better, here.'

Miranda caught sight of Casey the first day she arrived in the post. The young reporter was swearing fluently as she rushed to print out Ross's story list for conference. A flame of energy, grey eyes missing nothing. Casey had glanced across at Miranda, just for a second, scepticism in every line.

But Casey had pounced on Dash later, as he was showing Miranda around the newsroom.

Me. Casey had insisted. *I can do it. Please.*

'And this is Casey.' Dash had waved a careless hand.

'I can be invisible,' Casey said. 'I promise. I can do investigations. I'd be good.'

'You can't cross the room without starting a riot.' Dash was smiling at the junior reporter.

'I could serve you breakfast, and you wouldn't notice' – insisting, half-joking.

'Casey,' the news editor had bawled just then. 'I need that bloody research for PMQs right fucking now.'

And Dash and Miranda had smiled at Casey, and her nerve.

The next morning, Dash had taken Miranda to the Wolseley. Introducing her to the newspaper's owners, over smoked salmon and scrambled eggs. Their new trophy, all polished up.

At the end of the meal, the owners swept off to another meeting. Dash and Miranda had been waiting for the receipt, because journalists always get the receipt.

'Hope you enjoyed your breakfast, sir' – a laugh in the voice.

They'd looked up, startled, and it was Casey, in the black and white Wolseley uniform. With the smart tie, and half the staff grinning across the restaurant.

Afterwards, Miranda had laughed aloud, walking through the early morning, down Piccadilly. And after that, she had believed in her. Put her faith, such as it was, in Casey.

And then a few months ago, Hessa had joined the team. One of the most junior reporters at the *Post*. Shy, at first. But that same determination they both recognised.

Miranda looked round the little room, and smiled.

They worked into the early evening, and finally Miranda looked at her watch.

'I have to leave,' she said, although she often worked until midnight, a modern Cinderella.

'Go home,' said Casey. 'And you too, Hessa. I know you were on an early shift today.'

'A little bit longer. I've just got a couple more things to do.'

‘Fine,’ Casey sighed. ‘I’ll go and get us another coffee.’

‘It’s my turn.’ Hessa made to stand.

‘I need the walk.’

‘How is the Manchester project coming along?’ asked Miranda as she packed up her bag.

‘Slowly,’ said Casey. ‘Not the most exciting to be honest.’

‘Keep plugging at it.’

‘Course.’

Waving at the room, Miranda headed out. A few minutes later, Casey stood, stretched and began to walk across the office. It was mostly empty now, the night news editor alone at his desk. The light on the coffee machine was flashing: empty.

Casey wandered through the doors, down the escalator, past the security barrier: out to the coffee shop, those familiar steps, day after day.

But this time, a surprise.

Cressida, standing in the bright lights of the foyer, hesitating in her high heels. The sleek fashion editor looked oddly unsure of herself, wavering to and fro. In one hand, she was clutching a carrier bag: black with long silk ribbons. When she saw Casey, she made as if to move towards the exit, heels clicking on the grey marble floor.

‘Cressida?’

‘Casey! You’re here …’ Cressida’s voice trailed away to a silence as she jerked to a halt.

‘What’s the matter?’

A hesitation, then Cressida smoothed down her purple silk dress firmly. ‘You’re going to think I’m an idiot.’

‘I won’t.’

‘Promise?’

'Yes.'

Cressida shoved her hand into the carrier bag. She scrabbled for a second, and pulled out a tangle of material. It was a skirt, Casey saw. Scarlet taffeta over layers of ivory tulle, fit for a fantasy ballerina.

'Here.' Cressida held the skirt awkwardly, as if she couldn't stand to touch it.

Casey reached out. She could see something folded among the petticoats: a piece of white silk, with a pattern of pale blue. It was only when Casey looked closely that she saw the fabric was stitched with lines of words.

'What . . .'

'Just take it.'

Cressida almost threw the skirt at Casey, and backed away, her usual glamour cracked like a glass.

The piece of silk was hard to read, some of the embroidery torn into meaningless threads. Casey peered at it, and turned it sideways. Looked closer, held it up to the light.

A jolt.

They take the girls.

Casey bent closer, the entrance hall around her disappearing.

She read it again. *They take . . .*

Part of the embroidery was snarled on a layer of ballet-girl tulle. Slowly, Casey tried to pick it apart without tearing the material.

'I've got to go.' Casey realised Cressida was still standing there, uncertain. 'I'm late. And I've got a lot to do . . .'

'We can talk tomorrow anyway.'

'It was just there, in the middle of the shop.' Cressida sounded shocked. 'In part of Rhapso's diffusion range, right in the middle of that big new shopping centre. I was looking through all the skirts – they've got some really lovely ones at the moment – and I picked up that skirt, and it just . . .'

'It fell out?'

'The piece of silk was stitched into the petticoats very loosely,' said Cressida. 'You wouldn't have seen it unless . . . I was checking the seams' – Cressida, the consummate professional under all the sparkle. 'I've been to hundreds of shops, Casey. Thousands, probably. Tried on a million outfits. You never think . . .'

'Were there any other notes? In any of the other clothes?'

'I don't know.' Cressida sounded hopeless. 'I didn't look. Didn't want to.'

'I'll go and check,' said Casey. 'Now.'

'The shopping centre is open until ten.'

'Thank you for bringing me this, Cressida.'

'I've got to go now,' Cressida said more firmly, tugging her coat around her.

'Sure.'

They said an awkward goodbye. Casey watched Cressida disappear out through the doors, before whirling back to the escalator.

'Where's my coffee?' Mock outrage from Hessa as Casey walked back into their office.

'Hessa, look at this.' Casey gestured her over to her desk. 'Can you read this?'

Hessa leaned over. 'Where did . . .'

'Just read it,' said Casey.

Hessa picked up the skirt, and concentrated on it, her fingers careful, her face taut with concentration.

'*The Rohingya*,' Hessa struggled with the blue embroidered letters. 'They're the refugees in Bangladesh. I don't understand . . .'

'What do you think that bit there says?'

'It's all tangled.'

'I know.'

'It doesn't make sense.'

'Try.'

Hessa peered closer, and Casey saw her flinch.

'It says "factory".' Hessa's voice shook. 'It says they take them to a baby factory.'

The shop's music was a shield of noise, drowning out the scramble of the shopping centre.

'You have a nice evening.' A beaming smile from a beautiful girl handing out diamante-studded baskets at the entrance. A security guard stood vigil.

Rhapso's lightning-flash logo was everywhere. The neon letters shouted on the wall, and the music pounded. Two girls, killing time. Beside them a shop assistant folded jerseys, as women queued up to change.

Hessa and Casey paced through the shop, stroking the silks and the satins and the lace. The changing rooms were hidden behind theatrical red velvet curtains. The shop assistant, spiky hair and ripped jeans, smiled at them indulgently.

'Let me know if you need anything, yeah?'

'Thank you.'

They walked on, then drifted apart.

As Hessa marched down serried ranks of clothes, Casey checked the piles of skirts. Scarlet taffeta, folded fun, nothing else to find in dozens of identical skirts.

Casey began unfolding a different pile of skirts, then shirts, then trousers, then cardigans. A shop assistant followed her, refolding as she went.

'Sorry.'

A snap of gum. 'S'fine.'

Until finally Hessa caught Casey's eye, and Casey headed over to a quiet corner, breath shortening. Hessa was carrying a grey velvet jacket, beautifully cut, and thrust a piece of silk into Casey's hands. 'Look.'

It was the same white silk, the words embroidered in a pale blue thread. Casey turned the piece of material cautiously.

'They take the babies,' she read aloud. 'They take the babies for the women.'

2

'Do you think it's possible?' Miranda was prodding at the red skirt. The three of them were in the little investigations office early the next morning. Casey was sprawled at her desk, chin in her hands. Hessa was leaning against the scuffed cream wall, the shiny black shop bag at her feet.

From some odd sense of propriety, Hessa and Casey had queued up to buy the grey jacket just before Rhapso closed the night before. They had watched like hawks as the assistant folded it into a bag, tying the ribbon with a professional smile.

'The shop assistants would never have noticed a piece of silk among the petticoats on that skirt,' said Casey. 'Or fastened into that velvet sleeve.'

Casey was playing with a little silver bird that hung around her neck. It dangled there to give her something to fidget with.

'But isn't it such a strange way of getting a message out?'

'This sort of thing happened a few years ago.' Hessa was flicking through her notepad. 'There were stories about labels being added into clothes in shops on the high street. Someone inserted a label into a Primark dress in Swansea: "Forced to work exhausting hours." Then there was: "I made this item you are going to buy, but I didn't get paid for it." That label was found in something from Zara. The Swansea labels were a hoax, probably, but people obviously know that it might be a way of getting a message from the factories to London.'

'Isn't it a bit scattergun?' asked Miranda. 'Anyone could have picked up that skirt or that jacket. Or that little piece of silk could have fallen out, and just been swept away. Or it could have been found long before it reached the shopfloor.'

'Sure,' Casey shrugged. 'It's not the most obvious way of doing it. Cressida said the piece of silk in the skirt was very loosely stitched into place. Same for Hessa's jacket. I'd guess that only a customer trying it on would have noticed.'

'So it's a risk,' Miranda went on, 'packing it like that. If that piece of material had been found by the retailer, presumably the jacket and skirt could be traced to whichever factory it came from. Maybe even the shift.'

'But I suppose,' Casey continued, glancing sideways, 'that whoever put it there might have inserted messages into more than two pieces of clothing.'

Miranda stood up. Beside Casey, Miranda was blonde and confident. A few years older than Casey, in her mid-thirties. She had a slow smile, and a knowing laugh. Chic, Cressida admitted once, crossly. Really elegant.

Hessa and Casey watched as Miranda walked out of the little room, towards the newsdesk.

'Ross,' they heard her saying to the news editor. 'I need someone to go the branch of this shop, Rhapso, the one just off Bishopsgate, and turn it upside down ...'

'Fine' – the quick Scottish accent.

Hessa and Casey smiled at each other.

Miranda walked back into the office.

'So where was that skirt made then?'

'It doesn't say on the label,' said Hessa. 'But probably Bangladesh, especially given that this is their diffusion line. Loads of the high street clothes come from there anyway. And Bangladesh would tie in with the Rohingya.'

'And even with Rhapso's premium brand,' said Casey thoughtfully. 'They're just as likely to make the clothes in Bangladesh, fly them to Italy, stitch on a couple of buttons and stick on a "Made in Italy" label.'

'You ever been?' Miranda was looking at Hessa.

'A few times. When I was younger.'

Hessa had grown up just off Brick Lane, by the mosque that had been a synagogue and a church before that. All her life in a neat little flat, too small for her family now. Inside it was a quiet home, despite the graffiti on the door and the street noise outside. Sometimes, to escape her family's questions, she wandered the beautiful Huguenot streets nearby, peering in through the wide windows where the silk weavers once worked.

But Casey knew that Hessa's mother had been born in Sylhet, up near the Indian border. And that her mother told stories of tea gardens in the mist rolling for miles, green on green. But Hessa had shied away from those old stories, and fought her way to the *Post* instead.

'That skirt was most probably made in Chittagong, in fact,' Hessa went on. 'That's where a lot of the big garment factories are. The whole industry began there, really. From nothing.'

Miranda turned to Casey.

'You went out there last year. To the Rohingya camps.'

'Yes. Down in the south, next to the border with Myanmar.'

Casey didn't want to think about those camps.

The yellow dust, that was what she remembered. Yellow dust, and two little girls laughing.

They were prancing, giggling, in the strip of sunlight between two grey-patched tents.

So tightly packed, the tents in those camps. Miles of them, just a shoulder width apart, and far too low for anyone to stand up. Row after row, so it looked as if the whole hillside wore a carapace of canvas. Each tiny space, for a whole family.

And in the middle of it all, two little girls twirling.

All the rest was hell.

Those creaking bamboo bridges, over slow trickles of shit. A water pump, spitting brown drops over a crying toddler. A little boy with a badly burned face, trying so hard to smile.

One day, Casey had watched a puppy scramble down one of the narrow paths. There were only paths in these camps, not roads. The puppy snuffled, here and there.

And Casey realised: he was trying to find a place to die.

One place of stillness, that was all. To lay down his head and give up. And she glanced around, and saw the camp children watching too. Because there was nothing else to watch, not today.

Bored faces, and yellow dust, and a desperate, dying puppy.

And everywhere, the signs, handwritten: 'Don't go outside at night, not on your own.'

In the cartoon red letters: 'You will never be asked for favours, not for food. Not ever.'

And, underlined, again and again: 'Never be on your own.' 'Never be alone.'

'Could it happen there?' Miranda was asking. 'In Bangladesh. This sort of farm.'

'I don't know,' said Casey. Then: 'Maybe.'

Because there had been rumours, all over the camps.

A child disappeared in the night. They want the eyes, went the whisper. And the girls, so young, watched for every minute of every day.

There were stories about Kunming, too, not far over the border, in China. The transplant capital of the world, Kunming, a city where no one asked questions. Not the doctors, and certainly not the patients. Not when your kidneys are shutting down, a bit worse every day, and every other fragment of hope is gone.

'The area around Cox's Bazar has always been known for trafficking,' said Hessa baldly. 'For decades. The girls get moved on everywhere from that region. To India, mainly. But all across Asia, too. Europe, even, some of them.'

Although there were thousands of eastern European girls in London already.

'Would the Rohingya women be working in the garment factories?' asked Miranda. 'Is that how the message could have been packed into the skirt?'

It was mostly the women who worked in the factories in Bangladesh. Hour after hour, piece after piece, on the pretty little dresses they would never ever wear.

'I don't know how many work in the factories,' said Casey. 'The Bangladeshi government doesn't want the Rohingyas to assimilate with the locals. So the refugees are banned from learning Bengali, quite deliberately, to keep them isolated from the rest of the population. And then there are the checkpoints along the roads outside the camp. The camps aren't fenced, but the refugees can't move about the country freely either. Bangladesh won't give them passports, of course.'

Again, Casey felt that flare of anger. They had moved around for decades, the Rohingya. From Myanmar to Bangladesh, and back again. Never settling: always hunted.

'So could they be in the factories?' Miranda asked.

'They might be,' said Casey. 'The men certainly get work outside the camps, although legally they aren't supposed to. Day labourers. Salt farming. That sort of thing.'

Back-breaking work, all of it.

Dash appeared at the door.

'Ross has packed Tillie off to Liverpool Street,' he said, rumpling his dark hair as he spoke. 'What's going on?'

Dash always raked at his hair when he was thinking. Ross managed the day-to-day of the newsroom. Dash – more cautiously, gaming out every step first – was in charge of strategy for the *Post*.

Dash was quiet, compared with his news editor. Watchful, and instinctively secretive. He could be very funny, inconspicuously, and he had an uncanny ability to predict where a story might go next. He spent all day negotiating. 'The Tories'll give us a good interview with the pensions minister if . . .'

When the newsroom was chasing the biggest stories – a bomb ripping apart a Tube station, a cabinet minister on the brink – it was Ross who dispatched reporters, screamed at recalcitrant subs, blitzed through copy. Dash, a few steps away, would assess, calculate, anticipate the next move.

They worked well together, Dash averting his eyes from the worst of Ross's temper, and sometimes exploiting it when a reporter slipped up.

The structure meant Dash managed the investigations team, and their long-running inquiries. Or just kept out of their way, more often.

Miranda explained, Hessa and Casey listening carefully.

'They take the girls,' Miranda finished crisply. 'They take the girls to a baby factory.'

'Haven't I heard about that sort of thing?' said Dash. 'Don't they do surrogacy stuff out in India?'

Dash was glancing across at Casey. He worried about her, she knew, ever since that journey to the Sahara.

'That sort of surrogacy has been banned in India.' Casey ignored Dash's concern. 'And those women had a choice in the matter.'

'Or as much of a choice,' said Miranda, 'as you have, when you have almost nothing.'

'And children to feed,' Hessa added.

'But couldn't it be straightforward surrogacy?' asked Dash. 'Bangladesh taking over where the Indians left off. I know they don't allow it in the UK, paying for surrogacy. You only get expenses, don't you? But it wouldn't surprise me if someone found a way round the rules. People always do.'

'We know surrogacy happens in countries all over the world,' said Miranda evenly. 'With variations in the rules. They pay a fortune in America.'

'So it may be something like that,' said Casey. 'But from what we have seen in the embroidered notes I don't think these women have any choice. At least in America, there are rules. A factory, this says. A baby factory.'

Casey paused, fiddling with the skirt, crumpling the scarlet taffeta.

Dash looked across at Casey. Next to her, Miranda shrugged at him.

'Do you really,' Dash asked, almost gentle, 'want to get stuck into this now, Casey? You could do something else, for a while. Defence or politics, or something. You can come back to investigations in a bit.'

'I'm fine.' Casey was staring past him at a faded print tacked quite incongruously to the wall. *The Fighting Temeraire*, a grand old warship off to be pulled apart in the sludge of Rotherhithe.

In the silence, they could all hear one of the reporters, walking past the investigations office. 'Got sent on a bloody doorstep in sodding Shropshire yesterday.' Casey could hear that it was Eric, one of the junior reporters. 'And the bugger pulled a fucking gun on me. I rang the newsdesk, and Ross just said, "Give him an hour to calm down and knock again." God, I hate him. And then I got marooned in twatting Newport for hours. Drink?'

Casey and Miranda tried to suppress their grins.

'Why would anyone bother snatching refugee girls?' Dash asked. 'There must be thousands of very poor women in Bangladesh. Surely whoever is behind this could pay them a pittance. Wouldn't this just create an unnecessary risk?'

Hessa managed to keep her face expressionless. 'It might be partly because of the perception of the Rohingya in Bangladesh,' she said lightly. 'They've been denied everything – education, basic human rights, homes – for decades. In the last few years, hundreds of thousands of Rohingya have been trafficked into slavery. Certain Bengalis would find it odd, the idea of negotiating with them.'

‘Fine,’ Dash shrugged. ‘Easier to snatch than to pay.’

Hessa stared at him. ‘Something like that.’

‘OK,’ said Dash, after a pause. ‘Spend some time working on it if you want. But you haven’t got much to go on, you know.’

Dash’s mobile rang. It rang every few minutes, all day, all night. He ignored it.

Casey glanced across at him. ‘We’d have to find the clients in the West,’ she said slowly. ‘Find out who is coordinating it all. And where they are.’

Her eyes were hazy now, the calculations almost blurring her sight.

‘And none of that,’ said Dash, ‘will be easy.’

He stepped out of the room, leaving a silence behind him.

‘He’s worried about you, you know,’ Miranda said to Casey.

‘I know,’ Casey shrugged. ‘I know. But I am fine.’

They sat in the small office for hours.

‘Right,’ Miranda began. ‘Let’s work out how we would do it.’

One of the old reporters at the *Sunday Times* had explained that trick to Miranda after the fourth bottle. *Put yourself in their head. Work out what you would do, and then flip it.*

And he – half crook himself – had tracked down rogue after rogue.

‘Where would you find the clients in the first place?’ Miranda asked. ‘In London?’

‘Wimpole Street?’ said Casey. ‘Harley Street?’

Patients flew from all around the world to those elegant Georgian roads cutting through the heart of Marylebone. Where Elizabeth Barrett searched for a cure, and only ever found love.

Rhinoplasty and ophthalmology, dermatology and podiatry. There was no part of the body that couldn't be tweaked, so carefully, with a soothing smile. Hundreds of doctors worked along those streets, most expensively.

Most discreetly, too, behind their little brass nameplates.

'But where would we start?' said Casey. 'There must be dozens of places that offer fertility treatment on Harley Street alone. How could we guess the right one?'

'You'd probably have to go through all sorts of hurdles first too,' Miranda thought aloud. 'It's not the sort of thing you'd be offered on your first appointment, surely? Unless, maybe, if we asked the right questions ...'

'We could ask about surrogacy,' suggested Casey. 'And just see where that led.'

'Or perhaps someone in India is referring clients on to Bangladesh?' suggested Hessa. 'After the surrogacy programmes got shut down in India?'

'Because we're not even sure if the scheme only operates in London,' said Miranda, drawing doodles. 'Whoever put that message in the skirt might be sending others to Germany, Australia, wherever.'

Casey turned back to her computer again. The afternoon had worn away. Miranda glanced at her watch, and looked up, worried. 'Tom will go spare if I'm late again.'

Miranda and Tom lived together, just, in a pretty house in Queen's Park. In a three-wishes life that Miranda never wanted.

'Don't stay on too late, Casey,' said Miranda.

She knew Casey would stay for hours.

'I won't,' Casey lied. 'You go too, Hessa.'

Hessa and Miranda left Casey there, in the glow of the investigations room, head bent over her notepad, as she raced through all the possibilities.

The start of an investigation: Casey had been here before. Within just a few years of joining the *Post*, she had been all over the world.

Beijing. Nairobi. Lisbon. Los Angeles.

Kandahar: just another army base. Dusty rows of tents, sprawling to the horizon. Ugly prefab blocks, fading into the sky. The quickstep of the military, at every turn. The strangeness of English snacks and American candy, out in a dusty desert. McDonald's and Starbucks and Burger King. The Afghans, who belonged here, looking as if they were wrong here. And beyond the fence, that unknown enemy. They didn't know, then, that he would never really fade.

Delhi. São Paulo. Madrid. Singapore.

The Promenade des Anglais: that familiar stretch of beauty, torn apart. The blue of the Mediterranean, sparkling to the horizon, and the patches of blood, black in the sun. The families, searching. That's the worst part, really. Because the families don't give up. Not when the phones – out beyond the police tape – stop ringing, one by one. Not when they're told, kindly meant: *there is no hope*. It's when they see the bodies. That's when they break.

Montreal. Jakarta. Geneva. Dar es Salaam.

Minsk. Rome. Shanghai. Amman. A meat thermometer, plunged into flesh, the red digital flicker viewed coolly through heatproof glass.

Interlaced with boredom, of course. The coroner's court in Surrey, just round the corner from Woking station, for some pointless, careless, thoughtless death.

Three days outside a redbrick house in Hertfordshire, hoping to talk to a murderer's wife. Who didn't want to talk to anyone, not ever again.

And the endless nights in hotel rooms, all designed to look just the same.

When Miranda had joined the *Post*, Casey knew at once: *this*.

It suited her, this job. Dissolving into roles, day after day. A flick of eyeshadow, and a touch of lipstick: then she drew the eye. Other days, she was nothing; forgettable and forgotten.

And an answer, at last, to the question: *Who am I today?*

Casey bent over her notes, biting into a stolen apple because it was all she could find to eat in the newsroom. Years ago, she remembered some distant aunt warning her, *Don't eat the seeds or they'll grow in your head.* She imagined the rustling leaves, the rosy apples, filling her brain like a story. And her head drifted down to the desk.

'Casey.' It was the night editor, shaking her arm. 'Time for you to go home. Have this.'

Blearily, Casey looked up. Cory was smiling down at her, a horrible coffee from the machine in his hand. Behind him, the newsdesk was a pool of light in a dark room.

If a big story broke after hours, it was Cory's job was to assess the importance of the story. He decided who should be kicked out of bed: the reporter, or the specialist, or the head of news.

A dead MP meant the political editor got the call. If a plane crashed, the transport correspondent was jerked awake. 'But only if it's filled with Brits,' the transport correspondent had bawled once. 'If it's thirty-five Indonesians into the South China Sea, leave me to fucking sleep.'

For the biggest stories, Cory called the editor himself. No one wanted to be the editor who got a call at 2 a.m. to say that Princess Diana had been in a car crash in Paris, and shouted, 'So what?' and crashed the phone down. That episode had taken years to live down.

'Sorry, Cory,' said Casey. 'Must have drifted off.'

The night editor pulled her to her feet.

'Passports,' Casey said.

'What?' Cory looked at her. 'Are you all right?'

'They would need passports, to get the babies back.' Casey was speaking almost to herself.

Cory stared at her, and almost laughed. 'Go home, Casey.'

'I will.' She was scribbling herself a note, on her keyboard for the next morning. 'I will, now.'

3

The first daffodils were bobbing in the park as Casey walked towards the office, the snowdrops shy beneath the trees. There was a shimmer of frost on the grass, fading as the sun crept over the skyline.

'Casey.' Tillie leaped up as she walked into the newsroom.

'Hello,' Casey started.

'I went all over that Rhapso near Liverpool Street last night.' Tillie's voice was breathless, as if she had been rehearsing the words. 'And finally, just as they were chucking us all out at ten … Anyway, here.'

It was the same white silk, the words embroidered in the same pale blue thread. Casey stroked it flat.

They take the babies for the English women.

Well, at least that meant it was happening in London. Probably. Someone must have smuggled them into a whole consignment of clothes, destined for London, or who knew where?

'What does it mean?' Tillie's brown eyes were worried. Behind her, the newsroom was unfurling. Ross was bawling at the education correspondent, some missed story about university access. The newish editor of the *Post*, who regarded the investigations team with deep suspicion, was arriving in the office. Flunkies trailed him, seagulls following a tractor.

Archie, the *Post*'s avuncular political editor, was leaning against the newsdesk. 'How shall I quote you on this?' he was saying. 'Are you "sources close to"? Or "good friend of"?'

Those odd friendships, based only on favours.

'It's probably nothing,' Casey said reassuringly, her pulse leaping. 'Thank you though, Tillie.'

Casey walked towards the beige of the investigations room. Past the Business desk, past Sport and past the rows of news reporters' desks. Tillie was half-following her, hesitating, and then quickstepping to catch up.

'The shop assistants hated me. I unfolded so many things. I tried to put them back right, but they must still have been so annoyed with me,' Tillie faltered. 'I'd love to work with you on any project ...'

They were just outside the investigations room now.

'Thanks, Tillie,' Casey said. 'I'll check with Ross. Maybe you can go to another branch today.'

'Great!' said Tillie. 'Brilliant. Amazing.'

Casey smiled at the enthusiasm as she unlocked the office. Miranda and Hessa arrived minutes later.

'Right.' Casey didn't waste time on hello. 'Surrogacy. It's a business.'

Casey had her notes from the night before in front of her. Her first call had been to the *Post*'s health editor, a quick-tongued blonde who had three-year-old twins, and no time for Ross's moods.

'I'm right up against it,' Heather had bawled down the phone. 'But, yes, international surrogacy is a whole can of worms.'

Heather had sprinted Casey round the industry at high speed, as she spooned Calpol into one of her children.

Back around 2004, Heather said, the whole industry got started in India. Well, we outsource everything else, don't we? Who do you speak to when you call up your bank to scream about a lost credit card? You might as well do the same with kids, I suppose. Maybe. Anyway. So surrogacy in India became a massive business: 25,000 children a year was a low-end estimate, which made it an industry worth billions. Well, you can't put a price on hope, can you? But gradually, the Indian government went off the idea. A few big stories about problems. Kids not being handed over by the surrogates. Dodgy parents, all that. Cold feet about the whole thing. Gradually, India brought in more rules, more regulations. They banned gay couples, who are a big part of the market. So the industry moved over to Thailand, and Nepal too. Then those countries changed the law. The industry moved to Cambodia, which was especially popular with the Chinese. That got shut down too. Then on to Laos. Ukraine's a big market too. It's meant to be more regulated, these days. But is it? Fuck knows.

You should talk to Alicia Dalgleish, Heather went on. You know, the chair of the Foreign Affairs select committee. She's very hot on it all. Believes in a woman's right to do whatever she wants with her body. And that sort of makes sense too, if you think about it. But who knows really?

'Thanks so much, Heather.' Casey had rung off, before digging back into her research again.

Now Casey spun her laptop round towards Hessa and Miranda. A website smiled back, swirly pink writing over a pretty couple on a beach, strolling hand in hand with a toddler.

No problems: your journey. No hassles: your dream. Come as a couple, leave as a family.

Hessa and Miranda studied the computer.

'This was an old website I found in Thailand.' Casey clicked around the photographs.

'What's an IP?' asked Miranda.

'An intended parent,' said Casey. 'At that place, they threw in bonus sex selection too.'

'Some of these families use surrogates because of serious health problems, you know,' said Hessa. 'Ovarian cancer, uterine cancer, hysterectomies. I read about it at home last night.'

Miranda looked at Hessa thoughtfully. 'And now the industry has migrated to Bangladesh?' She turned back to Casey.

'Maybe. Who knows? Thailand cracked down after baby Gammy,' Casey explained. 'That was when an Australian couple hired a Thai woman to carry a child. Then they found out she was having twins, and one of them had Down's. The surrogate claimed she was told to abort the Down's baby, but wouldn't, and she ended up keeping the Down's baby and handing over the other one. Then the Thai surrogate found out that the Australian father had been done for child abuse, and things really went downhill. The IPs kept their child though.'

Miranda tipped her chair back, sipping her coffee.

'I rang Savannah too,' Casey said.

Savannah was an aid worker who had guided Casey around the Rohingya camps the year before, down in the south of Bangladesh. Red-haired and tough-eyed, she strode around the camps, her rage flickering about her. In Lambasia, one of the sprawling encampments, Savannah had pointed out a child with a horribly swollen throat. 'Diphtheria,' Savannah had shouted in her broad New Zealand accent, flinging her hands in the air. 'We had beaten fucking diphtheria right the way around the world. It was basically gone, for Christ's sake. Rammed into history, where it belonged. And now it's back, for fuck's sake. Who does this? Who does this to people?'

'Does Savannah know anything about it?' Miranda asked now.

Casey hesitated.

You know how fucking dark things are here, babe. You know what it's like. But I'll ask, course I will. I'll talk to the women I know well. And I think they'll tell me, if they know anything.

'Savannah doesn't know much,' said Casey. 'Not yet.'

There was a light tap on the doorframe. It was Audrey, the *Post*'s legal affairs correspondent, with a tired smile on her face.

'Casey,' she said. 'You were looking at the legalities around getting surrogate babies back to the UK?'

'Yes.' Miranda pulled out a chair for her. 'It seems so complicated.'

Audrey slumped into the chair. 'Long day yesterday,' she apologised. 'Old Bailey for a murder, and then out to Woolwich for more of that grisly terror trial.'

Audrey ran her hands over her neatly braided hair, visibly pulling herself together.

'Right. The legalities of surrogacy are a nightmare.' Audrey handed round copies of a Foreign Office document, reading aloud random sentences. 'International surrogacy is a complex area … The process for getting your child back to the UK can be very long and complicated, and can take several months to complete. Strongly recommend specialist legal advice …'

Audrey looked at Miranda. 'Basically, it's fiendishly complicated, takes ages and varies from country to country. You need to get the child a passport, and separately you need to get something called a parental order to transfer various legal rights from the surrogate to you. There are different rules depending on whether the surrogate is married or not, and whether the British father is actually genetically linked to the child or not.'

'So, for example, if you use a surrogate in the US . . .?'

'If a child is born to an US citizen, they get American citizenship. That means you can apply for a US passport and you can usually bring the baby back quite soon. Then you go through the other hoops back in England.'

'Why wouldn't everyone just go to the US?'

'California is the centre of the industry,' said Audrey. 'It's very expensive though. I've heard quotes of £50,000 just for the legal side, and that's before you even start paying the surrogate or any of the medical costs. On top of that, British couples are meant to ensure that their international surrogacy agreement complies with UK law. Clearly, because of the big payments made to US surrogates, that isn't the case. So it's a grey area, and potentially vulnerable.'

'And, say, the Ukraine?'

'That depends. In most countries, the baby doesn't get automatic citizenship. So a baby born to a surrogate doesn't get Ukrainian citizenship. If the father is British, and the surrogate isn't married, you have to apply for a British passport, which takes four or five months. But if not, it gets much more complicated. Anything to do with the Home Office is always a nightmare, anyway. It's a Byzantine system.'

Audrey sighed to herself. Casey remembered that Audrey's parents had been part of the Windrush generation: dropped into a bureaucratic chaos after decades of happy life in London.

'And commercial surrogacy is only legal in a very few countries?' said Casey.

'Yes,' said Audrey. 'It started up in several places around the world, but then each of those countries quickly realises that there is a reason why there is a lot of regulation around surrogacy. I can't see any record of legal surrogacy in Bangladesh. It never really got started there. Certainly, if someone found a way to fast-track the other routes, they could make a chunky profit from it.'

'What if they had someone out there who could provide them with Bangladeshi birth certificates?' asked Casey. 'If it had just the intended parents' names on it, rather than the actual birth mother, might it be much easier to get the British passport?'

'Possibly,' said Audrey. 'And that may be easier to achieve in Bangladesh. I don't know.'

'If they did that,' Casey was thinking aloud, 'it might be quite straightforward for someone to issue the passport from the High Commission.'

Audrey stood up, giving them a glint of a smile.

'Good luck,' she said. 'I must get going.' She disappeared. There was a momentary hush.

'OK,' said Miranda. 'Then what's the approach?'

4

'Passports,' said Casey firmly. 'If the babies are being born illegally in Bangladesh, the organisers of this scheme must be finding a way of getting them back into this country. A baby's no use unless you can bring it back to the UK for the IPs. And as Audrey says, that process usually takes months, and there are a lot of legal hoops. To make any sense of operating in Bangladesh, there may well be someone manipulating the system in Bangladesh somehow, possibly with the emergency passports.'

Miranda was playing with her scarf.

'The High Commission in Dhaka,' Miranda agreed. 'There must be someone there who at least has some idea about how the parents are getting British passports. Or are issuing the passports themselves. It would be very hard to traffic a newborn into the UK without a passport, even using a private jet. Then there would have to be a legitimate doctor in the UK who can sign off all the standard documentation.'

'Whoever is organising the passports would probably have the names of everyone who has ever been out there,' Hessa followed. 'And they might know who is coordinating the whole thing.'

'So I rang Luke,' said Casey. 'In Delhi, last night.'

Currently the *Post*'s India correspondent, Luke Armitage had had to leave London for Delhi quite abruptly after a misunderstanding over the Home Secretary's phone bill during the last general election. Following that eruption, Dash had decided Luke should spend a bit of time as the *Post*'s Delhi correspondent.

Out of sight, out of mind, just for a year or so. You'll like Delhi, Luke.

I bloody won't.

Get on the sodding plane, Armitage.

Luke and Casey got on well.

'I need a list of anyone dodgy in the Dhaka High Commission,' Casey had said to Luke the night before. 'Someone who could get people passports, when they're not supposed to.'

Bangladesh, part of the old Commonwealth, had a High Commission, not an embassy.

'Passports are a nightmare when you're travelling with babies,' Heather had agreed. 'Haven't taken my husband's name, have I? And the kids have his surname. I had to show a border guard my flaming C-section scar to get the twins past one joker when I was travelling on my own. Tell you what, they let me through pretty quick when I started taking my top off. Sodding patriarchy.'

They were tough, border controls, with an eye out for a trafficked child all the way around the world. They still got through, of course.

'When' – Luke rarely wasted words – 'did this passport lark get started?'

'Let's say some time in the last five years,' said Casey. 'They may not be there any more.'

Diplomatic staff moved on to a new posting every few years, skimming around the globe, oh so politely.

'It would probably have to be someone quite senior,' Luke thought aloud. 'Without many people checking above.'

'Yes,' said Casey. 'It takes months to get passports in normal surrogacy cases.'

'For cash or blackmail?'

'Could be either.'

'You' – there was amusement in Luke's voice – 'don't ask for much.'

'I know,' said Casey. 'Sorry.'

'Any time.'

This morning, Casey had arrived in the office to an encrypted email from Luke. *Call me when you get in. Doesn't matter what time.*

Luke had answered the phone immediately.

'I trod carefully, I promise,' he said. 'But I've got a mate who has a good line into the Dhaka High Commission. He won't say a word to anyone, I guarantee it.'

Casey didn't ask, didn't need to know.

'Anyway, my pal said they had a changeover of high commissioners, just a few months ago,' Luke went on. 'Sir William Cavendish, the old high commissioner, was a peach, by all accounts. Much loved by all. He's retired to a Greek island, or something. The newly arrived ambo is most correct. Very much believes in dotting the Is and crossing the Ts, and everything else by the book.'

'Doesn't sound like your mate likes him.'

'You guess right. But my buddy also reckons the new high commissioner is clean. Too saintly for words. Dull as ditchwater, were his precise words.'

'How about the deputies?'

'That's what my mate suggested. He says the new high commissioner is running things on such a tight rein that it would be hard to get anything past him. But he said all sorts of alarm bells were ringing about the last deputy out there. Gabriel Bantham.'

'Never heard of him.'

'You know how low-profile they are, the Foreign Office lot. You never hear about them until they're right at the top of the tree. But apparently Bantham had been flagged up quietly as being a bit too sharp for his own good.'

'How?'

'Nothing too dodgy,' Luke said. 'Getting swept off for very ritzy weekends by a company that wanted an introduction to, say, a Foreign Office minister. A lifestyle that was just a bit too grand for a Foreign Office salary.'

Casey felt her interest flare, a shiver in her spine.

'Might be family money?'

'Not, apparently.'

'He get caught?'

'Not quite,' said Luke. 'My mate reckons the old high commissioner, Sir William, didn't want to drop him in it. Cavendish just wanted a quiet life, towards the end of his career. So Bantham's next move was a step sideways to Washington. That's where he is now.'

The huge British embassy on Massachusetts Avenue, thought Casey. A long way from the backwaters of Dhaka.

'Could there have been anyone else organising passports through the Dhaka outpost?'

'It's not a big mission, the Bangladeshi operation,' said Luke. 'Not exactly a focus for the Foreign Office, is it, Dhaka? But I don't think you could hand out several passports in a row without one of the main officials knowing.'

'And your friend hadn't heard of passports being doled out?'

'I didn't get that specific. Do you want me to go back to him?'

'No,' said Casey slowly. 'Not yet. But he's sure Bantham is the guy?'

'He said that he would put his house on it.'

'OK,' said Casey thoughtfully.

Now she summarised the conversation quickly.

'Right,' Miranda decided. 'It looks like you and Hessa are going to DC.'

5

Casey waited until Hessa was out of the room.

'You're not coming to DC?'

'You can do it without me, Casey. Take Hessa.'

Why? Casey didn't need to ask.

Two weeks earlier, Miranda had found messages on her husband's mobile.

What sort of an idiot thinks about cheating on an investigative journalist? Miranda had spat in their little office the next day, trying to laugh. Casey had put an awkward arm around her shoulders, not knowing what to say.

'There's nothing too incriminating on his phone,' Miranda had said. 'Nothing conclusive. I don't even know if anything has happened.'

Not yet.

'Who is she?'

'He met her at work.' Tom was a corporate lawyer. In-house now: better hours, less stress. 'Some girl in business development. Whatever the fuck that is.'

'Do you want me to find out about her?'

'No. Yes. I don't know.'

And it was so unlike Miranda, that uncertainty.

Tom and Miranda had met at university. Back when everything was possible. They laughed their way into marriage, soon after, too early. And realised, too late, that their dreams were so very different.

They had moved to a pretty house in Queen's Park, all the same. With patterned tiles cold underfoot in the hallway, and roses round the door. Surrounded by prams, and smiles, and school fetes.

This is what I want, he whispered.

I know, she said. *I know.*

And he'd waited, a kind man, as she fled to Nigeria and Russia, Libya and Iraq.

When will you be home? he would ask, calling from a back garden just right for a Wendy house. Again and again, until the pretty house became a prison.

I wish your dreams were enough.

'Rebecca, she's called.' Miranda snarled the name. 'Becky.'

'And what do you want?' Casey bit a fingernail.

'I don't know. I think Tom might have finally had enough. And I don't know that I can blame him.'

Miranda turned away.

I'm going to save my marriage, Miranda had said to Casey a few days later, knowing the words were ridiculous. As if her marriage were a drowning damsel, caught in a rip tide.

'Are you sure?'

'Yes.' A pause. 'No. Let's talk about something else.'

Casey looked across the bustling restaurant. Le Diplomate, appropriately enough; Washington's interpretation of a French bistro. Casey stared at the mosaic-tiled floors disapprovingly, as the noise rose around them. Tiles were the worst for undercover work.

They were in the heart of America's capital, just off the thoroughly gentrified Logan Circle. All around them, gossip ebbed and flowed. The lobbyists, the politicians, the journalists: they all came here.

Hessa was sitting across the table from Casey, awkward in a big wicker chair.

'Relax,' said Casey. 'You've got to look like you belong here.'

'Sorry.' Hessa tried to adjust.

'And never apologise.'

From her red leather banquette, Casey was watching the entrance. Anyone walking in would only see the back of Hessa's head, anyway. It didn't matter that she was nervous.

After landing in Washington, it hadn't taken Casey long to find out where Bantham would be for lunch today.

There was a delegation of British MPs in DC, over to discuss trade relations. A jolly, they all knew. Cross-party, very cosy. A Labour MP had happily handed over the delegation's schedule to the *Post*'s political editor, hoping he was dropping his Tory colleagues in the soup. It would never occur to an MP that Bantham was the target.

Lunch, today's schedule read. *DC restaurant tbc.*

It had taken ten minutes to ring round; only a few restaurants fitted the bill.

A smart English accent and a mumbled title never failed: I'm calling from Lord Gidleigh's office. Just ringing about the VIP party today. The British parliamentarians, yes. The Foreign Affairs select committee. Just checking you knew two of the guests were gluten-free?

There was confusion at Cafe Milano. Polite bemusement at Fiola Mare. And a casual, oh sure, I'll make a note about that, from Le Diplomate.

'You have a good day now.'

'You too.'

And here they were.

Casey watched the MPs crowding through the entrance, full of noise and importance. They wouldn't recognise her face, she knew. She kept away from Parliament for exactly that reason. She identified several MPs, pontificating loudly. In the heart of the throng, she could see Alicia Dalgleish, the bright young thing of British politics, with an interest in surrogacy, smiling and chatting. She was talking to a pretty blonde woman, probably some backbench MP.

Now Casey waited for the group to settle, in a flurry of menus and water, still or sparkling, and would-you-like-some-bread?

She had spotted Bantham in his smart suit and green silk tie as he walked through the doors. Light brown hair was smoothed back from a neat parting, above a sharp, pale face. It had been hard to find a photograph of him; diplomats were careful. Casey had trawled his university archive in the end. Oxford, of course. Sepia pose, distant eyes.

The consummate diplomat, Bantham's eyes darted around the restaurant, noting all the Washington players. Casey felt his eyes on her for a second, before they flicked on. When the Tory MP sitting next to Bantham dripped a spot of olive oil on her shirt, he whisked out a silk handkerchief.

Hessa's nervousness had disappeared, Casey noticed, as soon the MPs arrived in the restaurant. The actress, on her stage. Now

Hessa was an elegant young executive, graceful in a navy suit, her shiny dark bob gleaming in the light. Casey smiled at her.

A few tables beyond Hessa and Casey, an up-and-coming Texan congressman was holding court. Casey knew that Bantham would not be able to resist a quick hello.

She waited.

It didn't take long. Just after the starter, she saw Bantham push back his chair. At once, Casey was on her feet, strolling down the restaurant, smoothing her expensive suit, with its charcoal pencil skirt.

'Gabriel Bantham?' As they passed, Casey held out her hand with a smile. She watched him fumble for her name. 'Katie Faraday. We met in London, a few years ago now.'

Katie was a favourite name. Same first syllable, enough to make Casey's head turn. But it could be Catherine or Catrina, Katherine or Kathryn. Katja, even, at a push. Katie turned an easy research trawl into a lengthy challenge.

'Of course,' he said smoothly. 'How lovely to see you again, Katie.'

'And I see you're here with Ali Dalgleish,' Casey glanced across at the table of MPs. 'I bumped into her at Congress yesterday.'

Because Alicia Dalgleish, tipped for promotion in the next reshuffle, would have met a hundred people in a couple of hours, and would nod automatically at the mention of a Katie.

'She enjoyed her day there,' agreed Bantham, a flex of American in his voice.

'And now you're based at the embassy in DC?' Casey spoke with a smile, halfway between business and flirtation. He reflected it.

'Yes.' Bantham was unsuspicious. 'I've been there for a few months now. It's a fantastic city.'

'You know' – a careful pause – 'that could be interesting to my client. He's having a slight problem with his UK citizenship at the moment.' A brief smile. 'We like to get things right for the client.'

The client. Definite article. One man, anonymous, who could monopolise a whole team. The family office, the private office: those were for the truly astronomical fortunes, and everybody knew it.

'Might you be free for lunch soon?' Casey went on. 'It could be so helpful to have a chat.'

As she spoke, she handed over the business card. Heavy cream card, embossed in gold.

Bantham handed over his own card, without even thinking about it.

'Great,' she said: always be the one to break the contact. 'I'll be in touch.'

And he watched her strut away across the restaurant.

The next day, she was waiting in the palatial restaurant of the Four Seasons, poised in one of the big comfortable chairs.

'The Four Seasons?' Dash had asked. 'Really? The editor is kicking up about expenses already.'

'It's what Bantham would expect.' Casey was firm. 'And it's got carpet to blot out noise, and nice big gaps between the tables so no one else can overhear anything. It's perfect.'

I'm so sorry to bother you with such a bizarre request about carpets of all the wretched things, she had summoned the same voice from Lord Gidleigh's office, *but I am trying to find a restaurant to take my mother for lunch. She's very deaf these days, and I was worrying about the sound levels.*

Oh, sure, don't you worry. Yes, ma'am, it's all carpeted in our restaurant. We look forward to hosting you. You have a nice day now.

'Well, write a sodding review of it for the paper, at least,' Dash grumbled. 'We can publish it after the story runs.'

If it runs, he didn't say. Casey knew Dash didn't quite believe in this story. Not yet.

Now Casey straightened a fork, twitched a napkin and moved a vase of white irises an inch to the left. She glanced in a mirror to her left, checking the camera, and that all the wires were carefully hidden. In the mirror, she looked like any other glossy businesswoman. *Mirrors reflect the soul*, she'd read once. *And vampires have no soul, and no reflection.*

Sitting to Casey's right was a polite Indonesian man, in a very expensive suit. He turned to Casey, and adjusted his Rolex.

'I'm good to go,' Ibrahim said, in a strong New York accent.

'All Bahasa from now,' she warned, with a grin. 'Mr Halim.'

'Sure,' he said. 'My granny would be proud.'

Gabriel Bantham didn't speak Bahasa, Casey knew.

She knew that because the day before, she had called the embassy, and asked to be put through to Bantham. While the call was transferred, she passed the phone to Ibrahim. When Bantham answered from his office, Ibrahim had spoken in the Bahasa language of millions of Indonesians.

'I'm terribly sorry,' Bantham had apologised, so politely. 'I don't speak ... Do you speak any other languages? I'm so sorry about this.'

Bantham had tried Mandarin and Japanese and Hindu on Ibrahim, but it was clear that the diplomat didn't have a word of Bahasa.

It hadn't taken long to build the rest of the story. First, Casey had called a stringer pal in Djakarta who laughed and posted a few photographs on her popular blog of Mr Halim, the celebrated philanthropist.

I'll send through some photographs of Ibrahim.

I'll backdate them. When can I delete them?

A couple of weeks? I'll call you. Coy references to billions would be helpful.

You owe me.

I do.

Next, Casey put up a brief article on the *Post* business section about wealth management. The article listed several world-famous family offices. It noted, in passing, that the Halim family's vast fortune was being invested through a new, but impeccable office in Zug. Casey had found a name for this new family office by stealing an English-Latin dictionary off one of the *Post*'s more pompous columnists and opening it at random.

A glossy website for Gradibus Capital AG – it was password-protected naturally, with a generic photograph of Lake Zug as its backdrop – offered Swiss and London phone numbers.

Tillie answered the London number with a Cheltenham Ladies' sneer; the Swiss line connected straight to Hessa's burner mobile: Gradibus, *wie kann ich dir helfen?* In both cases, Bantham had ended the calls almost immediately, apparently convinced.

A cheerfully resting actor, Ibrahim lolled back against his seat now, as Bantham hurried towards them.

Casey watched him approach, picking her character like a book from the shelf. She would reflect his mannerisms now. Terse to terse, flirt to flirt, nudged along so carefully. A blank canvas, a broken mirror, and very bad luck.

'I'm not late, am I?' Bantham knew he wasn't.

'May I present you to Mr Halim.' Casey bowed her head respectfully towards Ibrahim.

'How do you do?' Bantham half-bowed.

Ibrahim nodded his head.

'I am afraid Mr Halim does not speak much English,' said Casey. Turning her head, she spoke the few words of Bahasa Ibrahim had taught her on the way to the restaurant. Ibrahim nodded thoughtfully at Bantham.

For the first half an hour of lunch, Casey and Bantham made idle conversation. Although Bantham chatted easily to her, Casey knew his attention was on Ibrahim.

Ibrahim largely ignored them, occasionally making phone calls in rapid-fire Bahasa.

After three-quarters of an hour, Hessa approached the table.

'I am very sorry to interrupt, Ms Faraday, but you wanted to be reminded about Mr Halim's phone call with the Prime Minister. At 2.30 p.m.'

'Of course,' Casey waved her away.

Hessa sat down a table away, pulled out her laptop and started tapping.

'I always enjoy lunch here,' said Bantham. 'You get to see everyone in the end.'

There was a hush as a woman with long blonde hair strutted in, almost bouncing out of her tight black suit.

'Goldie Robinson,' said Bantham. 'She's claiming to have had an affair with that California senator, and well ...'

They both pondered the blonde's lively film career.

'Do you know how you come up with your porn name?' Casey grinned. 'Your first pet, and your mother's maiden name. I'd be Bunny Beeching. How about you?'

'Beau,' Bantham screwed up his face, smiling. 'Kilmartin. Beau was a dog. A little Jack Russell.'

'That's a good name,' Casey laughed. 'Why are the MPs out here, anyway?'

'Cross-border trade discussions.' Bantham faked a yawn. 'But quite coincidentally, they're out here at the same time as a certain African president. There's been some kerfuffle over an oil well, apparently. Some British company wants to get drilling, but a rival bunch also have a claim.' He laughed. 'And if the MPs happened to bump into the president at, say, a function at the Washington Ballet tonight, I am sure there will be a discreet nudge.'

And the situation would be resolved, Casey thought. She grinned broadly at Bantham. He was almost advertising his skills.

At a quarter past two, Ibrahim stood up. He nodded his head to Bantham, and struggled for the words: *Good – bye.*

They smiled him away.

When he had gone, the waiter brought out coffee, topped up wineglasses, folded the thick linen napkins. Patiently, Casey waited for him to go.

'Mr Halim has been having some difficulty getting a visa for Britain,' Casey said, baldly, when he did.

'Oh dear,' said Bantham. 'I am sorry to hear that.'

'There are,' Casey spoke in careful transatlantic syllables, 'misplaced concerns about his businesses back in Indonesia.'

'It can be very tricky,' nodded Bantham.

'Would you have any advice?' asked Casey.

They talked for a while, Bantham giving the advice that any diplomat would dole out.

Time. Patience. Top immigration lawyers.

But there was a hesitation, now and again. Almost a suggestion. His words trailing away into a silence.

Finally, Casey turned towards him.

'Is there a way, Mr Bantham, that we could streamline the process? Mr Ibrahim is such a very busy man. And' – a pause – 'a most generous one.'

Bantham had done this before, she knew at once. The awkwardness gone in the smoothest stream of words.

It was simple, Bantham's plan. Easy.

A junior minister. A pet project. The most generous dollop of sponsorship. And afterwards, he would be helpful, the minister. The quietest of words, that's all this sort of thing would need.

'It doesn't take much, I assure you.'

'You make it sound so easy.' Casey met his eyes.

'It is.' He was blunt.

And for Bantham, the consultancy fee, at first. And a success fee later, maybe. It always sounds so proper. A bonus. A signing fee. Nothing so vulgar as a bribe.

All paid into an offshore account, of course.

'You spend so much time abroad,' she nearly winked at him. 'Anyway.'

She was signing the bill to her room, partly because that meant she didn't have to pull out a bankcard, emblazoned with her real name.

They were smiling now. They understood each other.

Upstairs? The quick suggestion in his eyes.

Not today. But she added a hint of regret.

They parted with a handshake, a nod.

'We'll talk soon.'

'We will, Katie Faraday.'

'A pleasure.'

'All mine.'

6

When Casey got back to her room and flopped on the grey velvet ottoman, there was a message waiting for her. *Call me.*

'One of the women in the camp found me.' It was Savannah, the words pouring out of her in a rush. 'I had been asking around, Case. I could hear you really needed to know.'

'Thanks, Savannah. It's so kind of you.' Casey imagined the aid worker sitting in her small hotel room in Cox's Bazar. She was short, Savannah, and fizzing with energy in her charity-branded T-shirt and bright pink jeans. Her long red hair pulled back into a plait, her face plastered in suncream because her skin burned so easily.

'The thing is,' Savannah went on. 'I wasn't really getting anywhere. To be honest with you, I've never been convinced the people in the camps know details about trafficking. There are lots of rumours, sure. But if you think about it, by the time someone's been trafficked, and realised what they've got themselves into, they're miles away from the camp. And they never come back.'

'Yes,' said Casey. 'But I suppose they all know enough to be scared.'

She thought of a group of teenage girls, in their brightly coloured dresses, giggling by one of the wells in the camps. They wore the thick eye make-up that all the Rohingya girls wore, even the small children.

A man had smiled back at them; just a smile at first.

But there was a sudden explosion of fury from a mother, as she charged down the slope. *Get away! You get away from my daughter. We'll get you … We'll …*

He would be back, though, that man, the next day, and the next. More friendly, and less shocking, every single time.

'Sure,' said Savannah. 'The refugees know to be scared all right. But the who, and the how, I don't think they know that, really. It's in the interests of the traffickers that no one knows exactly how they operate. Stop it, you bugger.' A slam. 'Sorry. Cockroach.'

But the refugees had guessed some of the routines. Casey had spoken to a mahji, one of the refugees' leaders, in the Balukhali camp. So casually, he had pulled out his phone, and scrolled through the photographs. *This is what we did to a kidnapper*, the fixer had translated coolly. *Look. See.*

The man – she thought it was a man – was mangled far beyond survival, his face unrecognisable. A pearly gleam of bone showed through, here and there.

We sorted him. A smile.

'And there's the shame too, for the families.' Savannah was still talking. 'Even if the mothers know what has happened to their daughters, and where they are, it would bring such shame on the whole family to acknowledge that their girls have been taken that they don't want to talk about it. They hide it, usually.'

'So what have you heard now?'

Savannah's voice changed. 'One of the mothers came to me this afternoon, just as I was walking out of the camp. She was waiting on the path, right away from her section. I'd spoken to a few of the women that I work with regularly about what you wanted to know. Asked them to put out the message.'

The charities had set up systems to communicate with the camp residents, usually about health advice. Trained refugees went from tent to tent, recommending vaccinations and sharing other bits and pieces of advice. It was a crucial system, in a semi-literate society. Private, too.

'Anyway,' Savannah went on. 'This woman's daughter had gone missing a few weeks ago. She just disappeared one morning. The mother's devastated, of course. But today, she told me she had a call from her daughter, out of the blue. Romida, the girl was called. Is called, I should say. I used to know Romida. I'd see her around the camp. Shamshun – that's the mother's name – told me Romida had managed to call her. She had managed to get a phone from somewhere, God knows how. Romida was crying, Shamshun said. Romida couldn't stop crying.' Savannah's voice dried up.

'Where was she?' asked Casey urgently.

'Romida didn't know where she was.' Savannah's words were tight. 'She said a man had driven her, in the dark, for miles. She was tied up in the back of a van or something. With a blindfold, so she didn't have any idea where she was. But now,' Savannah hesitated, 'she was in a big room, with some other women.'

'And what?' Casey said. 'What was happening to Romida?'

'Romida said she didn't know what was going to happen to her,' said Savannah. 'Just that she was being held in this room.

She said …' Savannah paused, cleared her throat. 'It sounded from what she described like they were doing medical tests on these women. Like you might do before IVF.'

Casey stared around her beautiful hotel room, at the hazy painting of a lake on the wall above her bed.

'Did they say how?' Casey kept her voice clipped.

'The other women have told her that some of them have been inspected.' Savannah took a second to answer. 'Scanned. Blood taken. Someone gives them injections, over several days. At other times, they're ordered to take tablets. Pessaries, sometimes. Then they're taken off somewhere, and they don't come back. It doesn't seem like anything has happened to Romida, yet. But she may not have wanted to say to her mother.'

'Oh Christ,' said Casey. 'How can …'

'I don't know.' Savannah gave a long sigh, cleared her throat again. 'Romida said they were fed well though. I suppose that is one thing they would do …'

'How did the phone call end?'

'Shamshun said Romida started crying. Shamshun was screaming at her, begging her to say where she was. But Romida just didn't know. And then the phone … It just went dead.'

'Did Romida say,' Casey spoke fast, 'how long she was in the van?'

'She thought maybe six hours,' said Savannah. 'They stopped in a small street somewhere, and drugged her in the van. She woke up in a room with these other women.'

'Could she hear anything outside the room? Were they in a city? Street noise? By a river? By the sea?'

'I'll ask Shamshun,' said Savannah. 'Tell her to ask this if Romida calls back. But I can't imagine she will, if I'm honest.'

'No,' said Casey sadly. 'I don't suppose she will. Did Shamshun get the number Romida was calling from?'

Savannah read it out. 'It's just a Bangladeshi mobile.'

'I'll see what I can do with it,' Casey said. 'How many women did Romida think were being held there?'

'Only four or five,' said Savannah. 'At the moment. The women said other girls have been taken somewhere else. They are sleeping on mats on the floor. There's only one bed, which some of them share. But they can't open the windows, Romida said. And the lights are only switched on a couple of hours a day.'

Casey stared out of the window of the Four Seasons. 'Savannah, how old is Romida?'

There was a pause.

'Thirteen,' Savannah said quietly. 'Her mother said she's thirteen years old.'

'Right,' said Casey, because there was nothing else left to say.

'Casey.' Savannah's voice was urgent. 'You've got to get these fuckers, OK? You have got to find these girls. The police won't do anything here, you know that. Shamshun was beside herself when she was talking to me. And there is nothing she can do.'

'I will,' Casey promised. 'I'll do everything I can.'

'All right,' said Savannah. 'You do that. For Romida.'

Savannah rang off. And Casey sat there for a long time, in the elegant suite of the Four Seasons, trying not to scream.

7

It was a grey day in London. Miranda dragged open the door to the sagging shed at the bottom of the garden. Loose on its hinges, the door screeched over the paving stones and then stuck hard. The shed smelled of damp and mushrooms. Miranda peered unenthusiastically at grimy bottles of weed-killer and half-empty paint pots.

Sighing, she reached for a heavy pair of gloves, a small gardening fork and a sack of compost.

There was the pretty sky-blue watering can she had bought during an eager trip to the garden centre just after they moved in. It sat next to a piece of broken trellis, covered in dust and spiderwebs. Miranda glanced at it resentfully.

Hurrying now, she made her way through the house. There were four terracotta pots by the front door, all of them filled with dead plants.

Miranda dumped down the compost and stared balefully at the selection of plants she had bought from the nursery the day before. She began to scratch at the surface of one of the terracotta pots.

'You're going to do what?' Tom had stared at her in surprise that morning.

'I'm going to do some gardening.' Miranda had met his eye firmly.

'Aren't you supposed to be working?'

I'm going to save my marriage.

'I'm going into the office a bit late. They won't mind.'

'And are you sure you know how?'

'Of course,' she had lied.

'All right.' She had felt a surge of affection as he began to laugh. They had laughed together, just for a moment, everything left unsaid.

The affection had echoed on as she waved him off for the Tube station. As she watched him walk down the pavement, he stopped to talk to old Mrs Markovic from three doors down on the right, who blossomed under his smile. Tom had always been able to do that, Miranda thought as she watched: remember small details about people's lives, ask them about their day and really listen to the answers.

Miranda remembered details when they would make good colour for a story, and asked people about their day to start them talking.

She only knew Mrs Markovic's name because Tom had been talking about her grandchildren – *Boris got scouted by Arsenal, isn't that amazing?* – at the same time as Miranda had been investigating some Serbian war criminals.

When Mrs Markovic had pottered back into her house, Tom glanced back at Miranda. 'Off to hunter-gather,' he said, and laughed. And she watched him hurry down the road.

He'd never offered to stop his job, she thought, with a flicker of anger.

Rebecca. Becky.

Miranda forced herself to concentrate on the terracotta pots, tugging at the dead plants.

How do you fix something you only want to break?

'Hello, Miranda!' It was Verity Taylor, right on schedule, off to drop her six-year-old twins at the primary school just down the road.

'Verity!' Miranda just managed to mirror the enthusiasm. 'How nice to see you.'

'You're gardening!' Verity's china blue eyes opened wide. 'What fun.'

'Thought I should get stuck in. Do you fancy a coffee?'

'After I've dropped off the kids? Why not? I'll be back in five.'

Verity, two doors down on the left, had stopped working at the BBC to bring up her children. Within a day of Miranda and Tom moving into this house, Verity had insisted that they come to a barbecue 'just to meet a few people, you'll love them'. Within five minutes of Miranda arriving at the barbecue, Verity had told her all about her twins being born 'with the help of an amazing surrogate'. Verity believed in 'honesty and openness about it *all*. Because I *really* think it helps people to see that *everyone* has a different path.'

Miranda had decided that this honesty and openness might be helpful; especially if Tom believed she was actually doing some gardening.

'I like what you've done with the blinds,' said Verity, so that Miranda was startled into noticing the blinds for the first time as she switched on the coffee machine.

It only took a few minutes to get Verity talking about surrogacy, and then the words spilled out of her.

'We went for Ukraine in the end, and they were so great.' Verity took a sip of her cappuccino. 'Couldn't do enough to help.'

'But didn't you start off in the US?'

'Yes, we did. How clever of you to remember!' said Verity. 'We did several rounds over there, with a surrogate from Minneapolis, of all places. But the embryo transfers just kept failing for some reason. They never worked out why.'

'The embryo transfers? I don't know anything about it. How do they work?'

'Jonty and I flew over to a clinic in Miami,' said Verity with all the enthusiasm of the obsessive. 'And I stayed out there while I went through egg collection before the transfer.'

'Gosh, how does that work?'

'Oh,' Verity waved. 'It goes on for ever, and everyone has slightly different protocols. It's a nightmare. For example, our clinic made me take the pill – just an ordinary contraceptive one – for the month before I travelled out to the US, so that they knew exactly where I was in my cycle. Then once your period starts, they check to make sure your body is doing roughly the right thing and then you have lots of injections of FSH – that's follicle-stimulating hormone – to make you produce lots of eggs. You'd normally only produce one a month, you see.'

'How long does that go on for?' Miranda winced.

'They keep scanning you to see how the eggs are developing,' Verity rattled on. Bored and bright, thought Miranda. It led to encyclopedic levels of knowledge. 'And eventually you have a trigger shot, usually hCG – that stands for human chorionic gonadotrophin' – Verity was showing off now, Miranda thought – 'and then exactly thirty-six hours later, they do the egg collection. Legs up in stirrups; none of it is glamorous, Miranda, I tell you.'

'Amazing.'

'And then the eggs are mixed up with Jonty's – well – contribution.' Verity blew her thick blonde fringe out of her eyes, 'And, fingers crossed, some of them are fertilised. And there's your embryo.'

'The science is extraordinary.'

'So then' – Verity was ticking off options on her fingers – 'you either have one or two popped straight back in after a couple of days, or you freeze them. With standard IVF, they often freeze them anyway now because they think there is a slightly better chance of implantation after your body has had a month off to recover from all the drugs. Or you might freeze embryos while you are waiting to find a surrogate.'

'Because that can take a while?'

'That' – Verity looked suddenly bleak – 'can take a lifetime.'

'And then how do you get them back ... in ...?'

'Ah.' Verity perked up. 'That's the frozen embryo transfer. Or FET, as you start to call them after a while. Everything has an acronym, Miranda. *Everything*. The FET is relatively straightforward, especially if you're using a surrogate, because – hopefully – the host is super-healthy and hasn't got any fertility issues. It's basically just a matter of ensuring someone is at exactly the right point in their cycle, and then defrosting the embryo and going for it.'

'So that bit,' Miranda thought aloud, 'could happen more or less anywhere?'

'I suppose so,' Verity said. 'It's definitely the more lo-tech bit of the whole process.'

'And why Ukraine? Why not – I don't know – Bangladesh?'

'Surrogacy breaches sharia law,' said Verity crisply. 'Most Islamic rulings have concluded it isn't acceptable, certainly amongst the Sunnis. The Shiites are slightly more open to it, which is why there is some surrogacy in Iran, but not much.'

The brisk summary reminded Miranda of Verity's years at the BBC.

'Do you ever miss journalism?' Miranda asked without thinking. She saw the regret flicker in Verity's eyes, the enthusiasm draining away.

'Every day,' Verity said tonelessly. Then she rallied: 'But of course, I love the children more than anything . . .'

'But why did you—'

'Quit?' Verity was fiddling with her coffee cup. 'I thought that stress must be part of the problem. We'd been trying for years by then, and it just took over everything. Should I eat this? Should we book that holiday? Will we both be in London for the right forty-eight hours this month? Especially with Jonty's job, travelling too.'

'So you decided to reduce stress? I thought you'd stopped working to bring them up. I didn't realise . . .'

'Yes, we decided I should quit. We? I did. Or did Jonty? I don't even remember any more. But it meant I could go off to Florida. For weeks, if necessary.'

'It must have been tedious.'

Verity's jaw was clenched. 'Tedious is one word.'

'I'm sorry.'

'I know I am lucky,' Verity's voice was sharp. 'And it worked out for us, while some people never get there. But it's all so bloody unfair, isn't it? Everything falls on the woman, time and time again. The ridiculous thing is that half the time, they reckon it's the man's problem anyway. Jonty's life is ... Well, it's barely changed, has it? Apart from a couple of delightful children, whereas mine ...'

'And then quitting didn't help anyway? Before you went for IVF?'

'No. Although who knows? That's the problem with this whole "miracle of life" business,' Verity made quote marks with her fingers. 'No one really knows anything.'

'But you got there in the end.'

'Just about.'

Verity was gazing out at the garden. 'It's all madness, when you think about it. And so oddly medieval. Men don't have to kill each other to prove they're men any more, do they? So why do women have to have children to prove themselves? It's insane.'

They sat there for a moment, staring at the dank garden shed.

'It's our battlefield,' said Miranda.

'Are you and Tom ...' Verity let the question drift.

'Oh no,' said Miranda. 'Not yet. No.'

8

A few hours later, Casey was waiting for Gabriel Bantham. On the street outside his Georgetown apartment block, as the birds sang into the dawn.

Hessa had followed him home from the embassy the night before, to this home close to Rock Creek.

This is a test, isn't it?

Not really. Yes.

I'll find his address.

I know.

Casey was neat now, dark hair tied back, waiting for Bantham's door to open. She had felt her throat tighten, as his neighbours left for work, one by one. Every time the door opened, Casey wished she were somewhere else. Anywhere else.

Usually, she and Miranda had a rule: whoever did the undercover escaped the front-up.

Casey always hated the front-ups anyway. It was the change in the voices; that was the worst. From buoyant and brash, confident and ebullient, to uncertain and panicked and broken. The undercover front-ups were the worst. As they realised, so slowly, that it was a lie. All of it.

It was you, all along. Wasn't it? Whoever you fucking well are.

Better, always, that it was an anonymous voice. So the humiliation and the shame were at least impersonal.

Casey hated it. Hated it every time.

But today, it had to be her, because Miranda was thousands of miles away. So Casey thought about Romida, the little girl living in the dark, and dug her fingernails into her palms.

Above her head, the lights flicked on and off in Bantham's building. It was a townhouse divided into apartments, smartened up recently. Casey waited and waited and waited.

Finally, the door opened, and Bantham took the steps down to the street in a rush. Late. Hurrying. Cross. And Casey stepped into his path.

For a second, Bantham's eyes swept over her, narrowing as they took in the tied-back hair, the jeans. Hessa was beside Casey, ice-still.

'Katie?' Bantham tried.

'No,' said Casey. Then, almost meaning it, 'Sorry.'

'Who are you?' His voice was almost a shout. 'What do you want?'

Wordlessly, Casey handed him a silver tablet. A tremor started in his hands, and Bantham pressed play almost involuntarily.

There he was, leaning back in his chair, smiling. He was neatly framed by the Four Seasons's white irises and a bottle of mineral water. The words clear, the picture sharp.

It was almost artistic.

Miranda had been known to move glasses, salt and pepper, a bottle of wine, into a shot. *People love the undercover filming, you know. You want it to look the part, in the clips.*

But Casey just wanted a clear line of sight, and peace and quiet.

And now she watched as Bantham crumbled.

It doesn't take much, I assure you.

You make it sound so easy.

It is.

Around them, Washington's commuters slammed out of their houses and set off for the metro.

'Who are you?' Bantham's voice was ragged. He leant against a burr oak, as if he might stumble and fall. 'What's happening?'

For Romida.

'Shall we go into your house?' Casey suggested politely.

'No.' He glanced around, thought of the neighbours. 'Yes.'

Bantham's hand shook as he put the key in the door. There was a narrow shared corridor with polished floorboards, and a flight of stairs at the end. One floor up, his apartment was elegant and neatly tidy. Old political cartoons were framed on grey walls. In the sitting room there were dozens of books, an expensive television and a very lavish sound system. There was no sign of anyone else living in the few rooms.

Bantham collapsed onto a brown tweed sofa in the sitting room. Casey waited for a second, then perched unasked in one of the armchairs. Hessa lingered in the doorway.

In the bedroom behind him, Casey could see that Bantham had made his bed before setting out for the day. She imagined him smoothing the blue-and-white striped duvet cover, just before the sky fell in.

'Who are you?' His voice was choked. 'Journalists, I suppose?'

'Maybe,' said Casey.

'You're like vultures,' he hissed. 'Going for the eyes.'

'Maybe.'

They gave him time to think, though, because they didn't want his first, panicked reaction. As they watched, his hands slowly stopped shaking.

'What,' he said, in the end, 'do you want?'

'Bangladesh,' said Casey.

'Bangladesh?' She watched him recalibrate, reassess. Not what he had expected, she could see. Her thoughts recalculated, again.

'We want to know exactly what happened out there,' she insisted.

'I don't know . . .' The words caught in Bantham's throat. 'I don't know what you mean . . .'

But there was a hesitation somewhere.

'I think,' Casey said coldly, 'that you do.'

Bantham's eyes roved around the comfortable room, and everything he had to lose. His back straightened.

'This is ridiculous.' He tried anger. 'You're completely mad.'

'Don't,' said Casey patiently. 'Don't.'

'How dare you?' The outrage bubbled up, real now. 'How dare you approach me like this? It is absolutely disgraceful.'

Bantham leapt to his feet, his movements still jerky, and took the few steps to the fireplace. A mirror hung above the mantelpiece, and Casey knew he was watching her in it.

'None of this needs to go any further.' Casey didn't meet his eyes. 'This is all just between us, at the moment. But we do need to understand a few things, my colleague and I.'

And it might be their secret, partly because Ross would have wanted the minister, not the nameless girls in some faraway country.

‘What do you mean?’ Casey glanced up and Bantham’s eyes were sharp in the mirror. Almost hopeful. He turned around.

‘I want to clarify exactly what happened,’ Casey said smoothly, ‘in Bangladesh.’

‘I don’t know anything about Bangladesh.’ Bantham shook his head. ‘You’re fucking mad.’

‘Tell us.’ Casey made it an order. ‘Right now.’

Bantham was scuffing his shoe against the floorboards.

‘I can’t imagine why you’ve targeted me like this.’ It was almost a plea.

‘You do.’ It was Hessa now. ‘You know exactly why we came for you.’

She pressed a button on the tablet again.

It doesn’t take much, I assure you.

You make it sound so easy.

It is.

Hessa stopped the recording. ‘That’s why.’

‘We just want to clarify a few things,’ Casey’s words floated across the room. ‘You’d be a source on our story. And we look after our sources, Gabriel.’

They let the silence run, and quite suddenly, Bantham disintegrated.

‘Do you mean it? That it’s just to help you clarify things.’

Casey tilted her head, in what might have been assent.

‘I may have organised a few meetings.’ Here was the desperation, so familiar. ‘Meetings that helped out a few companies, once or twice. I can see – now – how that might have been misinterpreted. Maybe. But nothing … Nothing …’

‘And the weeks away?’

Bantham's eyes widened.

'There was a weekend here and there, maybe,' he said. 'Ten days in Koh Samui, once. But you're absolutely right, I shouldn't have done it.'

The admissions were coming easily, thought Casey. Too easily.

'And did you think no one would ever find out?' she asked.

'They were just research visits, really,' he floundered. 'Just to meet people, build contacts. You know how it is.'

The political cartoons sneered down from their cherrywood frames, the ignominy looming so close.

'It was helpful for everyone,' he finished lamely. Casey thought of the MPs, trundling out to DC for a quiet word. It happened everywhere.

'Who was paying you?' Hessa asked.

Bantham reeled off three companies busy building empires in the east.

'I'll never do it again,' he promised, blindly. 'And I suppose you're recording this too, now … Oh God. I should never …'

He was almost in tears, the sophistication ravaged.

'My parents,' he begged. 'There's only me … They couldn't bear …'

For a split second, Casey thought of an old lady, shamed by her son. The silver head bowing, everything lost. *But he is still my son.*

Casey forced herself to focus instead on those companies, so ruthless, seizing the opportunity and ramming it home. It wasn't fair, no.

'The passports,' said Casey. 'What about the passports?'

It puzzled him, she could see that at once.

'The passports?' he asked. '*Passports*?'

Bantham was fidgeting with a paperweight now, shifting it from hand to hand, like a magic trick. The paperweight had a pale yellow rose in it. Trapped in glass, preserved for ever, gleaming as Bantham fidgeted.

'We know about the passports, too.' Casey kept her face stern, but she could feel the ground slipping away.

'I don't know what you mean.'

Bantham put the paperweight back on the fireplace, and turned to Casey.

'Stop it,' Casey snapped at him, bullying now. 'Tell us.'

'No.' His eyes were wide. 'Really … I don't …'

And she didn't know enough to trap him, this time. Had to tread so carefully, because if he guessed her ignorance, he would surge off the back foot at once, and they might lose it all even now.

'You do know,' she said flatly, risking it. 'You know about the British couples, and the babies.'

There was a long pause.

'Oh,' he said. 'That.'

'Yes.' Casey's confidence flooded back. 'I need to know about that.'

'But I don't know,' said Bantham. 'I don't know what was going on. Not really.'

'Yes, you do.' Casey was headmistress-firm. 'And you're going to tell us all about it.'

'I don't,' he said. 'It wasn't me. I had nothing to do with any of that business.'

'Then who?' Hessa couldn't contain herself. 'Who was doing it?'

'I don't know,' Bantham choked.

'Tell me,' Casey spat. 'Right now.'

'I promise it wasn't me,' Bantham swore. He glanced around one more time, and crumbled. 'It was the old ambassador. It was Sir William Cavendish.'

9

'Do you think he was telling the truth?' Miranda leaned her chair back.

They were in the *Post's* offices, straight from an overnight flight into Gatwick.

Casey looked across at Hessa.

'I thought he was,' Hessa offered. 'He was feeling guilty about some of the visits and things. The trip to Koh Samui, and so on. But he went blank when we asked about the passports. There wasn't any guilt there.'

'We could check up on him,' Casey said carefully.

Miranda raised her eyebrows.

'How?' asked Hessa.

'His business card has his private email address on it,' Casey said delicately.

'And his first pet was Beau, and his mother's maiden name is Kilmartin,' Hessa realised. 'I wondered what you were ...'

Because with his birthday publicly available, it would only take seconds to crack into an account from some anonymous internet cafe.

Only *in extremis* though, that sort of thing. Only when there was no other way.

For Romida.

'Would it help?' asked Miranda.

'Probably not,' said Casey. 'I think I could tell when he was lying, and I think that he was telling the truth when he was talking about Cavendish.'

'I thought Luke said that Cavendish was clean,' said Miranda. 'One of the good guys.'

'We've been told that before,' said Casey.

Casey was watching Hessa. Hessa had asked – quietly, sleepless in the airport – as they waited for their plane: 'What happens to Bantham now?'

'Nothing happens to Bantham now,' Casey's voice was cold. 'Not now.'

Casey had ground it into Gabriel before they left the apartment: *You tell no one about us. There is no quiet warning to Cavendish. No guilty confession.* Nothing. *Don't forget what we have on you.*

And he'd looked up at her, from the depths of his brown tweed sofa. *I promise. I promise. I'm sorry.*

'But Bantham admitted it, that stuff with the companies.'

'Do you think,' Casey had turned to Hessa, surrounded by the endless marble of Dulles airport, 'that he will ever do anything like that again?'

Hessa thought of the broken man, tear tracks on his face.

'No,' said Hessa slowly. 'It'll be the straight and narrow for Bantham, from now on.'

'Well then.'

A form of justice, maybe.

And Bantham might be useful one day, Casey didn't say to Hessa. He might even end up a sort of friend. It happened, oddly often. There was a relief, sometimes, when someone already knew the worst about you.

'Well done, back there, Hessa,' Casey said aloud. 'I know they aren't easy, those front-ups. You did well.'

'Thank you,' said Hessa, very quietly.

Luke, annoyed with himself out in Delhi, had already found an address for Cavendish, safe in his Greek retirement.

'Paxos,' Luke wrote. 'It's a little island, one of the Ionians. Fly to Corfu, and then there's a ferry the rest of the way. Not much there. Especially not at this time of the year.'

'Can you come?' Casey asked Miranda, when Hessa was out of the room.

'No.' Miranda was looking down at her screen, so Casey couldn't see her face. 'Not this time.'

Days before, Casey had caught Miranda staring at a picture of a pretty girl on a corporate-grey website. Curling highlighted hair, coy little eyes and a how-can-I-help-you smile. Rebecca. *Becky*.

'OK.'

Changing the subject, Miranda told Casey about the conversation with Verity Taylor, and the rest of her research into surrogacy. 'As Audrey said, there are different rules and regulations all around the world.' Miranda spoke quickly. 'Surrogacy divides approximately into altruistic and commercial procedures. Very few people will go through an entire pregnancy, not to mention the birth and all the tests, out of the kindness of their hearts. So that leaves commercial. The Kim Kardashian route.'

'Right.'

'California is the epicentre of US surrogacy,' Miranda went on. 'They're seeing a rise in social surrogacy there – that's if you just don't want to be pregnant for whatever reason. Too busy running your company, or you're a bikini model who doesn't fancy a year or more out of the business. It's hugely expensive though, and the price is rising, partly because there is more competition for would-be surrogates. Some of the brokers have started targeting military wives, because they're often stuck in the middle of nowhere and struggle to get into employment.'

'How nice,' said Casey.

'So it's quite possible that our man in Bangladesh has spotted a viable market. If they can do surrogacy on the cheap in Bangladesh and get passports, while broadly maintaining appearances for the hopeful parents, then there's the potential to make a lot of money.'

'OK.' Casey rubbed her forehead.

'The other complication is that different religions take different approaches. IVF isn't acceptable to some Catholics, partly because of the creation – and potential destruction – of embryos. The more conservative Jews don't accept it either.'

'Endless problems.'

'Quite. It would most likely be regarded as unacceptable in Bangladesh, which could be why it has to happen under the radar.'

Hessa reappeared, with a tray and three cups of tea.

'I think I found out about that British company operating in Africa,' Hessa said. 'The one that Bantham mentioned.'

She passed over her careful notes to Casey.

'Tartarus Energy,' Casey read aloud. 'Registered in the Isle of Man, chaired by a South African oil man and owned through a Bermuda-based company. But there are a couple of Tory grandees on the board, and a serviced office with a brass nameplate on the door near St James's Park, and so of course our MPs go into battle for it.'

She clicked on their website, a row of smiling suits under a logo of a charging bull.

Casey sighed, and put the notes to one side, swallowing a mouthful of tea. 'Good work, Hess.' Casey turned to her. 'Now, can you call this number?'

It was the number that Romida had used to call her mother. Untraceable, Casey had discovered. Almost certainly a burner.

'Are you sure?' Hessa looked nervous.

'You'll be great,' said Casey. 'You know how to do it.'

And Hessa took a deep breath, and dialled the number.

Hello, can I speak to Anu please? In her best Bengali.

This is not his phone. A rough voice, a man's voice.

Oh, silly me. Who is this then?

Don't call this number again.

The line went dead. Hessa looked around at them in a silence. 'Sorry.'

'Why?' Miranda was smiling at her. 'You did brilliantly.'

Casey had stopped the recording. 'Can you tell where he was from, that man?'

'I think it was a Chittagong accent,' Hessa said. 'They speak Chittagonian further south. It's a dialect, I suppose. Closer to the Rohingya language.'

'Would your mother know for sure?' Casey asked.

'Yes,' said Hessa. 'She likes working out stuff like that.'

'Like her daughter,' Miranda grinned. 'I wonder if this man dropped his mobile somehow, out in the building, wherever they keep the women.'

'Something like that,' said Casey. 'And now he's got it back. Which means that Romida won't be able to call her mother ever again.'

10

It was beautiful, the house of Sir William Cavendish. There was a perfect symmetry to the old stone front, the shutters faded to the softest blue. Jasmine sprawled around the front door, reaching up to the cracked pink tiles of the roof. Around the house, the overgrown olive trees drifted like ancient green ghosts.

The house was on the west side of Paxos, above grey cliffs that fell hundreds of feet to the sea. Nothing for a hundred miles, all the way to Italy.

The old man sat there as if he was waiting for them, under a threadbare violet parasol. He watched them picking their way up the ruined limestone steps, past the fallen stone posts that would once have held a gate. He got to his feet as they drew near, steadying himself on the slab of the table. Only just over seventy, Casey knew, but he looked older, with the habit of secrets in his eyes.

'Good morning,' he said, with a nod of his head. He was so polite, raising his tattered straw hat, that Casey hesitated.

'It's a beautiful day,' she said.

'It's always glorious on Paxos.' It was as if he were talking to someone else, a half-smile on his face. 'I've lived in so many places, all over the world, but this has always been my favourite.'

For a moment, it was the polite conversation of a hundred receptions, and a thousand cocktail parties, and maybe something else.

Cairo, Delhi, Beirut, Jeddah, Casey thought. A lifetime of service, before, finally, Dhaka.

'We found this house together, my wife and I,' Cavendish went on. 'On holiday. A few decades ago, now. We walked all the way along the paths, through the lavender and the bees, and one day we found it, just waiting for us around a corner. We loved it from the first moment we saw it.'

Lady Cavendish died a few years ago in Sri Lanka, Luke had told them. Not long before Sir William had meant to retire. She just didn't wake up, one morning. Nothing to be done. An Englishwoman, buried thousands of miles from home. Cavendish had stayed on with the Foreign Office, after that. Gone to Dhaka, alone.

Casey looked around at the old house, and the dream it had once been.

'Have you walked out along the cliff path?' Cavendish went on. 'There's a spot just along from here where it looks as if a giant took a bite out of the cliffs. Like a huge scoop of ice cream. The swifts arrive there in the spring. Thousands of them, pausing on their journey from Africa to who knows where in the north. It's like witchcraft, watching them dip and dive. The Greeks take potshots at them, of course, especially during their Eastertime. I very much hope they don't hit them.'

'It's a magical island,' said Casey uncertainly.

'It's so peaceful,' he said. 'Busier during the summer, of course. The villas fill up with people complaining about the sewage system and the potholes, which are troublesome, of course. Terribly hot, too. Although there is usually a breeze up here.'

Cavendish looked out over the sea again. The gardens ran to the edge of the cliffs, a crumbled stone wall marking the land. Two donkeys were grazing in the next field.

'I haven't walked out along that path yet,' said Casey. 'To the cliffs.'

'You must,' he said. 'You must.'

He sat down at an old stone table, waved to wooden chairs. 'Please.'

Hessa hadn't spoken a word. They sat down. Yesterday's newspaper was folded neatly under a green teapot. Pale pink geraniums straggled out of chipped urns, and a stone lion, curled up nearby, had lost half of his paw.

'Now,' said Cavendish, almost patiently. 'Why are you here?'

Casey turned to him, squarely.

'I understand that you signed off on a series of passports, Sir William. Out in Dhaka. For families going through illegal surrogacy in Bangladesh.'

The silence wrapped around them, stifling as a scarf. The old ambassador's face didn't move.

'That would be most improper,' he said calmly.

'I know,' said Casey. 'But I think you did it, all the same.'

'You know I wouldn't tell you,' he said, 'either way.'

A man shrouded in secrets, Casey though. Entombed, even. A lifetime of silence, fashioned into an armour that she would never pierce.

She tried, all the same.

'Gabriel Bantham,' she said. 'He knew about it. And he told us. He told us everything he knew.'

A flicker of sadness crossed the old face.

'Gabriel,' said Cavendish, and there was almost an affection there. 'A young man in a hurry.'

They waited.

'I sent him off to Washington, you know.' Cavendish said. 'I knew he was close to the wrong people out in Dhaka, and I warned him. But I sent him to Washington. Gave him a second chance, one might say. And not everyone gets a second chance.'

And he betrayed you, Casey couldn't say. Not that he wanted to, but he betrayed you all the same. And I can never explain why, not to you.

'How many?' Casey asked.

But he shook his head, waving her away like a fly.

'You know I won't tell you, Miss ...'

'Benedict. Cassandra.'

'That organisation?' He nodded to the teapot and the folded newspaper.

'The *Post*,' she said. 'How many passports?'

'Silence' – he smiled the apology – 'is just too old a habit.'

'But we know,' Hessa's voice was unsteady, but firm, 'that you did it. We just don't know why.'

Cavendish looked from Hessa to Casey and back again.

'The eternal question,' he said. 'Why?'

They waited. The sea pounded against the rocks, far below.

'The wind is getting up,' said Cavendish. 'I do hope your ferry back to Corfu isn't delayed. You can get awfully isolated over here, at this time of year. The ferry doesn't come over for days. Or have you got a place to stay? Lakka, maybe? It's the nearest village. Best not stay there, ideally. It's known locally as Lakka facilities.'

A half-wink, and he smiled to himself, sending a creak of laughter towards his feet.

'Please tell us,' said Hessa.

She needed to be liked even when it was all a lie, thought Casey. It made the job so much harder.

'If I had done all that you say,' said Cavendish to Hessa, 'surely these children would have gone to good homes? Loving homes?'

'They might have done,' said Casey. 'But you couldn't possibly know that. And what about the women left behind in Bangladesh?'

'We want to know who was coordinating it all,' said Hessa. 'Who is behind everything.'

'Ah,' said Cavendish.

He stood up, stepped away from the table, lost in the curved mirrors of memory. A pear tree stood there, just starting to bud. Cavendish ducked his head towards it.

'Have you ever seen a Poire Williams?' said Cavendish. 'Eau de vie. Or brandy, really. With a whole pear trapped in the middle of the glass bottle. Now, I ask you, how do you get the pear into the bottle? That whole perfect pear? My permanent secretary asked me that question on my very first day at work, many years ago.'

'I don't know,' said Casey.

'You place the bottle over the growing pear,' Cavendish gestured. 'Right from the very start. And the pear grows inside the bottle. And, when it's ready, you just snip the stem, and it is done.'

He looked west, across the blue of the Mediterranean. There was an immeasurable sadness in his eyes.

'You don't realise you are trapped until it's far too late,' he said, almost to himself. 'I should have been firmer with Gabriel, right from the start.'

A bird sang in an olive tree beside the old stone wall. Cavendish took a few more steps away from the table.

'The Venetians had all these olive trees planted,' he said. 'Back in the sixteenth century. Thousands and thousands of them, all over the island. In the summertime, the fireflies flit between the trees in the dusk, and that's when you know there is an old magic here.'

Hessa was staring at Casey, her eyes wide.

'I wish my wife could have lived with me in this house.' Cavendish took a few more steps. 'We dreamed of it a thousand times. She never enjoyed any of those places. Dusty and chaotic, she'd say. Exhausting, all of it. I should never have taken her away. Not for a lifetime.'

He looked back towards the house, and the jasmine reaching up to the cracked pink tiles.

'Still,' he said. 'I hope I did some good.'

He gazed out to sea, east across the waves, then shook his head. He turned back to Casey. 'I am sorry not to be able to help you more,' he said. 'You must have known I would not be able to tell you anything useful.'

'We will find out some other way,' Casey told him firmly.

'Maybe,' he said. 'Maybe not.'

The old eyes met hers steadily. Sir William Cavendish would not tell her, Casey knew. She ducked her head. 'Come on, Hessa. Let's go.'

'Goodbye, Miss Benedict,' he watched them leave. 'Good evening.'

'Some people just won't.' Casey sipped at her glass of wine, staring moodily out at the sunset.

'Will Ross be cross? That we've come all the way out here, and got nothing?' Hessa sounded nervous.

'I don't care.'

They were sitting on the terrace of an old hotel, high above the cliffs, a mile or so south of Cavendish's house. The sun was setting in a blaze of gold scarlet, the cool of the night drifting in.

'I care,' Hessa told her lemonade.

Casey contemplated Hessa, remembering her own days as the most junior reporter, terrified of Ross every day. It was difficult, this job. Ordered to override, day after day, the human instinct to be polite, to not intrude, to avert one's eyes so civilly.

Painful, almost, for someone like Hessa, naturally shy, instinctively courteous. Some reporters – ruthlessly pushy, brutally assertive – never seemed to care. But Hessa would always struggle, Casey thought. The intuition, the perceptiveness, the intelligence: crucial to the undercover work. But they made it harder to approach a witness, or an unwilling source. When the intrusion was unbearable, and every hint of body language was screaming: *I am a human being in distress, please leave me alone. Please.*

Ross, knowing this, would be brutal. Targeting her, bullying her, kill or cure. Ensuring – quite deliberately – that Hessa was more scared of him than of the questioning. Forcing her through the habit of good manners to extract an answer from anyone.

Two small fisherman's boats were hurrying around the promontory, heading up the coastline. Casey watched them idly.

'Did you always want to do this?' Hessa asked.

'I don't remember.'

'And why do you do it now?'

'So that' – Casey was watching the sun disappear – 'no one can ever say, "I didn't know."'

There was a sudden howl of sirens to the north, unfamiliar on this holiday island. A few minutes later, a waiter hurried across, filled with the excitement of news. He refilled the peanut bowl, wiped the table and hovered until Casey asked the question he wanted: 'What's going on up there?'

'The old man …' he said. 'They have called all the fishermen to come and search for him out in the sea …'

'Why?' asked Hessa, her face suddenly taut. 'What's happened?'

'Old Sir Cavendish.' The waiter's eyes were wide. 'He fell … He fell right from the top of the cliffs.'

11

Hessa cried on the flight, all the way home. The tears came suddenly, in Corfu airport, as she stood next to a huge red I-heart-Kavos sign.

'I'm sorry,' said Casey, not quite meaning it. 'We don't know what happened though, Hessa. He might have tripped.'

'Do you believe that?'

'I don't know. We'll never know.'

A fisherman, bobbing past, had seen the old man, high up on the cliff. Alone, staring out at the sea. *There was something that made me keep watching him*, he had told the police, with a certain relish, enjoying the circle of fascinated eyes. *I don't know what exactly. And then I saw him fall.*

'He was living such a peaceful, beautiful life,' said Hessa. 'And we destroyed it, just like that. In a few words. Like smashing an antique vase.'

'Sort of,' said Casey. Then: 'You don't have to do this, you know, Hessa. There is a choice.'

'Is it always like this?'

'No,' said Casey. Thinking: sometimes, it's worse. 'But you don't have to do it at all. Tillie's desperate to work with us. You can go back to the newsroom. No one would blame you.'

It sounded more brutal than she meant.

For Romida.

'We didn't,' Hessa's eyes were puffy, 'even get anything out of it. He took all his secrets with him.'

'Yes.' Casey's thoughts were stuck in a groove, going over the conversation, and over and over. Because something didn't quite fit. 'But if he did jump, he made a choice, Hessa. He'd spent years in the Foreign Office. He knew how this all works. He could have told us what he knew, been a source. We'd have looked after him.'

Off the record, deep background, all the old codes.

'But he didn't.'

'No.'

'He wasn't doing any harm to anyone out there on the island,' said Hessa. 'No matter what he might have done before.'

'No.'

'Has anything like this happened to you before?'

'Not like this, no.'

'But it could have. It could happen every single time. You never know what you're walking into. What's gone before.'

A hen party clattered past, pink sashes, squealing. *What happens in Kavos, stays in Kavos.*

'Every time you knock on a door,' Hessa watched them cackle. 'You never know what you're going to find.'

Back on the hotel terrace, as the sun faded to a memory, Hessa's voice had stuck like a record. *He jumped. He jumped. He jumped.*

Until the words lost their meaning, and Casey shook her, quite hard. 'He's gone, Hessa. I know. And I'm sorry. But you have to pull yourself together.'

Staring at the peanuts, the scene was already clear to Casey: they had rambled past the old house, isolated in its few acres of bleached grass. There was nobody else around. Exchanged a few words, maybe. But nothing more.

Nothing more, OK?

A gasp. OK.

In her mind's eye, Casey saw the old man plunge through the air where his beloved swifts danced. The straw hat ripped away, the half-smile frozen.

All the way down to the waves, and oblivion.

Her heart felt as if it were being squeezed by a hard fist, and she turned away from Hessa. They had sat silently among the excited burble of theories, as the waiters reminisced about old Sir Cavendish.

It took the coastguards a few hours to find the old man, drifting in the blue, blue sea, and there was nothing anyone could do. The policemen shrugged, filled out some paperwork and headed back to the taverna. No one ever asked Hessa and Casey a question.

'You never give up, do you?' Hessa said, sharp upright on the awkward airplane seat.

Casey stared at the flight manual, the neat instructions for disaster. 'No.'

'Don't you feel bad?'

'Of course I do. We couldn't have known.'

There were tears in Casey's eyes, quite suddenly. She looked away, so Hessa didn't see.

'He's dead, Hessa,' said Casey. 'Dead. Of course I …'

The plane hit turbulence, heaving up and down in the sky, and the hen party's cackles dissolved into screams.

Now the plane was slowing into the long arc into Gatwick. Casey thought of the other planes lined up, ahead and behind, a necklace of lights flickering home through the dark.

'It's up to you, Hessa,' said Casey. 'You have to choose.'

12

Hessa was there the next morning though. She hadn't slept, Casey could see. But she was there, eyes swollen, in the little investigations room.

'So that line of inquiry's closed down,' said Miranda, quite brutally, so that Hessa's eyes flicked to Casey, just for a second.

Miranda had already spoken to Dash that morning.

So he might have tripped?

He might.

Fine.

Dash had moved quickly through shock to suspicion. They hadn't told the editor.

Need to know?

Not really.

All right.

'It's probably closed down,' said Casey now.

'But . . .' Miranda was watching her closely.

'It doesn't quite make sense,' said Casey. 'Luke Armitage said that Cavendish was liked by everyone, and generally seen as a good sort.'

In her hand, Casey held a rough draft of the *Post*'s obituary of Cavendish. The reminiscences, all of them, were glowing.

'He and his wife bought that house years ago,' said Casey. 'And that's where they planned to live out the rest of their lives. It was beautiful, yes. But it wasn't the lifestyle of a retired gangster.'

She thought about Cavendish's battered straw hat, the chipped urns, the lion without a paw.

'It was hardly,' Hessa agreed quietly, 'the lap of luxury.'

'Maybe the fight went out of him when the wife died,' suggested Miranda.

'But she died in Sri Lanka,' said Casey. 'Before he even went out to Dhaka. And it doesn't make sense that it was then that he suddenly decided that he wanted to retire to gold taps and caviar.'

'Luke said he adored her, didn't he?' said Miranda. 'People do stupid things when they're sad. You just don't know. He might have been vulnerable. To a pretty girl in a bar, or just a kind ear.'

'Maybe,' said Hessa. 'My mother says that man is from Chittagong, by the way. She listened to the recording, said she was sure of it.'

'Thanks, Hessa,' Miranda nodded at her.

'What if Cavendish was doing it for some other reason?' asked Casey. She sat forward and punched an extension into her phone.

'Harry?' Casey said. 'You couldn't pop in here for a second, could you?'

The obituaries editor sat in the newsroom, just a few desks away. Tall, gangly and impeccably polite, Harry de Villiers spent his days charming amiable anecdotes from weeping widows. 'Although sometimes no one can remember a single nice thing,' he said once, eyes wide with horror behind dark-rimmed glasses. 'Can you imagine? Not a single nice memory about a person.'

'Probably a news editor,' the Home Affairs editor had growled.

'Harry,' Casey said now. 'Sir William Cavendish's family. Who are they?'

He is survived by ...

Harry glanced down at his notebook. 'One son, forty-three, lives in Hong Kong at present. Unmarried, no children. Works in insurance. A daughter, Vivienne. She is married, to a Mr Hargreaves. Two children, three and tiny. They live in rural bliss, down in Devon. The daughter's forty-one.'

'Photographs?'

'A few,' Harry handed her printouts. 'A nice one from his time in Cairo. And that one was taken at his daughter's wedding.'

Casey studied it: a pretty girl in white lace, young, carefree, smiling on a proud father's arm. Casey looked closer.

'Have you spoken to the daughter?' Casey asked.

'Not yet. She didn't pick up the phone half an hour ago.'

'What does she do?'

'Nothing much, I don't think,' Harry shrugged. 'Been a housewife since she got married from what I can tell.'

'Do you mind if I speak to her instead of you? I'll say I'm calling about the obituary. I can file you everything you need.'

Obituaries were often the only section of the newspaper that some people didn't mind speaking to, for hours sometimes.

'Course not,' said Harry.

'Thanks.'

'That all?'

'Yes, brilliant.'

Harry half-bowed away. He didn't know they had been out on Paxos when Cavendish died.

And so Sir William Cavendish's death would merit a polite obituary. *Distinguished. Respected. At his home in Greece.*

'It's the daughter,' Casey told the investigations room. 'Down in Devon. I bet that's how it all started.'

'How do you know?' Hessa still sounded shivery. She had her hands tucked into her sleeves, and was chewing on a strand of hair.

'A hunch,' admitted Casey. 'She looks young in her wedding photographs, but she didn't have children until her very late thirties. She wasn't some hectic business type either. So what was she doing during all that time?'

They contemplated it.

'Make the call,' Miranda decided. 'But keep it gentle for now.'

Casey was charm personified on the telephone to Vivienne Hargreaves.

Sorry to bother you, at a time like this.

Not at all, I want people to know about his life. His achievements.

People are flattered – in all walks of life – to be asked for their opinion, or their story. It is a very human urge, the record of accomplishments chipped into the walls of the cave.

People want to tell their story, Ross had told Casey early on. Just give them the chance. Hold up the mirror.

In a leisurely manner, Casey and Vivienne ran over the biographical details, and gradually Casey edged the conversation round.

'It must have been fascinating for you, growing up in all those places? But difficult too, I imagine. Never being in the same place for long.'

'Yes,' agreed Vivienne. 'But my parents were so good at making a place feel like home. My brother and I were sent to England, for school. I missed my parents very, very much.'

'And did you visit him often in Greece? Since he retired?'

'The children love it out there.' Vivienne's voice was light, with an echo of boarding school. 'Paxos is always a bit chaotic, but it is such a special place. All our friends go out there too, of course.'

'It sounds wonderful.'

'He always loved walking along those cliffs. But the paths are terribly crumbly. He must have just missed his footing,' Vivienne said firmly.

'Of course,' said Casey. 'Did you visit the other places he was sent?'

'Some of them, yes. Cairo, once or twice. Delhi. Robin and I went on the triangle around Agra and Jaipur not long after we were married. Daddy always enjoyed showing us new places.'

'And Dhaka?'

The slightest hesitation. 'Once.'

'When was that?'

The shortest pause. 'Two or three years ago? Not long after he had moved across there. Not long after my mother . . .'

They chatted on. And finally, Casey said, 'Thank you so much, I won't take up any more of your time, you've been so very helpful.'

She hung up, typed up a few paragraphs for Harry, and then turned to Miranda. 'I'm quite sure of it,' she said. 'It's her.'

13

Vivienne Hargreaves lived in a Devon longhouse, on the edge of one of the prettiest villages. The house made up one side of a cobbled courtyard, and old stone barns another two. Casey and Miranda admired the slabs of granite, the daffodils bobbing in a stone trough. Pink and red camellias climbed the north wall. A black Labrador, sunning himself on a mounting block, barked what might have been a welcome.

'I'm a bit busy . . .' Vivienne opened the door, a child squalling behind her.

'It won't,' Casey smiled automatically, 'take very long.'

Her father's just died, Casey had said to Miranda, before leaving the office. Shouldn't we wait?

For how long? Miranda's jaw was set.

I don't know.

There we go.

Is everything OK with . . . You know.

Yes. Fine.

'We're from the *Post*,' Casey spoke to Vivienne. 'Actually, we talked yesterday. About your father.'

'Oh,' Vivienne smiled. 'His obituary. Of course.'

The hall was dark, with small windows and granite flagstones, uneven in places. In the kitchen behind Vivienne, Casey could see rows of bottled fruit, and strawberry jam prettily labelled. Two canaries hopped around a cage.

'Shall we go into the sitting room?' Vivienne was polite, but not instinctively warm. 'They're so inconvenient, these old houses. Impossible to heat. But we do love it here.'

Vivienne had thick dark hair and a strong jaw. Her green eyes were small, with firm eyebrows in a straight line above. She would be pretty, glossed up in London, Casey thought.

'Your house is very beautiful,' Casey said obediently.

Vivienne smiled around at her. She was prodding the fire, kneeling down without a thought for her sensible blue jumper and grey cords. The mantelpiece was covered in copperplate invitations, and there was a framed photograph of Vivienne, beaming, holding a tiny baby outside a beautiful church. Toys were scattered around the room. A wooden xylophone here, a stuffed lion there. An illustrated Snow White lay spine up on the floor, a pretty girl smiling on the cover.

'Thank you.' Vivienne sat back on her heels. 'Can I get you tea, coffee?'

'Tea would be lovely,' said Miranda. Because a hot drink always slowed the pace.

'I won't be a moment.'

Vivienne crossed the hall to the kitchen, and they heard her switch on a kettle.

Casey and Miranda looked at each other, thoughtfully. They didn't speak.

'Theo's out for the day with my husband, Robin,' Vivienne came back in. 'And Josie is meant to be asleep in her room, although she doesn't seem too keen on that.'

The grizzling continued from upstairs. Vivienne handed around flowered teacups and saucers. *How do you take it? Milk? Sugar?*

'Now,' said Vivienne, in the end. 'How can I help you?'

'We're researching,' Miranda said, quite calmly, 'surrogacy in Bangladesh. We have reason to believe that your children were born out there, and that your father helped you get a passport for them to bring them home to England.'

Vivienne froze, perched on the edge of her armchair. The saucer fell from her hands, smashing pink and white chips over the flagstones. Vivienne put her hands to her mouth, holding back the scream.

'What do you mean?' Vivienne just managed to control her voice. As Miranda began to speak again, the scream burst out. 'Get out of my house. How dare you? How *dare* you? Go to hell.'

'Here.' Casey stepped forward to help, but Vivienne was pushing her away with a sudden violence. *Don't touch me.*

The room was silent, for a moment. Vivienne's eyes flicked to the photograph, the baby wrapped in the long white dress. Her hands clenched.

'I am very sorry to ask you about this, Mrs Hargreaves,' began Miranda.

'No,' Vivienne spat. 'You're not. You're not remotely sorry.'

But there was no denial in her voice. Vivienne slid out of her seat, down to the floor, automatically feeling for bits of china.

'I don't . . .' She tried for calm too late. 'I don't know what you mean . . .'

'We're just trying to find out what is going on in Bangladesh,' said Casey softly. 'We have heard some very disturbing things, and we need to understand. Careful,' she put out a hand again, 'you'll cut yourself.'

'What do you care?' Vivienne looked up from the floor, crouched among the shards. Her lips were pulled back from her teeth, almost a snarl. 'You'll never be able to prove a thing. Even if the clinic was raided by the police, our names wouldn't be on anything. Theo is my child, mine and Robin's. And that's the end of it. The DNA ... Everything.'

'Look.' Casey kneeled down on the floor beside Vivienne. 'We can keep you and your family out of this. But we think terrible things are happening to women in Bangladesh, right now. And it may have got worse after Theo was born, for all we know. If you tell us what happened, it could help us find out what is going on.'

'I want you to get out of my house.'

'That,' Miranda said quietly, 'won't help anyone.'

There was a long silence. Vivienne looked at Casey, across the old Persian rug. She pushed herself backwards to sag against the armchair.

'We would, ' Casey repeated, 'keep you and your family out of it.'

A gust of wind blew around the courtyard, sending a door banging outside.

'Why should I trust you?' Vivienne's voice was sullen.

'You don't have to,' said Casey. 'But we will have to go to the police with what we know already. And then it will be the police that come for you, not us.'

'No,' said Vivienne. 'Please. You don't understand. We were so desperate for Theo. We would have done anything. *Anything.*'

'I know,' said Miranda gently.

'How,' said Casey, 'did this all begin?'

'Do you promise?'

Casey looked at her. 'I promise.'

Vivienne stared at her, for a long time. Then she climbed back onto the armchair.

'It was Dr Greystone.' Her voice was dull. 'In Harley Street. We had been seeing him for months. Years. And nothing was working. Not the drugs, not the IVF. Nothing. It becomes your whole world. You can't think about anything else. And every month, it gets worse, as time slips away. And one day you get one more call from one more friend – "We're pregnant!" And you can't stop crying.'

'I'm sorry,' said Casey automatically, thinking: Dr Greystone. *Dr Greystone.*

'It cost a fortune too,' Vivienne said. 'An absolute fortune. And people, who really mean the best, start saying, "Shouldn't you and Robin get a move on? You've been married for years now." And you can't believe anyone could be so stupid, and thoughtless, and cruel.'

'As if it's so easy,' said Miranda.

'Exactly.' Vivienne spun towards her. 'When you're growing up, and you're reading *Just Seventeen* and *More*, they all imply a man just has to look at you . . . And then . . .'

'So what happened,' Casey asked gently, 'with Dr Greystone?'

'We had been trying and trying,' said Vivienne. 'And I could get pregnant. I just couldn't stay pregnant. No matter what they did. They tried everything. And one appointment, Dr Greystone just asked, had I considered surrogacy? And I hadn't. I mean, I knew that some people did it. In America, and places like that.

But it's different in the UK. Much more complicated. I could never understand the idea of women just giving up their babies. To go through all that and then just give them away. What if they didn't hand them over? I just couldn't take anything more, not then.'

Vivienne had picked up the stuffed lion without thinking, stroking its golden coat.

'So what did he recommend?' Casey was lining up china chips on the coffee table. 'Dr Greystone?'

'First, he suggested Nepal,' said Vivienne.

'Why Nepal?' Miranda's voice was calm.

'Dr Greystone said surrogacy was becoming much trickier in India.' Vivienne was sounding more confident now. 'He said you didn't quite know what was going to happen in India, that it would be much more straightforward in Nepal, and there was a woman ready to do it. Keen, even. It would be really helpful to her and her family. And we thought about it, and we knew we had to try. After that, we just got more and more excited. But just when we were counting down the days to start, Nepal changed the rules.'

'Their supreme court banned it for everyone except Nepalis,' said Casey thoughtfully.

It was the earthquake in 2015, oddly, that shone a search-light on surrogacy in Nepal. To avoid the Indian ban on gay couples, some surrogates were being inseminated in India and then shipped back over the border to Nepal. When the earthquake struck the Himalayas, killing almost 9,000 people, foreign governments rushed to save the babies. One 747 landed in Ben-Gurion with twenty-six brand-new Israeli babies on board. Of course, there was no airlift for the surrogate mothers.

Nepal wasn't the only workaround the Indian industry had identified either, Casey knew. By the time of the earthquake, women were being recruited in Kenya, and flown over to Mumbai to be inseminated. When they were 24 weeks pregnant, the women were flown back to Africa, to give birth in designated hospitals in Nairobi a few months later. The parents then picked up their children in Kenya. Three continents, working in an odd sort of unity.

'Dr Greystone called us into his office one day,' said Vivienne, gathering pieces of china in the palm of her hand. 'He said that if we went ahead, he couldn't be sure we would be allowed to bring the baby home from Nepal, after all. He warned us that it might turn into a complete nightmare. I just collapsed, right there in his office. I remember crying and crying. I said I just couldn't go on. It had felt like we were so close, finally. But now it was all going to be taken away, just like that.'

The baby had stopped crying upstairs. The house was silent.

'Then what happened?' asked Miranda.

'Dr Greystone called me a few days later,' Vivienne said. 'He knew who my father was, you see. It must have come up, in one of our chats. He was nice, Dr Greystone. And we had been seeing him for so long that he knew that my father had moved from Cairo to Dhaka. He had been very kind when my mother died. He knew that she was desperate to be a grandmother.'

Vivienne's eyes filled with tears again. She looked much younger when she was crying.

'What did Dr Greystone say when he called you?' Casey edged Vivienne forwards.

'He said he'd been thinking,' said Vivienne. 'He said they might have found a way to do it in Bangladesh. But that it would need my father's help to get a passport for the baby.' Vivienne stared into the heart of the fire. 'I suppose I knew there was something wrong. Why would they need my father if it was all being done by the book?'

She turned and looked Miranda straight in the eye. 'But I didn't care any more.' She spoke each word with precision. 'I didn't care what it would take.'

'So you rang your father?'

'Yes.' Vivienne raised her jaw. 'I begged him. I pleaded.'

'What did he say?'

'He was furious with me,' said Vivienne. 'He said he could never countenance anything like that. That I should never even have asked. He put the phone down on me. And he would never do that normally … Never.'

'But you called him back?' Miranda was watching Vivienne intently.

'The next day,' said Vivienne. 'I told him that Hugh – that's my brother, he's in Hong Kong at the moment – was never going to settle down. Not for years. Not ever, if we're all honest with each other. And didn't he want grandchildren? And of course my father did, desperately. But he still wouldn't agree.'

'Did he put down the phone again?' Casey asked.

'Not that time,' said Vivienne. 'No.'

Casey imagined it: the daughter weeping down the phone, frantic to her father. Sir William, shaking his head.

She saw him again, the old man in his tattered straw hat, in the green shade of an old olive tree.

'Robin wasn't sure either,' said Vivienne. 'He wanted to be a father, always had. But he thought we might end up in trouble. By then, Dr Greystone was promising us that the situation was under complete control. Total control, he said. Every step of the way. And so I begged Robin. In the end, I threatened my father. I know it sounds awful, but I did. I said I just wouldn't go on ... Couldn't bear it ... I half-meant it, in the end.'

That was when he snapped, Casey knew. The emotional blackmail. A lifetime of honour laid aside for his daughter.

'You don't know what it is like.' Vivienne's eyes were dull. 'Your life divides into segments. Two weeks of misery, because it hasn't happened, yet again. Then two weeks of slow-growing hope. Convincing yourself that *this* is the month. Then that despair, crushing, again. Another month gone, another month older. It's the same circle, again and again. Because a month is just enough for the whole trajectory. From hope to despair and back again. That's one of the things you learn. Hope and despair, and hope and despair. And everywhere you look, there are pregnant women, and babies. Even calves and lambs, for God's sake. On every street corner, in every magazine, in every single conversation. Because everyone can do it, except you. It starts to feel like some terrible sentence, for a crime you haven't committed. A sentence that gets a month longer, and then a month longer, every single time. And every month is worse. And one day, you realise that it's never going to end. That you're just going to be sad, for ever.'

'And what happened' – Miranda brought her back – 'out in Bangladesh?'

'I don't know,' said Vivienne, and they could see she was telling the truth. 'I didn't want to know, not really. We had frozen embryos already, of course. They had been made in Harley Street, months earlier. Always seemed like a strange thing, that my first act as a mother was to have those embryos shoved into a freezer.'

Casey thought of those little half-lives, in test tubes, trapped in ice, stashed in long metal rows.

'I suppose the embryos were flown out to Bangladesh,' said Vivienne. 'God knows how they organised that. They must have found a way. And a few weeks later, Dr Greystone told us that the surrogate was pregnant. And I remember the feeling when we got to twelve weeks ... The glory ... The absolute wonder ... That was when I started believing it might actually work. That it might happen.'

'And then you flew out to Bangladesh?' Casey tried to imagine Vivienne in the sprawl of Dhaka. The endless traffic, the tuk-tuks everywhere, the beggars at the lights.

You get to know them. Casey's fixer had turned to her once, gesturing. That had been in Gulshan, at a particularly chaotic junction, five roads tangling like wool. This girl here, you see her? Cleaning the windscreens. I have been seeing her at this crossing since she was a baby. She's always here, at this junction. And she'll always be here. Unless she is hit by a car, of course. That happens. That happens a lot.

Vivienne glanced around her sitting room, at the silver glowing in the cabinet in the corner, and a painting of a stern Edwardian lady over a crammed bookshelf. Next to the Edwardian matron there was a watercolour of Vivienne, hopeful at twenty, untouchable behind glass.

'It was extraordinary, Bangladesh,' Vivienne said. 'I've visited my father in all sorts of places, of course. But never anywhere as chaotic as Dhaka. Have you been there?'

'Yes,' said Casey. 'A couple of years ago.'

'Dr Greystone told us when to fly out to Bangladesh,' said Vivienne. 'He was very precise.'

He could be, Casey knew. Those babies would be carefully timed, for the convenience of the new parents. Induced, quite ruthlessly, to a strict schedule. Or a C-section.

'We were staying at a hotel in Dhaka,' said Vivienne. 'It was meant to be five-stars, but it was still pretty grim. No one from the clinic was there, so it was all a bit nerve-racking. But one day, a man just walked into the hotel lobby, with this tiny scrap in his arms. And there he was, our beautiful baby. Theo. I could hardly touch him. I couldn't breathe. I loved him, right from the start. Loved him so much. Everything changed, just like that.'

'Just like that,' Miranda repeated.

'You didn't go to the hospital?' asked Casey. 'I know that in some surrogacy cases, the baby is handed over immediately.'

'No,' said Vivienne, a wrinkle between her eyebrows. 'They brought Theo to us.'

'So you never met the surrogate?'

'No.'

'You didn't need to check he was yours?' Miranda asked roughly. 'That they hadn't brought you some random baby?'

'He looks . . .' Vivienne stalled.

'And then your father arranged the passport?' Casey asked.

'Yes,' said Vivienne. 'We flew home as soon as we could. We just wanted to get Theo back here, safely into our house. There was no problem at passport control. Not in Dhaka, not here. It was easy, really. Dr Greystone provided all the paperwork we needed for Theo to fit into the British system.'

'Can you remember anything about the man?' asked Casey. 'The man who brought Theo to you?'

'Not really,' Vivienne compressed her lips for a second. 'He was taller than the average Bangladeshi.'

'So he was Bangladeshi?'

'Oh, yes,' Vivienne said. 'I suppose so. I remember thinking he was taller than you might expect. But I wasn't looking at him. The only thing I could see was Theo.'

'Did he speak English?'

'Yes.' Vivienne realised she knew more than she thought. She pondered for a second. 'I can't remember his name though.'

The Labrador padded in, contemplated the room, then flopped down on a rug in front of the fireplace.

'And then Josie?' Miranda asked.

'After all that, she just came along naturally,' said Vivienne. 'It can happen like that, they say. It felt like a miracle.'

'So your father didn't help you again,' Casey paused. 'But he did help other people.'

'I don't know,' said Vivienne. 'He never mentioned other people. And I'm sure he wouldn't have … He was so angry when I first suggested it …'

The flood of realisation rushed into Vivienne's face.

'He had to do it,' she said haltingly. 'Once he had done it once for me, they made him do it again.'

'Maybe,' said Casey. 'We don't know that.'

'Oh God,' said Vivienne. 'Oh my God.' The tears spilled down her face. 'I made him,' she said. 'He never wanted to do it. He hated it so much. And I forced him.'

She stared around the room again. 'And now he's dead,' she whispered. 'He's gone for ever. And I never once said sorry.'

14

They left her for a few minutes. Walked around the garden, teacups in hand. The willow was just coming into leaf, drooping gently over a pond. The clouds were low, a shaft of cold sunlight here and there. A little stream chattered past, on its way to join the river.

'Nice place,' Casey said, 'for a child to grow up.'

'Indeed.' Miranda was distracted. 'Did you see Jessie Miller's article this morning? About that Labour MP.'

Jessica Miller had taken over Miranda's old job back at the *Argus*. The rivalry was superficially friendly.

'I didn't think you'd like that,' Casey grinned.

When they got back to the house, Vivienne had washed her face. She stood there, pink-cheeked, dry-eyed, the laundry basket at her feet.

'I've told you everything I know,' she said, as they came into the kitchen. 'And I'm asking you, please, don't do anything to my family. Robin would be terribly upset, to know you had even come here.'

The sun flooded through the leaded windows, the shadows a cage on the wall.

'You don't know where she lived, this woman in Bangladesh?' asked Miranda.

'They never said anything about her at all.' Vivienne looked exhausted. 'I know I should have asked. But you just don't.'

'Not when you don't want to know,' said Miranda.

One of the canaries chirped loudly.

'I know,' said Vivienne. 'And I know what you must both think of me. If it's my fault that my father … If I can think of anything else, I will call you. I promise. But you want to get the person behind all this, don't you? You want to stop it happening again. So do that. Don't come for me. Don't come for my son, please, for God's sake. He's only three. He doesn't deserve any of this.'

There was ice in Vivienne's eyes as she spoke, her back straight. The diplomat's daughter, Casey saw.

'You definitely never knew anything at all about the mother?' asked Miranda.

'I'm Theo's mother.' The words were sharp. 'And, no, I never asked.'

'Is there any way that there might be more information at the house on Paxos?' Casey asked.

'The Foreign Office archived my father's papers,' said Vivienne. 'He was never interested in writing his memoirs, or anything like that. And I am sure he would never have written down anything about this.' Her face crumpled for a second. 'He would have been so ashamed.'

'He just wanted to live a quiet life,' said Casey.

'I don't know what we will do with that house now,' said Vivienne, almost to herself. 'I am sure the children would love it so much when they are a bit older. It is so very beautiful.'

'It is stunning,' agreed Casey, without thinking.

There was a pause.

'Did you go there?' Vivienne's words came slowly. 'Before he died? Out to the house on Paxos?'

Casey hesitated a long moment. But there was no way of lying: 'Yes. Yes, I went out there.'

'When?'

'Not long ago.'

Vivienne was watching her face. 'You were there' – there was an eruption of rage – 'when my father died. You were there!'

Casey looked across the room at Vivienne. Upstairs, the baby started to cry again. The awareness was growing, creeping across Vivienne's face.

'You went to my father, with all your accusations. With all your threats and menaces. You …'

'It wasn't—'

'Get the hell out of here,' said Vivienne. 'Get away from me.'

She spun away from them, out into the hall, and paused for just a second. 'You killed my father,' she said over her shoulder. 'You can leave the rest of my family alone.'

15

'You think he jumped, don't you?' Miranda was climbing into her car. They had left it, parked neatly in the village, beside the thatch of a Ring of Bells.

'Of course he jumped.' Casey was staring at an old tree. It had grown so slowly around a barbed-wire fence that the steel was completely embedded in the wood. Like a flawed relationship, Casey thought. Digging in so gently that nobody noticed.

'She's wrong, though, you know,' said Miranda.

'Is she?'

'If anything' – Miranda was firm – 'she destroyed her own father. She knew what she was doing, when she asked for his help.'

'She didn't know the consequences.' Casey watched the hedgerows slide past.

'No one ever does.'

By the time they got back to the office, Hessa had pulled together a package of research on Dr Greystone.

'A Dr Greystone operates out of one of the big Georgian houses on Harley Street. The building itself is owned by a company in the British Virgin Islands.' Hessa was reading from her notes. 'Aceso Limited. There are several doctors operating from different sets of rooms in the building, which is quite usual in these properties. Greystone is the only fertility specialist in that building. I've found a house, wife and kids in Hampstead. Huge place, must have cost a fortune. There is a website for Greystone's clinic, pretty standard stuff. Bouncing babies and big smiles, and however-can-I-thank-yous?'

'Heartwarming. He's British?' asked Miranda.

'Seems to be.' Hessa sounded more enthusiastic about her work now.

'GMC register?'

'Yes.'

'Cuttings?' Casey's voice was quiet.

'Nothing,' said Hessa. 'He has no profile at all. There are whispers on the chatrooms though. They say he can work miracles.'

'How much does he charge?'

'If you have to ask . . .' Hessa shrugged. '"It's a baby," I found on one forum. "I'd give anything. Everything." It's a good industry to be in, when the customers have that sort of mindset.'

'Can't put a price on life,' Casey said flippantly.

'Well, it turns out,' Hessa replied, 'that you can.'

'And I suppose babies,' Miranda said almost to herself, 'are the closest thing you can get to immortality, even with all of Harley Street at your disposal.'

'Did you scout out the building?' Casey glanced at Hessa.

'Yes,' Hessa's mouth twitched. 'I went along and rang the top bell, and then I had a good look at each floor, before – oops – realising I was in the wrong building. There's a big basement, in those buildings, and then four floors of doctors. Smaller rooms in the attic. There's a plastic surgeon on the first floor of Greystone's building, and then a dentist. Greystone is the next storey above, up a couple of flights of stairs. There's a secretary on the landing, who shows people into a big waiting room. Greystone's office is to the left, and there's another room on the same floor too. A lab, maybe? Or perhaps a small surgical theatre.'

She stopped.

'Well done,' said Casey. 'Great work, Hessa.'

'I suppose,' Miranda said, 'that it's time for a visit to Dr Greystone.'

16

It was immaculate: the shiny grey door, the grape hyacinths spilling out of the window boxes, the polished brass door number and the glossy black railings. A Harley Street townhouse impeccably repurposed. Miranda paused on the marble steps, and rang the doorbell.

'After all,' she had said to Casey as she left the office, her mouth twisted to the side, 'I am the right age for a visit to Dr Greystone.'

Miranda was wearing a sensible skirt and a fawn silk shirt. 'Drab,' she had moaned to Casey. An upside-down Cinderella.

The shiny grey door unlocked with a purr. On the second floor, the receptionist was beautiful in a black linen suit, half-hidden behind a sleek computer and a huge bunch of lilies.

'Miranda Lancaster.' She gave her married name, almost unfamiliar. She was Miranda Darcey in her head; she forgot that Miranda Lancaster existed, too often. That Miranda Lancaster was brought out for the lie. 'I'm so sorry, I'm terribly early,' Miranda went on. 'My previous appointment was cancelled. Would you mind awfully if I just sat in your waiting room and read my book?'

'Not at all.' The professional polish gleamed. 'Can I bring you a cup of tea?'

There were only a few women in the waiting room. Miranda smiled around the room, and then sat down to leaf through piles of *Country Life* and *Good Housekeeping* and *House and Garden*. Not *Mother and Baby*, though. Not here. There were more lilies in the waiting room. The sofas were a soft pink, with framed watercolours of flowers on the wall.

Miranda sat down, and waited. It never took long to learn a routine.

The receptionist came for the women, some of the appointments taking just a few minutes. Only one of the women was accompanied by a husband. He was awkward, not sure quite where to look. Several women were pregnant already, touching their bumps self-consciously. Not them, thought Miranda. Not them.

Miranda began chatting to the women as they arrived. *Have you come far? Aren't the lilies lovely? I've heard he's brilliant, Dr Greystone. You hear such encouraging things.*

And then gently: *It's just not working, not for us. No matter what we do. You too? I know. It's devastating.*

The receptionist popped in. 'I'm sorry to keep you waiting, Mrs Lancaster. It's just such a busy day that I haven't been able to squeeze you in earlier.'

'There's really no rush,' said Miranda. 'I would have to wait somewhere else anyway, and it's much nicer here. My husband and I are getting the train home together, you see.'

'Of course.' That gleaming smile. 'Another cup of tea?'

'Thank you.'

Just then, a woman came out of Greystone's office, crying. She stood on the landing, tears trickling down her face. A sound like an animal in pain came from her throat, as she stared blankly at the stairs. And the other women in the waiting room looked away, because this horror was too raw.

Miranda's heart twisted for this woman, crying outside an anonymous waiting room. She stood up sharply.

'Are you all right?'

'It's failed.' The woman could barely speak. 'It's failed, again.'

It wasn't fair, talking to her. Not here. Not now. Not ever.

But Miranda hugged the woman, because she was there. *I'm sorry. I'm so sorry.* She felt the thin shoulders shake, the despair physical.

The receptionist had her routine. She patted shoulders caringly. She handed out tissues. She called a taxi. *Don't cry, Mrs Abbott. Next time. Next time. Next time.* And the woman was ushered away, still crying, out of sight.

Forgive us our trespasses.

Miranda sat there for a long time, staring at the white lilies in a silver bowl, orange stamens stripped, seeing nothing at all.

'Another cup of tea?' the receptionist asked.

Miranda looked up only as a pretty girl slipped shyly into the room. She was tall and slim, her long brown hair falling out of a ponytail. She wore a loose blue-and-white tunic, sailor-striped, over black leggings. In her late twenties, Miranda judged. A wedding ring, and a big diamond on her left hand. The woman moved delicately, as if she had been a trained dancer, once.

Flat stomach, Miranda noticed, disguised. 'Hello,' she said.

They smiled at each other across the quiet of the room. 'Gorgeous day,' said Miranda.

'Have you been waiting long?' The woman had a soft voice, so that Miranda had to lean close to hear her.

'Not too long.' A big smile. 'Are you waiting for your results?'

'Not really. No.' The smile gone, the woman was staring at the lilies with solemn grey eyes. 'At least … No.'

'He's so good, isn't he? Dr Greystone. Everyone says he's a genius.'

'Yes.' A sweet smile. 'That is what people say.'

The woman picked up a magazine. Flicked through it, without reading the words. She jumped at a bang from the street.

'Actually' – Miranda dropped her voice confidingly – 'we are thinking about surrogacy.'

The woman glanced up, eyes wide. She hesitated, for a moment. Then: 'Yes. Actually, that is what we decided, too, in the end.'

'How lovely,' Miranda smiled at her. 'When is your baby due?'

The woman's face lit up. 'Just a few weeks now. Dr Greystone wanted to talk over a few last things. I can't … I still can't quite believe it.'

The words were flooding out of her, the joy overwhelming.

'How wonderful,' said Miranda. 'Where will you go to pick up the baby?'

The receptionist came into the room. 'Emily Burton? Dr Greystone is ready for you now.'

The woman got to her feet, smiled at Miranda over her shoulder.

'Bangladesh,' she said, the joy overflowing for a moment. 'We're going out to Dhaka.'

17

Miranda and Casey watched the Burton-Smiths pick their way down the cobbled street. They were hand in hand, smiling in the light at the end of the day.

'Thank fuck,' Miranda whispered, 'for that.'

They were in Bath, just next to the great Abbey. The grand old church soared above them, the East Window like a frozen dream. The Burton-Smiths paused to look up, still holding hands.

They've gone to Bath for a few days, a neighbour had said. *A babymoon, that's what they call it nowadays. At Elton House, or something, she said. Not long now, they say. It's lovely news.*

It had taken days and days to find Emily Burton. *We're running out of time*, Casey had fretted, curved over her desk.

There were hundreds of Emily Burtons, right the way around the country. And dozens of them were about the right age. Miranda had travelled hundreds of miles. Not an Emily Josephine Burton, near Ludlow in Shropshire. Not Emily Rose Burton, just off the Royal Mile, in the heart of Edinburgh. Not an Emily Nugent, married – unhappily, from the quiet sag in her shoulders – to a choleric Nigel Burton, a chartered surveyor from Ipswich.

'It's taking up so much of your time,' said Casey to Miranda, late one night.

'But I'm the only one who saw her,' said Miranda. 'And Emily Burton was the only woman at Dr Greystone's to fit our profile. It has to be her.'

And finally, Hessa had done one last search. 'Emilia Burton-Smith,' she announced to the room. 'She's an artist. Lives in Surrey, with her husband.'

Miranda studied the website Hessa had found. She worked in oils, Burton-Smith, huge splashing canvases, red on red. The photograph of the artist was small, though, black and white, blurred, half turned away from the camera.

'It could be her,' hesitated Miranda. 'Maybe.'

'She looks beautiful,' said Hessa. 'But that website is old, now.'

'I should have asked one of you to wait outside the clinic,' said Miranda. 'So that at least you would have seen her too.'

'I like her paintings,' said Casey. 'How long have they been living in Surrey?'

Hessa tapped at her computer.

'They moved there a few years ago,' said Hessa at last. 'Out from Notting Hill.'

Waiting for the babies, Casey thought, that never came.

Hessa, tapping databases, found out more about Emilia and Dominic Burton-Smith. His family owned a swathe of Gloucestershire, it turned out. 'Very low-profile,' Hessa said. 'But smart. They got married ten years ago. When she was twenty-one, and he was twenty-nine.'

'Photographs?' Miranda asked. 'Of the wedding?'

'No.' Hessa sounded apologetic. 'I can't find them anywhere. There's an address though.'

As Hessa read it out, Casey turned away, gouging at her desk with a pen.

'I'll go,' said Miranda.

But when Miranda got to Surrey, an hour from the office, the house was still, empty.

'They travel a lot.' A neighbour ambled past, with a small terrier. 'I keep an eye on it for them. I can let them know they missed you? Here, Choccy.'

Miranda smiled at the neighbour, and the terrier, and chatted on. And finally Casey and Miranda reached Bath, and the busy little square beside the Abbey. Now they watched, invisible from a small café, as the Burton-Smiths explored a little longer, and then turned away down the little street that ran next to the Roman Baths.

The man whispered something in Emily's ear as they walked off, and she laughed up at him, stroking his face affectionately. And Casey and Miranda waited, and then they got up to follow.

As they made their way down the cold streets, Casey stopped sharply.

'Miranda,' she said. 'Are you sure we should be doing this?'

Miranda turned around, scowling.

'These people have set up a factory in Bangladesh, Casey. An actual human farm. Exploiting some of the most vulnerable people in the world. And these two, this pretty little couple, wandering down lovely Georgian streets, they know exactly what they're doing.'

'We *think* they know what they're doing,' said Casey. 'They probably haven't had the details spelled out to them.'

'You mean they haven't asked the right questions?' spat Miranda. 'Like Vivienne, sitting in her old farmhouse? Half these people probably think that having a baby made in Kenya for forty-five thousand dollars a pop is an absolute bargain. They'd spend that much on a boob lift and getting rid of the stretch marks after a standard delivery. Plus it doesn't interrupt their busy schedules.'

'I know,' said Casey. 'But maybe if we just went to Greystone? Told him we knew what he was doing. Told him we knew about Romida.'

'We don't have anything linking Romida to Greystone,' snapped Miranda. 'We're not even sure if they are part of the same operation. For all we know, Romida's disappearance is a complete coincidence.'

'We could tell him that we knew, though.'

'It wouldn't work,' said Miranda. 'I've met Greystone, and I know. And we can't have a baby made to a formula just to prove a story. Not even us.'

Back in the Harley Street clinic, the receptionist had finally called Miranda's name.

'Again, Mrs Lancaster. I am so sorry for the wait.'

'It really is no problem.'

'He does work such very long hours, Dr Greystone.' The receptionist looked supportive. 'He's here day and night.'

Miranda had been shown into the elegant room across the landing. Dr Greystone was sitting behind a beautiful walnut desk, half-rising as she came in.

It was a large room. Intricate old medical devices lined the shelves, juxtaposed by glistening technology worth millions.

On a side table, a large ship in a bottle, a schooner in full sail. Next to Greystone's desk, Miranda could make out a silver-framed photograph of a ravishing blonde woman and two immaculate children.

'Good afternoon, Mrs Lancaster,' Dr Greystone had said. 'How do you do?'

He had sharp eyes and a weak chin. He must have been a good-looking teenager, thought Miranda, but his forties were being less generous. His hair was thinning and greying. His tan had faded, as if he had been back from skiing for a few weeks. He was quick though, and unctuously charming. They talked about the weather, just for a minute, and then ran through some of the treatments and problems Verity Taylor had described.

'I got OHSS in the last round of IVF,' Miranda ended, with a brave smile. 'I was in hospital; it was pretty awful.'

Ovarian hyperstimulation syndrome, when a woman's ovaries are forced into such chaos by all the drugs that they swell catastrophically. It can kill, and gets mentioned in passing, quite casually, in the long list of side effects.

'I'm sorry.' Greystone made a note. 'It must have been very hard for you.'

Miranda nudged forward.

'Really, after all that, I am most interested in surrogacy. My husband and I have considered all the options, and we have decided it's the best way for us. It's been … a struggle.'

He had nodded, glancing just for a second out of the window across Harley Street.

'And we would be delighted to enable you in that, Mrs Lancaster.'

The smooth explanation followed, punctuated with the occasional discreet nod. Dr Greystone took off his gold-rimmed glasses when he was being especially reassuring.

'It's all quite straightforward, I assure you,' he ended.

'And where?' Miranda asked. 'It would obviously be very important to me to know as much as possible about the person carrying my child. It's such a crucial thing.'

'Of course,' he smiled. 'I can promise you that every precaution would be taken at every step.'

'Which country would the child be born in?' Miranda persisted. 'I know it is all becoming more complicated, these days.'

He had a habit of steepling his fingers and pressing his thumbs to his mouth. Somewhere between a prayer, and a gesture to silence. He did it now, eyes fixed on hers. Wily, she thought. Cautious.

'I can take you through it all, Mrs Lancaster, as we go along.' He changed the subject smoothly. 'Surrogacy is such an excellent solution. And the money you give is so gratefully received abroad. It makes a huge difference to the people there. You'll have heard the phrase, it takes a village to raise a child?' He was smiling, as if at a private joke. 'Well, now, they say, it takes a child to raise a village.'

'Wonderful,' said Miranda. 'I am so glad you are able to help.'

'We don't have any real proof,' Miranda said now, in the cold little street in Bath. 'Greystone would deny everything, and what do we have? A scrap of silk? Some blue embroidery? An angry mother, out in the camps. Greystone wouldn't even name the country to me.'

'But the Burton-Smiths are happy now,' said Casey. 'And they just want this baby. And they will give their child a beautiful life.'

'That happiness is built on someone else's misery,' said Miranda.

Casey took a deep breath. 'Miranda, are you sure we are doing this for the right reasons?'

Miranda twisted away from her, long black coat swirling. 'Casey ...'

They stood there, for a few minutes, next to the old Roman Baths. The crowds pottered around them, oblivious. One woman was carrying the *Post*, tucked neatly under her arm.

'Come on,' said Miranda. 'You know what we have to do.'

18

Dominic Burton-Smith opened the door of the beautiful Georgian house. 'Can I help you?'

'Could I come in?' Miranda arched her eyebrows.

'This isn't actually our house,' he said. 'We're just staying here for a few nights. City break.'

Dominic was good-looking, with dark brown hair, boyishly ruffled. He was wearing an old blue shirt and frayed jeans. His grey cardigan – chunky knit – was just right for a weekend away. He pushed his hair back as he looked at Miranda, all easy charm.

'I know,' Miranda was abrupt. 'But I was hoping to speak to you and Mrs Burton-Smith.'

He was confused, opened the door wider. 'I'm sorry, have we met?'

'No.' Miranda took a step forward.

She was past him before he realised, stepping into the hall. Casey was left on the doorstep, while Dominic gave her a rueful half-shrug. 'I suppose …'

'Who is it, Dom?' Emily was on the stairs, pretty in her flowing silk dress. 'Oh.' She stopped as she saw Miranda. 'Don't I know you from somewhere …'

'We met at the clinic on Harley Street,' said Miranda. 'Dr Greystone's.'

'Of course,' said Emily, puzzled. 'How odd to see you here.'

'Your surrogate in Bangladesh,' Miranda said bluntly. 'We have a very strong reason to believe that the woman carrying your child is a Rohingya refugee, trafficked out of the camps in Bangladesh.'

Miranda stopped. Dominic took three quick paces towards his wife as she wavered on the stairs. Emily's jaw had dropped open.

'That's impossible,' said Emily. 'Who are you?'

'My name is Miranda Darcey. I'm a journalist at the *Post*.'

'You can't come in here,' said Dominic. 'You can't just burst in like this—'

'She's a refugee girl,' Miranda said again, speaking straight to Emily. 'A child who escaped all sorts of hell in Myanmar. She has been snatched out of the one place where she should be safe, and now she is being exploited by Dr Greystone, and his clients.'

'That can't be right,' Emily voice went higher. 'Dr Greystone said …'

'We are sorry to be intruding like this,' said Casey. 'Really sorry.'

'That's not much help, is it?' Emily snapped at her. It was only when she took a step forward and almost missed her footing that Casey saw how much she was shaking.

'Did you ask him' – Miranda turned to look straight at Dominic – 'who the surrogate is?'

'Dr Greystone is a highly respected professional,' said Dominic. 'He assured us that everything is being managed impeccably in Bangladesh.'

'But you didn't ask for details?' Miranda pushed him.

'We wanted to know about the woman.' The words burst out of Emily. 'We did ask Dr Greystone who the surrogate would be. He just said that the girl didn't speak English, and that it would be impossible for us to speak to her. There wasn't much else we could do, after that.'

'But did you ask where she lives? Where she came from?' asked Miranda. 'Did you ask where she would be staying over the nine months?'

No.' Emily hesitated. 'Dr Greystone said that his team out there would arrange for everything.'

'She is being paid,' Dominic insisted. 'Part of our payment is going directly to her, they promised us that.'

'But didn't you want to know,' Miranda asked, 'who this woman actually is? This is the probably the most important event in your whole lives, and you didn't even ask?'

'What could we do?' Dominic said, almost angry. 'I don't know anything about Bangladesh. It's thousands of miles away. But Greystone promised us it would be done properly, that the girl would be well looked after while she was pregnant.'

'To guarantee you a healthy child,' said Casey.

'Well,' said Dominic. 'Yes.'

'These women,' Miranda said, 'are being kept in a factory. A farm for human beings. They are forced to get pregnant, and then they are forced to hand over the baby. It's barbaric.'

'That can't be true,' Emily mumbled.

'It is,' Casey said. 'It is.'

'Well,' Dominic said, 'even if it is true, what can we do about it?'

He was so quick to dismiss them that Casey realised that he had known all along. Or guessed, at least. Miranda's eyes were slits.

There was a long silence.

'Casey will go out to Dhaka instead of you.' Miranda's voice was like ice. 'And while she's out there, she will find out where they are keeping these women.'

'No.' Emily leapt to her feet in horror. 'You can't do that. That's my baby out there.' Her voice rose to a scream. 'Our daughter.'

'It's the only way,' said Miranda.

'You can't.' Emily's legs gave way and she slid into an armchair. 'You mustn't.'

Dominic had his arms around his wife now, was crouching down beside her. 'You're mad,' he said to Miranda. 'Of course we won't do that. Never.'

'I can't . . .' said Emily. 'No . . .'

'How are you planning to get that baby home?' Miranda was like a viper striking. 'You know the clinic won't be able to get a passport for the baby if the authorities find out. It will take months to resolve, this sort of thing. You don't want your daughter stuck in Bangladesh for years while you try and sort this.'

'But what if something goes wrong?' screamed Emily. 'You don't care about our child at all. You only care about your bloody story. We have to go out there to get her. We need to bring her home.'

There was a primitive rage in Emily's voice, and a fast-rising despair.

'The loose clothes, the big winter coats,' said Miranda stonily. 'You'll just say she was early, and that everyone carries them differently, and that I felt so awful all the time – I suppose I just haven't seen you for a while.' As Miranda spoke, they could all hear Emily. 'But you can't keep that going, not if there's a proper investigation.'

'You wouldn't do that.' Emily was pleading now. 'You wouldn't do that to us.'

'I would.' Miranda's eyes were dead. 'Oh, I would.'

There was a long silence. A grandfather clock somewhere upstairs clanged the hour.

'This is blackmail,' said Dominic. 'What you're doing is illegal.'

Miranda met his eyes. 'What you've done is illegal. And I think you knew it, all along.'

'Never.' Emily looked up, wiping away the tears. 'I will never let you do this.'

'Get out,' said Dominic. 'Get out of this house and get away from my wife. Stay away from us.'

'Mr Burton-Smith ...' Miranda tried one last time.

'Get out.' The veins stood out on his neck. 'Get out, or I will call the police.'

19

‘They won’t call the police,’ Miranda said.

They were in the Pump Room, incongruously, just around the corner from Elton House. Jane Austen’s ghost hovered in the corner. A waitress had brought them a tower of little cakes and cucumber sandwiches, which Casey was ignoring.

‘They might. It’s as if we’re throwing hand grenades into people’s lives, one after the other. Eventually, someone will fight back. Or ...’

A straw hat ripped away, a half-smile frozen ...

‘I think Dominic knew something,’ said Miranda. ‘He guessed things weren’t right with Dr Greystone.’

‘He might realise,’ said Casey, ‘that he’s screwed either way. And that means he could go to Dr Greystone, and tell him we’re on the hunt. That would blow the whole thing.’

‘He might,’ Miranda shrugged. ‘It’s always risky at this point.’

Casey was staring at a table of tourists, posing with a woman in a Georgian dress.

‘They knew,’ said Miranda flatly. ‘The Burton-Smiths couldn’t get it done here, because of the strict rules in place, and they know those rules are there precisely to keep people safe. To stop people being exploited. And because they couldn't get it done here, they went there. And they're paying a big chunk of money, partly so they don't feel too bad about it.'

The woman, picturesque in her Empire-line dress, smiled and bobbed her head. She was wearing a pretty little bonnet, and carrying a posy of roses.

'Are you OK?' Miranda asked. 'Not like you to have a *crise de conscience*.'

'It's nothing.' Casey pushed it away.

'Is it Cavendish?' asked Miranda. 'Has Hessa been OK?'

'Yes,' said Casey. 'No.'

Hessa had sidled up to her in the investigations room the night before. 'How do you make it right in your head?'

'By not thinking about it,' Casey said. Then she saw Hessa's face, and dropped the flippancy. 'You have to make your own rules, Hessa. And make sure they make sense for you. That you can live with them.'

Speaking to Hessa, Casey had remembered Miranda's words, years earlier: 'Remember who your friends are. You've got a billion possible sources, and a finite number of friends. Never screw over a friend.'

'Anything else?' Hessa had looked hopeful.

'Decide what you're happy with, and don't break your rules,' said Casey. 'And if someone is a source, you never, ever throw them under the bus. Never.'

'But isn't that so artificial? Just giving us an excuse to keep secrets.'

'I suppose so.' Casey pondered it. 'Like barristers insisting on the cab-rank rule, so that they can nod and shrug to each other,

"You know how it goes. Everyone needs representation." But there has to be something. Some truth.'

'But we lie' – Hessa hesitated on the word – 'all the time.'

'I know,' said Casey. 'But that is why it matters. If I give my word to a source, I don't break it.'

'Never?'

'Never.'

She didn't tell Hessa the indescribable truth: it will be hard. It will be hard, and it will change you, for ever.

Casey looked up at Miranda now. 'Hessa's fine,' she said.

'Good.' Miranda gave her a long look.

'I'll go to Emily,' Casey said. 'I'll talk to her, just the two of us.'

'In Surrey? Are you sure? You hate Surrey.'

'Yes.'

It was in the car, driving back to London, that Casey spoke.

'You're being too hard on them,' she said.

'Given what they've done?'

'You know,' Casey said carefully, 'that it's irrelevant right now.'

Miranda was silent, watching the columns of cars on the other side of the road. Headlights, blurring in the rain. She knew it was irrelevant. Facts, not opinion: all that mattered. Usually, it was Casey who struggled.

'All right.' Miranda forced down the anger.

'Is everything OK?' Casey's voice was expressionless.

I am going to work on my marriage. As if it were a tapestry, for some lofty medieval altar.

I'm going to save my marriage . . .

'I don't know.'

‘I’m sorry. But that’s not their fault.’

‘I know. I *know*.’

The car fell into silence. Miranda stared out of the window, clenching her jaw, and abruptly felt her throat close up, the memories overpowering as cheap perfume.

He’d caught her one Sunday morning. Not one Sunday morning: the Sunday morning her father died. Crying in that grand old court, in the dawn, the blossom still wet from the dew, as everyone quietly slept.

Are you OK?

I’ve got to … I’ve got to get the train … My father … I don’t know …

I’ll help.

He helped her pack. Then the trains were chaos. Sunday: of course.

I’ll drive you.

Don’t be ridiculous, it’s the other side of the country.

It doesn’t matter.

You can’t. It’ll take hours.

Anyone would.

‘No,’ she had told him later, as his car purred down the motorway. ‘Anyone wouldn’t.’

And he’d looked surprised.

‘Of course they would.’

‘No,’ she said again. ‘They wouldn’t.’

‘So cynical.’ His hands were steady on the steering wheel. ‘Miranda, isn’t it? I’m Tom.’

She’d known then: looking at the neatly cut hair, the hazel eyes, the carefully cleaned car. No one cleaned their car back then. No one. Cars a chaos of McDonald's wrappers and Lucozade bottles and fumes of a hangover.

Known that this might be foundations for happiness, at last. Maybe.

He'd stayed. Her mother crying on his shoulder, the stink of gin in the air. After a day, it was as if he had been there for ever.

But now the foundations were slipping away. It was never *No*; just *I'm not ready yet.*

Unforgivable, really.

If a man had done this ... She knew.

But I meant not yet. And it was only as I got closer ...

He'd waited, a kind man.

But now ...

And one Sunday morning, it was *No.*

20

Casey sat on a train, gazing out of the window. She stared into the sitting rooms of a thousand houses, all the way down the railway track. These gardens were neat in the morning sun: a trampoline here, a cherry tree there. Casey shuddered as a single magpie hopped away from the onrush of the train.

The train pulled into the station and Casey couldn't breathe. Surrey, and he was everywhere.

A brilliant mind, people had always said, smiling. And such charisma. They would remember meeting him, just once, twenty years ago.

She remembered sitting on a knee, in front of a fireplace. Suit trousers and crisp white shirts. Clever grey eyes, dark hair and electric bursts of attention. Jigsaw puzzles, and a fizz of excitement when he arrived. The flat shrank around him. Her mother laughing, which she never did normally.

Coming and going. Mainly going.

He's away for work, her mother would say, almost bravely.

When she was older, he liked her mind. Quizzical, he said. Sharp. There was pride there, for a while.

Too sharp, like him. He taught her chess. There were games, too. Treasure hunt, hide and seek. Murder in the dark.

And then, one day, he left his book behind. The bookmark, a photograph.

Three blonde children, sitting on a big navy sofa. On holiday, she guessed, by the shorts and swimsuits and tans. One boy waving a small tennis racket.

Three golden faces, laughing with the confidence of love. Picture perfect, and safe. And she'd known, at once, that she was the other. That she was the secret. That she was the one who wasn't real.

These were the treasured three. The real family. The proper ones. And that made her the intruder.

She listened at doors, after that. Put it together, bit by bit.

He was a barrister. A QC, no less. Although she didn't understand the initials, not then. Her mother, his pupil. An affair, many years ago. So normal. Almost mundane, really. But this time, a child.

He hadn't cut them loose, not completely. There was the flat. The flickering, flustering visits. A present, at Christmas. But not him. Never him. Not for Christmas. And her birthday present could be a week late, or two.

There'd been a fight, in the end. Squalls over money, and a fading beauty, and he disappeared one summer day. She was seven, when he dissolved into that August morning. Pawn sacrifice, maybe. She wondered, later, if they had begun to bore him.

Her mother hid her tears, sort of. Afterwards, there'd been others. Worse. Always the other woman, her mother.

Only years later, she understood. Love refracted through a marriage. Somebody else's. That was the only bearable sort of love.

Peering at the eclipse, through the pinhole.

Then another man, crueller, this one. My wife doesn't understand me, it began. We never fuck, any more.

One morning, a black eye.

It's nothing, darling.

Frozen peas and silent sobs.

She'd hunted him down, when she was thirteen. The man who had been her father. To here. This town.

The house had been easy to find, down a road, studded with trees, a walk between each house. Sprawling expensively, with fake Tudor beams and bay windows lighting up a grey afternoon.

It was just after Christmas. The road a forlorn Dunsinane, littered with pine trees, stripped of sparkle and forgotten.

She followed the five of them from the house as they pottered to the high street, lazy Sunday, Weybridge respectable. Watched, from a distance the life that might have been hers.

Then she crossed the road to them. I'm so sorry, do you know the way …

Just the right touch of innocent confusion.

The blonde mother had been so kind. Pointing directions, gold bracelets clinking. A beautiful voice: now, are you sure you've got it?

She watched the rings. A diamond glittering in the low winter sun, and a band of gold. Wealth and security, love and recognition. Honour, such an unfamiliar word. Everything she'd never had, in small golden circles.

And just for a second, she'd shifted her gaze, and he'd known her for who she was. The other. The threat to everything. The smiling child who could shred all the tissue layers with just one tiny word.

Daddy. Daddy. *Daddy.*

And destroy all that perfectly flawed beauty.

She held his stare just for a second, and then looked away. In his nightmares for ever.

A brilliant mind, they said.

Was I not enough?

Thank you so much, she echoed the woman's voice, so easily. Yes, I understand exactly. You've been most kind.

The woman wasn't watching for her husband's grey eyes and careless smile. She didn't see.

And the secret one turned, and walked away, and understood mysteries, and power, and layers of knowledge, for the very first time.

She kept the book, though. And the photograph of the three children, a big blue sofa. And the pack of cards, he'd taught her to count. There wasn't much else.

A few scrappy presents, which she laid out once a year, on an August morning.

She'd monitored them, the three of them. Knew their names, and their schools, and their first jobs, several rungs up from the start of their careers.

She was almost exactly the same age as the second child, a girl, and she wondered about the days and weeks, in between.

She saw one of the daughters at a party, years later. Silver dress flowing to the ground. A girl who saw everyone else as walk-on characters in her life.

She watched the confidence, built on the frailest of foundations, and sheltered only by ignorance.

Sister, such an unfamiliar word.

And Casey thought: I could break you. Because I know you. And it would only take a second.

But she ducked away, so the girl wouldn't see her, the spectre at the feast. She was the other girl, the mirrored girl, the girl who wasn't there at all, not really.

She used the twirl of the hair later, of course. Magpied that imperious happiness, for just a few minutes.

And blazed with anger at the brilliant mind that made her a secret.

21

Casey walked out of the station, through the clatter of people and noise and Costa coffee. The Burton-Smiths lived just over a mile from the station, but Casey wanted to walk. She had looked up the house already, the particulars five years old. *An exceptional location. One of the most desirable private roads. Superbly appointed.*

The road was wide. A few smaller houses here and there, but most had been flattened and rebuilt, sprawling as far as the plots would allow, with indoor swimming pools to the rear. Casey shuddered. It was the sort of road she only visited when a husband had battered his wife to death with a piece of gym equipment.

The Burton-Smith house was empty though, behind the shiny black gates. Casey wandered up the street, glancing around. A silver Audi was grumbling as an Ocado van struggled through a three-point turn. Most people drove, round here.

But Emily walked. Casey soon saw her, walking down the street, eyes on the pavement. Her bulky navy coat was buttoned to the neck. She was carrying a big cotton shopping bag, and a bunch of tulips, buds tight shut. She looked tired, worried, fragile as a daisy chain.

You don't belong here either, thought Casey suddenly, a brief burst of sympathy.

'Emily.' Casey stepped into her path.

Emily glanced up from the pavement, and flinched when she saw Casey.

'Oh please,' Emily whispered. 'Please, no.'

In a single movement, Casey had pulled out her phone.

'Here.' It was a photograph, sent through by Savannah.

I went through my pictures, Savannah had typed. *The girl in red on the left, that's Romida.*

'Romida is thirteen,' Casey said. 'She was taken from the camps just a few weeks ago, so she isn't the girl carrying your child. But we believe that your unborn daughter's mother is being kept with her somewhere with a group of other women.'

Your unborn daughter's mother ...

Emily stared at the photograph. Romida was looking slightly away from the camera, excited and shy all at once. Her red dress was covered in roses, and her shawl – also red but with a different pattern – was wrapped around her head. The girl's eyes were patient, and her mouth not quite used to smiling. Sitting on the floor of a makeshift playroom, she had one arm curled behind her, half hiding away. Next to Romida, her friend was more confident, beaming at the camera from beneath an orange headscarf. They had folded into each other, as teenage girls do, awkward with laughter.

Emily looked up at Casey, and her eyes were full of tears.

'I am sorry,' she said. 'If I could undo it all ...'

'We need to find out who is snatching girls like Romida,' said Casey. 'I can't do it without your help. We don't know where they are being kept in Bangladesh, and who is in charge of it all out there.'

'But I ... I can't ...'

'We know that Dr Greystone is probably the person managing things from London,' Casey went on. 'But we don't know anything else.'

Emily was staring at the photograph of Romida, the tulips dangling by her side.

'As far as we know,' Casey went on more gently, 'nothing has happened to Romida yet. But it will, unless we can get to her, and stop it. You can keep her safe.'

Two small boys cycled past slowly, plainly proud of their bright new bikes, their laughter echoing down the street.

'You don't understand.' Emily was struggling to get the words out. 'We've been counting down the days until we could go and pick up our baby. The hours, even. I look at the scan they sent us every five minutes. I love her. I love her, as if she were already here. I couldn't bear it if anything went wrong ... If I wasn't there ...'

'We would be very careful,' promised Casey. 'We would bring her home to you, Emily. You wouldn't lose your baby. But these are refugee girls. Girls, not women. Being forced to carry babies for foreigners. They are girls just like Romida. You must see that it's unbearable. That it can't go on.'

'But this is my baby,' Emily's voice broke. 'I know it's awful, and I know I should be thinking something different, and I am so sorry about that. But I just can't. I want my baby.'

'Emily ...'

'Will she go the authorities?' Emily asked. 'Your colleague.'

'I don't know,' said Casey. 'She might.'

'She will,' Emily murmured. 'I saw it. She was so angry.'

Emily slumped, turning towards her house. Casey watched her go.

As Emily reached the gates, wearily punching in the code, she paused.

'I'll always think of her now, won't I?' Emily said, without turning around. 'That girl, Romida.'

'I don't know,' Casey said honestly. 'But only you can stop Romida being hurt.'

Emily turned towards Casey.

'Do you know the name? Of the girl who is …' Emily shrank away from the words. 'The girl who is having our baby.'

'No.' Casey met her eye. 'She's just an anonymous girl, somewhere in Bangladesh. You never need to know a thing about her, if you don't want. You can just pick up your baby, like a bunch of flowers.'

Emily looked down at the tulips. She had crushed the stalks, Casey saw.

'We used to be different, you know, Dominic and I.'

In her mind, Casey flicked through the documents that Hessa had pulled together. The bright young artist. The good-looking husband, in advertising, highly successful. All backed up by a solid wall of family money behind them. Anything possible.

'We used to have so much fun. But I wanted a family. Everyone wants a family, don't they?' Emily waved at the twee grandeur. 'It's ridiculous all this, I know. But I wanted it so much that I gave up everything else … And then we were stuck … Halfway to a dream.'

Casey felt a sudden wave of fury at the beautiful woman, standing outside her desirable home.

'I know what you're thinking,' Emily almost smiled. 'Romida, stuck somewhere out in Bangladesh. Terrified, homeless, and in real danger. And then pathetic me, here. Complaining.'

'A little.' Casey let the anger flicker.

'I'm sorry,' said Emily. 'But I can't do it.'

'Sleep on it.'

'I won't sleep.'

22

Emily called a day later, as Casey had known she would.

'Meet me by the Round Pond? In Kensington Gardens?'

Emily was waiting as Casey walked up. It was cold today, with a shiver in the air. Emily wore an elegant black coat, long and flowing, that caught the wind and billowed. The swans drifted in slow circles, under the solemn watch of Kensington Palace.

'Hello,' said Emily.

'Hello.'

They stared at each other for a second.

'I have no idea' – Emily had to unclench her jaw to speak – 'what to do.'

Casey was silent. Emily kept her eyes on the swans, turning in their graceful swirls as the wind whisked across the water.

'Has your colleague' – Emily struggled with the words – 'gone to the authorities yet?'

'No,' said Casey, watching Emily relax, just slightly. 'Not yet.'

The tension returned. 'But she will?'

'I don't know.'

Miranda had spun in angry laps around the office, whirling past Business, Sport, Production. *These people. These fucking people.*

'On the way here,' Emily said, 'up on the train, I thought I would know what to do. At one station, I was going to tell you to do your worst. Bloody call whoever you'll call. Get on with it. But then at the next station, that girl, Romida' – Emily hesitated over the name – 'would be there. It was as if she were just waiting on the platform. I can't get away from her.'

A small child scooted up to the pond, and began throwing bread for the ducks. Raucously cheerful, they crowded round.

'Romida,' Emily said again, turning the syllables over in her mouth. 'Romida.'

The little girl was throwing the bread with an intense concentration. Wide eyes and freckles, she was neatly buttoned into her tiny red coat. Green mittens on a string dangled from her sleeves. Emily's eyes followed her hungrily.

Emily pulled out a photograph, shoving it blindly at Casey.

'They sent us that, you know. The clinic.'

Casey looked at the photograph. A young Rohingya woman, standing in front of a pale-blue painted wall, a shy smile on her face. To her left, there was a poster: a grinning child in the arms of a beaming nurse, with some stern advice about vaccinations. To the right, a Doppler machine sat on a white steel filing cabinet. A neat bed, crisp sheets, was partly hidden by bright curtains.

The room looked immaculate, cosy.

'They send us regular scans,' said Emily. 'They look after these girls, you know.'

'What is her name? That girl.'

'I don't know.' Emily looked back at the swans. 'They never... But Dr Greystone said he can provide all the documentation we need from the Harley Street clinic... All the...'

Her words drifted into silence. Greystone, the man who must be forging pages of documents to allow the babies to slip into the British system.

'I can't sleep.' Emily cleared her throat. 'Dominic said to forget you ever came. That you wouldn't just tell the police. That you would find another way to do this story. He said that what you're doing is just as bad, in its own way.'

He probably wasn't wrong, thought Casey. But aloud she replied: 'We have a duty to report things to the police. When we know that something terrible is happening. We can't just walk away.'

Emily flinched, tugging the belt around her waist tighter.

'Why us?' she said. 'Your colleague could have picked anyone walking into that waiting room. Why did it have to be us?' The words trailed into a silence. 'I know what you think of me,' she said again. 'You despise me, I imagine. But you don't know what it is like.'

Emily had turned away from Casey, was looking across the green stretches of the park.

'No. I don't know what it's like.' Casey waited. 'But I do want to understand. If you'll be a source on this story, I promise the *Post* will protect you. We'd anonymise your story, keep your secrets.'

That everyday trade: protection for knowledge, knowledge for power. *Sources close to, good friends of.*

'This wasn't even our first try at surrogacy, you know.' There was a defiance in Emily's narrow shoulders. 'After all the Clomid, and the rounds and rounds of IVF, we found a surrogate in England. It took years to find her. Not many people will . . . We had all the agreements written up, everything signed and done. We paid the surrogate as much as we could under the rules, which isn't very much in England. Just expenses. But still. I couldn't believe that it was happening. At last. *At last.* I was so excited. I dreamed about this baby every night. She was in my dreams. She was in my head. I *knew* her.'

Emily stopped talking. She gazed across the pond, to the chestnut trees in the distance. The sky was cold pastels.

'She lived in Yorkshire, and we would drive up and down for the scans and everything. I got to know her really quite well. I'd go up for some of the midwife appointments. I heard the heartbeat.'

Casey imagined Emily picking out baby clothes, appraising the candy-coloured prams.

'We got the call late one night,' said Emily. 'The surrogate – Naomi, her name is – had gone into labour. Dominic and I, we drove through the night. We were so excited. Thrilled. Grinning, like a couple of idiots. And we got there, to the hospital, just after the baby was born.'

The wind caught the chestnut trees, sending branches rustling like secrets.

'And then Naomi decided that she didn't want us to see the baby.' Emily spoke as if she were reciting a story. 'Not that night, she said. We tried to stay calm. We went to a hotel. The Premier Inn, just down the road. It's funny, what you remember. Plastic carpets, and a bored teenager on reception, and windows you couldn't open even a crack. We lay on the bed all night, the two of us. Eyes wide open, face to face, promising each other again and again that it would be all right. That Naomi would feel differently in the morning. That there was hope.'

Emily rubbed her face for a second.

'But the next morning, Naomi hadn't changed her mind. The nurse said that she was keeping her. And that was that. She was keeping our baby. I fainted, right there in the hospital entrance. When I came to, I was looking up at all these pale faces. They were staring down at me as if I were some sort of experiment.'

'Couldn't you have fought it? If Dominic was genetically the father?'

'Our lawyers said we could,' said Emily. 'But the law is so hazy. Legally, Naomi was the mother, and that was the end of it. They lived in a lovely house, right up near the moors. Nice enough place, nice enough family. It would have been very hard to show that they weren't the perfect parents. Brutal, the lawyers warned us. Recent court cases have been more sympathetic to the intended parents, but back then ... I could have killed Naomi. I *hated* her, and I've never been that person.'

'I'm sorry,' said Casey.

'I drove up to near where they lived once,' said Emily. 'Parked the car just above their house. You could look down at the house from the road. I could see the washing on the line, and two cars parked in the little driveway. It looked *normal*. I imagined our child, my child, just learning to walk.'

Casey imagined it. The car parked awkwardly up on the moor. The gorse, and the heather, and the beautiful girl crying over the steering wheel.

'I went a bit mad,' said Emily. 'I saw her everywhere, our baby, the girl she would be. I kept seeing glimpses of her, in every face we saw. By the time the courts started finding in favour of the intended parents, it was too late. She would have been a child, by then. You couldn't ... You couldn't just take her.'

'I'm sorry,' Casey said again.

'I thought about it though, you know. A baby, somewhere. Anywhere. Just grabbing, and running. I can see how people get to that point. How women end up … But then I imagine another woman glancing up, one morning. To that empty pram in the front garden. And I couldn't. I couldn't …'

'I'm sorry.'

'I know. Everyone is terribly sorry.'

In the park, all around them, women pushed prams, wiped noses, lost tempers. Everyday, every day.

Emily turned towards Casey, meeting her eyes. 'So you see why I can't give up this child. Not again. I can't bear it. When Dr Greystone suggested this, it seemed like a miracle. Thousands of people have gone to places like India and Thailand and Nepal. And they don't ask all these questions, so for all they know, anything could be happening there. We thought we would *help* people. I was promised that the women volunteered, that they wanted to do it. I had no idea …'

I, not we.

Casey was silent.

'Oh God.' The words burst out of Emily.

The little girl in the red coat had run out of bread. Gently, her mother tugged at the tiny hand. A swan lumbered past, awkward on the paving stones.

Emily's shoulders slumped.

'I have to do it, don't I?' It was as if she was talking to herself.

Casey stared across the park, to where the children came to play.

'I'll talk to Dominic. I promise. I will talk to him.'

23

Casey bit her nails to the quick, waiting for the Burton-Smiths. Wait, and wait, and wait. Over the years, she had learned patience, quite against her nature.

Dash stopped beside her desk. 'I'm just back from lunch. Everything OK?' He waited for her answer.

'I'm fine.'

'You sure?' Ask the same question all the different ways, he told her once, and really listen to the answers.

'Yes.'

A pause. 'Anything new on this story?'

'I went to see Greystone's house this morning,' Casey leapt on the change of subject. 'It's up in Hampstead. Amazing place.'

The avenue was even more opulent than the sprawl of Surrey. The Greystones' house was a mansion: pillars and dark brick, peering suspiciously down a driveway.

Next door to the Greystones, a house sagged. Windows barred by thick steel plates, the roof beginning to go. The grounds were a riot of brambles and green, a secret garden forgotten.

On this Hampstead street, the houses were so valuable that they were allowed to rot. Mere bricks were almost worthless.

This was a land of gold taps and thirty pieces of silver, maybe, where foreign princes bought sanctuary for ever, as an expensive refuge, far from the mob. A safe room from the world. There, always, just in case.

As Casey walked again past the Greystone house, a black Porsche Cayenne powered down the street towards her, the gates purring open at its approach. The Porsche jerked to a careless halt in front of the house, and for a moment, Casey caught a glimpse of a woman stepping up to the front door. Greystone's wife, Casey thought: Clio Greystone. Understated elegance. A black jersey and grey capri pants, blonde hair caught back by her sunglasses. The woman walked quickly to the house, a bounce in her step, the sun glinting off her hair.

'Greystone seems to have a lot of money then,' said Dash.

Follow the money, still the battle cry of any reporter.

'Yes,' said Casey, 'there's certainly a lot of it there.'

'Good. What else is—?'

'Look over there.' Casey dodged more questions.

Dash stared across the office at Eric's desk. An angry woman in a furry cat disguise was sitting on the floor beside his desk.

'What,' Dash raised an eyebrow, 'is that woman doing there?'

'It's Xav's fault.' Eric scowled at the columnist a few desks away. 'He wrote something about vegans that the vegans didn't like, and she came rampaging into the office this morning, shouting and screaming. She shrieked, "Which one is Xavier Crittenden?" Xav pointed at me, and now she's chained herself to my bloody desk. It's not fair.'

'Where the hell was Jose?' Dash asked, knowing the security guard had been flirting with the trainee barista next door.

'Fuck knows.' Xavier was enjoying himself hugely.

'Is she pro-vegan or pro-meat?' Dash asked.

'I' – Xavier flicked through his English-Latin dictionary – 'have no idea.'

'It's all right for you.' Eric glowered at the woman, who glowered back. 'But I've got to write six hundred words on potato farming and I'm on deadline. It's very distracting.'

'Six hundred words on potato farming?' Xavier looked appalled. 'Christ, what is this paper coming to?'

'Piss off back to doing your expenses,' Eric snapped. 'About the only time you get creative.'

'For fuck's sake,' Dash cut them off. 'Has someone called a locksmith?'

As he turned back to the investigations room, Casey's phone rang. She pounced on it.

'Casey?' Emily's voice.

24

The kitchen was sleek, glossy, hardly used. Most of the room was an extension, built out into the dark, spotlit garden. The roof was a cage of white steel and glass.

The tulips – stems cut down, flowering pink now – were in a blue vase on the table, looking oddly out of place.

'I don't really cook,' Emily said vaguely. She was looking for wineglasses, opening and closing cupboards. She smiled at Casey, almost conspiratorially, and Casey found herself smiling back.

Casey tried to imagine Emily painting in this house, surrounded by buff and biscuit, tan and taupe. She couldn't.

Dominic was sitting at the kitchen island, glowering at Miranda. Miranda met his eye, her smile quite empty.

'How?' Dominic stared at Casey. 'How can you possibly pass yourself off as Emily?'

'They look similar enough,' Miranda said briskly. 'Same general description. Brown hair, grey eyes, quite tall. You would give us your passports, and Casey and one of our colleagues would travel out to Bangladesh together. They can carry their own passports for border control. But they would take yours too, in case whoever you meet up with wanted to check. Unless someone had met both Casey and Emily, they wouldn't know the difference.'

'Was that all?' Emily sounded wondering. 'Was that all you were looking for? Back in that waiting room?'

She was quieter than she had been in the park, almost distracted. Oddly likeable, even now, Casey thought. A naive charm, too trusting.

Dominic stared at the ceiling, his anger visible in glints, like white-topped waves in a storm. Casey wondered what it was like for him, living in this house. That hollow key sound, every evening.

There had been a floorplan, in the estate agent's particulars. Casey had glanced at it. Up the elegant staircase, down a corridor, third door on the right: *a lovely bedroom, windows to the garden*, photographs of toys, a cot, clouds stencilled on the ceiling.

I know too much about you, Casey thought, *and far too little.*

'What happens,' said Dominic, 'when you get her home? Our daughter. Would you go to the authorities then?'

'You'd be our source,' said Miranda. 'We always protect our sources.'

'How can you be sure? We'd end up all over the *Post*.'

'You have my word,' said Miranda.

Dominic looked at her with near-contempt.

'How,' Emily said wonderingly, 'do you get to make that decision? What gives you the right?'

Miranda tilted her head and stared at her.

'Who,' Dominic straightened up finally, 'would stand in for me, if we go ahead with this mad idea?'

Miranda glanced at Casey. 'I know someone. He's excellent at this sort of thing. Done it before.'

'No one from the Harley Street office actually travels out to Bangladesh with the couples.' Casey seized the opportunity to drag the conversation back to logistics. 'We know there is a fixer who organises it all on the ground. You wait in a hotel in Dhaka, and they just bring the baby to you.'

They were nodding, Casey realised. They knew this already.

'Greystone said they didn't keep notes,' Dominic said unwillingly. 'Our names would never be connected to all this. They don't have photographs of us to send out to Dhaka.'

You knew, thought Casey, and she watched Emily's eyes swoop to her husband.

'I go out there instead.' Casey moved the conversation on swiftly. 'And find out as much as I can about the whole operation. Where they keep the women, who they are, how they find them. And I'll try and work out who is organising the passports at the High Commission now, too.'

'You don't,' Miranda asked Dominic, 'have any idea who organises the passports at the moment?'

But he only shook his head. Casey wondered if he might lie out of habit.

'And would the passport be all right,' Emily's nerves surged, 'doing it this way?'

'We've worked it out,' Casey didn't quite answer.

'Couldn't we go?' Emily begged again. 'I'd ask all the questions, I promise. I would find out everything you wanted to know.'

'We only have one chance,' said Casey. 'It would be far too risky, you doing it. And it could be dangerous.'

'You don't know what you're doing, Emily,' said Miranda bluntly.

'I could try,' Emily whispered.

'It wouldn't work,' Miranda flattened her.

The Burton-Smiths turned to each other.

'Dominic?' Emily's voice was high, wavering.

'I love you.'

And Casey saw that he did. It was for Emily that he had rammed together the pretty little jigsaw pieces of their lives, although he knew they would never quite fit.

'You promise?' Emily turned to Casey. 'You promise that if we do this, you will protect us for ever? Never give up our names? Never tell anyone about our baby? We can just live our lives, and forget this ever happened?'

'Yes.' It was the only promise Casey could make. 'I promise, I will keep your involvement a secret.'

'But you can't tell a soul either,' Miranda warned them. 'Especially while they're abroad. Anything that endangers Casey risks the baby too.'

Casey saw the shudder run right through Emily's frame.

'I promise you,' Casey said to Emily again. 'We will keep her safe, your baby girl.'

'Poppy,' Emily whispered. 'We are going to call her Poppy.'

'Poppy,' said Casey. 'I promise you I will bring Poppy home to you.'

25

'Ed?' Miranda asked. 'Can you work with him?'

Will he work with you? she didn't quite ask.

They were back in the office.

Casey looked up. 'I have no idea.'

A few years earlier, Casey had been packed off to chase pirates around the Indian Ocean.

The Ministry of Defence allows journalists to 'embed' with armed forces around the world. Hacks fly all over the world, right alongside British troops. Over the years, Casey had travelled to Afghanistan and Iraq, deep among the fighting units.

Then piracy around the Horn of Africa became a story.

For years, a plague of international trawlers had systematically stripped Somalia's coasts of all marine life. Finally, furiously, the locals started to retaliate. Desperate Somalis began to set sail on tiny, inadequate boats, bobbing around the coast until they tracked down one of the slow-moving tankers cruising through the Red Sea.

Then somehow, madly, they fought their way on to the huge ships.

Kidnap and ransom, K&R. A booming business, quite suddenly. Billions of dollars of goods forced to cat-and-mouse through one of the busiest shipping lanes in the world, from the Indian Ocean to the Mediterranean, only to be snatched, one by one.

A bottleneck, just where the world couldn't afford it.

Cash ransoms – millions and millions of dollars – were parachuted onto the decks of vast supertankers.

It was the spiralling insurance premiums that finally caught the attention of the international community. That, and the rage of the shipowners who dotted Eaton Square. The government listened to that, fast.

British Navy ships were dispatched to the Indian Ocean, to police thousands of miles of ocean. Casey was dispatched too.

Ed had been the captain of the group of Royal Marines, on board the HMS *Apollo*. By the time Casey joined the ship, from a scruffy port in Oman, his team had been at sea for almost six months.

Having joined the ship in Salaleh, Casey found herself stuck on board for three weeks.

Ross had not been delighted by her prolonged absence.

'Where are you?'

'Several thousand miles from the coast of Kenya, by all accounts.'

'Can't you fucking swim for it?'

'They've mentioned sharks. And the pirates I've just filed about. Why? You missing me?'

'Fuck's sake.'

'Turns out these things don't have to go back to land for ages,' said Casey, admiring her suntanned arm.

Both oddly shy, Casey and Ed avoided conversation for the first ten days.

She noticed him, of course. Dark hair cut close, and a smile that flickered for a second. Rainbow eyes turned down at the corners, and when she looked closely she saw his eyes had flecks of grey and green, blue and brown. He moved with a careless grace, swinging down the ship's ladders.

In the evenings, she watched him playing cards. He was so good that they accused him of cheating, and he would laugh, and smack away the hands that reached for his chips.

Later she watched from the bridge, high above the ocean, as the Marines stormed a little pirate ship, knifing through the water in splinters of spray. She only realised the danger when an officer holding binoculars relaxed. 'They've got her. Surrendered. All safe. Nice job.'

That evening she went to what she called the back of the boat and the Marines called aft. The Somali pirates were being held there, in a huge black cage. Fifteen of them, all silent. They were dressed, incongruously, in padded black nylon jackets, crouching on the desk, feet flat to the floor. They had separated into groups, even then divided by the Somali fight-to-the-death clan system.

Ed was keeping watch there, reading a book. He was always reading. A habit picked up in one of those bases in the wilds of Afghanistan, with no television and no fun.

Casey tried to speak to one of the pirates, who had a few words of French. This man seemed to have a brother in Manchester, a cousin in Glasgow, an uncle in Marseille.

He was friendly; they all were, trying to bridge the language gap.

Eventually, having exhausted her French and her sign language, Casey flopped onto a pile of rope to write up her notes.

'We found a beacon on their ship,' said Ed.

'What?' She looked up, surprised that he was speaking to her.

'A solar-powered beacon in their dhow. The trawlers round here dump the huge dragnets overboard, and attach a solar-powered beacon. Then they keep going, drop more nets, keep going. A few days later, when all the fish are tangled in the nets, the trawlers go back to that first solar beacon, and bring the nets in. Everything gets caught in those nets. Dolphins, turtles, tiny fish no one will ever eat.'

'Right,' said Casey. She liked his voice, she decided.

'Anyway, these pirates worked out that if they snatch the beacons and wait around for a bit, the trawlers would come looking for them. It saved chasing the trawlers around.'

'Clever,' said Casey.

'But not always lucky,' said Ed. 'A month or so after we started out here, one of the Chinese trawlers called us over the radio. Said that they had caught ten pirates, and would we come and take them off their hands? They thought we could pass them to the Seychelles or Kenya, where they have something approximating a justice system.'

'There are worse places.'

'We started heading towards the trawler. The fishermen were in a hurry though. Impatient. I think they thought we were holding them up, and wanted to get back to fishing. As we got nearer, the number of pirates in captivity fell … Ten. Nine. Eight. By the time we got there, they were all gone. The fishermen hadn't quite finished cleaning down the decks. There was a lot of blood.'

He wasn't looking at Casey as he spoke. He was looking at the horizon. The ship was heading east; the sun setting in an extravagantly pink farewell to the day.

‘That’s awful,’ said Casey. ‘Couldn’t you do anything?’

‘What could we do? Out here. This lot’ – he gestured towards the pirates – ‘were actually quite relieved to be caught by the British. The Russian navy caught some of the pirates a few weeks ago. They put them back in their little boat, two hundred miles from the shore, with no diesel and no food. They were laughing about it.’

‘That’s barbaric.’

‘You know, one in three pirates never make it back to Somalia from one of these trips,’ said Ed. ‘Two weeks ago, we found one of their little dhows. We pulled up alongside it, this huge ship and that tiny boat. They’d run out of water. Been dead for weeks.’

Casey shuddered.

‘Can you imagine how bad it must be, back in Somalia, for people to take those odds?’ said Ed. ‘The desperation.’

He fell into silence. Casey shifted on the pile of rope.

‘What will happen to this lot now?’ Casey asked. She waved at one of the pirates. ‘They seem pretty friendly now.’

The pirate waved back at her.

‘They’re almost certainly killers, this lot,’ said Ed. ‘You can be both, quite easily, it turns out. We’re taking them to the Seychelles.’

They sat in silence for a moment, with only the creaking of the huge ship. The deck was stained with oil, the heavy smell mixing uneasily with the sea air.

‘They’re not amateurs though,’ Ed grinned at her. ‘This lot had RPGs on board their dhow.’

Casey had seen rocket-propelled grenades being fired, long ago in Libya.

'Did you know that, when you were zooming up to their little boat?'

'No.' He smiled briefly. 'Better that way, really.'

Casey looked at him and thought that she might fall in love.

She'd seen him, just once, after he flew home from the Indian Ocean. Sunburned from his long tour. Waiting for her at the train station.

'Hello.'

'Hello.' So familiar, unfamiliar.

They had wandered through the streets of London all day, hands almost touching. It was so hot, an odd quirk of that spring. He bought her red peonies, from a flower stall vivid with colour.

Later the rain came, people splashing through puddles, their shoes ruined, cross, the sky spiked by black umbrellas.

'This way.' They ran to the top of Primrose Hill, as the storm flickered around them, the city below like a game. 'It feels like you've climbed into the thunderstorm,' he shouted over the wind. 'Into the wilderness.'

'Madman.'

He kissed her then, just for a moment, the rain hammering down, the city lit up by the storm.

But then he jerked away. 'I can't. I'm sorry, Casey. I'm so sorry.'

And he ran. Down the hill in the rain, slipping and sliding in the mud. And she stood there alone, the red peonies falling from her hands.

She knew what had happened to the Royal Marines, of course, out in the heart of the wars. The bootnecks were sent into the worst of it, time and time again. She had watched as the flags dipped for the long drive home. Talked to the women waiting back at the base. And she had interviewed the veterans, afterwards, as doctors battled to fix splintered bodies.

The minds, though. They were different.

He'd left the Navy soon after the Indian Ocean, and found a new sort of life. He was in charge of security for journalists, out in Gaza, in Cairo, Mosul. Watching for trouble, as the hacks searched it out. Yanking them backwards out of danger, as the crowds roared, hungry for blood.

He painted over the cracks, with an artist's care.

Until one day, she had called him again.

Come with me, please, to the Sahara. We need you.

And he'd come.

'Ed would know what to do, out in Bangladesh,' Miranda said now.

'But he doesn't look like Dominic Burton-Smith.' Casey turned away, thoughts of Ed clashing with that expensive Surrey road.

'He does, you know. Dye his hair a bit darker. He would do.'

'Miranda,' said Casey. 'No.'

'We will have to find someone though,' said Miranda. 'I wouldn't trust Dominic out there.'

'No,' said Casey. 'Never.'

26

'You could lose the baby,' Dash said baldly.

They sat there in silence, watching the rain spatter against the window of the investigations room.

'It's very unlikely,' said Miranda.

'A newborn,' said Dash. 'In the middle of Bangladesh.'

'Children are born there all the time,' said Miranda.

And they die there all the time, Casey thought.

'If the Burton-Smiths go to the police ...' said Dash.

Blackmail, thought Casey. Attempted murder of the soul, a judge had called it once. It came with a long sentence.

And what would it look like, a murder of the soul?

Something like this, maybe?

Yes, something like this.

'You should have asked me first,' Dash said. He jumped to his feet, paced the room.

'You would have said no,' said Miranda.

'Exactly,' said Dash. 'I've looked up the Burton-Smiths. His mother's a magistrate, for Christ's sake. If they mention even a word of it to her, the mother will have to report you.'

'The neighbour thought Emily was pregnant,' said Miranda. 'If the neighbour thinks that, everyone will think that. They obviously wanted to avoid the questions from all the chatty friends. Be the perfect family. They're not going to tell anyone about the surrogacy.'

'Is this because of Salama?' Dash turned to Casey. 'I should have taken you off this job, after that. I knew it.'

'No.' Casey's throat filled. 'I am fine.'

'You're not,' said Dash. 'I've been watching you, Casey. You look as if you're seeing ghosts.'

Casey stared at him, eyes hard. 'Don't worry about me.'

'And you said' – Dash turned to Miranda – 'that you still need someone to go out there with Casey.'

'I want Ed to go with her,' Miranda said. 'But we can think of someone else if he can't make it.'

'How about Luke?' said Casey hopefully. 'He knows the area from working out of Delhi. And he's good at all that stuff. Done it before.'

'Too well known in Dhaka as the *Post*'s man,' said Miranda. 'Luke could have been identified to anyone during a trip to Bangladesh.'

It was why Casey avoided Parliament. Because you never knew who was whispering in a corner, and pointing like a curse.

'I'd be happier if it were Ed going out with you,' said Dash. 'There's a huge amount of organised crime in Bangladesh. It's vicious. You can't know what you're going to be walking into. Ed's pretty tough.'

They all heard it in his voice. Dash was planning the journey.

He was waiting for her under the bridge. Casey watched him as he idled through the second-hand books. He paused at one, an old hardback about Churchill. Leafed through it, glanced about – that quick glimpse around, always – and caught sight of her.

'Hello,' she said.

Ed looked at her, eyes narrowed, and for a second, she thought that he might walk away. But he smiled, and stepped towards her. Kissed her, cheek to cheek for the briefest of moments. She almost flinched away, and almost turned towards him, and fought for a second to smile.

'Hello, Casey.'

He was wearing an old waxed jacket, zipped up, and faded jeans. And the solid boots that they all wear, the former military men, slightly battered, neatly tied. Despite the cold spring, his face was tanned and he looked older, with lines round his eyes from squinting under the sun.

'I've always liked it here.' She gestured round at the rows of second-hand books, safe from the rain below Waterloo Bridge.

'Me too.'

'Shall we walk?'

'Sure.'

He put Churchill back on the table and they wandered along Southbank, towards the City. The air was full of mist, and the threat of rain. There were only a few people walking beside the grey of the Thames, hand in hand or hurrying with their briefcases. The skateboarders clattered, bright as graffiti, while another huge building soared up, room by room, gouging scoops of air from the sky.

'How are you?' Ed looked sideways at her.

'Fine. You know. You?'

'Fine.'

The pause lengthened.

'Are you working ...' She gestured back towards the Savoy on the other side of the river.

His stride hesitated. 'How did you know?'

She shrugged. He smiled.

'It's a good job, you know, working for him. I know his reputation, but ...'

'Good,' she said. 'Really, I am glad.'

'And what are you working on?'

'You know,' she gestured. 'This and that.'

'I saw that you got some of the shooters.'

'Some of them, not all.' Casey scowled towards the city. 'We couldn't prove a few of them had definitely done it, and they lawyered up fast. Others we never even got near.'

Ed watched a seagull wheel over the river. Casey shook her head, dispelling her thoughts. 'How's your shoulder, anyway?'

'Fine.' Ed spun his arm as if he were bowling. 'Those doctors were brilliant.'

And your mind? She didn't ask. Because she didn't know how. 'I'm very glad,' she said.

They walked on, towards Blackfriars. It was raining properly now, the rain pattering across the river.

'What do you want, Casey?' Ed's voice was abrupt.

'I don't want ...'

'You must want something.'

Is that what you think?

'I'm working on a new project,' Casey admitted. 'We've been told that there are women ...'

Her voice stalled for a second, her eyes prickling unexpectedly. Ed kept walking, waiting for her to speak.

‘They’re stuck in Bangladesh, these women,’ said Casey. ‘Refugees from Myanmar. Or what used to be called Burma. They’re been trafficked to a farm somewhere, forced to be surrogates … For British women. I think they’re being held near Cox’s Bazar.’

‘Cox’s Bazar?’

‘Down in the south of Bangladesh.’

Ed stopped walking, turned towards her. She couldn’t look at him.

‘And what are you planning to do, Casey?’

‘There’s a couple in England.’ Casey couldn’t meet his eyes. ‘Their baby is due any week now. They say I can travel out to Bangladesh, instead of them. Meet up with the traffickers, and try and find out where the women are being kept.’

‘Why would they let you go out there in their place?’ asked Ed. ‘They must know the risks are …’ He turned away. ‘Oh, Casey.’

A car horn blared from the bridge. The Shard was knifing the sky in the distance, glistening layers of apartments and hotel rooms and money.

‘What about the Rohingya women?’ Casey sprang in front of him. ‘We can’t leave them out there, just being used as incubators.’

‘But what gives you the right to get involved in all this, Casey?’ Ed tried to step past her. ‘What gives you the right to play god with these people’s lives?’

Thousands of readers, a strange sort of democracy.

‘Nothing.’ She blocked his path again. ‘But it’s the right thing to do, Ed. Surely you can see that?’

‘The right thing to do?’ Ed stared at her in disbelief. ‘How can you possibly judge what is or isn’t the right thing to do? You, of all people?’

Casey flinched away.

'Don't you remember, Casey?' Ed scrubbed at his eyes. 'Don't you remember walking up that hill towards Salama?'

His voice was rising. A couple walking along the river with a pram turned towards them, eyes sharply interested.

'Of course I remember,' Casey tried to hush him.

'How was that the right thing to do?' But his voice was quieter. 'How ... We could have done something, and we didn't.'

'You know we couldn't do anything else out there.' Casey's words sounded meagre, even to her. 'They would have killed us, without blinking. We came back, and we wrote about it, and we stopped it all.'

'As far as you know.'

Her eyes dropped to the pavement. 'It was all we could do.'

'Was it?'

'These are young girls,' said Casey. 'Children. You'll regret turning a blind eye, Ed. I know you will.'

She saw him flinch. His shoulders tensed as he straightened up. 'Maybe.'

'This is different.' She tried to soften. 'We can make things better, this time.'

'Casey.' Ed looked exhausted, all of a sudden. 'It doesn't work like that.'

He pushed past her, faster than she could react. And she could only watch him walk away down the river, back straight, long strides, leaving her far behind.

27

Casey stamped into the office.

'Not' – Miranda looked up – 'going well then?'

'No.' Casey threw herself at her chair. 'Disastrous, if you want my professional opinion.'

'I wonder if it would work, telling him how you feel.' Miranda contemplated her keyboard, her face all innocence. 'Imagine the novelty.'

'Stop it. Where's Hessa?'

'Sandwich.'

'I'm not going to tell him,' Casey scowled at Miranda, 'just to get him out to Bangladesh.'

'Why not?' said Miranda. *I would*, she didn't say. She pushed some notes towards Casey. 'I've been doing more research about surrogacy. Did you know one Japanese guy fathered thirteen children with surrogates in Thailand? He was only twenty-four himself. That was on top of four more children in Japan and two in Cambodia. Apparently he wanted a thousand children in total.'

'Did anyone stop him?'

'No,' Miranda sighed. 'He's the son of an IT billionaire, and they decided he just wanted a lot of children. He got custody.'

Casey was staring out of the window, only half listening. 'We will just' – she stabbed her pen into the desk – 'have to think of someone else who can be Dominic.'

'Easier said than done.' Miranda picked up a photograph of Dominic, snapped surreptitiously in Bath. 'Dave Accardi is far too short. It would never work, if they've given the Bangladesh team even the briefest description of Dominic.'

Accardi was a tough private detective, who could do a dozen accents with ease.

'Just ringing up about my bank account,' in a perfect Scottish accent. 'Could I just check my mortgage balance?' a day later, in the Queen's English. 'Thank you so much,' a polite West Country burr would wrap up the last call. 'You've no idea how helpful you've been.'

'Not Dave,' Casey agreed. 'How about Austin?'

'He looks the part,' Miranda blew out her cheeks, as she pondered the *Post*'s own social affairs editor. 'But he gets stressed about a bloody deadline. He'd never cope in Bangladesh.'

'Could Calvin help us out?'

Calvin had quit his staff job at his old tabloid suspiciously soon after a new managing editor with a keen interest in expenses had started working there. He now charged newspapers four times his old salary for undercover work, and spent the rest of his time clubbing.

'Do you really want to go abroad with Calvin?' Miranda started to laugh. 'He's such a sleaze. Didn't you hear about what he's got up to most recently? Some kiss-and-tell girl came to him, to stitch up some Premiership dimwit. Calvin had worked with her before, and didn't trust her as far as he could throw her. So he announced that he needed to hook up a camera in their hotel room to make sure what she said was happening was roughly right. So Calvin and that idiot sidekick of his were in one hotel room, and the footballer and the girl were in the next one.'

'Calvin can be such a creep,' said Casey.

'Unfortunately,' Miranda went on, 'the equipment went berserk for some reason and the television in the footballer's room somehow started picking up Cal's signal. All of a sudden, the footballer can see himself, with this girl, up on the bloody widescreen.'

'Christ,' said Casey, trying not to smile.

'So Calvin and the idiot are in complete meltdown next door. Even the kiss-and-tell girl is looking a bit jumpy. But then Cal jumps on the hotel phone, and gets reception to put him through to the room next door. The footballer's phone rings and "I'm terribly sorry, sir," Calvin says, in his most upmarket tones. "There seems to be a very minor glitch with our automated babysitting service right across the hotel. Slightly bizarrely you may be able to see yourself on your television at this time! But don't worry, sir! We'll be right back to normal soon." '

'Honestly.' Casey started to laugh.

'So the footballer looks a bit baffled, and then carries on as before.'

'Grim.' Casey grimaced, scrubbing at her face.

'You probably don't want to spend days and days with him.'

'No. Could Hippy help us out?'

Rhys Hipkiss had been their opposite number on the *Sunday Enquiry* until quite recently. He had left the paper, abruptly, a few months ago. The *Enquiry* was one of the racier tabloids, skating raucously over legal niceties. Hipkiss also specialised in kiss-and-tell girls. A world where *I'll go to the* Enquiry *unless you give me a hundred grand* would land you in jail. But *They're offering me a hundred grand. I don't want to take it, but …* was quite different.

That careful ellipsis would land the cheque. But the tabloids would be there, manoeuvring, all along. *You'll get all the deals, we'll make you a star …* 'Hippy? Didn't you hear about what he got up to?' Miranda started to laugh. 'He got axed over Amners. You must have been away.'

'What happened?'

Amners, a big accountancy firm, had collapsed in chaos a few months earlier, amidst tears and recriminations.

'Rhys decided,' Miranda went on, 'that it was a good idea to hack the chief executive's phone.'

'Who still does that?' Casey rolled her eyes.

'And he got such good stuff out of the voicemails that he decided to change the chief executive's password so that the *Banner* couldn't listen in too.'

'I despair,' said Casey drily, 'of our profession.'

'Anyway, the *Banner* had clearly been doing the same thing,' said Miranda.

The battles between the *Banner* and the *Enquiry* were notorious. They scheduled their Christmas party on the same evening every year, just so their subs could track each other down for a punch-up later on.

'Oh dear,' said Casey.

'When the *Banner* found they'd been locked out of the voicemail, they trotted off to the Amner chief exec, asking him about dirty tricks. As you'd expect, he had had it up to his eyeballs with the lot of them. Nevertheless, he let the *Banner* chief reporter leave a long, complicated message on his phone about some crazy insider-trading scheme going on at Amners. Naturally, Hippy listened to the whole thing, and then splashed the *Enquiry* on it.'

'Bloody hell,' Casey grinned. 'What's happened to Hippy now?'

'The *Enquiry*'s fired him,' Miranda sighed. 'They had to, really, for appearances' sake. They gave the Amners chief exec such a vast sum that it covered the pay-out he wasn't getting from Amners after they'd gone bust. He was quite pleased, in the end, and didn't bother with the police. Amners was going down in flames anyway, so he was past caring. I'm sure the *Enquiry* will take Hippy back by the end of the year. He's off sailing round the Med in the meantime. Sounded quite chirpy when I last heard from him.'

'How,' Casey asked, 'did the *Enquiry* know it was the *Banner*'s chief reporter who left the message?'

'Oh …' Miranda waved a hand airily. 'They dropped enough hints. The *Enquiry*'s news editor is swearing vengeance in this life or the next. To be honest, Hippy thinks that's why they'll need to bring him back in the end. To do over the *Banner* once and for all.'

'Fine.' Casey crossed a name off her list. 'Not Hippy.'

'So.' Miranda sobered up. 'Who?

'It's going to have to be Ed.'

28

The room went black. For a second, there was complete silence, hundreds of people holding their breath.

Then a laser stabbed the darkness, twisting and dancing. Another sparked, and another, building up into an explosion of light, carving out a wilderness of brilliance in the dark. One more split-second of total darkness, and then all the lights dazzled at once, the music erupted, and models prowled out from the four corners of the huge room.

'I need to get into the Mercutio show.' Casey had sidled up to Cressida the day before.

'Getting extra tickets for that is always a nightmare.'

'It's important.'

'You always say that.'

Casey hovered until Cressida got irritated. It was London fashion week, one of the fashion editor's busiest times of the year. While Casey had been in DC, Cressida had been in the flurry of New York. Next week the circus would roll on to Milan, then Paris, in a swirl of glitter and champagne, Cressida and her team alongside.

'Please, Cressida.'

'Sod off.' A long pause while Cressida tapped at her keyboard and ignored Casey. Then, quietly, 'Is it to do with ...?'

'Yes.'

Cressida glowered.

'You're not having my ticket. You'll never get past the door. Everyone knows who I am.' A hint of complacency in Cressida's voice as she glanced round. 'You can take Tosca's ticket' – a squawk from a pretty blonde sitting nearby – 'but you are not to get caught, and you are not to embarrass my team, do you hear me, Cassandra Benedict?'

'Yes,' Casey had grinned.

'And Tosca will style you first,' Cressida said firmly. 'You're not bloody turning up dressed like that if you're going from the *Post*.'

As the music pounded, Casey gazed around the room. From Tosca's seat, several rows back from the catwalk, Casey could see everything: the photographers crouching at the end of the stage, the PRs rushing around nervously, the emaciated models. The photographs from this show would be far more glamorous than any reality.

Mercutio's creative director was nowhere to be seen. He would be backstage, giving a final check to every girl before they strutted out on the stage. Across the room, Casey could see Cressida, sat primly in the front row, between the editor of *Vogue* and a blogger whose followers ran into the millions.

There he was: just a few seats down from Cressida. Declan Bentley. Laughing broadly for the cameras, flanked by one of the most famous supermodels in the world and an Oscar-nominated starlet. The most powerful man in the room, and Casey watched as his hard blue eyes followed the models around the catwalk.

Models weren't his type, she knew. There were many rumours about Declan Bentley's tastes, some of them true.

Casey waited impatiently until the show was finished. As soon as the last model disappeared, she hurried down the steps towards Bentley. He was making his way backstage already, the crowd skipping out of his way as he marched along.

Ed saw her too late. She heard his voice – 'Casey, for God's sake' – but she was already holding out her hand to Bentley.

'Mr Bentley, I'm Casey Benedict.'

It took him less than a second to place her.

'You wrote that fucking article about fucking Ethiopia.'

'Yes.' Mercutio was only one of the brands in Bentley's international conglomerate. Two years ago, a whistleblower had approached Casey about appalling conditions in one of Bentley's garment factories in Ethiopia. That factory provided clothes for Bentley's high street label, Juniper, and Casey had been on the first plane out to Addis Ababa.

'Didn't really work out for you that one, did it?' Bentley smiled nastily. 'I shut that entire fucking factory down, and now the whole village is out of work.'

Bentley emphasised his Cockney accent as he was speaking. He had lived in Monaco for a decade, but still liked the image of bad boy made good. Today would be one of only ninety carefully allocated days a year he spent in the UK, his private jet flying into the country first thing in the morning and out again last thing at night. When in Britain, he lived in the Savoy: no private home for the taxman to link him to the UK.

'I know.'

'So what the fuck do you want? And how the hell did you get in here anyway?'

Out of the corner of her eye, Casey could see Cressida sidling away.

'I need your help, Mr Bentley.' For a second, Bentley was almost surprised, his face freezing into a near-laugh. Then he snapped back. 'Tough. Fuck off.'

'It'll screw up Rhapso.'

The rivalry between Juniper and Rhapso was notorious. After a long-running row over trademarks, Rhapso had poached Juniper's team of senior buyers two years earlier. Two weeks later, Rhapso's brand director had received an offer he couldn't refuse. Within days, a series of articles about Bentley's tax arrangements had appeared, sparking protests outside Juniper's flagship Oxford Circus branch.

The Ethiopia article was the final straw, with Bentley threatening to personally break the legs of everyone involved, 'a task I usually fucking outsource, to be honest. But for you, darling, I'll make an exception.'

Casey had been followed around by private detectives for three months after the Ethiopia article appeared.

'No fucking way,' said Bentley now. 'Now fuck off.'

'Fine.' Casey stretched, arms over her head. 'I'll be off to Vietnam then, if I've got time on my hands. I hear it's delightful at this time of year.'

Juniper's operations had been shunted across to Vietnam shortly after the Ethiopian factory closed down. Chasing the cheap needle, they called it. Factories across the world bidding against each other to offer the lowest rates.

Bentley hesitated, and Casey raised an eyebrow, making it almost a joke. Bentley gestured, ordering his team of people to back off. They fell away at once.

'What's your plan for Rhapso?' he spoke quietly.

'It's complicated,' said Casey, 'but I've got a tip about one of their factories in Bangladesh, and I want to check it out.'

'What do you need from me?'

Casey's eyes met Ed's over Bentley's shoulder. He narrowed his eyes at her.

'He's probably not mentioned it, but I've worked with Ed Fitzgerald on a story before. And I need his help on this.'

'Ed?' Bentley's face opened into a laugh. 'Fuck's sake. He's kept that very quiet.'

He gestured Ed over. Very unwillingly, Ed came across. Behind him, the Oscar-nominated actress and the supermodel were hugging ostentatiously for the cameras.

'I understand that you've been working with Miss Benedict.' Bentley raised an eyebrow.

'A long time ago,' Ed protested. 'Just after I left the Marines.'

'You dark fucking horse.' There was affection in Bentley's words.

'I should have told you.'

'Damn right.' But Bentley was laughing. He turned back to Casey. 'What have you got on those twats at Rhapso?'

'That's confidential.' Casey met his eye.

'Who was the fucking source for the Ethiopia story?'

The silence stretched out in the air-kissing chaos of the room.

'Ed?' Bentley turned to him.

'I don't know.'

Bentley's personal assistant was trying to get his attention, waving two phones. Bentley looked around, remembering the crowds, the actress, the supermodel.

Bentley laughed. 'Fine,' he said. 'Give them a few shitty days. Ed, you're off to Bangladesh. See you back in Fontvieille.'

And he was gone, in a tidal wave of PAs and PRs, and Ed looked at Casey. 'You're shameless,' he said.

29

That night Casey lay in the dark of her new flat in London. Lost in the wilds of the Sahara, the sun burning down like a curse. Out where the desert shimmered, as if none of it were real. But it was, it was, it was.

She had pleaded with Ed to go out there with her and to pretend. To find the men who killed refugees, just to find out how it felt.

He had kissed her, out there, but it was just a part in a play. An actor saying his lines.

You can't be a spectator, he had pleaded, the night before. *That child is out there right now, with a whole life ahead.*

But she had forced him, out along the path, up into the hills. Because without proof, there was nothing. Or there was no story, anyway, almost the same thing.

She had turned to him, in that beautiful room, in that magical palace lost out in the sands.

I am going, Ed. Even if I have to go up there on my own.

Knowing he would never let her go alone.

And so he had walked beside her, step by step, and watched, eyes blank, as the tiny figure crumpled.

You got her. Clean kill.

The trader's arms raised in triumph.

Casey had stepped across to Ed, hugged him close. And he had gazed at her, lost, as if he had never really known her at all.

They had had to run across the desert, hunted, like rabbits. The rifle shots, one after the next, closer and closer. Ed had been hit, blood spattering, the car crashing down the bluff.

The nightmares followed them home, of course. Just a few paces behind, like old acquaintances. There, in the corner of the eye. Slinking closer as the nights drew in.

Her new nightmares, and the old. Back again, worse than before. Fragments of glass slicing up through the dreams.

I did this to you.

30

Miranda was tense the next morning. 'Have you heard from Ed? Maybe we should try Calvin. He's a professional, at least . . .'

Casey's telephone jingled. She read the message and was on her feet.

'I'll be back in a bit.'

'Everything OK?'

'Yes.'

Meet me at the top of the hill. She read it again and again.

The London sky was grey as she climbed Primrose Hill. A seagull shrieked overhead, twisting higher and higher into the sky.

He was waiting in a cold swirl of wind.

'Hello.' Casey sat down on a park bench, rubbed smooth, and covered in years of graffiti. *Liv loves Charlie.*

Ed stayed on his feet. A jogger panted up the hill. Teenagers – smoking with a careful precision – ambled past. Casey waited.

'I come up here when I'm not sure what to do,' he said.

'It is beautiful,' she agreed. She shivered, and pulled her jacket closer around her.

'Do you want mine?'

'I'm fine.'

Two middle-aged tourists stopped, asking for directions. Ed pointed, explained, smiling easily, *No, it's no trouble.*

Casey waited.

'I'm not coming because of that business with Declan yesterday,' he said at last.

'OK.' Casey felt the gloom settle around her. Checkmate.

A fat spaniel waddled past. A father, impatient, scooped up his toddler son and marched down the hill, ignoring the bawls. It had rained recently, black puddles sprinkling the maze of paths.

'You talked about turning a blind eye,' said Ed.

'What?' Casey's memory blurred. 'When?'

'Down on Southbank. You said that I'd regret turning a blind eye to those girls.'

'Oh,' Casey remembered. 'I'm sorry about that. I know you …'

'I can't stop thinking …' He paused. 'I've never told anyone … We never spoke about …'

'Spoke about what?'

'Afghanistan,' Ed said. 'My unit was out there with the ANA,' he went on. 'The Afghan army.'

'Yes.' She kept her voice even.

'We were sent out to a small base, not far from Bastion. Just a dot on the map.'

Casey waited.

'And then we were stuck there for weeks on end.'

Casey remembered those bases, out in the wilderness. The Chinooks screaming in low, ducking and diving, racing scared of the missiles. She remembered the patchwork of canals, the scrappy little villages, the fluttering pink of the poppies. The smiles from the locals that weren't smiles at all. And the patrols through the fields, against every instinct, when the danger is so real that it must be ignored.

'We were training the Afghan soldiers out on that base,' he said. 'We were working with them. Alongside them.'

'Yes.'

'We needed their help. We couldn't do it alone. There were too many Taliban. Too many enemies.'

'I know.'

'We had to get the Afghan security forces trained up, so that we could leave. That bloody country . . . But we needed to leave a decent force behind.'

'I remember.'

'So we were working with the Afghans, day after day. Teaching them what they had to know. And giving them guns, of course.'

Casey remembered the monotony on those bases: the endless rules, the hours on stag, the crunch of the boots on the gravel. She remembered the men waiting for orders. And the boredom, and the high bombproof walls, as the world got smaller and smaller.

When the only interesting thing is: you might die today.

'We were miles from everything,' said Ed. 'It felt like we were completely alone. Just us, forgotten. The Afghans were fed up too. They'd had enough.'

For a second, oddly, Casey remembered the latrines where everything was bagged and incinerated, as if they were never really there at all. The smell, swallowing you whole.

'Some of the Afghans, at night . . .'

London grumbled around them. A siren, sharp, wailed along the edge of the park. Ed watched the blue lights skitter along, safe and threatening all at once.

Ed cleared his throat, spoke quickly. 'Some nights, the Afghans would go to one of the villages nearby. They would go there … and snatch one of the little boys … They would grab one, and …' He forced himself to carry on. 'At night, we could hear the little boys screaming, out in the darkness.'

Casey sat in silence, watching the lights flicker over the city.

'They raped them. The boys …'

'Oh, Ed.'

'Don't.'

'What did you …'

'We didn't do anything. We just *listened*. One night, we had a bonfire going all jolly. Some of my men were singing, and when they stopped … When they stopped, we could hear this little boy crying out beyond the circle of light.'

A plane tracked across the sky towards Heathrow. Casey's eyes followed it aimlessly.

'But what could you have done?' she asked quietly.

'I don't know. We didn't know. We had a job. Orders. These were our *allies* …' His voice hardened. 'In the morning, the Afghans would be all bright and breezy. As if it was normal, just what they did. And maybe it was. And we needed them. We were miles from anywhere else. We needed them, and they knew that.'

'I'm sorry.'

'Sorry for who?' He still had his back to her. '*Bacha bazi*, that's what they called it. Boy play. We just looked the other way.'

Across the park, London spiked into the sky. The Shard, the Gherkin, the BT Tower, tens of millions of lives.

'We didn't do anything,' Ed said tightly. 'We just got on with it.'

'It wasn't your fault.' The words were automatic.

'And then when we went out to Salama together,' he spoke very quietly, 'again, you and I. We just watched. We didn't *do* anything …'

'I'm sorry,' Casey said. 'So sorry. I didn't know.'

He spun round towards her.

'So I can't ignore those girls now,' he said.

Despite herself, she felt that flood of relief. 'Do you mean …?'

'I mean I'll come to Bangladesh.'

For a second, she couldn't speak. 'Thank you, Ed.'

'One condition,' he said.

'What?' *Anything.*

He glanced round. 'Sure?'

'Yes.' She didn't have to think, agreed blindly.

He sat down on the other end of the bench, stared across the city.

'This is the last time, Casey. Do you understand?'

She knew what he was asking.

'After this, I don't want to know anything more.' He had turned towards her, his eyes hard. 'I can't know any more. It's too much. It's endless.'

So that no one can say, 'I didn't know.'

'I just want to get on with my life,' he said. 'You have to promise me, Casey. You have to choose. I'll come to Dhaka, but this is the end of it.'

Casey ducked her face away.

You have to choose.

'Casey?'

She looked up, London blurring.

'All right,' she said. 'All right.'

As soon as the words were spoken, she felt the shock of regret. But his shoulders relaxed.

'You think I'm a coward.'

'No. Never.'

He was staring past her. 'I will never forget, you know. I will never forget those screams out beyond the light.'

31

Just a few days later, they flew into Dhaka.

The day was slowing into evening as Ed and Casey walked down the long corridors of the old airport. A golden light sloped through the windows, and men clustered in glass smoking-rooms, clogged like lungs of soot.

The airport was sweltering, the Bangladesh spring burning into summer. There would be a few more months of searing heat, and then the crackling flood of the monsoon.

Casey was wearing a long loose dress over baggy trousers. Bangladesh was a Muslim country, and believed strictly in modest dress for women. The gold wedding ring was tight on her finger. She smoothed down the pale blue cotton, trying to breathe easily.

She straightened her shoulders, the surge of excitement coming from nowhere: *I'm here, really here, all on red.*

She glanced across at Ed, unfamiliar with his darkened hair.

'It'll be all right.' He touched her arm, just once, because they could never be sure. And Casey grinned up at him as they approached passport control, carefree, happy, easy.

Never talk to strangers, that old chant. *Never get into their car.*

But she did it time and again. And every time could be her last. A roll of the dice too far.

Casey glanced around the airport, looking for spies. The Bangladeshi faces stared back, indifferent.

'You're playing on their turf,' Dash had said, just before they left. 'Are you sure about this, Casey? Really?'

'We have to,' she'd said. 'We have to take the chance.'

'We don't.'

'I do.'

And she stepped forward through the airport.

Dominic and Emily had met them at the airport back in London, to hand over their passports. Casey could see that Emily had been crying.

'I have to be there,' Emily had tried one last time. 'I have to be with Poppy as soon as she is born. Please don't make me wait here, Casey. Please.'

But she handed over her passport all the same, Casey staring down at it. Pretty Emily, seven years ago, smiling in an elegant shirt and jaunty earrings. A photograph taken before the smile was blurred by sadness. Casey felt that pang of sympathy again.

'Dominic's passport is quite old,' said Emily. 'It's nearly full, actually.'

'It's all helpful,' said Casey. 'I am sorry you can't travel with us. But if they spotted you … If they guessed …'

'I know. And you need our passports anyway.'

They placed their two passports side by side for a second. Emily and Casey, Casey and Emily. There was a smudge of blue paint on Emily's wrist, and she scrubbed at it, almost angrily.

'They'll do,' Emily admitted, glancing between the two photographs. 'We could be cousins.'

Casey stared at the grey eyes, the long brown hair, the scattering of freckles, and wondered about all the lives she might have lived.

The airport babbled around them.

'I know what you must think of me,' said Emily again.

Dominic and Ed had stepped away from them, separated momentarily by a caravan of baggage trolleys, trundling past in a long line. There were children shrieking, a mother wiping a nose. *Come* on, *Mia, for heaven's sake.*

Emily stared with a naked jealousy that almost hurt.

'I know why you did it,' said Casey. 'It's all right.'

'The worst thing,' said Emily, almost to herself, 'is that you never even know when to start mourning. "It can take ages," people say, trying to help. "You've only been trying a year!" Then it's two years, three years, four. And then there are the miracles. "Great-Aunt Jennifer, she didn't have her first until she was forty-three! She was convinced she couldn't! Imagine!" ' Emily swallowed. 'You don't even know when to grieve.'

The line of trolleys had passed.

'Have you ever lost a baby?'

The question startled Casey, and she recognised the irony as she flinched away from the intrusion.

She looked across at Emily. 'No,' she said.

'Have you heard of phantom limb syndrome?' Emily asked. 'It's almost like that, losing a baby. Rationally, you know they're gone. But some dark recess of your mind won't quite believe it. Can't quite believe that the world could be so cruel. It's a shock, the memory, every single time. That something so intrinsically a part of you just disappeared one day. Ceased to exist, just like that. Your mind sends back those flashes, bursts of pointless pain. *There she is.* In a playground, as you pass a school. *There she is.* Just waiting for me.'

They stood there in silence.

'I am glad though.' Emily tried to smile. 'That you are going to find out about these people. It is horrendous. I can't imagine what it must be like for that girl, Romida. Her life.'

Her voice was interrupted by an announcement over the loudspeaker, a bored woman listing delayed planes.

Emily crouched down. She had brought a huge suitcase with her, unzipping it now. It was filled with baby paraphernalia, and she showed it to Casey now. The tiny pink babygrows and the Pampers. The milk formula and the baby wipes. There was even a book about looking after a baby for the first few days. 'If you've got nothing better to read on the flight.' Emily tried to make it a joke. 'But it does come very highly recommended.'

Casey kneeled down, picking up a little changing mat.

'We will take very good care of her, Emily.'

'I know.' Emily repacked a grey baby sling. 'I know. There's also a car seat. And the travel cot. The instructions are included ...'

Her voice trailed away.

'Remember,' said Casey gently. 'You have to stay low-profile now, both you and Dominic. Don't answer your phone. If someone from the clinic calls you, I will ring them back from a Bangladeshi mobile. And you can't stay at your home for a bit, either. I'm sorry. If the clinic somehow realises you're still in this country ...'

'I know.' Emily wiped her eyes. 'We were going to go away anyway. Go away and come back – surprise! – with a baby. Tell everyone she came a bit early. Somewhere in England though.' She almost smiled. 'Because I'm not allowed to fly any more, of course.'

Now, Emily handed over a bankcard too. 'The *Post* will reimburse you,' Casey promised automatically.

Emily shrugged, gave her sweet smile. 'It hardly even matters any more.' She looked across at Casey curiously. 'Are you scared?'

'No,' said Casey. Then: 'A little,' she admitted.

'Please don't take any risks,' begged Emily. 'I can't bear it.'

'I won't,' Casey lied.

Then a smile that was almost a conspiracy spread across Emily's face. 'There's a payment due to the clinic after the baby gets safely back to England. Quite a big one. They'll want you to get back here, for that.'

'Thank you,' Casey smiled. 'That is helpful to know.'

'Please hurry back,' said Emily. 'As soon as you have got Poppy. Please.'

'We will come home as soon as we can,' Casey promised. 'I don't want to be out there any longer than we have to be.'

'I've been reading up,' said Emily. 'About bonding, and attachment, and emotional transfer. It all just seems so ridiculous now.'

'As soon as possible,' Casey repeated.

Emily stared across the airport. At the crowds, the orange signs, the clumsy clutter of suitcases. 'None of this,' she said, 'was ever in my dreams.'

She turned to Casey. 'We never meant to hurt anyone.' Her voice was more urgent. 'We were just like everyone else. We thought the good outweighed the bad.'

Those decisions, a million taken every day.

'It won't be long,' said Casey. 'We'll be back soon.'

Emily's eyes were fixed on Casey's. 'Please,' she said. 'Please just bring me back my baby.'

32

There was a long queue at passport control. The airport was filled with tired Bangladeshi men travelling home. Ed and Casey had flown to Qatar first, and on the flight to Bangladesh they were surrounded by the poorest workers, looking awkward on plush airline seats.

Going home, though. *Going home.* Because they might have been in Qatar for months, these men. Years, even. Building the palaces and the towers, the stadiums and the follies, all in that blazing heat. For decades, Bangladesh has sent its workers abroad, for some sort of chance. Any sort of chance, really.

Now Ed held Casey's hand as they got closer to passport control. She glanced down for a second, seeing their fingers intertwined, her knuckles white.

'OK?' she asked.

'I'm fine.'

On the other side of the border, Casey hid their own passports deep in her luggage. Dominic's and Emily's passports were in her handbag, easy to reach. Casey slid her hand into her bag for a second and traced the gold lettering, just for a second.

In the Name of Her Majesty ... to allow the bearer to pass freely without let or hindrance ... Always taken for granted, those most precious words.

And then they walked out into the chaos of the airport, staring round the crowded room as the mosquitoes buzzed about them.

A man glanced at them, looked away. *Burton-Smith*, read his sign. Casey felt the surge of adrenalin as they walked towards him, with those nervous smiles. *Would he guess? Would he know? Would he bite?*

'Dominic and Emily.' Ed held out his hand, the words solid, so respectable. 'How do you do?'

As he spoke, Ed wrapped his arm around Casey, and she melted into his side, smiling round at the man.

The man lowered the sign, black eyes flickering over them. Casey forced herself to breathe, the nerves twining in her throat. *Please.*

'Welcome to Bangladesh,' the man smiled, with a half-bow as he swept the sign across his heart.

And Casey's smile was real, at once.

He was wearing a beautiful black suit, his English impeccable. This must be the man who brought Theo to Vivienne, Casey thought, in that hotel lobby those years ago. Taller than most of the Bangladeshis, and looking down at the airport as it rushed around him.

'I am Raz,' the man grinned.

Raz clicked his fingers at an elderly Bengali man beside him, who snatched up their luggage.

'Please, Mr and Mrs Burton-Smith, do come with me.'

There was a sharp intelligence in Raz's eyes, and the sense of a snake uncoiling as he began to move across the concourse. *Do not underestimate this man*, Casey thought.

Raz led them through the crowds, to a shiny black Land Cruiser. In the stale heat outside the airport, the traffic was chaos. There were no road markings, cars flooding along haphazardly. The green tuk-tuks slipped through impossible gaps, forcing their way past with shouts and squawks. The hooting was relentless: a toot on the horn instead of indicating, always. Everyone kept out of the way of the brightly painted buses – so battered already, the victors of a thousand clashes – as they thundered along.

Many of the buildings along the airport road were unfinished, the steel rebar springing into the sky like a metal fountain. The main road into the city was lined with shacks, smoke lingering in the air.

Raz sat in the front seat, beside the old driver.

'I will take you to the hotel.' He smiled back at them. 'You must be exhausted after your long flight.'

'Thank you.' Ed nodded his head once, as Dominic might. 'It's a bugger of a journey.'

'You are early,' Raz said. 'I thought you were coming in a few more days.'

They had only called him from Qatar, unstoppably late, hoping that the confusion would tilt the balance their way, very slightly.

'We couldn't wait any longer.' Casey put a giggle in her voice. 'I am sorry if it is inconvenient. But we just had to be in Bangladesh. We had to be near our daughter.'

'It is no problem at all,' said Raz. 'I am just worried you will have nothing to do. Dhaka is not exactly designed for tourists.'

He laughed to himself, as if it were a private joke.

'There are elections coming up,' he went on. 'That means demonstrations, curfews. You shouldn't travel to some parts of the city at all, because it might be dangerous. Bangladesh is not always an easy country to operate in, as I am sure you know.'

'Poppy,' said Casey. 'Where is she?'

The hint of desperation was so easy.

'Everything is coming along just as it should,' said Raz patiently. 'But she is not here yet, of course. She will be born soon. You mustn't worry yourself, Miss Emily.'

A person, made to measure. Not here, not yet. No.

'I would like to meet her,' said Casey. 'The lady carrying our child.'

'I am afraid that is not possible right now.' Raz looked apologetic. 'You must understand, the woman is very tired at the moment. These last days are hard.'

'Of course,' Ed interrupted Casey. 'We understand completely.'

'Is she in Dhaka?' tried Casey. 'Or somewhere nearby?'

Raz turned round, and gave her an easy smile.

'The baby will be brought to Dhaka in a few days,' he said. 'It is all as we promised.'

The driver dodged round a tuk-tuk, which was trundling the wrong way down the motorway towards them, a Bangladeshi flag flying from its roof.

'Have you ever met Dr Greystone?' Casey asked lightly.

'Dr Greystone?' Raz sounded blank. 'I have never met this Dr Greystone.'

Casey stared out of the windows. There was water everywhere in this city: in puddles, in canals, in pools under motorway bridges. A dilapidated lorry hurtled by, piled high with sacks, a small boy clinging to the very top. The lorry's driver was old, with a beard that would have been white, had it not been dyed the startling henna orange. The small boy waved at her.

'We were thinking,' Casey said brightly, waving back, 'that as we have a few days here, we might head down to Cox's Bazar.'

Chittagong, Bangladesh's industrial powerhouse, was 150 miles south-west of the capital Dhaka, further down the Bay of Bengal. Cox's Bazar was beyond Chittagong, another four hours along the coast.

Not far north of the Burmese border, Cox's Bazar was the closest thing to a tourist resort in Bangladesh. Named after Captain Cox, hero of the East India Company, the ramshackle town sprawls along one of the longest beaches in the world, almost a hundred miles of sand.

The Bangladeshis thronged to Cox's Bazar at this time of the year, the women swimming fully dressed in the sea, the hawkers hustling to and fro. *Photo? Sunhat? Photo?*

'Cox's Bazar is a nice place to go,' said Raz cautiously. 'Certainly, for a few days, you might enjoy yourselves there.'

The Rohingya refugee camps were an hour's drive further on from Cox's Bazar, spreading over hundreds of acres just to the north of the Myanmar border. Cox's Bazar itself had been flooded with aid workers, who had been commuting down to the camps for years now. The big humanitarian agencies blockbooked the holiday hotels for months at a time, almost smothering the tourism.

'Those women will be somewhere in the area around Chittagong and Cox's Bazar,' Casey had insisted to Miranda, back in the office. 'The man Hessa spoke to had a Chittagong accent, according to her mother.'

'Maybe,' Miranda had shrugged. 'You can't be sure. They could be anywhere. In the outskirts of Dhaka, wherever. And just because he has a Chittagong accent, it doesn't mean he still lives there.'

Snug in the black Land Cruiser, Casey cracked open a bottle of ice-cold water, and leaned her head back against the plush headrest. 'Would you arrange a car for us down to Cox's Bazar tomorrow?' Casey put on Emily's confidence like a coat. 'It would be so helpful.'

Raz would expect them to be driven. In Dhaka, the Bengali elite were driven everywhere by a chauffeur. With at least one bodyguard, and the horn blaring. Quite often they travelled in convoys, in a cloud of weed and coke.

'If you want to go to Cox's Bazar,' said Raz, 'it would be much easier for you to fly. The highways, they can be very dangerous.'

Casey stared out of the car window. Men sat on white plastic chairs in the shade of the motorway bridges, watching the world go by.

'Oh, but I would so love to see some of the countryside,' Casey protested. 'You don't see anything from the plane. You might as well be anywhere. In fact' – she dipped her head like a princess – 'could you arrange for us to take the train from Dhaka down to Chittagong, and then a car onwards? It'll be an adventure.'

'Of course,' Raz smiled round at her. 'It would be no problem.'

In the smart Dhanmondi district, they passed through airport sensors before checking into the hotel. Security in Dhaka had jumped after an attack on a restaurant just a few years earlier, when the militants stormed in, and sprayed the crowd with bullets, not champagne. So now a bored security guard ambled round the car, checking for bombs with a mirror.

'He would never find a thing,' Raz whispered back at them, so that Casey almost grinned.

A tired hotel receptionist stared at Emily's passport for a long moment, and Casey felt her heart rate surge.

'It's so exciting to be here at last,' Casey beamed at the receptionist, lighting up the room. 'Have you worked here long?'

The receptionist smiled back, not understanding the patter of English.

'You are most welcome to the Rose Petal Inn,' she recited. 'Here is your keycard.'

'I will message you later,' Raz said. 'About the train journey.'

And he was gone.

Their room was generously sized, and could have been anywhere. There was one bed. Ed looked at it.

'I can sleep on the floor again.'

They laughed, Casey meeting his eye for the first time since they got off the plane. *You promised.*

'I can go downstairs and tell them that Mr Burton-Smith snores like a train if you want,' offered Casey. 'And that I must sleep alone.'

'It's fine,' said Ed. 'I don't mind if you're OK.'

'I'm so shattered,' Casey yawned. 'I'll just pass out.'

'And we won't be here very long anyway,' he said.

'No,' she said, thinking. 'Raz said the baby would be brought to Dhaka. And that means the mother is somewhere else at the moment.'

It was odd, averting her eyes as he changed. When Ed went for a shower, Casey hurried to the mirror, peering at herself pensively.

'Why didn't Miranda come out to Dhaka?' Ed came out of the bathroom, rubbing his hair dry. 'I think some of that bloody dye is coming out, you know. I'm going patchy.'

'She's tied up in London,' Casey said quickly. 'And she thought Hessa could use the experience, anyway.'

'Sure.' He tugged off the silky bedspread. The air conditioning sighed.

Casey lay down beside him, careful not to touch.

'Are you sleeping all right at the moment?' she asked into the silence.

'Are you?'

'No,' she said quietly.

'Well then.'

They lay side by side in the dark. He was so close, solid in the dark. The room fell into silence. Casey listened to his breathing, and longed to reach out and touch him. The traffic roared outside, and she knew that he lay awake for hours.

33

They jumped awake when the telephone rang beside Ed's head.

'Mr Burton-Smith?' It was Raz. 'I am sorry to bother you, but the express train to Chittagong, it goes very early.'

'That's OK.' Ed was rubbing his eyes. 'We'll be down in a minute.'

Even at this early hour, the traffic in Dhaka was solid.

'There are fewer crashes than you'd think,' Raz shrugged. 'But still a lot of crashes.'

In the dawn, the station was packed.

'How will we get on board?' Ed said, as a train pulled into the station, and the huge crowd surged forward.

'Not this train,' said Raz. 'This one is for Sylhet.'

That was where Hessa's family was from originally, thought Casey, where the tea plantations rolled green for miles.

A wave of passengers flooded across the platform as the train stopped. They crammed through the carriage doors, pushing their way further and further into the train, squeezing into every inch. Packages, parcels, a baby, all were passed over the heads of the crowd. As the train pulled away, so slowly, men were still wedging themselves on board, hanging on to the doors with all their strength.

But the people fell away for Raz, Casey saw, when the next train arrived. The crowd edged back, as he paced through towards their carriage.

'No problem, you see,' he smiled, as they stepped into a first-class compartment. 'And at the other end, our driver will meet you.'

'You've been so kind,' said Casey. 'Thank you very much.'

It was beautiful, travelling slowly through the Bangladesh countryside. The rice was growing in the paddies now, impossibly green in the neatest of rows. Between the lines of emerald seedlings, water glittered in the sun. Here and there were small villages perched high up on embankments, peering out among mango trees and date palms. Between the villages, raised roads snaked through watery fields. Occasionally, the roads meandered all the way to solitary shacks built out on tiny islands, right in the middle of the paddies.

Low-lying Bangladesh, delta nation, half-needing, half-dreading the floods.

In the little villages, minarets poked out above stands of bamboo. Small boys raced the train, giggling to themselves. Casey pointed out the brick factories to Ed, with the high chimneys belching smoke into the air.

The station names were like charms. Srinidhi, men bent double in the rice fields. Gangasagar, detergent bubbling in a waterfall. Laksam Junction, a goat wandering down the platform. The train rolling on, waved forwards, solemnly, by a stationmaster in a black suit with a green flag. He kept his red flag firmly wrapped up. At lunchtime, a man came down the train, selling the sweet milky coffee that made Casey's brain fizz. And finally, the buildings grew closer together, and, slowly, so slowly, the train rolled into the suburbs of Chittagong.

The man who met them off the train was a surprise.

'Dylan.' He shook Casey's hand hard, audibly Australian.

He was dark-haired, very tanned, with shocking blue eyes. A Bangladeshi parent, Casey guessed.

'How was the train?' he asked curtly. 'It's a long way.'

'We wanted to see the countryside.' Casey smiled at him. 'It was fascinating.'

'I've organised a car to take you down to Cox's right now.' Dylan was brisk, tough, wasted few words. 'It's just outside the station.'

A Rolex gleamed on Dylan's wrist, as he gestured towards the car. Another black Land Cruiser, again with no markings. A Bangladeshi man hopped out, and rushed towards them. The driver was very nervous around Dylan, Casey saw, quite subservient.

'It's about four hours to Cox's from here.' Dylan tapped on the roof of the car, as soon as their bags were stowed. 'You've sorted a hotel?'

'Yes,' said Ed. 'It's all done.'

The car accelerated away.

In a drifting sea mist, Cox's Bazar was apocalyptic. At some point, years ago, the property developers had rushed here, hoping to make their fortune from the old resort.

They began building high-rise hotels, dozens of them. But then some crisis erupted overnight, and the hotels were left abandoned, half-built.

They looked haunted, now. Some of the buildings had rows and rows of blank dead-eyed windows. Others had just a few concrete storeys completed, and an empty skeleton of steel sagging above. Rubbish piled up along the road.

One hotel, almost finished, had been squatted by dozens of families. Bright clothes fluttered on a balcony, where some architect had probably dreamed once of all-modern-comforts, a-magical-seaview. Children grinned down from the hotel roof as Casey and Ed passed. *Hello mister, hello mister.*

Here and there, a few labourers worked sporadically, their drills on concrete jagging the air. Further down the street, fishermen paced to and fro in what would have been an huge ornamental lake in the fantasy version of Cox's Bazar. A curve of hotels, half-built, circled the lake. The fishermen smoked as they hunted. The catch was sold in the market just a few yards from the lakes. All along the road to their hotel, the fish were hung up to dry in long lines. The stink was overpowering.

The NGO signs were everywhere. Save the Children in one hotel, Oxfam in the next.

'This,' Ed looked around him, 'is the country's resort?'

The beach was beautiful though, golden sand rolling south towards the Burmese border. The fishing boats, sailing home through the dusk, were half-drowned crescent moons.

'Watch out for the quicksand,' grinned one of the hustlers. 'We lose a few tourists every year at Cox's.'

At the hotel, Casey rushed up to their room, switching on her laptop.

'There.' She pointed at the screen.

As the car was driving down towards Cox's Bazar, Casey had edged a tiny tracker between the car seat and the floor.

'Isn't that risky?' asked Ed now.

'I think these men must have quite a big operation,' Casey explained. 'With different divisions running out of Dhaka and

Chittagong. I thought that they might send a different car for us, if we got the train down to Chittagong. A car based down this end of the country, rather than up in Dhaka. And with any luck, that car will now head back up to Chittagong. And then it might be parked up overnight, somewhere near wherever those girls are.'

'I suppose it might,' Ed put the same emphasis on might. 'But what if they find the tracker?'

'Did you see how the driver reacted to Dylan?' asked Casey. 'Fear. I reckon that Dylan has plenty of enemies. Even if they find it, they won't know the tracker came from us.'

Tapping her computer, Casey updated the tracker location again. It was 20 miles up the road, at Eidgaon, stuck in slow-moving traffic.

'OK,' Ed lay back on the bed, exhausted. 'Let's see where it goes.'

She nudged him awake five hours later.

'It's arrived,' she whispered. 'It's parked in Sagorika.'

Sagorika was a sprawling industrial zone, just to the north of central Chittagong. Dozens of factories lined the dusty roads, and thousands of workers poured in and out of them every single day.

They aren't as bad as they used to be, the factory bosses say defensively. But Casey had heard the stories about the Bangladesh garment factories for years.

Small children, splashing through so much bleach that their hands and feet turned white. Women coughing in the chemical air, until the blood spattered red.

And the Rana Plaza, of course, when eight storeys pancaked down into one. Over a thousand people died that day in Savar, when the vast factory collapsed.

All around the world, people wore clothes from the Rana Plaza. It had supplied so many shops, from Bonmarché to Benetton, Mango to Monsoon. They found so many pretty rags in the rubble.

The workers had tried to protest, that morning. They were ordered back to their machines, although you could see the cracks in the walls by then. *A month's salary gone, if you miss just one day*, they were told. *Get back to work. Get back to work. Get back to work, right now.*

The overseers carried sticks too, just in case.

And down came the factory, with a mountain's roar.

The rescue took days. One woman, afterwards, told how she was passed a hacksaw to cut off her own arm. It took hours, she said, trapped under a steel beam. She would saw a bit, pass out, come round.

Casey was back in Chittagong before dawn, driven through the night in an old taxi she found a few blocks from their hotel. On her screen she had watched the Land Cruiser manoeuvre round the north-west of the city, before coming to a halt in the industrial area. And the moment it parked, Casey was on her way.

Hessa was waiting in a faded business hotel, near the centre of Chittagong, her face lighting up as Casey arrived.

'Welcome to Chittagong,' Casey grinned. 'We've got to hurry.'

34

It had been odd, flying into Dhaka on her own, Hessa thought. Odd not to have her whole family around her, bickering, squabbling, and being met at the airport by a dozen more relatives. Waiting for Casey's call, she had drifted around and around Gulshan Park. Clockwise, the way they always had. Hessa stared at the pink flowers, and the red roses, and the steep, lush banks sliding down to the sludgy green lake, and wondered.

You have to choose.

She crossed back and forth over the bridges as the joggers ran past. All around the park, she noticed the old buildings replaced by the new. She felt a jolt of sadness at the loss, even though she barely remembered the old ones.

I never had this life, so why do I miss it?

It was easy to blend in, almost. She went to the shops, bought some clothes. A sari, orange and pink. A shawl, the chips of diamante glittering as she moved. Gold earrings, dangling nearly to her shoulders.

You have to choose.

Three girls were in the changing room, chatting about last Saturday and next Saturday and the Saturday after that. Hessa's conversations, in London.

I never had those friends, so why do I miss them?

She wondered about her mother, a lifetime ago. Did she gossip with her friends, just like this? Hold up the shiny earrings, the long bright sari? *I was never here, so why do I have these memories?*

Hessa was relieved to hear from Casey. *Fly to Chittagong, Hessa, as soon as possible.* She had barely unpacked a thing. It took her only a moment to leave that dark hotel room.

In the Chittagong dawn, Hessa and Casey focused on the building where the black Land Cruiser had parked for the night. It was a big white structure that took up a whole block, five floors high. The windows stretched from floor to ceiling, to let in as much light as possible.

A wall of blue corrugated iron, 15 feet high, ran right the way round the factory. Casey tried to peer through, but couldn't make out any of the factory's features. The Land Cruiser was there though, parked up right next to the entrance.

'What's the factory called?' Casey couldn't read the Bengali alphabet.

'Arakny …' Hessa struggled with the word. 'Incorporated. It doesn't mean anything, I don't think. It's just a word.'

The company's logo was a stylised oak leaf. Casey photographed it, just in case. 'I wonder if this is where the red skirt and your grey velvet jacket were made.'

They were sitting in a rainbow-painted tuk-tuk. The grille that fitted around the passengers was closed up. The grilles were usually shut to deter bag-snatchers, who preyed on the traffic as it slowed, but it shielded them well here. Pink plastic flowers with big green leaves were twined through the steel mesh.

‘The women might be in there,’ said Casey.

‘They might,’ agreed Hessa.

The tuk-tuk’s driver was staring into space, exhausted by a night of driving across the city.

‘Do you think you can …’ Casey began.

You have to choose.

‘Of course,’ and Hessa’s eyes slanted into a smile.

35

Two hours later, Hessa was at the gate to the factory. The workers had crowded in by then, flooding through the door in their hundreds. One woman sat close to the gate, hands out in the international gesture of desperation. Her face had been terribly burned, the skin pulled tight, her mouth a slit. She turned blank eyes at the sound of Hessa's steps. *Please, please, help me.*

Hessa was wearing an old blue sari, bought in a dusty shop a few roads away. She had a pale orange shawl wrapped around her head, and fraying grey sandals on her feet.

'What do you want?' The door clanged open and a man stared her up and down.

'A job,' Hessa said quietly. *Talk quietly*, Casey had taught her. *It's harder to pin down an accent from a whisper.*

'This is not how we employ people here,' the man said. 'We have proper agents.'

Not the voice, Hessa thought. *You are not the voice on the telephone.*

The man moved to close the gate.

'I beg you.' Hessa put a choke into her voice.

The man paused. He made a show of staring at his watch, and gave a long sigh. 'All right,' he stood aside. 'Maybe it is possible, this once. We may have some vacancies.'

They walked towards the factory. There were no other buildings in this compound. Rust stains ran down the white walls from cheap windows, like red tears. Rubbish blew in circles, chased by a hot wind.

'You have skills?'

Hessa bowed her head.

'Where are you from?'

'A little village near Sylhet,' whispered Hessa. 'You wouldn't know it.'

'I thought I didn't know your accent.' He was pleased with himself. 'You are not from Chittagong.'

'No.'

They walked into the factory, and the noise hit Hessa like a slap. It was brutally hot, the air choked by desperate sweat and sour chemicals.

The women, packed together in row after row, sat crouched over their sewing machines. The girl closest to the door glanced up. She wore a small dust mask, her eyes above dark with exhaustion. She was very young, Hessa thought, probably lying about her age. No one would check if she was really eighteen: that much they all knew.

On the table to one side of the girl's sewing machine, a pile of floral material lay in neat shapes. Pink hearts, blue arrows. The girl picked up two pieces, tucked them together and whirred them through the machine. *Mummy's little princess*, read a tiny T-shirt.

The woman picked up another two pieces of material, whirr. Pick, whirr. Pick, whirr. Pickwhirrpickwhirrpickwhirr.

'This is a good factory,' said the man.

Smile, Casey had said. *He has to enjoy showing you around. You need him to flaunt it at you.*

And Hessa smiled.

The girl's hands were rough, nicked here and there by the machines. The air was filled with tiny wisps of thread, gold in the sunlight.

Hessa glanced up at the big windows. The sun sloped in, so that every tiny stitch could be checked. As Hessa gazed up, a supervisor in a black suit paced past, peering at the little T-shirts, the pink hearts, the blue arrows.

Hessa stared around the rest of the room. Huge cardboard boxes were piled up against the fire exit. She imagined this room if a spark caught. Nylon goes up like a torch, she knew. For a second, Hessa saw the place filled with smoke, the sewing machines crammed together making an impossible obstacle course in the dark. She heard the screams. One staircase and a thousand desperate women. That beggar outside: a pleading face, her mouth a gash.

There were no addresses on the big packages, anonymity a habit. Hessa peered and squinted, feeling the camera belt bite her side.

The man was running through the terms. Thirteen hours a day, six days a week, fifty dollars a month, maybe. Bangladesh's selling point to the world, that figure. They took pride in it even. Pickwhirrpickwhirrpickwhirr, forever.

Hessa leaned against a work table for a second, forcing herself to breathe.

The second woman along the line looked as if she was in her late fifties, but was probably only forty. Her body had shaped itself into a crouch over the sewing machine. She could barely look up, must have sat there for years, in just that shape. A wisp of human in a line of appliances.

At the far end of the room, Hessa saw one of the supervisors stop by a machine, grab a pair of indigo jeans and fling them to the floor. A woman cowered and the supervisor slapped her, very hard, straight across the face.

None of the other women around her reacted. The woman bowed her head, just for a moment. Then she reached out, and picked up two more pieces of denim. Pick. Whirr. Pickwhirr.

'What is on the floor above us?' Hessa smiled so sweetly. 'I have never worked in such a big factory before.'

This man was bored today, she could see. Tomorrow she would disappear into the crowd, bent for ever over her sewing machine. But today … He gestured to the stairs.

It was the same on the next floor, and the next. On the fourth floor, they were cutting material, the grey pinstripe stretched tight. Hessa thought of the red taffeta skirt, a piece of silk tucked into its petticoats.

'Where do they go, these clothes?'

'All around the world' – a showman wave. 'Germany, England, France, Australia.'

Hessa thought of these clothes, first sprayed with formaldehyde, for mildew and moths. Unpacked, with pursed lips, at their destination. Steam-cleaned quickly, and rammed on hangers, in those long bargain rows.

Here you are, darling.

I don't liiiike it, Mummy.

Chucked in a corner, and forgotten. And a year later, *gosh, this is far too small.* Landfill.

They climbed the stairs. All the floors were open-plan, clattering with racket as the bright sunlight streamed through.

'Thank you,' said Hessa, at the end. 'I will come back tomorrow, sir, to start my work.'

Hessa fled out of the factory, and down the hot dusty streets to where Casey was waiting. She scrambled into the tuk-tuk without words.

They were half a mile away before she could speak. 'It's not there,' she said precisely. 'Not there.'

'Are you sure?' Casey forced her face to stay calm.

'Every floor is the same,' said Hessa. 'They're huge open-plan rectangles. There isn't space for any other women to be held in there. And Romida would have mentioned the noise. It is like the roar of a dragon.'

Hessa pushed the grille open as the tuk-tuk moved off again, gasping for air.

'Could you see who they were producing for?' Casey asked.

'No,' Hessa admitted. 'I couldn't get close enough. I don't know if those blue silk messages could have been sent from there either. There was no way to tell.'

She looked apologetic, sheepish.

'It doesn't matter,' said Casey. 'You've got the footage.'

The tuk-tuk purred on.

'I suppose Romida might not have been grabbed by Greystone's lot anyway,' said Casey. 'She could be part of a different operation altogether.'

'Romida is not there,' said Hessa. 'None of them are. I am quite sure of it.'

They passed a rubbish dump, a line of flames licking through the stench. Two small boys were playing a sort of cricket beside the garbage sprawl.

'But where then?' asked Casey. 'Where can they be?'

Hessa sat there for a long time, staring out of the tuk-tuk.

'We should go down to the refugee camps,' Hessa said. 'Go and talk to Romida's mother, and anyone else who might have seen this man. You never know. They might know something.'

'OK,' said Casey. 'I'll call Savannah. Let's go and see tomorrow.'

36

As soon as they were back at the hotel, Casey downloaded the footage from the factory. Hessa sat in silence as the computer screen filled with her recording, and looked away as the camera approached the factory gate.

'We need to link this factory to Rhapso,' Casey decided. 'I'm sure a factory on this scale will supply several other retailers too, but we need to start proving the connections between Dylan and the factory and the traffickers.'

'How' – Ed was staring at the sea-rough footage – 'is anyone going to know from this where these clothes are going?'

Casey's quick smile lightened the room: 'I know someone.'

It had been the day before a huge royal wedding that Casey had discovered the hidden skills at the *Post*. As the nation twirled out the bunting, and the papers exhausted every story angle, Casey had been wandering round the office, thoroughly bored by the whole thing.

She was scouting the fashion cupboard once again when she overheard a bustle of excitement from Cressida's desk.

'It is,' Cressida was saying. 'That's Lalla Finsbury's belt.'

Casey had joined the small group around the fashion editor's desk. The knot of women were staring at Cressida's computer screen: a paparazzi shot of a woman, blanket over her head, running up the stone steps of the Alperton Hotel in Knightsbridge.

'Isn't that where she's staying tonight?' Casey asked. She: tomorrow's new princess.

'Yes,' grinned Cressida. 'Lalla must be going in for a final fitting. They'll be so thrilled at Manaton's. They've had a rough couple of years.'

Lalage Finsbury was chief designer at Manaton's. One of the more cutting-edge London fashion houses, Casey remembered vaguely.

'But how can you possibly tell just from that?' Casey was staring at the carefully anonymous blanket, the inch of brown belt barely visible.

'Oh,' Cressida waved. 'I just know.'

Cressida had tapped her keyboard, dozens of thumbnail pictures spreading across her screen.

'There,' Cressida pointed. 'Lalla wore that belt last year when she was in LA for the Oscars. It's the precise colour, that stitch here, the turn of the leather there.'

Casey stared back at the inch of brown belt running into the Alperton, awed. Cressida's knowledge was encyclopedic.

'Have you told the newsdesk yet?'

'Oh no. Manaton would be furious if we revealed they were doing The Dress.' Cressida managed to capitalise the words as she spoke. 'They'd be catatonic. It's their secret.'

'Yes,' said Casey cheerfully.

'They're one of our biggest advertisers,' Cressida bridled.

'Mmm.'

'It would spoil the surprise for everyone.'

'That,' Casey said, '*is* what we do.'

'I can't.'

'Cressida, I'll give you a thirty-second head start, or I'm telling the newsdesk and taking the byline. It'll be tomorrow's splash either way.'

'Oh.' Cressida had kicked out at Casey with her satin heel. 'Bloody hell. All right, I'll tell them.'

They contemplated the photograph for a moment longer, Casey surreptitiously admiring Cressida's glossy highlights, perfect nails, immaculate make-up.

'What's your role for the royal wedding?' Cressida had asked. 'The newsdesk seems to have a minute-by-minute plan, starting long before dawn.'

'Miranda and I are on deathwatch,' Casey said cheerfully.

'Deathwatch?'

'If a bomb goes off in the massed cheering crowds,' Casey explained. 'We trot towards it and try and work out what's going on.'

'To each their own.' Cressida arched a perfect eyebrow. 'I think I'd rather be analysing the bridesmaid dresses.'

'Fair enough,' Casey grinned. 'Good to have the experts this time.'

Casey remembered the last royal wedding, when half the fashion team had actually been invited, leaving the 15-stone Home Affairs editor bawling, 'That's sodding ecru, I tell you,' at the television screen.

'That's not bloody cream,' still got chanted at him when he was late on a deadline. 'That's sodding ecru.'

The trials of that royal wedding had been compounded by the *Post*'s lip-reader going rogue and catastrophically misinterpreting a conversation between the Prime Minister and the Home Secretary as they sat among the congregation. Ross had fired the lip-reader halfway through the ceremony with a newly invented form of sign language.

'It's all going to go much more smoothly this time,' Casey said.

'At least,' Cressida had sulked. 'You've got a proper splash now.'

Now Casey took screengrabs of Hessa's footage, sending the clearest shots back to Cressida.

'Rhapso.' The message came back in seconds. 'We'd have to wait for those jeans to reach the shops to be 100 per cent, but that won't take long.'

'How can you be sure?'

'The positioning of the rivets.' Casey didn't need to see Cressida's eye roll. 'The angle on the pocket. The curve of the looped seam. I could go on.'

'That's OK.' Casey hoped the sarcasm came across. 'Thanks, Cressida.'

She thought about the dusty factory with the beggar outside. And she thought about the red velvet curtains and *you-have-a-nice-day* of the Rhapso shop.

She turned to the others. 'We can be fairly sure the message came from that factory.'

37

The car jolted into a rut and stalled beside a line of scruffy tents. 'It was beautiful here, once.' The fixer gestured carelessly across the crowded refugee camp. 'And now it is all gone for ever.'

Hessa and Casey stared across the miles and miles of tents, the scale of it still shocking. The car had stopped on a small rise, and from this point the camps spread as far as they could see, in every direction, every single inch used.

'It's crammed so tight,' Hessa murmured. 'All of these people.'

The Rohingya camps were especially chaotic. In her years of journalism, during her travels to Jordan, to Lebanon, to Turkey, Casey had spoken to dozens of Syrian refugees. In Syria, it had taken the refugees months to leave their country.

A barrel bomb hit my neighbour's house. Then my brother disappeared … He was taken at a checkpoint, and we never saw him again … And then … And then … And then …

Until finally, *finally*, the Syrians packed up their most-loved possessions, and started the long walk to the border. That meant they crossed south into Jordan in threes and fours, fives and sixes. A big family group, now and again. Even at the peak of the crisis, the Syrian refugee camps grew slowly enough that there were rows of tents, blocks of latrines, some sort of a plan.

But the speed of the Rohingya crisis of 2017 took everyone by surprise. The Rohingya moved in whole villages, hundreds of people in hours. Blamed for everything for years, and attacked on all sides for decades, when the militia rolled in, the Rohingya rushed for the border. Thousands in a day.

The soldiers came with rockets. They burned our village, they burned our people. They burned everything, and we ran. We just ran.

As the crisis erupted, the Prime Minister of Bangladesh, in a gesture that was part generosity, part panic, offered up great tracts of the reserve jungle, the beautiful forest that sprawled across the low hills of southern Bangladesh.

'There were huge trees here, and it was all so green, once,' the translator grumbled. 'Now there is nothing. Nothing left at all.'

The translator had turned to Casey with a sigh, as they climbed out of the car. She was called Layla and had developed a tough half-smile after weeks of escorting journalists around the camps.

The Rohingyas cleared this land in days, Layla recited laconically. Like ants. Chopping down trees, hacking away at undergrowth. Total deforestation of whole hills, in an afternoon. She pulled a face.

And now it was April in the shadeless camps, and the sun punched down like a fist.

Layla stopped talking, shielding her eyes from the sun. She was tall for a Bengali woman, her movements both angry and graceful. She wore a simple white shirt, with the charity's lanyard round her neck. Thick eyebrows came together in a scowl as she made her way down the narrow path between the tents. Her face was an odd combination of compassion and distaste, as if she couldn't quite decide on her emotions.

'These camps are just about OK right now.' Savannah followed Layla along the path. 'But in a few weeks, the monsoon will come.' The aid worker stared around the steep-sided valleys of the camps. 'They're all built on dust, these tents. Delta silt. When it dries out, there's nothing there. It crumbles at a touch now all the trees are gone. When the monsoon comes, the tents at the bottom of the hill will flood, while landslides wipe out the ones at the top.'

Casey tried to imagine living for years in this endless camp. A little girl peered down at them, as they passed by. She was leaning against a bamboo railing, loosely tied to an upright pole, above a 15-foot drop down to a dried-up riverbed.

'It was the British who encouraged the Rohingya to go to Rakhine in the first place,' Savannah murmured. 'When the map of this part of the world was all pink.'

'Quite,' Hessa nodded.

'Some of the Rohingya have been in these camps since the early Nineties.' Savannah spun in a circle. 'That was when the first wave of refugees arrived in Bangladesh. In the older parts of the camp, no one under the age of twenty-five remembers living anywhere else, ever. This is all they know.'

'And probably all they will ever know,' Hessa sounded harder, tougher.

They had parked up near the Balukhali camp, in the shade of a sweeping acacia that had somehow survived. Ed had stayed behind in Cox's Bazar.

'It'll be easier, just two women reporters,' Casey had explained. 'I think Shamshun might be happier talking to us. And it's useful, you being in Cox's, just in case Dylan checks up on us.'

The camp stretched for miles all around Balukhali, the tents loosely constructed from chopped-down bamboo and tarpaulin. The colour of the tarpaulins depended on the donor, so one stretch of the camp was patterned in pink, the next aquamarine, then coral. A strange plastic Babel, Casey thought.

'This way.' Savannah pointed. 'Two refugees were killed by elephants down there a few months ago. In the most recent rush of refugees, the tents were built too close to one of the old elephant paths. The elephants have gone now, deeper into the forest. Or maybe they're just gone.'

Occasionally, looking between the tents packed together on the steep hillsides, Casey could see all the way down to the rice paddies. The flagrant green of the rice was a shock against the browns and greys. Below them, the Bangladeshi farmers still worked, near the heart of the camp.

'And in England, they rage about refugees at Calais.' Hessa half-smiled.

They could hear the children chanting in madrassas as they walked up the path.

'There's always the money for the mosques somehow.' Savannah chewed at her lip. 'They're the best buildings in the camps, always. It's Saudi money, every time. Still,' she brightened. 'Somewhere more solid for the refugees to hide if a cyclone comes.'

After Casey's phone call the night before, Savannah had asked Romida's mother to meet them at a feeding centre, half a mile from her tent. The refugees queued up at these centres in the mornings, clutching their ration cards. But the big blocks were locked and abandoned at this hour.

Casey had asked to meet Shamshun at a distance from her tent. 'Because we don't know if the people who took Romida are still operating here. And we don't want them to know that journalists are searching for Romida. It could be dangerous for us. And it could be fatal for Romida.'

'Sure,' Savannah had said easily. 'I did ask the women to keep it quiet, when I asked around. And they keep their secrets, the women of this camp.'

But when they got to the feeding centre, Shamshun had not come alone. As the little group crowded into a small office, Shamshun pointed to the teenager beside her.

'Shamshun says this girl is called Jamalida,' said the translator. 'Shamshun arrived in the camp from Rakhine just a few months ago. Jamalida's family came across at the same time.'

Casey looked at Jamalida, familiar somehow, and realised. She was the girl in the orange scarf, next to Romida in the photograph. Casey had stared at that photograph, again and again. Jamalida was the girl with the big wide smile and bright red lipstick, as Romida turned shyly from the camera.

But Jamalida was crying now, shrinking away from Shamshun, smearing the black kohl that lined her eyes. She looked much younger than thirteen.

'Speak,' Shamshun snapped, Layla translating impassively. 'Tell them about my daughter.'

Wiping her nose, staring at the floor, Jamalida started to speak.

'They were so friendly, at first. They brought us food, sweets even.'

The refugees got a fixed amount every month of lentils, rice and cooking oil. Enough not to starve, in theory, although many of the children across the camp had the skinny limbs and the hollowed eyes of the perpetually malnourished.

'We eat the same thing, every single day,' a woman had told Casey, on her last visit to the camps. 'I dream of the food we used to eat back in Rakhine. The spices. Fruit. The vegetables. Fish. Meat, even, can you believe it? I dream of that food. It drives you mad, after a while.'

'We talked to them often, these men.' Layla translated Jamalida's words. 'They came every day. They were our friends.'

'How many times …' Shamshun's eyes filled with tears. 'How many times have I told you girls …'

The words trailed away. Too late, too late, too late.

'And one day, they said, "Do you want to come for a drive? It will be such fun." '

'Did they say,' Hessa asked urgently, 'where they might go?'

Jamalida shook her head.

'But then I was late on the day of the trip. I had to get water for my mother, from the big pump. The well had run dry, the one near our tent. So I ran when I was finished. I ran all the way down the paths, as fast as I could. I was shouting for them to wait. But they had gone … I must have just missed them.'

Casey imagined the men waiting for a few minutes. Romida beside them, excited, skipping from foot to foot. A shrug, impatient. Well, one's better than nothing. Dangerous to hang around too long anyway.

And the little girl climbing into the car, grinning as the car accelerated.

Romida, thrilled, for a few minutes.

And then the slow-growing worry. The car, moving too fast. Bumping along the road, hooting other cars out of the way. The hesitation, not wanting to be rude: not to these kind friends. Then the fear, prickling down her neck. *Please stop, I should be going home by now.* Nothing. And then the sudden rush of real terror. Where am I? Who are they, these men? And what have I *done*, going like this? The car stopping, at the edge of the jungle, somewhere far from the busy main road. Where am I? I don't recognise anything. A punch, maybe. That was when she knew it was over, really over. A blindfold, maybe, and into the van like a sack. Please. Please. *Please.*

And a little girl, lost, for ever.

'When Romida called me from wherever she is, she told me to move tents,' said Shamshun. 'She said that I was in danger.' Shamshun made a flicking gesture with her hand. 'But what more can they do to me? I don't care any more. And besides, if I moved, Romida might not be able to find me again. The camps are so chaotic. And she might … She might.'

'Did they say where they were from?' Hessa could just about make herself understood, speaking to Jamalida.

'No, I don't know,' the girl answered. 'They talked about Dhaka. Chittagong, too.'

'Did you know their names?'

'Jeetu, he was the friendly one. Jeetu.'

Jamalida was crying again. Hessa was adapting to the Rohingya dialect now, understanding more of the words, the cadences. *Romida was my friend. We did everything together. We wanted to be tailors, together, when we were grown up. In a shop. A proper shop. She was my friend. And now I will never see her again.*

'Have you seen them in the camps again?' asked Savannah. 'Either of these men?'

'No,' Layla translated for Jamalida. 'If I see them, I will tell the mahji. And he will have them killed.'

The blunt hatred filled the tent.

Casey saw Shamshun staring at Jamalida. You survived. You survived, by a twist of nothing, and it is my daughter who is lost for ever.

Shamshun clenched her fists. She rocked to and fro, mouth tight, and then all at once the words poured out of her, Layla racing to keep up.

'I was glad when my house burned,' said Shamshun, and it was as if she were speaking to herself. 'Back in our old village, I heard them come. The army, in the middle of the morning. I was out in a field, a few hundred yards away from the houses. I could hear the screams. They were setting fire to the houses, one by one. And I knew Romida was in our house, all alone. So I ran. You never know how you can run, until you run for your daughter. I got to our house, and the soldiers were there. Crowding around, a dozen of them. And Romida, there in the middle of them all. But she was struggling, screaming, begging. She fought, my daughter. She fought so hard. But I could see their hands on her. Their hands and their eyes. They do it to ruin the women. They do it to break us.'

Shamshun stared across the tent, eyes blank, plaiting her fingers together until they twisted. 'My house caught fire. The soldiers in the street had fired a rocket to make it burn. The soldiers turned and ran, and they were laughing as they ran. *Laughing*. And only because my house was on fire, I could grab Romida. And we ran the other way, away from the soldiers, through the smoke and the flames. Because I would rather burn than …'

Shamshun was running her thumbnail back and forth over her wrist, hurting herself deliberately. 'We ran through the flames, Romida and I, and we ran and we ran … It took days to get here. I thought we would die. We had no food. All I had, I gave to Romida. But then we were here, in this camp, in our little tent. It was just me and Romida. And I thought we were safe, here, at last. Maybe. And we were happy here, for a while. My daughter …'

A child was screaming in a tent, just a few feet away. The noise of the camp was endless, relentless, unbearable. There was the sound of a slap, followed by tears.

'My husband died, years ago. At least he never saw this.' Shamshun's voice was an angry whisper. 'He could never bear any of this. I was glad when my house burned, because it saved Romida, and she was all that mattered. And I am glad that my husband is dead, because at least he can never see this.'

Shamshun sat up straight, wiped away the tears.

'She's gone, isn't she? I've lost her. I've lost her for ever.'

Shamshun stared out into the chaos of the camp.

'I wish I had died,' she whispered.

38

There was a long silence, and Hessa was the one to break it.

'Jamalida?'

Jamalida tore her eyes from the floor.

'Did you see the car? Before the men took Romida away.'

A slow nod.

'Do you remember what colour it was?'

Another nod. 'Black.'

'And do you know what kind of car it was?'

Jamalida shook her head.

'There's seventy per cent illiteracy in these camps,' Savannah interjected. 'She won't know car brands. It's impossible.'

The car was big, Jamalida gestured, her eyes sharp. She was sketching a shape with her hands.

'Could you look at photographs of the cars,' Hessa went on patiently, 'and tell me which one it was most like?'

She had searched for three photographs on her phone. A Hilux. A Ford Ranger. A Land Cruiser.

Jamalida considered the photographs for a long time, one by one. And then very carefully, she pointed: the Land Cruiser.

'Are you sure?' asked Hessa.

A firm nod.

'Thank you, Jamalida.' Casey kept her voice steady. 'That is most helpful.'

'And anything else?' Hessa asked. 'Jamalida, do you remember anything else at all?'

Jamalida crushed her head into her hands, thinking, the bright smile a memory. Then she looked up, spoke rapidly.

'They said Teffy was coming,' Layla translated. 'One time, they said Teffy was coming soon.'

'Teffy?' Hessa stared from Jamalida to Layla. 'What does that mean?'

Layla shrugged. 'I have never heard this word.'

'What did they mean, Teffy?' Hessa tried again. 'Is it a person?'

'I don't know what it means. Jeetu just said it once. He was talking on the phone one time, and after he hung up, he said it.'

They all stared at her. Thrown by the attention, Jamalida blushed.

'Teffy?' Casey repeated. 'Are you sure?'

Layla was staring at a poster above her head, a sad-looking child, with a warning about malnutrition.

'I have never heard of this name,' the translator said flatly. 'It is not a Bengali name.'

Hessa and Casey watched Shamshun and Jamalida leave, Jamalida with her arm around the older woman, a comfort that was almost a curse. Shamshun was crying.

You never know how you can run, until you run for your daughter.

'Teffy.' Casey and Hessa were back in the Cox's Bazar hotel room with Ed. 'What the hell does that mean?'

They had run variants of the word through every search engine, every database they could think of. Nothing showed up.

'We're running out of time,' Casey said despairingly.

Raz had called, voice unctuous. 'Miss Emily, not long to wait now. Are you enjoying beautiful Cox's Bazar?'

'It's delightful,' Casey lied. 'The beach is beautiful.'

And there was a despairing message from Emily herself. 'Is there any news, Casey? Anything at all? I don't think I can bear it, Casey. Please.'

Casey deleted Emily's message and turned back to her laptop. Teffy. *Teffy.*

Hessa glanced up at her, eyes worried. 'What if we can't work it out?'

39

As the day sprawled towards night, Hessa and Casey went for a short walk out along the beach, enjoying the breeze off the sea. One of the hotels, even seedier than the rest, had a neon pink sign hanging over the door. Men slipped in and out of the door.

The town's brothel, Casey thought. There was always one, at least, in most cities in this country. Bangladesh was unusual, among Muslim countries, in permitting prostitution.

'I remember' – Hessa waved at the pink neon – 'my cousin telling me about Daulatdia, when I was about eleven.'

Children giggling in a corner. Have you heard? Have you heard? Showing off, in a whisper. And then the round eyes. And the shock. No. No. No.

'Daulatdia?'

'It's a vast place, Daulatdia,' Hessa went on, a sudden anger in her eyes. 'Just to the west of Dhaka. They think almost two thousand women work there. It's basically its own town, with shops and streets and everything. Children are born in Daulatdia, with no idea who … And then they grow up there, and they spend the whole of their lives there. And, one fine day, those little girls, they go into the business too.'

'Grim,' said Casey.

The Bay of Bengal looked blue in the distance, but lapped brown against the sand. The neon was glowing brighter as the evening closed in.

'I read up about Daulatdia properly a few years ago,' Hessa went on. 'When I first started working at the *Post*. The average age of a girl arriving in Daulatdia is fourteen. Some of them are only ten years old when they start working.'

Casey sat down, kicked her heels into the sand.

'It's hideous, everywhere.'

'The gangs grab girls from wherever they can' – Hessa squatted down next to Casey – 'and sell them into bonded labour for, what, two hundred and fifty dollars? Chukri, it's called. I read somewhere that the Daulatdia girls are forced to take Oradexon. That's a steroid normally used to fatten up cows for market, for God's sake. The girls in Daulatdia are forced to take it so they look right for the men. Plump and healthy. Three thousand men visit that place, every single day.'

'And the younger the girl,' said Casey, 'the more the men will pay.'

'Of course,' said Hessa. 'And, of course, that's where the Rohingya girls ended up, too. Where the Jamuna river meets the holy, dirty mother Padma. It's so convenient for the customers, that location. There's the boat terminal, and the train station. And the roads, for the truckers. It's so advantageous,' she pronounced the word deliberately, 'that port position.'

'Hessa ...'

'The pimps were waiting on the beaches.' Hessa was speaking faster, the words sharp in the dusk. 'As the refugee boats arrived from Myanmar, the men were waiting for the orphaned girls.'

Hessa jumped to her feet, took a few steps down the beach. The fishermen, home for the day, were fixing their nets, and calling to each other.

'Why are they so different, Greystone's girls?' Hessa turned to Casey. 'Why are you so determined to help them especially? What's different about them?'

Casey gazed at the setting sun.

'I don't know,' she said, a lie.

'What about the girls of Daulatdia?' Hessa's voice rose. 'What about the thousands of women forced into prostitution all over this bloody country? Why don't we care about them?'

Casey's hands were digging into the sand. 'I know, Hessa.'

'There are lots of girls' – Hessa eyes were on the horizon – 'who might even prefer the Greystone life. A medicinal rape,' she spat the words out, 'rather than a thousand different men, night after night, for ever. A neat little human incubator, kept comfortable for a few months.'

Casey scrambled to her feet.

'What do you want me to say, Hessa? You know why we are chasing Greystone. And you know why we are trying to find Romida, wherever the hell she might be.'

'Because Romida is interesting,' Hessa said carefully. 'Because she's got a strange little connection to Britain. A connection that our readers can understand, all the way back in London. That makes her interesting to us. The little girl, born in a town-sized brothel, we know all about her already. That little girl, trafficked out of the camps and forced to start fucking men when she's just ten years old, we've all known about her, all the way through. She's a bit dull, that little girl in Daulatdia. She's an old story.'

'When I was doing my research,' Casey said, 'before this trip, I was reading an article about a surrogate who presented for a routine examination over in Delhi. She was eight months pregnant. As she was waiting for the doctor, she collapsed. They delivered her child by C-section, on the spot, cutting the foetus out of her just like that. And they rushed the baby to the best hospital they could find, money no object. That meant the baby survived. That precious little baby lived. The mother wasn't even taken to hospital. And who has the right to do that to another person? Who gets to make that choice?'

'That choice is made every day in Daulatdia.'

'Fine, Hessa.' Casey spun towards her. 'You know exactly why we are interested in the Greystone girls. Because our readers are interested in Greystone, and Harley Street, and well-groomed wives in Hampstead. Because our readers know someone who knows someone who might have visited Greystone. And they don't give a shit about the girls in Daulatdia.'

There was a long silence, two women staring out to sea.

'Yes, I know,' said Hessa quietly. 'Greystone is a story.'

Hessa turned, walking back up the beach, trudging past the hawkers.

And Casey sat, for a long time, folded up on the sand.

When Casey looked up, one of the huge supertankers was tracking across the horizon. She knew she should get back to the safety of the hotel, but she watched the ship just the same. It must be heading south, from Chittagong's huge port. Tonnes of cheap Bangladeshi goods, off to Indonesia or Malaysia or Australia. As the night closed in, Casey watched the ship lumber along, its lights flashing. Red and green, port and starboard, ponderous as a funeral. There was another ship, not far behind, and another, and another, and another. Hypnotic, a chain of lights where the sea met the sky.

She heard a movement behind her, and Ed sat down beside her on the sand.

'I thought you might be out here. Everything OK?'

'Not really.'

For a few minutes, they watched the ships together in silence. Little glimmers on the horizon, vast engines dragging the world along.

'It's strange, isn't it?' Casey said. 'Almost every element of international trade depends on those huge ships, and we barely ever even see them.'

'Always just over the horizon.'

'Yes,' said Casey. 'I suppose it is telling, that one of the biggest industries in the world exists invisibly.'

She thought about the vast ships, riding the tides, into every corner of the world.

Ed laughed. 'Cynic.'

'They say there are two paradoxes in blackmail,' said Casey, almost to herself. 'Revealing a secret is legal, and asking for money – or whatever else – is legal. But when you do both simultaneously, it becomes a crime. And the other paradox is that if the blackmailer initiates the sequence, it is illegal. But if the blackmailee asks for secrecy in return for money – it is the chief executive who groped the secretary who makes the offer – then it is legal. Odd aren't they, the economics of secrecy?'

'Two rights make a wrong,' said Ed. 'Two wrongs make a right.'

'I suppose so. Yes. I've upset Hessa.'

'I thought so.'

They watched two ships track across the horizon. One heading north, the other heading south, red and green lights flashing.

'I suppose,' Ed said, as the lights crossed over, 'those ships are the reason we first met.'

The memory stabbed at Casey. That night, all those years ago, out on the wilds of the Indian Ocean. Sitting on a pile of ropes on the deck of the *Apollo*, idly watching the captured Somali pirates.

'I have no idea how they get on board those huge supertankers,' Ed had said then. 'The risks they take to survive. Those big ships go like the clappers through the risky areas now, and the wake they generate is crazy. How do you get close enough in a tiny little boat?'

'Wilful determination?' Casey wondered aloud.

'Supertankers are designed not to have access points below a certain height,' said Ed. 'The pirates are looking up at, say, ten storeys of steel. But they zoom along in those tiny boats and just go for it.'

'It should be impossible.'

'You should see the official guide to defending yourself from pirates,' Ed had said. By then, he was enjoying speaking to her, she could tell. 'Issued by the authorities. They recommend barbed wire. And they note, quite politely, that pouring boiling water over the side of the ship can be helpful too.'

'It sounds medieval,' Casey had said.

'It is, really.'

The sun was a line of fire over the Bay of Bengal. Ed pulled Casey to her feet. 'Let's go for a walk.'

Talking quietly, they wandered down the beach. The straggle of high-rise hotels slowly fell away, leaving just the coast road, and a fringe of palm trees.

The sunset, the beach, the whispering palms. For a second, Casey saw Ed's profile dark against the sky, and spiralled into the impossible.

'How can you work for Declan Bentley?' Casey forced the thoughts away.

'There aren't that many billionaires with a perfectly clean sheet,' Ed protested. 'I like the south of France. I get on fine with Declan. I know he comes across as a prick, but compared to some ...'

'But his factory in Ethiopia,' Casey protested. 'And God knows what the new Vietnamese factory is like.'

'Who should I work for then?' Ed rolled his eyes at her. 'I was with one of the Saudi princes before Declan, and I know just what you'd have made of that.'

The dozens of Saudi princes, Casey thought, the playboy billionaires who commuted to London for their fun. The wives stayed at home, of course.

'You should have stuck with the prince,' Casey admitted. 'I would have found it harder to turn him.'

'You'd have found a way, with your blackmailing habits.'

The children in Yemen with their round stomachs and cavernous eyes. And the bombs, scattering death like blossom in a field. British-made, of course.

'Yes,' she admitted. 'I know.'

'Ruthless,' he said again. He was smiling though, scraping his hand over his head. 'Do I need to dye it again?' He was laughing. 'I stained my pillowcase last night. Disgusting.'

'It looks fabulous.'

They stared out across the ocean. The sea was indigo now, a shade darker than the denim blue of the sky.

'It's so beautiful here,' Casey murmured.

'But we'll always remember it for those trafficked girls.'

Casey thought about all the places that would always be the jab of a memory now, a spreading patchwork of misery. A beach in Spain: a toddler drowned. A Christmas market: the roar of a truck. A hilltop in London: *this is the last time*. The thought was a jolt.

'Are you OK?' Ed was watching her. Her mood had shifted, like a breeze drifting over the sea.

'I'm fine. I have to get back to the hotel.' Casey turned away abruptly, heading back towards the hotel, trying to hurry in the deep sand.

'Casey?' He was confused. 'Wait . . .'

She ignored him, almost stumbling in her haste. He caught up with her easily.

You have to choose.

'I need to get back . . .'

'Why?'

She faced him, almost angry, and he pulled back, waiting.

'What's the matter, Casey?'

'I'm very glad you came out to Bangladesh,' she managed. 'But I have to get back to the hotel.'

'Casey.'

'What?'

He was watching her face, and let her go. She stepped away, hesitated, turned back. They stared at each other.

'I didn't come out here,' he said guardedly, 'just because Declan told me to, you know.'

She twisted away from him. 'I know. You told me why you came.'

'Yes. Casey—'

'It's fine,' she interrupted him, almost a shout. 'I needed you. For the story.'

'For the story,' he said. 'Yes.'

He folded himself down on the sand as she stood stubbornly. A silence settled, but Casey's anger was gone. She scraped shapes in the sand with a piece of driftwood. Spades, diamonds, clubs, hearts, then stared out to sea. The ship lights glowed. Red and green, port and starboard, again and again and again, and suddenly Casey was hurrying down the beach towards the hotel.

'Casey—'

'Come on, Ed,' she raced towards their dingy hotel, grabbing his hand in a burst of her excitement. 'Quickly.'

'Steady on.' But he was laughing again, as she dragged him along.

'The Teffy,' Casey gasped. 'What if she is a ship?'

40

To the north of Chittagong, the city straggles away along the coastline. All the way up this shoreline are broad mudflats, hundreds of yards wide, the slope down to the sea almost imperceptible. The mudflats are so wide that a pier has to be hundreds of yards long just to allow the boats to float.

There was almost nothing in this muddy part of the world, for years. And then one day, in the wilderness of a cyclone, a Greek ship washed up on the flats. She sat there for months, the MD *Alpine*, sinking slowly into the sediment. And then quietly, secretively, the locals began to gouge away at her.

Finally, in 1965, five years after she first ran aground, the battered old wreck was sold for scrap.

A new industry sprang up overnight. Because the huge ships that circumnavigate the globe need a place to die, in the end. And the mudflats of Chittagong became their graveyard.

The ships came in their hundreds, beached side by side on the silt. Thousands of workers hacked away at them, the glitter of the oxyfuel sparkling blue-orange across the mud. As they worked, the men ripped the ships apart from stem to stern, carving away huge hunks of metal.

'We recycle everything,' the shipwreckers said proudly. 'All the steel and everything.'

But the workers died, in their hundreds.

One a week, a charity guessed, for years. Struggling with huge sheets of steels, and scrambling over the bulkheads. No ropes, no safety, plunging to their death.

And, quite often, those workers were children.

There is a strange sort of beauty to the dying ships of Chittagong. They are so proud, these ships, as they storm in on the highest of tides. They have fought the oceans for years, and survived the storms.

And one day, it all ends.

Sometimes, men build a bonfire in her path. Her last triumph, as a wall of salt water drowns the flames with contempt. But then the ship runs out of water, slamming full-speed into the mudflats. The magic of the sea captured in this most brutal of traps. The ship's weight and all her arrogant speed carry her onwards, upwards, skidding along the flats, carving through the silt. Until finally, she grinds to a halt, gravity irresistible.

There she is, grounded. Earthed. Stranded in the mud, all her dignity gone. The slow ignominy, as the tide goes out, and the ship is abandoned.

She waits.

And then they come for her.

She is chiselled apart, day after day, night after night. Butchered where she lies. Disappearing, scrap by scrap.

'The Teffy,' said Casey. 'I think that she is a ship.'

Back in Casey's room, Ed and Casey gazed at her laptop. They had raced through the hotel lobby, the night porter looking up blearily, surprised by the sudden movements.

'Come on,' Casey grumbled to herself, searching frantically. 'Come on.'

Casey had tracked ships around the world before. Almost all large ships sent out a signal, and on her computer she had trailed the colourful little dots for days at a time, as they swept across the map. The shipping lanes lit up like motorways: ships hurrying around the Cape of Good Hope, cornering around Cape Horn and shouldering up through the Strait of Hormuz. They clustered at the bottlenecks – at Panama, at Suez, at Malacca – queuing up impatiently, every minute costing.

In the past, as she worked, Casey had watched the pirated ships, drifting aimlessly off the coast of Somalia. Still sending back their hopeful signals, *we are here, we are here*. Even though no one would ever go to their rescue.

Once, Casey had hunted down a notorious billionaire, glorying on his superyacht, and he had lashed out at her photographer, in the pretty harbour of Cephalonia. *How the fuck did you find me?*

The *Post*'s business desk routinely tracked a few of the supertankers, because the giant ships unwittingly telegraphed the traders' expectations about the price of oil. Sometimes, the vast tankers would be filled with oil, enough to fill a hundred huge swimming pools. But instead of beetling off busily, in their dead-straight lines towards Europe, and America and

Australia, the ship's huge engines would be switched off, drifting with the current out to sea. And there they dawdled, as the traders waited for the price of oil to rise. A strong vote of confidence, that was, with the tankers costing $50,000 a day just to leave out in the ocean.

Ships could switch off their trackers though. Casey had watched ships hovering in the Mediterranean, just off the coast of Syria. One second to the next, they would melt off the screen. Vanishing for a few hours or a few days before they reappeared, all innocence, heading back up the Bosporus towards the Black Sea.

Now Casey focused on the fleet of dots gathered around the port of Chittagong. The huge cargo ships came and went in their hundreds from Bangladesh. Whisking away the cheap clothes, the cheap food, the cheap goods.

She checked the ships, one by one. The *Kristina*. The MT *Scorpio*. The *Somerset Lady*. The *Dolphin Blue*. And at last she saw it.

'There,' she breathed. 'The *Tephi*. That is what they were talking about.'

Ed and Casey stared at the tiny dot. The *Tephi*'s beacon had sent its last plaintive message close to the coastline by Bhatiari, 10 miles to the north of Chittagong.

'That's lucky,' breathed Casey. 'I thought they might have switched off her tracker earlier. They often do.'

Together, they looked up the *Tephi*'s history. Old photographs filled the screen, of a huge cargo ship, heavily laden.

'She's a Panamax,' read Ed. 'That's the biggest ship that can fit through the Panama Canal.'

Casey glanced at him, mouth turning up. 'Geek.'

'It's true.' He nudged her away. 'There are others too. The Suezmax, which just fits down the Suez Canal. The Q-Max, that's the biggest sort of vessel that can get in and out of Qatar. The Seawaymax, for getting down the Saint Lawrence Seaway into the Great Lakes in America.'

'All right,' Casey was laughing. 'I get it.'

They looked at the photographs of the *Tephi*, huge and blue, piled high with containers like Lego blocks. A distinctive red stripe had been painted all the way around her hull, a few feet below her decks. Below her waterline she was a dark forest-green. In the photographs, the green showed through as she battled through waves. Shipping enthusiasts had snapped her in Guangzhou and in Rotterdam, in Long Beach and in Mombasa, loaded with containers filled with new cars or bright dresses, toothpaste or prams.

'She's certainly notched up the miles,' said Casey.

She thought of the old ship, slapped over the nose with champagne at the start of her journeys, now trapped in the mud of Chittagong, her knickers showing shamefully.

'The shipping companies sell them off when they get too old,' she explained to Ed. 'To the highest bidder. Cash buyers, usually, who sell them on straight away. The shipping companies know full well that the ships will end up in the wrecking yards of Bangladesh, but what do they care? They shrug their shoulders and say, "Gosh, we had no idea" when it emerges that their old ships are being disembowelled by eight-year-olds.'

'A couple of steps removed,' said Ed. 'Deniable.'

'It's simple maths.' Casey was nodding. 'If you have your ship taken apart somewhere in Europe, you have to pay the scrapyard to do it carefully. In Bangladesh, they pay almost three hundred dollars a tonne for the steel.'

'Who,' said Ed, 'could possibly say no?'

'So this Jeetu character, who we think works closely with Dylan and Raz, bought up the *Tephi*,' Casey said, 'when she was on her last journey, and had her brought up to Chittagong.'

'Jeetu might have been talking to Dylan or Raz when Jamalida overheard him, for all we know,' said Ed.

The *Tephi*'s last movements had been small, edging to and fro just off the coast.

'Parked up, waiting for the tide,' Ed said. 'They wait for the highest tide, to get the ships as far up the beach as possible. It makes the breaking easier if it's not wallowing in water.'

'So wherever the *Tephi* is now,' Casey was thinking aloud, 'Dylan and his team are likely to have some sort of base. We need to look there.'

She pulled up the Land Cruiser's trajectory around Chittagong, after it had dropped them off in Cox's Bazar on the first day.

'There.' The big black car had travelled up to Bhatiari, paused, then travelled across to the head of the long Sandwip pier that reached hundreds of yards out to sea, and paused again. It had made its way south along the coast road, stopping here and there. Then finally, it had headed back to the factory in Sagorika.

'And what,' Casey glowered at the screen, 'were you doing up there?'

41

Back in London, after a long day at the *Post*, Miranda turned the key in the door of the pretty house in Queen's Park. That hollow key sound, every evening.

'I'm home,' she called. The dream trappings, the trapped dream. 'Hello?'

I have to tell him.

I don't know how.

The front sitting room had been knocked into the back, like every other sitting room on the street. Tom had wanted to extend the kitchen, right the way across the back of the house. He liked the way the Adamsons had done it, at number 56. Family space, they called it.

He hadn't got round to it.

Not yet.

'Hello?' Miranda called again.

When she walked into the kitchen at the back of the house, Tom was sitting at the table with an expression she didn't recognise on his face. There was a bunch of pink roses, still wrapped in their brown paper, shoved awkwardly into too small a vase. The water had splashed on the countertop.

'Miranda ...' He jumped to his feet.

She was so surprised for a second that she had to lean a hand on the kitchen surface.

Not yet.

No.

'Tom?' Miranda couldn't keep the shake out of her voice. 'What's going on?'

'Miranda, I had no idea.' Tom was walking towards her, smiling, one hand reaching for hers. He had a leaflet in his other hand.

'What?' Miranda blinked at him.

'I'm so sorry, darling. So sorry ...' Miranda didn't recognise his smile for a second, realised that she hadn't seen it for years, not properly.

'What on earth are you talking about, Tom?'

Her husband held it up, a brightly coloured pamphlet. Miranda saw it with a thud of realisation: a leaflet from Dr Greystone's clinic.

The secretary must have handed it to her as she left her appointment. And Miranda had shoved it in her handbag, without thinking.

'You looked in my handbag?'

He was surprised for a moment. 'I needed a pen. You always have pens, in your handbag.'

The journalist's habit, it had been their joke for years.

'Right. Of course.'

'I didn't know, Miranda. You should have told me. We could have ...'

Tom was opening the leaflet, peering at a bouncing baby.

'It's not,' Miranda sat down heavily at the bleached pine kitchen table, 'what you think.'

But Tom wasn't listening. He pulled up a chair beside her, reaching for her hands again.

'I thought you didn't . . .' There was that smile again, so familiar, unfamiliar. 'I didn't know what to do . . . I so wanted . . .'

Miranda felt exhaustion descending like a blanket. 'It's not . . .'

She stared down at her hands. There was an ink stain on her right hand, she noticed. And her gold wedding ring. Bangles jingled on her wrist, a memory of love.

Tom interrupted her again. 'They can do so much, these days, Miranda. I spoke to Reuben . . .'

'Reuben?' The mention of one of his colleagues confused her. 'Why on earth were you talking to Reuben . . .'

'I just' – he peered at her face, shrugged – 'did. I've been so desperate for this to happen, Miranda . . . We never . . . talked.'

Not yet.

'No,' Miranda almost shouted the word, suddenly desperate to cut him off. 'It's not what you think, Tom. It's just . . . That leaflet is just for work.'

The words took a moment to reach him, and then his face shattered.

'Work?' Tom stared down at the leaflet. 'How can this be work?'

'It just is.' Miranda snatched the leaflet off him, rammed it into her handbag. 'Don't go through my bag again, Tom.'

'I wasn't . . .' Tom turned towards the window, looked out to the dark garden. 'You mean, you're not. You don't want . . .'

He was staring through the security shutters, still pulled across. Outside, the cherry-tree branches rattled in the wind.

'No,' Miranda heard a new cruelty in her voice. 'I don't think I do, Tom. No.'

She felt an odd flood of regret and relief. A blaze of guilt too, as his shoulders sank. From her chair, Miranda watched his back. He was tall, Tom. His dark hair thinning slightly in a patch at the back. He was still wearing his suit from work: the blue shirt, the navy pinstripe, the black shoes.

'Never?' He turned, and for a second, the movement twisted her heart, so that she almost reached out for him. But she placed her hands flat on the kitchen table.

'I don't think so.'

'But we've said ...'

'We haven't.' It was almost true. It sounded true.

Tom folded his arms, almost hugging himself. He bowed his head, staring at his shoes.

I will never lie to you, she had promised him, long ago. That one promise in a life full of lies: *I will always tell you the truth.*

A lie.

'You know I love you, Miranda.' Tom spoke into a silence. 'But this ... I need this.'

'I can't, Tom.'

'But you can,' he said. 'You can.'

The kitchen was silent. Miranda stared at the pink roses, in their crumpled brown paper and the pretty blue ribbon. She thought about shaping herself, time and again, to what the world wanted.

My foundations.

Her fingers curled to fists.

'You don't get to fall in love with shards of me, like everyone else.' The words rushed out of Miranda, flooding from nowhere. 'You can't choose the pieces of me to love, Tom.'

'I don't . . .' Tom looked up. There were lines across his face, lines she had never noticed before. 'Do you love me, Miranda?' The words startled her.

'Yes,' she said. A long pause. 'Of course I do.'

The words crept around the kitchen.

'Do you though? Really?'

'Why do you want this so much?' Miranda spoke quietly. 'This is who I am, Tom. Why can't I be enough?'

'You are.' He said the words as if by rote. 'Of course you are.'

'Well then.'

'But . . .' He leaned against the kitchen counter. 'Is it just going to be us, like this? Just the two of us? For ever?'

'You always knew,' she said. 'About my job.'

'Did I?'

She thought back to those early first days, a lifetime ago at university. The dawn after the balls. The cobbles, and the bubbles, and the striped lawns rolling to the river.

It was the kindness: that was what she remembered. Tea in bed in the morning, and supper waiting after a long day in the library. Learning to be normal, as if practising her timetables.

And she had learned kindness, too. For a while, by rote. Even enjoyed those little gestures: running him a bath after an icy game of rugby, buying cough mixture when he had a cold.

Oh, bugger, I've forgotten my mother's birthday.

Don't worry darling, I've sent flowers from us.

Us.

So close to normal, happy, contented. So close to a sensible job, well-behaved children, a decent pension.

And neither of them realised when she took that first job. He had made her a packed lunch that first morning. Her favourite sandwiches – expensive ham and that smelly cheese – and coffee in a brand-new thermos, bought specially. A note: You'll be brilliant.

The first step into a world with no value on kindness. Bad luck, really. Too easy to slip into old ways.

'No,' Miranda admitted. 'Maybe you didn't know then. But you've known for years, Tom. That everything I love about my job, it disappears, with …'

'But it's just' – he was plaintive – 'a job.'

Miranda thought of Casey, out in the chaos of Bangladesh. Of Hessa, battling not to cry.

'It's not,' she said. 'It's not just a job.'

'But it is.'

'Why?' She was standing now, meeting his eyes, and the growing rage. 'Why isn't this enough?'

'You're never bloody here, Miranda.'

'I am.' Her voice rose. 'I haven't been anywhere for weeks. I've been crushed into this house, saying no to everything.'

No.

Not yet.

'In your head, you're a thousand miles away.'

'But I'm not,' Miranda heard herself almost scream. 'I'm here. And I should be in Bangladesh, right now.'

'You might as well bloody well be.'

They froze, still in their beautiful kitchen.

'Fine,' Miranda spoke into the silence. 'I'll be on the next fucking plane.'

42

At the head of Sandwip pier there was a chaos of little shops. A small herd of black goats scrabbled among the litter, chewing on anything edible. By dawn, Casey and Ed were walking along the pier, gazing south down the coast. It was almost half a mile long, Sandwip pier, reaching right out over the mudflats to where the water is deep enough for the local ferry to chug in. Even this early, porters scuttled up and down, pushing wheelbarrows, or racing on motorbikes, swearing at people in their way. Beneath the rattling planks, the shallow brown water sucked at the uprights. The Sandwip ferry motored backwards and forwards, heading out to the 350,000 people who live on Sandwip island, far out in the Meghna river's huge estuary.

To the left and the right of the pier, vast ships slumped like drunks in the mud. A crowd of workers were already scurrying around thewrecks. As they walked along the pier, the locals peered at them interestedly.

'Ed and I will have to pretend to be a couple,' Casey had said. 'Tourists. The three of us together would look too odd.'

'I'll chill out in the hotel for a bit,' Hessa grinned, the anger of yesterday forgotten.

Now Casey felt peacock-conspicuous, trying to ignore the stares as she gazed along the coastline.

The boat to the south of the pier must once have been a supertanker, built for efficiency not charm. Oil rainbowed the silt below her: violet, orange, electric blue, gold. Casey could make out a worker climbing carefully out of the ship. The man jumped and landed, ankle-deep in the grey-brown mud, carrying some piece of junk for the breaking yard. As Casey watched, he slipped, falling to his knees in the mud.

The ship to the north had been enormous, once. Her wreckage dripped with rust, her name painted out for shame. This ship had been a cheery cherry-red once, apple-green beneath her waterline, but only fragments remained. She was picked to a carcass, the steel of her hull stripped away.

Casey ran her hand along the pier's rough and ready wooden barriers as a stray dog contemplated her thoughtfully. Ed was talking to a boy with a little fishing boat, maybe 10 feet long. The boy laughing, as Ed brought out his scraps of Bengali.

'He'll do it,' Ed triumphed in the end. 'Although I have no idea how many taka I have just agreed to pay him.'

A few minutes later, the boy's little boat was grumbling its way down the coastline. The smell of sewage was sharp in the air. It seemed to take hours to manoeuvre past dozens of beached ships, the outboard motor puttering like a sewing machine.

The white fibreglass boat was a dot beside the huge hulks on the beach, but they crept as close as possible to each vast blue shape, peering up for identifying marks.

Finally Casey pointed, with relief. 'There she is.'

Ed turned to see a familiar broad blue hull slumped in the distance. The *Tephi*. Her name was painted over in a splodge of black, but her shape was instantly recognisable from the photographs they had seen. The distinctive red stripe ran all the way around her, and her forest-green keel had buried itself in the mud.

They bobbed closer.

As she travelled the oceans, the *Tephi* would have been piled high with a Rubik's cube of containers. Now she lay empty, slumped sideways. Beside her lay another huge shape, the *Beauvallet*: Casey could just make out the letters on this ship's prow. From her shape, the *Beauvallet* must have once been a cruise ship. Casey imagined her in her heyday, holiday-jolly, skimming joyfully across the waves.

The *Beauvallet* had been hacked away in sections, bit by bit. Her bow, high up the beach, looked almost normal, but a hundred feet back the ship had been sliced cleanly from deck to mud. Patches of rust spattered the remaining hull, like a terrible plague.

The fishing boat sidled closer to the two beached ships. Compared with the other wrecks along the Bhatiari coastline, the *Tephi* looked new and intact. She had come to a halt in the silt, listing heavily to port.

'She looks like she might go over altogether,' Ed warned. 'Incredibly dangerous for the workers.'

Casey was studying her map, trying to work out exactly where they were. She pointed towards the mudflats, hoping the boy would take them closer to the shore. But the shipyard's workers had seen them already, and were peering down at the little boat from the height of the *Tephi*'s bridge. The boy flinched away.

Behind the *Tephi*, the coastline rose up to straggly grass that disappeared beneath some trees. Beyond the trees, Casey guessed it was only a few hundred feet to the coast highway. In the shipyard, two huge barns faced the coast. There were no signs giving away the name of the shipyard. Behind the barns was a long, low building, with no distinguishing features. It was built of grey bricks, solid, with a blue corrugated-iron roof.

'Could that …?' Trying to see better, Casey stood up in the little boat, almost tipping it over. Beside her, the boy was cringing down in the boat, trying to hide his face from the workers.

'Casey, come on,' said Ed. 'Let's get out of here.'

'But …'

'It's not fair, Casey.'

Ed signalled to the relieved boy, and the little fishing boat turned swiftly, chugging away, north towards the Sandwip pier.

'Ed … I need to …'

'What exactly are you going to be able to see from here anyway?'

'I don't know …' Casey flicked the water with annoyance. 'But we have to get closer …'

'Not now, Casey.'

They bobbed along with the tide, Casey scrambling through her thoughts.

'Do you know the name of that shipyard …' she tried, but the boy was blank. Finally, she brought out the name of the garment factory. 'Arakny?'

The boy glanced at her, eyes dark. Then he shook his head slowly. *No.*

He looked away, avoiding her eyes. Casey leaned back on his fishing nets. It was hot on the boat, with almost no breeze coming across the water. A surge of frustration. She flicked the dinghy's painter back and forward across the water and tried to make sense of it all.

They were almost back at the pier when Casey's phone jangled.

'Hello, Raz,' she answered it, her mind elsewhere.

'I've got good news for you, Miss Emily.' Raz paused, building the moment. 'It looks like your baby will be born tomorrow. The girl is in labour, right now.'

A baby.

A baby.

A baby, almost forgotten …

'Oh, Raz,' Casey managed to whisper. 'It feels like a miracle.'

'It is a funny sort of miracle,' agreed Raz. 'And it will be soon.'

A mist was rolling in, blotting out the oily rainbow of the sea. As Raz carried on speaking, Casey sat staring over the waves. 'Thank you, Raz,' she murmured when a silence fell.

'I am very glad for you and Mr Dominic,' Raz said politely.

As he spoke, the thought of another girl, so much nearer, crowded Casey's mind. A woman screaming, in a darkened room, as the sun disappeared from the day.

Right now. This minute. Would she be alone? Or would the other women be with her, helping her, the best they knew how? Would Romida be there too, dark eyes wide, a new fear growing?

Where are you, my girl?

'Shall we meet you in Chittagong?' Casey made her voice crisp. 'Where should we come?'

As he gave her the instructions, Casey reached for Ed's hand, and he squeezed it.

43

Although it had no windows, the room was far too bright. The hotel called this a banqueting room, but no one had feasted here for years. Strip lighting was tacked to a ceiling too low for elegance. Trestle tables were scattered here and there, with cream polyester tablecloths. Each table had a grimy blue runner down the middle, and a dusty bowl of red plastic flowers at the centre. A burble of noise came through double doors from the lobby. *Chittagong's Jalico Hotel* was spelled out in blue neon behind the receptionist's desk.

Ed and Casey sat on gold chairs, padded in faded scarlet. They were alone.

'He said ten o'clock.' Casey was fidgeting.

A digital clock flickered, red numbers on the wall. 10.47.

How can we go home if . . .

'Just wait.' Ed put his hand over hers. She stared blankly at his fingers.

But how can we go home . . .

Casey forced herself to gaze at the plastic flowers.

Where is she? The jolt again. *Where is this baby right now?*

10.49.

A woman screaming. Somewhere, out in this city.

Hands, clenching. Flesh, tearing.

And all the pain for nothing.

Casey thought of husbands. Waiting out in the corridors, beside cream polyester and red plastic flowers and strip lighting pinned to the ceiling. There, and not there. Vital, and quite insignificant.

10.50.

Who is she, this woman?

A mother, and yet not a mother.

What happens, in those last frantic minutes, when the pain is all there is? Gripping, and raging, and howling.

And that sudden first squall. *She's alive. She's alive.*

A baby, brought around, just for a moment: small, slippery, mewling. A hand reaching out, for a second. And the baby abruptly lifted away.

10.52.

Then the drugs, to stop the milk.

My child, and not my child.

All the dreams of a lifetime, and only a couple of seconds.

The love of a lifetime, gone. The cries, fading away down a corridor.

You never know how you can run, until you run for your daughter.

And Emily, somewhere. A mother, and not a mother.

10.56.

The double doors flew open.

Beyond the banqueting room, they were all in play. Miranda, just off the plane, was sitting in the hotel lobby, casual in jeans and an embroidered tunic. Outside, a tuk-tuk waited patiently. Up in Bhatiari, to the north of the city, Hessa was lingering just outside the gate to the shipyard, sitting on a low wall in her old blue sari.

Casey had called Savannah too.

'I need your eyes. Can you spare a day?'

'Well, I haven't had a day off since I arrived in this wretched country,' said Savannah, 'so I guess I am owed a few.'

'Can you come up to Chittagong?'

'Course.'

Savannah was sitting in the entrance to a hospital in Chittagong, the one that a woman might be moved to for emergency surgery. Invisible in her charity-branded T-shirt and jeans.

'Layla wants to help too,' Savannah had called back, a few minutes after Casey had spoken to her. 'She says she's seen too much in the camps, doing all her translating work. That she wants to do something proper.'

'That,' Casey had said, 'would be amazing.'

Layla was positioned a few steps away from the factory in Sagorika, queuing at a street corner, in her oldest sari.

'But it's still not enough,' Casey fretted. 'They could be being held anywhere, these women. In a suburb in Chittagong. Or out in a village in the hill tracts. Anywhere.'

'It's the best we can do,' Miranda had tried to reassure her. 'Let's work out the rest of the plan.'

They had all strategised for hours up in Casey's hotel room, eating endless biscuits and crisps. Casey hadn't questioned Miranda about her sudden arrival.

'I was a university student, you know,' Layla had told Casey, as they tapped on their laptops side by side. 'Before all this, before the crisis, we'd all work together on a class project just like this.'

The NGOs, paying Western rates, hoover in anyone who speaks English from across whole countries, causing ripples of difficulties in schools, in hospitals, in universities.

'Thank you for coming up here, Layla,' Casey said.

Layla shrugged. 'I have been talking about surrogacy with a friend of mine in India. She works as a journalist there. I suppose one day the technology will advance, and the babies will be grown in labs, all tidy. But for now . . .'

'It is so hard to know what's right,' said Casey. 'If the women choose to do it, then—'

'Do you really think the surrogates in India, or wherever, always get paid when they agree to carry these babies?' Layla's face grew fierce. 'Do you think that they get to keep the money to do whatever they want?'

'I know,' Casey said quietly.

'My friend said that the doctors in India needed donor eggs too.' Layla picked up a biscuit, bit into it. 'She said they harvest them like a rice crop. You get more money for a Caucasian egg, apparently.'

Casey met her eye. 'Yes.'

For a second, Casey thought of witches, saving locks of hair and clips of nail and tiny drops of blood. And what would they make of an egg, just like that? Too good to be true.

'She said the doctors put in several embryos at a time, to hurry things up,' Layla went on. 'And abort a few if too many take.'

'They've thought of everything now,' said Casey flatly.

'Mind you.' Layla rested her chin on her palms. 'In some places, the clients go through the whole thing, and quite a long time later realise that their baby is not actually genetically theirs. Because their own embryos just weren't working, so someone somewhere in the system just swapped them out.'

'I heard about that,' said Miranda.

'In the women's contracts,' Layla said, 'there is a clause saying that the girls agree be kept alive on life support if things go wrong, but there is still a chance the baby could survive.'

Emily, a thousand miles away, who wouldn't even know when her daughter was born.

'It's barbaric.'

'The things I have seen in those camps,' said Layla. 'Nine months after the crisis first broke out, I was showing journalists around one of the medical centres when a woman came in. She just handed over her baby, no words at all, and walked away. She had been raped by soldiers, before escaping Rakhine. Her husband had been dead for years, and there she was, pregnant. The shame of it, you know? I can still see the nurse, just holding this tiny baby, staring down in shock. Imagine it. Abandoned, as an orphan, in that camp.'

'Poor little thing,' said Casey.

'But another time a different woman came into the health centre, just for a check-up,' Layla went on. 'She'd also been raped, but was holding her baby so close. She said, "I carried this boy for almost ten months. I had all sorts of pain and grief for him. And I gave birth to him. He is a son of the Rohingya."' Layla shrugged. 'So which woman is right? I can't tell any more.'

'Does it surprise you?' asked Casey. 'These surrogacy arrangements?'

'Not really.' Layla pursed her lips. 'The Rohingya have always been seen as—' She gestured vividly, dismissively. 'It's different here,' she went on. 'The women in this country, they're treated like shit anyway. More than one in five Bangladeshi girls are married by the time they are fifteen, just for starters. When the Rohingya girls arrived in Bangladesh, a lot of them were married off as soon as they got here. It's not like they had any choice. Very young girls, and old, old men, sometimes.'

'At first, I didn't understand why the gang didn't just go and recruit these women,' said Casey. 'Just pay them a bit, make it easy. I didn't understand why they had to go to all the trouble of kidnapping them. Hessa understood it, right from the start.'

'It is what has happened for years with the Rohingya,' said Layla, and Casey knew it was true.

By one calculation, 170,000 Rohingya were trafficked to Malaysia and Thailand in just three years even before the current crisis. Sold off like cattle, at $2,000 a head. A nice little business for the traffickers, coining $100 million a year. Mass graves were found in Thailand: those who wouldn't follow the rules. Plenty more where they came from.

'No,' said Layla coolly. 'These men would never go and negotiate with the Rohingya. They'd tell a few lies, and grab them. And who would stop them? No one.'

As the banqueting room doors flew open, Casey jerked to her feet. It was Raz, beaming widely. He stood there for a moment, enjoying his entrance.

How should I be? Casey had asked Miranda. *I don't know how to play this part.*

Jubilant. Miranda's smile was crooked. *Ecstatic. Delirious. Don't you know what happiness looks like, Casey?*

Now Casey stood there for a second, unsure.

Her feet were clumsy. She took a step towards Raz, almost staggering.

'Here.' He hurried towards her. 'Your daughter, Miss Emily! Mr Dominic. Your daughter is here.'

Casey collapsed back in her seat, her legs unable to hold her.

Ed was beside her, staring down at the tiny bundle as Raz deposited the baby in Casey's arms, as if he were delivering a parcel.

'She was born just an hour ago,' said Raz, almost fatherly. 'And she is perfect.'

Casey stared down. She was beautiful, this little girl, and almost unbelievably tiny. The baby opened her eyes, just for a second, and stared up at Casey blearily. The little eyes were that strange clear blue.

'There were no problems,' said Raz. 'All was as it should be.'

The baby had a scattering of dark brown hair. *Those eyes*, thought Casey. *Dominic's eyes.*

'Hello, little one,' she murmured.

Casey glanced up, over the baby's head, and there was Ed, his eyes so solemn.

'Poppy,' he said, and there was a break in his voice. 'Her name is Poppy.'

Flowers fluttering like pale pink silk . . .

Underneath the white blanket, someone had tucked the baby into a babygrow. Pink with blue spots: *Mummy's little princess.*

The little girl kicked her legs, her fingers curling into tiny fists, and Emily's face, crying with happiness, flashed before Casey's eyes.

'Bloody hell.' Casey's smile glittered. 'Dominic! Our baby. Our *child*.'

Ed was staring at her.

We steal these moments, Casey thought. *And by stealing them, we lose them for ever.*

This baby, born of a lie, announced to a lie.

The old fairy, cursing over her cradle; a shadow, over her grave.

'Emily, my darling.'

Ed was reaching towards her, wrapping his arms around Casey and the baby. And she was stretching up, finding his mouth for the kiss.

'My love.'

He pulled back, just for a second, the rainbow eyes upon her. And then he kissed her, hard, and so familiar, yet unfamiliar.

'A baby,' she whispered.

'Darling Emily.'

For a second, the name was a shock. He saw her startle, and jerked her closer.

'I can't believe it,' Casey managed to beam at Raz. 'I never believed that this would happen. Never.'

Emily's smile, Emily's words.

'You miracle worker,' she said.

He spread his hands wide. 'For you.'

Hands, clenching. Flesh, tearing. The dark, becoming the world.

A body, torn apart. And the screams, and the screams.

And all this, for someone else's joy.

Casey pushed the screams away, quite deliberately. 'I can't believe it,' she said again.

Raz grinned down at her. 'I will leave you now, in peace. I will be back with a passport for her soon. But she is a good girl, that one.'

He backed away, still smiling.

As Casey looked down, a wave of protectiveness washed over her. 'We will get you home, little girl,' she whispered. 'We will get you home.'

And the baby opened her mouth, and started to cry.

44

It seemed to take ages to get to the hotel room, the lift creaking past the floors. The lift was small, Ed and Casey awkwardly close, Casey's head full of the kiss that meant nothing.

The baby was mewling, a small arm escaped from her blanket. She was stronger than Casey had expected, the little limbs wrestling in the babygrow.

'Shh.' Casey bounced the baby up and down, struggling to support the small head. 'Quiet, little one.'

Casey had read Emily's instructions, and looked through the bags and bags of equipment. But back in the room, it was Ed who sorted out a bottle, and held the tiny baby, and tried to get her to feed. After a few squawks, she took the bottle trustingly, her eyes two slits of blue.

'God.' Casey stood flat against the wall. 'How do people cope?'

He laughed up at her. 'It's not hard, you know. Just patience, and a little bit of love.'

'Not' – Casey was checking her phone – 'my specialities.'

They were racing back, all of them except for Miranda. *She's here. All done. Come back.*

Out in the city, Miranda was following Raz, her tuk-tuk slipping easily down the streets as the big Land Cruiser got tangled up in traffic. 'I'll be back when I can,' she messaged.

Savannah was the first back to the hotel room.

'I never even caught a glimpse of them,' she grumbled. 'I checked every person going in and out of that hospital. Never saw a thing. Hello, poppet. Aren't you gorgeous?'

Casey had shown Savannah photographs of the men beforehand, and given her the Land Cruiser's numberplate.

'It was the longest shot,' Casey apologised. 'There are several hospitals around the city. And they may well not have taken her to a hospital anyway.'

'Doesn't matter,' Savannah shrugged. 'How is she?'

'Ed just changed her nappy,' said Casey. 'I almost had to leave the room.'

'Casey' – Savannah was laughing – 'you're ridiculous.'

'She's very quiet,' said Casey approvingly.

They all stared at the baby, a tiny technological miracle.

'They often are,' said Savannah drily. 'For the first twenty-four hours. Then, God help you.'

'Time for you' – Ed picked up the baby – 'to have a kip.'

Very carefully, he settled the baby in a tiny travel cot in the corner. 'He's a good one,' Savannah winked at Casey, and Casey turned away, embarrassed, confused.

Layla bounded through the door, Hessa just behind her.

'The Land Cruiser left the Sagorika factory just after eight this morning,' Layla said briskly. 'It turned west, and shot off fast. I followed, but I lost it as it turned onto the Dhaka Highway. All the windows were rolled down as it left the factory, before the air con kicked in. I am sure the baby wasn't with them then.'

'The Land Cruiser got to the shipyard not long after that,' said Hessa. 'Layla texted me as soon as she lost sight of the car, so it must have come straight there. It stayed at the shipyard for almost two hours. I was starting to worry that there was another way out. But finally, it came out again, zooming off down the highway back to Chittagong.'

They were both elated, thrilled at chasing the car across the busy city. Hessa threw herself into a chair.

'I tracked the Land Cruiser a long way back here,' Hessa went on. 'One of the huge trucks on the highway had gone over on its side, so the traffic was total chaos.'

All along that road, scrap from the ships was sold off piecemeal. Boilers, life-jackets, odd lengths of tubing, it was piled high and sold cheap.

'So it looks like the Land Cruiser came straight to the hotel from the shipyard,' Casey concluded. 'The car would have had no time to go anywhere else. Hessa, could you see if the baby was in the back, after it left the shipyard?'

'No.' Hessa was serious now. 'Remember, the windows are tinted, so I couldn't see into the car. But the baby must have been with them by then. They must have picked her up from the shipyard.'

'It seems likely,' Casey said. 'Could the women possibly be on that site?'

'There are lots of buildings on the little track leading down to the shipyard,' said Hessa. 'But they are just shacks for the workers.'

'The way Shamshun described it, it can't be a shack,' said Casey.

She and Hessa had examined the shipyard online, zooming in and out. It was lush with greenery, this part of the coast, the little houses surrounded by trees, big pools of water here and there. The track off the main Bhatiari road led past some shacks and then down towards the entrance of the shipyard. At the entrance, the track forked. One branch meandered through the shipyard, towards the mudflats and past the big barns. The other track continued outside the perimeter fence, towards some more workers' homes. The shipyard's fence ran around a large area. Several acres, Casey estimated.

From space, they could see the narrow workers' paths, out to the *Tephi* and the *Beauvallet*. To the left of the barns was the grey brick building Casey had seen from the fishing boat.

'One of those buildings,' Casey pointed. 'There.'

As the others went out to find a restaurant, Casey drew a breath. Then she pushed the numbers on her phone.

'Casey?' The phone barely rang before Emily answered it.

'We've got her, Emily,' Casey said, and an almost animal noise came down the line. 'She's a lovely little girl.'

For a moment, Emily couldn't speak.

'Let me see her,' Emily pleaded. 'I need to …'

Casey angled the camera so that the tiny baby filled the screen. Poppy lay there, eyes closed, quite angelic, swaddled in a soft white wrap.

'My baby.' They were the only two words Emily could manage. 'My baby, my baby, my baby.'

Casey could hear Dominic's deeper tones somewhere in the background. She kept the camera pointed at tiny Poppy, listening as the tears flooded Emily's voice.

The baby's tiny arm jerked, almost a wave. She was lying on her side, a small comma. She looked alarmingly vulnerable lying there.

'She's a gorgeous baby,' Casey said after a few minutes.

'When ...' Emily struggled to speak. 'When will you be back?'

'As soon as possible,' said Casey. 'I'll have someone check flights.'

'Don't make promises,' Miranda had ordered. 'We may be delayed.'

'Please,' said Emily. 'Please, please hurry.'

'We will,' said Casey. 'But it will take time, getting flights back from Chittagong.'

'I know, I know,' said Emily. 'Is she eating a lot? Is she healthy?'

'She seems very well,' said Casey, thinking how oddly fitting it was that Emily should meet this baby – created by syringes and Petri dishes, pills and vials – through the toughened glass of a mobile phone. 'She's lovely, Emily. Beautiful.'

'I never thought,' Emily's voice echoed down the line, 'that this moment would come.'

45

Night had fallen when Ed, Casey and Hessa walked down the pier. Hessa had taken a tuk-tuk down to Sandwip earlier in the evening, and bought the small fishing boat from the boy outright.

'He couldn't believe it,' she had reported. 'He was delighted.'

While Hessa was out negotiating for the boat, the rest of them had moved a few streets away from the Jalico Hotel, to rooms in another dusty business hotel.

'Best to be out of the way,' said Casey, peering around the Grand Prince Motel. 'Just in case they come looking.'

They had left just enough luggage in the Jalico to avoid raising suspicion among the staff.

'Take care.' Miranda had waved them off.

Now, the little boat bobbed on the tide as they approached, straining at its painter.

'Let's go.'

The fishing boat headed south, shapes looming out of the dark. They floated past the silhouettes of beached trawlers, cargo ships, even the odd oil rig. Ed was steering, trying to avoid the jetsam that clogged the water. A piece of plastic sheeting caught across the boat's bows, and Casey dragged it crossly out of the way. Lights flickered here and there, on the shore, but the mudflats were silent. It was a still night, the water barely rippling.

Finally, there she was: the huge shape of the *Tephi*, slumped in the mud. Ed slowed the outboard motor to a purr. He steered the little fishing boat in between the *Tephi*, with her brave red stripe, and the remains of the *Beauvallet*.

As the boat bottomed out on the beach, Casey was out, splashing through the water.

'Casey,' Ed whispered. 'Wait.'

Hessa followed Casey over the side, grabbing the painter and hauling the boat up the mud. A few feet above the shoreline, a large chunk of metal lay half-buried in the mud, and they tied up the little boat.

The ships lolled there, just visible in the dark, awkward as swans on land. The *Beauvallet* had lain in the mud much longer than the *Tephi*, Casey saw.

This old cruise ship must have been over a thousand feet long once, but massive gas-torches had sliced the *Beauvallet*'s steel hull like a cake a few hundred feet back from her bow. More than half the ship was gone, only splinters of steel left on the beach.

So far, the workers had left the front third of the cruise ship almost untouched. Here and there, parts of her hull had been stripped of steel, leaving gaping holes in her sides, but she was still recognisable as an elegant old ship.

As Casey looked up from the shoreline, the remains of the *Beauvallet* were a strange marine doll's house. Sliced from top to bottom, side to side, her cabins were hacked open like some fantastical anatomy lesson. From the muddy beach, Casey could see her cabins, deck after deck of them, with only half a room remaining on each level. Half a floor, and half a wall, and half a balcony, jagging into nothing. Casey could even see curtains in the remains of some of the cabins, an advent calendar on Christmas Eve.

For a second, the old photographs of a blitzed London flashed across Casey's mind. A scattering of Londoners in a black and white dawn, stunned by a house half-standing, and a whole life gone. She remembered sepia curtains blowing awkwardly in the breeze, a table and chairs perched above a cliff of rubble.

'Poor old thing,' Hessa said.

Casey looked up at the darkness of the beach, the broken shapes of metal, and felt a shudder of dread.

She raised her chin. 'Let's go.'

Only one light shone in the shipyard, sending a sad half-beam over the mud. A warm breeze drifted in from the sea. As Casey peered up at the barns, clouds blew across the moon, and it darkened abruptly. She pushed away a shiver, superstition tightening her throat.

Anything might be here.

One step.

Be brave.

Another step.

A whisper back to the others: 'It's fine.'

The silence wrapped around her. Chunks of steel had been laid in a rough row up towards the shipyard. A makeshift path, scrambling towards the barns.

I have to try.

A breeze was blowing up from the south. A bird screamed overhead, and Casey jumped, the shudder clawing down her spine. That fear, so familiar.

She could sense Ed and Hessa behind her as she crept along, a pulse pounding in her throat. Her blood fizzed, and she almost laughed aloud. *Is this how I live? Why this? Why here?*

Another step, and she slipped in the mud, slamming face down into the ground to lie stunned for a second, knees bruised, eyes dizzy. The sea was a quiet splash in the distance, the endless dark above.

All I had, I gave to Romida …

You have to try.

'Casey?' Hessa's whisper, urgent in the dark.

'I'm fine.'

Casey forced herself to her feet, and they crept forward again.

A door banged somewhere. *Who was that?*

Another step. And another. Some animal whipped away, just in front of her, and her scream almost burst into the air.

But I'm alive.

Another step.

So alive.

Finally, she could sense the barns just ahead, a darker shape in the night. A last few steps, her hands in front of her face, and she touched the cold corrugated iron.

Everything was still. Casey felt her way along the barn wall. There were gaps here and there. Cracks, where the iron had peeled away from the timbers. Finally, a big wooden door.

Maybe.

A panic like vertigo: *I can't.*

You have to try.

Casey held her breath and pushed gently at the door. It swung open, lighter than she expected, creaking loudly.

'Casey.' An angry hiss.

She ignored Ed, stepping forward and peering across the barn in the faintest of hint of light.

Tables and benches. Piles of machinery, shrouded by darkness. Odd pieces of steel dumped here and there.

And two shapes on the floor.

Casey forced herself to breathe. Two men, asleep. Workers? Guards?

A jerk at her arm startled her; Ed had seen them too. His gesture was firm: no. But she pulled away, pointing to a walled-off section at the back of the barn.

They might be there.

Maybe.

I have to try.

He shook his head, more forcefully. *Come away.*

Casey jerked her arm out of his grasp, and stepped forward too fast for him to grab. She heard Ed murmur, too late.

One step. Another. Out of his reach.

And now the men were between her and the door: no escape, no way out. Casey edged across the floor, the demons dancing just out of sight.

She was halfway across the barn when the silence shattered. Casey froze, flat against the wall, unable to breathe or think as a phone shrieked, impossibly, unbearably loud.

One of the men half-sat, reached blearily for his phone. Casey saw the glow as he answered it. *Don't move, don't breathe, crush the scream in your throat.* There was a grunt, a rattle of words, the phone chucked down again.

Silence.

The man settled back into sleep.

Casey stood against the wall, forcing herself to breathe. The seconds ticked by. Forward, or back. Forward or back.

I have to try.

Forward.

She inched on.

Just a few feet to the inner door.

Nearly there. Nearly. There. Closed. Locked? No.

Very carefully, Casey pushed down on the handle. She eased the door open: tiny movements, almost tender.

A breath, and she peered through.

Nothing.

Despair like a slap.

Nothing.

'Let's try the other building,' she murmured, as soon as she reached Ed and Hessa, not letting them speak.

She heard a sigh from Hessa, a deliberate silence from Ed.

Very carefully, they crept towards the grey brick building.

This building was more solidly built, Casey could tell in the gloom. No creaking corrugated iron here, but solid construction, carefully done. No windows, and only one door: unyielding, padlocked closed. Casey tried to listen, but silence filled her ears.

'I'm going to pick the lock,' she whispered.

'There could be guards here too.' Ed spoke quietly, a hand on her arm. 'There could be anything in there.'

'I know,' she whispered. 'But the other barn is a workshop. This one . . .'

'You'll get us all killed.'

The trees rustled around them, the breeze inquisitive.

'We have to, Ed.' It was Hessa's voice.

Casey felt him drop his hand, step back. 'Go on then.'

Picking the lock took only took a few seconds, and Casey stepped back and pushed open the door.

The women stared at her.

Maybe fifteen of them, some still half-asleep, peering up from the floor. A few of them looked terrified, flinching away as the door swung open. For a second, there was complete silence.

'My God,' Casey whispered. 'My God.'

In the half-darkness, she could see that most of the women lay on rows of thin mattresses, wrapped in dirty sheets. As Casey gazed around, they began to sit up, some climbing to their feet, others cowering away. They weren't all women, Casey saw. Several of them were young girls.

And almost all looked pregnant.

'Please,' said Casey pointlessly. 'Please don't be afraid.'

The girl lying nearest to the door was fourteen, maybe. She had big eyes, and a nose that had been broken once, many years ago. This girl hadn't moved as Casey walked in. She just stared up, blinking in the light, her expression quite unreadable. She was pregnant too, Casey saw. Six months, maybe. And past fear, it seemed.

'Hello,' said Casey. 'Hello.'

The words dangled in the silence. Hessa stepped past Casey, and kneeled down beside the girl.

‘Hello,’ she spoke in Bengali, ‘my name is Hessa.’

The girl stared back at her, jaw clenched. Hessa tried again. ‘Are you all right?’

Silence.

‘Who brought you here?’

Nothing.

‘What is your name?’

The girl’s eyes flicked away.

Hessa turned back to Casey, with an expression of despair. ‘What can I say to her? What do we do?’

Casey stared round the room, tried again. ‘Romida? Are you here? Romida?’

There was a long silence. Casey pulled a small torch out of her pocket, and flicked it on. Some of the women flinched away from the brightness, others glowered back defiantly, their fear fading as the intruders just stood there. Ed was waiting outside, Casey could sense his tension. She looked around the room, scrutinising face after face. A thud of disappointment: Romida wasn’t there. Casey stared harder, willing the girl to appear.

Where are you, shy smiling girl? A red dress, covered in beautiful roses. Not here, not there, no.

‘Does anyone speak English?’ Casey managed.

A pair of eyes glinted towards her. ‘Do you speak any English?’ Casey focused on the girl who had looked up. ‘Any at all?’

There was a pause, and then a slow, resentful nod.

Casey stepped towards her. ‘Do you mind if I talk to you? I am sorry to break in like this.’

The girl considered Casey for a second. She was short, this girl, with dark curly hair and a gap between her front teeth.

Maybe fifteen, Casey thought, and pregnant too, a small bump just visible.

'What is your name?' asked Casey. 'My name is Casey.'

The girl looked away, and then met Casey's eyes squarely. 'I,' she said quietly, 'am Khadija.'

'What are you doing here?' A shrug.

'How did you come here?' A slow blink.

'Where did you come from?' Khadija stared at Casey, eyes narrowed. She bit her nails soberly, and finally she spoke slowly, carefully: 'We came from Rakhine. We were in the camps.'

Casey felt something close to relief. She gestured: *Shall I sit down?* and Khadija gave a brief, wary nod. The other women watched them closely.

Casey sat cross-legged on the floor next to the girl. Rushing, because there was no time, she explained their presence to the girl. 'We are journalists. From London. We are looking for women taken from the camps. We want to help.'

Khadija nodded again, carefully. Then – suddenly decisive – she turned to the other women, speaking rapidly. The other women nodded. They had all seen journalists around the refugee camps, many, many times. Smile for the camera, keep the aid flowing. Click, click, click click, click.

'Who brought you to this place?' asked Casey, when the room had fallen into silence.

Khadija spoke slowly, searching for the words. 'Two men went to my parents in the camp. One of them said they had a friend who wanted to marry me. My parents ... We didn't have anything ... My parents thought it would be best.'

Khadija's voice trailed away, and her head bowed.

'I am sorry,' Casey murmured. 'We understand that the gang who took you are forcing the women to be surrogates,' she went on carefully. 'Using IVF.'

Khadija didn't recognise the word, staring blankly at Casey. The confusion didn't surprise Casey.

'You don't understand how cut off they've been, some of the Rohingya,' Savannah had explained months earlier, walking around Balukhali camp. 'We had one of the most famous football stars in the world here. He was an ambassador for a charity, here for one of those photo ops a few weeks ago. But the refugees didn't know who he was. They had never heard of him; they had never heard of his club. Not once. Even in the most remote parts of Africa the kids always know the clubs: Chelsea. Arsenal. Manchester United. But here, nothing.'

Now, Casey tried to explain to Khadija: 'There is a procedure that makes the women have babies, and then the babies are taken away.'

Khadija understood now, a burn on her cheeks.

'Yes.' She gave a slow nod, staring at the floor. 'Yes.'

'Is that what has happened to you?'

Another careful nod.

There was a beat of silence. Then Casey went on. 'Was a baby girl born here, maybe yesterday?'

Tears filled Khadija's eyes. *Yes*, she nodded again.

'And where is the mother now?'

There was a long silence.

'Where is the mother now?' Casey spoke more urgently.

'What is the mother's name?' Hessa tried.

Khadija tipped her chin in the air, staring at the corrugated-iron roof as she thought. 'Zohra,' Khadija said. 'Her name is Zohra.'

Khadija was twisting her sheet back and forth between her hands now, almost tearing at it.

'And where is she now?'

Khadija looked at Casey, eyes carefully blank.

'*Mirta*,' she said, and Casey didn't need Hessa to translate.

'She's dead,' said Hessa. 'Zohra died giving birth.'

Khadija was crying now, tears running down her face. Pausing for a minute, Casey looked around. Then she stood up, peering closer. In one corner of the room, there was a neat bed, with a carefully tucked-in sheet. Someone had painted a few yards of wall pale blue, and stuck up a poster. A smiling child, a beaming nurse, advice on vaccinations. A Doppler machine sat on a white steel filing cabinet. And a bed, half-hidden by a colourful curtain.

It was the backdrop of Emily's photograph, Casey realised. That reassuring scene was all they had needed. A cheap clinic nearby would be able to do the ultrasounds, and the same clinic could probably perform the embryo transfer. It hadn't taken much to gloss the image, and who would ever check?

Just a few feet away from the white filing cabinet, a woman was sitting on the floor, staring blankly at Casey, her knees huddled protectively. Casey tried to smile at her.

She turned back towards Khadija.

'We can get you out of here.' Casey tried to make her voice sound confident. 'If you come with us, we can help you escape.'

Khadija looked up, a flicker of interest in her eyes. 'But where would we go?'

'We have a safe house.' Casey didn't know if Khadija would know the words. 'We have a house where you will be protected.'

'But what about . . .' Khadija gestured around the room.

'It's for all of you,' said Casey. 'But we have to be quick. We have to hurry.'

For a moment, suspicion flared in Khadija's eyes, the eyes of a child betrayed before. 'How can we trust you?'

'You don't have to,' said Casey. 'You can stay here, all of you. But if you come with me, I will try and make you safe. Please tell the others right now. We don't have much time.'

Khadija hesitated. 'You promise?'

'I promise.'

Khadija squared her shoulders and turned to the others, speaking quickly. There was a sudden burble of noise.

'You have to keep quiet,' Casey gestured. 'It's very important.'

One woman, the oldest there, was talking now, one hand on her hip, the other gesturing angrily.

'Can you understand what she is saying?' Casey asked Hessa.

Hessa listened, her face beginning to relax.

'That woman is saying they should go,' Hessa murmured. 'That they don't know what will happen to them here, but it is worth trying to escape. That they might even be able to get back to their families.' Another woman across the room interjected something sardonically, and Khadija's face broke into a cynical smile. 'That woman says some of them are only here because of their families,' Hessa explained.

Casey looked around, imagining all the lies told to these women. The sweethearts they trusted, the uncles they believed. All betrayed, all ruined, all abandoned.

'Let's go.' She gestured towards the door.

They made their way through the woods. At first, the women were buoyed up with rebellion, but Casey could feel their bravery ebbing as they forced their way through the bushes. In this darkness, every shadow was a threat, every rustle a jailer.

'Not far,' Casey whispered. It seemed much further in the night-time. They crept forward, Casey trying to smile encouragingly.

'Watch out!' As Casey whipped around at Hessa's whisper, she saw the jolting flicker of a torch off to the right.

Get down, Casey gestured frantically. Hide.

The women flinched low to the ground, the noise unbearably loud to Casey's ears. Sprawled in the dirt, Casey could hear a murmur of conversation, smell a waft of cigarette smoke. Very carefully, she peered up. Two men, walking along the fence line. Guards. Their torch beams bounced around, almost casual. They came closer. Casey forced herself into the ground, making herself as small as possible.

A bark of laughter from one man, and his gesture sent torch-light glaring towards the group. A gasp from one of the women, and Casey closed her eyes tight, waiting to be caught.

She lay there, hopeless, motionless. Treasure hunt, hide and seek, a murder in the dark. She imagined opening her eyes to find two figures standing over her. *Got you.*

But the voices wandered on. These men were chatting, not searching. Casey lay still, the minutes passing, until at last she had to move. She stood up, dusted herself down.

'Come on.' She tried to sound calm. 'Nearly there.'

Hesitantly, the women stood up. The moonlight glowed.

Let's go, gestured Khadija.

At last, the tall wire fence loomed up in front of them. The women stalled, staring up at the barrier. Khadija's head jerked towards Casey.

‘Here.’ Hessa and Casey pulled out wire cutters, clipping quickly. It took only a few minutes, and then Casey crawled through the gap. A few steps through some mango trees, and she was on the dirt track that ran along the perimeter of the shipyard.

There. In the distance, Casey could see a minibus parked on the side of the track. Casey flicked her torch, and without switching on its headlights the vehicle began to move towards her.

‘How’s it going?’ Miranda brought the minibus to a halt. She grinned down, elbow on the window frame. Layla was beside Miranda, also smiling with relief.

‘Get in,’ Casey gestured to the women.

They scrambled into the minibus without a glance backwards. They had made their decision, Casey saw, everything committed. For a second, the air around her sparkled with happiness.

As she glanced at him, Ed gave her a rueful grin. ‘Well done.’ He shook his head at her. ‘I never thought we would do it.’

‘Did you find Romida?’ Miranda interrupted her thoughts.

‘No.’ A flood of exhaustion overwhelmed Casey. ‘I don’t know what has happened to her.’

Layla twisted around sharply, speaking across the minibus. Casey heard the word Romida several times and one of the woman, who didn’t look pregnant at all, jerked her head up, the words spilling out of her.

Layla asked more questions, her voice rising slightly.

‘What is it?’ Casey asked urgently. ‘Where is Romida?’

Layla spoke a few more sentences, and sat back, eyebrows raised. ‘This woman says that she saw Romida.’

'Where?' Casey said. 'When did she see her?'

'This woman thinks that the main building in the shipyard had got too crowded,' said Layla. 'So when the women are first brought here, they are held separately, away from the others. They are given good food there, kept healthy. This girl was only moved into the main building a few days ago, after a medical procedure. I assume that means she is pregnant, but not showing yet. They may be being kept apart so that the new arrivals don't know what is coming next.'

'But where is Romida now?'

Layla scrunched up her face. 'This is the thing. There are only a few of them being held out there. They're locked up.'

'Where? Tell me, Layla.'

'You can't go there.'

'I can try.'

'She says it would be very dangerous.'

'That doesn't matter.'

Layla pursed her lips, and for a moment, Casey thought Layla might not tell her. Then Layla shrugged.

'They're out there,' Layla pointed. 'They're being held on one of the old ships.'

46

'We have to go out to the ships,' Casey said, and the others nodded wordlessly.

She was almost surprised by Ed's agreement, but he shrugged. 'We can't leave them behind.'

'We'll drive these women to the safe house,' said Miranda. 'Layla can stay with them there, and I'll come back as fast as possible.'

'We have to get them safely out of the way,' agreed Casey.

'Going to the ships is dangerous,' said Miranda flatly.

'We've still got a bit of time,' said Ed. 'We closed the door to the barn, so if you were just looking across from the workshops, it wouldn't show. But you have to get these women out of here, right now.'

'Yes,' said Miranda.

'Hessa.' Casey looked around. 'You can go with Miranda. This is too …'

'No.' Even in the dark, Hessa looked outraged. 'I'm coming with you.'

Now they had reached the top of the beach, the sea a shimmering black nothing. They scrambled back down the makeshift stepping stones towards the ships.

‘Which one?’ panted Hessa.

‘The *Tephi*,’ Casey decided fast. ‘The *Beauvallet* looks far too dilapidated.’

‘Right.’ Ed peered up at the *Tephi*, as she soared above them. ‘How the hell do we get on to that?’

The hull of the ship rose up, impossible to climb. For a second, Casey thought about the Somali pirates, racing across the blue of the Indian Ocean. Armed with grappling hooks, and praying for a chance.

She tapped the hull quietly, but no sound came back.

A Panamax can be 190 feet tall, Casey knew from Ed’s research, twenty storeys high. She peered up at the vast hulk. The *Tephi* looked easily that big, the proportions out of all human scale.

‘There must be a way in,’ she whispered. ‘There has to be.’

Casey splashed towards the bow of the ship, wedged high up the beach. As she hauled herself through the sludge, the smell was nauseating. A filigree of oil gleamed on the mud. At last she reached the bow.

‘There,’ Casey whispered in triumph.

As their first effort towards breaking down the ship, the shipyard workers had carved a hole in the *Tephi*’s side. It wasn’t large, just big enough for a man to fit through, but it was there. For a second, Casey imagined this hole if the *Tephi* were still afloat. The weight of the water smashing in, crushing any human body in its way.

‘Come on,’ she whispered.

Casey scrambled up through the gap, and tried to look around. The workers had sliced straight into the *Tephi*’s hold, the space impossibly dark. Inside the ship, the velvet blackness filled her eyes. Casey held her hand in front of her eyes, and saw no movement. For a second, she felt as if she had dissolved, disappeared.

She shook her head, dragging herself back to the present. It smelt of oil down here. It was colder, too. Dank.

She reached for her torch.

'Do you think we should use the light?' asked Ed, as Hessa climbed up beside them.

'It'll be impossible if we don't.'

And I can't. I can't. I won't.

For a moment, the three of them blinked, staring around the hold. The shadows flickered like ghosts as Casey glanced around. In the dusty torch beam, vast bulkheads rose up to the next deck. The walls and floors were painted a utilitarian khaki, a fretwork of salt covering everything, a memory of the ship's last life.

In the corner, a steep ladder climbed to the next level. Casey moved towards it, clipping the torch to her belt before she climbed, sending a madness of light bouncing round the hold. It felt like the old ship was lying in wait, watching for the next move. The light reached out into impossibly dark corners, and anything could be there. *Anything.* The silence closed in.

'Come on,' said Casey. 'Come on.'

She was out of breath by the time she reached the highest deck, bursting into the fresh air with relief. Once, this whole deck would have been piled high with shipping containers. Uniform in shape and slotted into place by derricks and brisk cargo winches, at port after port after port. Now, there was nothing except a couple of roosting birds that screeched away loudly as Casey and Hessa hurried down the deck, Ed following them.

Chittagong glowed orange to the south. The workers had already stripped away many of the *Tephi*'s fittings. The lifeboats were gone from this deck, along most of the railings. Casey peered up at the barns, but everything was still.

There was an abrupt clatter below decks, echoing up in the dark. Casey jumped.

Who is there? Who is there?

They stood frozen to the spot as the minutes edged past. Then Casey forced herself to move, legs like lead. One step, and the next, and the next.

'I don't think there's anything here,' she whispered. 'We have to keep going.'

She turned towards the bridge, at the rear of the ship along with the living quarters. Once, the bridge would have given the captain a clear view over the mountain of containers.

'I suppose they might be there,' whispered Casey.

But the quarters were empty. They peered into cabin after cabin, dragging open the heavy watertight doors, one at a time. Strange fragments of past lives tangled in the beam of torch-light. Here, a string bag of potatoes, growing delicate white tentacles. There, a toothbrush, above a cracked basin. In a room of bunks, a Page 3 girl peered over her shoulder, toothily, torn. Half-lives, frozen, and forgotten.

But everywhere, there was the strange silence, the steady stillness, only the dust demons at their heels.

'There's no one here,' Ed said, in the end. 'Just dirt and cobwebs.'

Casey turned to him, face smudged with dirt. 'You're right. It's empty. You can feel it.'

'This ship is a tomb,' whispered Hessa.

They climbed back down the layers of ladders, thick with khaki paint and salt, and clambered back out of the ship into the mud. The seashore was still, apart from the water lapping lazily as the tide slipped away.

'It must . . .' Casey spun in the mud, flicking her fingers with frustration.

'There's nothing in the *Tephi*,' said Hessa firmly. 'It was empty.'

'The *Beauvallet*.' Casey turned towards the other massive shape. 'She looks like a wreck, but they might be in there, maybe?'

'The *Beauvallet*?' Ed looked at the huge ghost ship. 'Casey, we are running out of time. It'll be dawn soon, the workers arriving.'

Ignoring him, Casey walked up behind the remains of the *Beauvallet*. The ship towered above her. On one of the decks, a string of orange lifeboats still clung to the *Beauvallet*'s side.

At the base of where the ship had been carved from top to bottom, the workers had leaned a strip of steel into the mud, to create a makeshift ramp from the beach to the lowest level.

'Come on,' muttered Casey.

Ed and Hessa peered up dubiously.

'Just to check,' Casey whispered again.

Hessa stepped forward, followed slowly by Ed. In a careful silence, the three of them edged up the ramp, slime slippery in the black. Casey flicked on her torch again.

'This way.'

At the top of the ramp, Casey moved gingerly down a corridor, into the dark of the ship. At the edges of the passageway, the old pattern of the carpet showed through, red with blue diamonds and green scrolls. Casey followed the muddy footsteps of the workers carefully.

The pace of the demolition was erratic. Lifts had been stripped out, leaving dank burrows, pitfalls running down through the ship. But there were still bright signposts on the walls, here and there. *Spa. Fitness Centre. Captain's Restaurant.* Half-ripped away: *Childzone.*

'There are dozens of cabins on this ship,' murmured Ed. 'It's going to be impossible to search.'

'But we have to,' said Casey.

'Hurry, then,' he whispered. 'There may be a guard.'

Without looking at him, she started on the first deck of cabins, methodically working her way down the row of doors. Spiders wove curtains of cobwebs in every corner. As the ship had smashed into the mud, the *Beauvallet* had tilted to starboard, giving everything a drunken, funhouse air.

Down the other side of the corridor, Hessa was also checking cabins.

'Nothing,' she said, as they met at the end. 'Just a lot of dirt.'

'Next level,' Casey demanded, then froze. A clang? A knock? Far in the distance? Or nothing stirring at all.

'What is it?' Ed whispered.

'Nothing,' Casey said in the end. 'Nothing.'

They kept going, climbing to the next floor, and the next. Dragging open double doors to a huge casino, the fruit machines ripped away. Then a bar like an airport lounge, a vast gym, and even a table tennis room. Nothing.

As she searched, Casey imagined the thousands of people on this ship, once. The staff scurrying, neat in their uniforms, the tinkle of music in every corner, the sea, all around, quite forgotten. She saw the bright smiles, the formalised fun, the scarlet umbrellas in cochineal cocktails.

Now, the air was stale. A coffin, opened. In one bedroom, Casey couldn't bear it any longer, sprinting to open a porthole, tearing at the catch. She leaned out into the night breeze, fingers digging into her palms.

Outside, the smell of oil was sharp, carried along by the wind. She guessed it must be from one of the old oil storage units, just down the beach. In 2016, one of those units exploded on the beach at Gadani, in Pakistan. Dozens of workers killed by just one mistake. Casey imagined the searing flames, the men trapped by steel designed to withstand an ocean. It took days to find all the bodies in the wreck.

'Come on,' she muttered to herself, and turned back to the next cabin.

Up another flight of stairs to *The State Rooms*, twirls and curlicues on a plaque. These rooms were larger, easier to search, the rats scuttling away as Casey yanked open the doors. She paused for a moment in a slight breath of wind, pushing her hair back from a forehead wet with sweat. Beyond double doors, the end of this corridor was sliced off, the black void gaping empty. From the corridor, it was a hundred-foot drop straight down to the beach.

In the next corridor, Ed was checking rooms methodically.

Casey pushed open another door. This dusty king-size bed still had its sheets and its blankets, the striped sofas gathered round a coffee table. Through torn curtains, the balcony peered out on the darkest of nights.

Still, nothing.

Up another flight of stairs, mould blossoming on sweeping treads. A chandelier glittered briefly in the torchlight.

The Emperor Suite, shouted a nameplate, and Casey turned towards it, feet heavy.

But there . . .

'Ed! Hessa! Look!'

A huge bolt had been welded onto the door, the steel scarred brightly new.

Casey and Hessa leaped towards it.

'Careful, Casey,' Ed caught Casey's arm. 'You don't know what's in there. It could be anything—'

But Casey pushed him away. 'I have to know, Ed. I have to.'

She grabbed the bolt. It stuck for a second, screeching, metal on metal, and gave way with a shriek. Casey pushed the door open, and stopped.

47

A girl's face jolted towards her.

It was the girl in Savannah's photograph, Casey knew at once. The wary eyes under the thick eyebrows, the fuzz of black curls at the hairline. The shy smile was gone now, the girl's eyes sharp with fear. No pretty red dress any more. Romida wore a ripped T-shirt, shrinking away as Casey took a step forward.

She was so very young.

There were just two other girls in the cabin. One of them lay in the grand stateroom bed.

'Romida?' Casey whispered.

Silence.

'Romida?' Casey forced herself to smile as she repeated the name. The girl stared, her eyes meeting Casey's and then flicking away, as she twisted herself into a tighter coil.

'I want to help you,' Casey tried. 'We all want to help you.'

Hessa was just behind her, moving forward. 'Are you all right, Romida?'

Romida gazed at Hessa, her expression solemn.

Casey and Hessa waited.

'How do you know my name?' Speaking to Hessa, Romida's voice was hoarse, as if she hadn't spoken aloud for days.

Hessa hesitated. 'Your mother, Romida. I spoke to Shamshun, back in the camp.' Romida's eyes filled with tears. Her head bowed. 'I'm sorry, Romida,' said Hessa. 'I'm very sorry to upset you.'

'My mother?' Romida cleared her throat, lifted her head. 'You spoke to my mother.'

'Yes.' They stood there, for a long quiet moment.

'How is she? When did you see her last?' The words rushed out of Romida, and Hessa tried to answer, in her patchy dialect.

'She misses you, Romida. She misses you terribly.'

The girl on the bed reached across to Romida, and Romida folded into her, just as she had curled into Jamalida's side all those weeks ago.

'Jamalida misses you so much too,' Hessa said gently.

'I miss her.' The words were a gasp. 'I miss her every minute.'

Casey stared around the cabin. This must have been one of the grandest rooms in the ship once. There was a writing desk in one corner, the dark polished wood from another world. Mirrored cupboards ran down one wall. The bedside lights had been torn out, and there was dust and grime everywhere.

The girl nearest the door was staring vacantly at an ugly painting, cheaply framed above the huge bed. Narcissus, enraptured.

Casey imagined all the girls held here: the healthy girls chosen and snatched from the camps. *All I had, I gave to Romida …*

Dragged away to this strange distortion of luxury, fed decent food for the first time in years. And then …

Casey leaned against the wall, knees shaky.

'You OK?' It was Ed, hovering in the corridor, and she stared at him.

'We found Romida,' she said simply. 'I never thought we would.'

'Yes' – Ed's mouth turned up at the corners – 'you did.'

'We have to get out of here,' Casey said to Hessa. 'Tell them we have to go as quickly as possible.'

Hessa began to explain, pointing to the door, gesturing with her hands. Casey moved across to the porthole, looking up the beach towards the woods.

A jolt, adrenalin flooding. There were lights: torches moving, up by the barns.

'We have to hurry.' Casey spun around, the fear flashing round the room. 'Hessa, tell the girls that if they want to escape, we have to go right now.'

Even as Hessa's voice rattled, Casey could see the lights shift, hurrying down towards the makeshift path.

'They're coming.' The girls looked up, as Casey whipped round again. 'They'll be here any second.'

'Oh God,' said Hessa. 'Oh God.'

'Tell these girls, Hessa,' said Casey. 'Tell them now is the time to run if they ever want to go … Right now. Because they may never get another chance.'

48

They crowded through the doorway into the corridor, carefully quiet. Ed pulled the door to the Emperor Suite closed.

The silence prickled around them. In the distance, the wash of the sea was lost beyond the hull.

'Is there . . .' Hessa breathed, silenced by a gesture from Casey.

They hesitated, statue-still. Just as Casey thought she might be able to move, there came a clatter below.

Casey slammed off her torch. Ed and Hessa followed her lead. The darkness swallowed them like a curse. Casey felt shapeless again, as blind as the night. Amorphous, as if she had never been.

As she stood there in the dark, listening to the girls' breathing, Casey felt herself falter.

She forced herself to breathe calmly. Maybe it was nothing. Maybe . . .

A child, covering her eyes to hide.

They're coming. They're coming. They're coming for us.

Casey took a deep breath. 'Hessa,' she muttered, 'we'll try and work out which staircase they are coming up. You take the three girls and go the other way. Ed and I will try and distract them.'

Ed nodded.

'But ...' Hessa tried.

'Do it.' Casey's whisper was fierce. 'Go to the little fishing boat. Get these girls away.'

'I'll watch out for you,' Hessa insisted.

'Keep them safe.'

For a second, Casey pressed the heels of her hands deep into her eye sockets, shooting lights across her eyelids. One breath. In, out. Then she reached out, touching the sleek banister of the *Beauvallet*'s grand staircase, and eased her torch back on.

'Let's go.'

Together, they crept down the first flight of stairs.

At the bottom of the grand staircase there was a lobby with two passages running parallel towards the back of the ship. On one side of each corridor, the cabins looked out over the sea. On the opposite side, the cabins on the inside of the ship – cheaper by far – had no windows.

Halfway down each corridor, there was a set of double doors. Casey knew that beyond them the ship had been sliced from deck to hull, during its slow, deliberate shipwreck. Those corridors led to nothing but a plunging fall in the dark.

'Make sure,' she whispered to Hessa, 'that no one goes that way.'

Next to the passages running along the ship, doors on either side of the lobby opened on to smaller flights of stairs that ran down both sides of the *Beauvallet*. Left or right, port or starboard – the toss of the coin that meant everything.

Casey hurried over to one of the gaping lift shafts. Silence. She crossed the lobby and listened at the other.

Casey felt the girls' eyes on her, their fear almost tangible. *Nothing. Please nothing.* But, far below, so far below, she heard the scrape of a door echo up the shaft.

'That way,' she whispered to Hessa. 'Down those stairs as quietly as you can. Go to the fishing boat.'

'But . . .'

'Go.'

'I'll look out for you.'

The girls moved fast. One chance, seized. Casey felt rather than heard the women scurry down the stairs. One second, she was surrounded by human bodies, and the next moment the air was empty, only Ed beside her.

Casey waited a second, then crossed back over to the other staircase.

'*Bonjour*,' she shouted down. '*Qui est là?*'

There was a shocked scuffle below, a Bengali voice, a man, shouting in anger.

'That's Raz.' Casey recognised the voice. 'He must have come from Dhaka.'

'Now what?' Ed whispered.

'We wait.' She tried to smile at him. 'We'll be fine.'

'You're lying.' His voice was light.

'Why would I lie to you?' For a second, Casey felt a shimmer of hysteria.

'Force of habit?' Their eyes met, that smile.

They could hear several people racing up the stairs towards them, shouting. There was pure rage in Raz's voice, the charm all gone. Here was anger, violent anger, and Casey felt her laughter drain away. Raz would kill, she knew, rather than let them escape.

She tried to calculate how long it would take the others to flee down the opposite stairs.

Please, she begged. *Don't let them have left a guard at the bottom of the stairs. Please.*

'*Qui êtes-vous?*' she shouted down the stairs again. Then she sprinted across the lobby to the staircase that Hessa had scurried down. On this side of the ship, the *Beauvallet*'s hull had been hacked away as the workers operated to some unknown schedule. Casey could peer out into the night air, fresh after the stench inside, and peer down the beach. Her heart skipped.

Far below, in the half-light of the moon, she could just make out a figure scrambling through the mud towards the little fishing boat. Another girl was behind her, scurrying along. Hessa was last, racing across the beach.

'Ed,' Casey gasped. 'They're getting away! Look. They're escaping!'

For the briefest second, joy surged through Casey.

'Now,' she said to Ed. 'Now we run.'

He looked at her, bewildered. 'How?'

49

They leaped down the stairs, following in Hessa's footsteps.

'This way,' Casey hissed.

No one was shouting now. They were all moving with a grim determination.

Above Casey and Ed, the moon was gleaming through the gap in the hull, sending a hint of light down the staircase. On each floor, a door opened out to an identical lobby. These doors were solid, with no glass panels, and no way of knowing what lay beyond. They crept down, step by step, until at last they ran out of stairs. This must be the lowest floor.

Casey hesitated. *Open the door and run? Into who knew what?*

Just as she was about to throw her weight at the door, there was a rush of words from the other side: Dylan. She couldn't understand the Bengali, but the tone was enough.

'Quick,' Casey whispered to Ed. 'Back up the stairs. Hurry!'

They fled up the stairs, diving through a door a few floors up.

'Shit,' Casey leaned against the wall. 'They must have realised the girls escaped. They're at the bottom of the stairs now. We're trapped.'

It was pitch-black on this floor, and she couldn't see Ed's face. He didn't say a word.

'Do you think they'll search the whole ship?' Casey felt as if she was speaking to herself.

There was a pause.

'Probably,' said Ed quietly. 'They'll have the workers coming out today anyway, so it'll be impossible for us to hide for long.'

They stood there in silence, as a shout from below echoed up the lift shaft.

'Let's get out of here,' Casey decided. 'They'll see us as soon as they come up the stairs.'

Carefully, she felt her way to a set of double doors. They led to one of the corridors that would once have run down the ship. As the double doors creaked open, Casey held her breath.

A cool breeze reached down the passage towards her, and she inched her way down, running her fingers along a panelled wall.

Halfway along, the corridor was amputated. A cliff: rags of carpet ripped away, sliced steel shining bright in the moonlight, the wash of the waves in the distance, 50 feet below.

She crouched down, in case anyone was looking up at the ship, but the seashore below was empty. Casey could see tracks in the mud, leading away from the *Beauvallet*. The fishing boat had gone.

Without speaking, they edged back along the corridor and into one of the cabins. It was small, this room: only a few feet spare around a dusty bed. The mirrored cupboards were at the foot of the bed again, but these mirrors had distorted in the damp, reflecting a twisted view of the room as Casey stared round.

Sliding doors had led out onto the balcony once, but the glass had been smashed long ago. Two beach chairs sat there incongruously in front of white steel railings. A blue hammock dangled gloomily, and the *Tephi* slumped in the distance.

Casey peered over the edge.

'Maybe we should jump?' she whispered. 'The mud might be soft.'

'You'd break your legs.'

Casey could hear movements in the ship. They would check the Emperor Suite first, she thought dully, then launch a proper search as soon as they realised all the girls had gone.

'We've got to get out of here,' she said.

'How?'

Silence. Casey's head jerked up. 'How would they evacuate this ship?' she whispered.

She yanked open the fitted cupboard at the end of the bed. Clipped into the cupboard under a sheet of perspex was a neat piece of paper. *The Beauvallet: How to evacuate*, it announced. Casey scanned it quickly and turned to Ed, eyes gleaming in the dark.

'Follow me,' she hissed.

There was a creak from the double doors at the top of the corridor.

'We're too late,' Ed whispered. 'They're coming.'

It sounded like several men, searching in a team. They could hear them moving quickly, throwing open the doors to the cabins one by one. After each door opened, there was a pause, just long enough to check the bathroom, behind the bed, in the cupboards. Then onwards.

'There's nowhere to hide in here.' Casey's eyes raced around the room. 'Shit. *Shit.*'

'Is there anything we can use for a weapon?' Ed muttered. He was searching for any escape: a loose ceiling panel, access to the ventilation system, anything.

Casey's eyes fell on the rotting hammock out on the balcony, and she leapt forward. 'Quickly, Ed,' she whispered.

Her hands shook as she untied the hammock from its attachments and knotted both ends to the lowest white railing. As soon as the hammock was tied there, she threw the bulk of the material out over the side of the ship.

'Here.' She climbed over the railings. 'Come on.'

In the darkness, the smooth steel of the *Beauvallet* fell away beneath her, no footholds, no handholds, nothing. Casey's vision blurred. She forced herself to look down. The hammock dangled three feet below the edge of the balcony. Casey hesitated, testing it with her weight.

'It won't hold both of us,' Ed warned. 'The ropes are fraying already.'

'Come on, Ed.'

'It'll kill us both,' he whispered urgently. 'I'll hand myself in. I'll . . .'

'We have to stick together.' In her head, Casey saw the hammock creaking, ripping, bodies plunging into the void. She forced the thoughts away.

Ed straightened up. 'I'll jump, Casey. You hide in the hammock. They won't find you.'

'If you jump, I'll jump too.' Casey's whisper was fierce. 'Try it, Ed. It's worth a shot.'

'Casey . . .'

She could hear the men getting closer, quieter now. They were thorough, these men. Hunters, trained.

Ed had a foot on the railing.

'Hurry' – as loud as she dared. 'Now!'

He vaulted over the railing, scrambling down into the hammock. For a second, it swayed beneath their weight, and Casey felt the emptiness gape below them as the material stretched and sighed. Fifty feet of nothing, right down to the beach. Casey imagined the hammock ripping, shredding. Their bodies slipping into space and falling, and falling, and falling.

It held, for now.

There wasn't enough space for both of them. Ed ended up half on top of her, his face a few inches from hers.

'I've been' – a sketch of a smile – 'on better holiday breaks.'

Despite herself, Casey grinned back at him. 'Next year will be better, I promise you. Somewhere quiet.'

She couldn't bear to look up at her hastily tied knots on the railings. She imagined them pulling apart gradually, shifting inch by inch.

She clenched her fists in the silence.

Cat quiet, the door to the cabin opened. A man walked in, carefully. He hesitated, as if he could sense the recent movement in the room.

The footsteps moved towards the bathroom. A cupboard door opened and closed. More steps. He must be by the broken windows, thought Casey. Just a few inches away.

Ed's eyes were boring into her. Casey couldn't breathe. And just then, she felt the hammock give slightly.

Go away – in her head it was a scream, quite primitive. *Get away from us! Go away!*

Another step.

From the room, all he would see was the ends of the hammock. In the dark, it could look like a few shreds of material just hanging from the railings. It might look like nothing at all.

Another step.

Silence.

'Jeetu.' A shout from down the corridor. Dylan's voice.

Abruptly, the footsteps swung away, retreated across the cabin. A heavy door slammed.

Casey let out her breath in one long stream. For a second, she felt hot tears spring in her eyes.

'Stay still,' Ed whispered.

Very cautiously, he raised his head to look into the room before putting a hand up to the railing. His other hand reached out to Casey's wrist, gripping her hard.

'Don't move,' he whispered. 'I can still hear them in the corridor.'

Casey peered out of the hammock, across the dark sprawl of the beach to the *Tephi*, dead in the mud. A wisp of wind crept round the ship, sending a shudder through the hammock. At last, Ed inched himself upright.

'I think they've gone,' he whispered. 'I haven't heard them for a while.'

Cautiously, Casey reached up to the railing with her spare hand. Slowly, very carefully, she pulled herself upwards, jerking as little as possible. One foot on the railing, then the other. The relief.

Ed waited until she was safe on the balcony, and then he pulled himself up over the rail with a quick athleticism.

Casey leaned briefly against the wall of the cabin, then straightened up.

'Let's go.'

As they reached the end of the corridor, Casey could hear men, loud in the staircase to her left. There seemed to be voices all over the ship, other men talking loudly below.

Casey nodded to her right, and dodged across the lobby, Ed close behind. She edged the door open, very slowly, waiting for any sound. The light from the lobby below spilled up the stairs. Casey hesitated, and then turned towards the flight of stairs leading up. Ed caught her sleeve, nodding downwards, vigorously.

No, Casey gestured. *This way.*

There's no way out, that way, she thought. *Trapped like rats.*

Ed stared at her for a beat, and then moved noiselessly up the stairs. According to the map of the ship, Casey remembered, on every floor there was a door from the staircase to a lobby in the middle of the ship. There were identical staircases on each side of the ship, both with doors onto the lobby.

They climbed three flights, Casey counting in her head. She stopped at a door, standing there for a long moment, waiting for any sound on the other side of the door.

Silence.

Casey glanced across at Ed, eyebrows raised.

Shall we?

A nod.

But as she was about to move, she heard the shriek of a door far below from the ground-floor lobby. The footsteps drew nearer, turning corner after corner with careless speed. Ed shoved open the door to the central lobby. It creaked, just too loud, and they heard the footsteps skid to a halt.

Ed pushed Casey through the doorway.

A shout in Bengali behind them.

'Run,' shouted Ed. 'Run.'

Casey rammed the door closed behind them, anything to slow their pursuers, and sprinted down the corridor, fear speeding her like flames.

Deck, read a sign, and she burst out into the night air.

'Careful.' Ed grabbed her arm. The deck wasn't wide here, and the railings had been stripped away. To her left was a sheer drop down to the beach, the deck tilting away as the *Beauvallet* sagged to one side. Casey felt dizzy, as if she might step into emptiness, almost on purpose.

'This way,' she whispered.

There were shouts behind them, as they edged out along the deck. The men were searching the lobbies, racing up the stairs, getting closer and closer. They were relentless. Confident. Killers.

'Where are we going?' Ed murmured.

'Here.' Casey stopped. They were next to one of the big orange lifeboats, hanging lazily between two steel davits. 'Get in.'

'Casey.' He turned to her. 'Are you mad?'

He stared up at the lifeboat. It looked like a solid orange bullet, the boat's hard top-cover almost the same shape as its toughened keel. You could survive for days in one of these, out in the ocean.

The voices were getting closer. Any moment now, the men would burst through the steel door, and out onto the deck.

'Quickly!' Casey pushed Ed towards the lifeboat's hatch. 'Strap yourself in.'

'How the hell do you know it will work?'

'I don't,' she almost grinned at him. 'Hurry.'

They threw themselves through the hatch, just as the door smashed open behind them.

'Go!' Casey yelled. She pulled some shoulder straps around herself, dragging them together, hitting buttons on a dashboard almost at random. Outside the lifeboat, there were shouts, and then the sudden, shattering blast of a gun.

'Hang on,' she screamed, and pulled a lever.

The lifeboat reacted at once, coming to life with an animal surge. Moving fluidly, the two cranes lifted the lifeboat sideways and out over the side of the *Beauvallet*. Casey's stomach turned as the boat plunged over the edge of the deck like a runaway roller coaster, the cranes releasing, the wires screaming through pulleys.

It's broken, thought Casey. *They've stripped out everything important. It's broken, and we're going to die.*

Ed was wrestling into straps as the lifeboat roared through the air.

'Hold on,' Casey screamed. 'Hold on!'

A smash, and everything went dark.

50

Casey opened her eyes, slowly. There was blood in her mouth, she realised blearily.

Where am I?

She blinked carefully.

What happened?

There was a sort of light, trickling towards her. Straps were cutting into her chest.

What are those?

No answer.

I want to sleep. I want to . . .

A slow fade. And then, abruptly, from somewhere far below consciousness.

Don't sleep. No. no. NO. Stay awake.

You must.

Staccato thoughts. Discordant as an orchestra tuning.

She could see her hands, she realised. She concentrated hard, and the fingers moved. *That's OK, then.* Thoughts were settling, snow in a globe.

It was very dark, in here, wherever it was. A sort of peace. She tried to look around. *My neck hurts.* For a second, she almost relaxed. *Someone will be along to help, I'm sure. Just wait. Be still. And breathe.*

Like a curtain going up in a theatre, it snapped back to her.

In a lifeboat. We fell. Ed. Oh God, where is he? The lifeboat swam around her, and Casey kicked out, trying to scramble loose of the safety harness. It gave way sharply.

Ed was a few feet away, still fastened in, and Casey crawled over to him on bruised elbows and knees.

He had hit his head as he fell, she saw. A trickle of blood curled down from his eyebrow. His eyes were closed, head lolling.

'Ed!'

All the first-aid lessons, those boring hours in a stuffy room, raced through her mind. But none of the careful rules would matter if they didn't escape right now. Because it would only take seconds for the men to race down through the *Beauvallet*, and out onto the beach. And then—

Casey tugged Ed hard.

Nothing.

'Ed,' Casey whispered urgently in his ear. 'If you don't move now, it's over. They'll catch us.'

She shook him. Carefully at first, and then with a sudden violence. The lifeboat rocked to and fro with an odd sort of movement.

'Ed, wake up!'

Ed came to, veering into consciousness like a car skidding on a road. His eyes opened, focused slowly on hers.

'We have to run,' she said. 'I'm so sorry. But we have to run right now, Ed.'

His limbs jerked. She dragged at the straps, trying to disentangle him. His movements became grew more coordinated.

'You run, Casey,' he managed. 'I'll be right behind you.'

'Never,' she said. 'I'm not going to leave you.'

'Casey . . .'

She was yanking at his harness, her fingers tearing at the clasps. And suddenly, he was falling free, struggling towards the hatch.

She scrambled after him, and stared around. Outside the lifeboat, the beach was oddly still, the moonlight a lace frill over strange shapeless shadows. In the darkness, the *Beauvallet* loomed above.

Casey looked down. The lifeboat had landed in a pool of tidal mud, deep enough to float. The pool had saved them in the fall, but to get away, they would have to jump down into the dark liquid mud. She couldn't make out how deep it was.

Casey stared around. *Which way to go?*

A noise came from the ship behind her, and her mind ricocheted through the options, a panicking pinball, thoughts fragmenting as she reached for them.

No way out. It was that endless nightmare, the terrible fear of the hunted. *They're coming, they're coming, they're coming.*

'We'll have to jump.' Ed's voice broke into her thoughts.

'Yes.'

Casey heard him take a breath and jump down into the mud.

Watch out for the quicksand. The words of the hustler on the beach ringing in her ears, Casey pushed herself off the edge.

Without a splash, the mud swallowed her up, smooth and overwhelming. Casey couldn't kick, couldn't swim, couldn't float. *Can't breathe.* She scrabbled for a foothold. Her legs slipped away as she lashed out. Like something living, the mud swamped her mouth and her eyes, blinding, choking, drowning her. She surfaced once into the darkness, and screamed as the mud pulled her down again.

I'm going to die.

No. No.

Yes.

Casey lashed out, the nightmare real. Thrashed around for something to grip, something to hold, anything to survive. Nothing. Her nails clawed the mud, running out of air, running out of time. Lungs screaming. Flashes before her eyes.

Her arm reached out into the night air, one last time, and someone grabbed her, and dragged her out onto the bank.

51

It was Ed.

Casey lay on the mud, fighting for air. Ed was lying on his back beside her, his chest heaving.

'Thank you,' she gasped.

He turned his head, face dark with mud. 'No problem.'

More sounds came from the *Beauvallet*, and Casey was on her feet.

'We've got to move.' The panic flooded back. 'Quickly. They're coming.'

She took a step away from the lifeboat, and the mud dragged her down. Another step, and another, and already it was exhausting.

She forced away the horror.

'There's no way round the *Beauvallet* to that path,' said Ed. 'Not before those men get down the stairs. We have to try to escape down the beach.'

Beyond the *Beauvallet*, vast blocks of steel were scattered across the mudflat, as if by a giant's rage. A propeller, cast away into the sand, was a colossal metal flower.

'Here.' Ed pulled Casey down behind a huge section of the *Beauvallet*'s hull. 'Get down.'

They crouched down behind the lump of steel, and then peered back at the ship.

Men appeared at the top of the ramp leading down from the *Beauvallet*'s hull. They were shouting, waving torches. Casey could make out the silhouettes of Raz and Dylan.

Looking for footprints, she thought.

Unerringly, the torch beam swung round in their direction. The voices quietened.

Now the torches started towards the lifeboat, sweeping backwards and forwards over the mud as they did. They were not rushing, these men.

The lights came closer, flickering to and fro. A low call floated across the beach, met by a few sharp words.

They came nearer.

'They're coming for us,' Casey gasped. 'We can't . . .'

'Stay still,' whispered Ed.

One torch beam crept closer. It flashed across the big propeller, gleamed over some old crates, and then stopped on the big chunk of hull. The torchlight shone straight into Casey's eyes, dazzling her.

'Run,' Ed cried.

As soon as they moved there were bellows, and the crack of a gun.

The mud was hellish as she and Ed struggled away along the beach. Every time she took a step the mud sucked her down, insatiable. A step, a step, and another step and she tripped, floundering in the slime.

Ed dragged her up. 'Come on.'

She threw herself forward again, and the mud took hold, each movement painfully slow, every step a pointless battle. 'We can't get away from them. There's nowhere to go . . .'

In the dark the beach seemed endless. A few hundred yards away, Casey could see the next huge ship, slumped deep in the mud, but she would never reach it. Never. And even if she could, what then? She gasped for air, lungs screaming as a bullet ricocheted off a shipping container sagging on its side.

'Hurry, Casey.' Ed pulled at her arm. 'Come on!'

She dragged herself on, the animal at the back of the herd that knows it's the one to die. Lumps of metal lay half-buried in the mud and ripped at her legs as she lurched past. The gun blasted again.

The men were chasing them, excitement in their voices, almost glee as they scrambled through the mud. They were so much faster, inexhaustible.

The sand was firmer here, and for a few blissful seconds, Casey could run, feet slapping, freed from the oozing grasp. But then she plunged into the mud again.

The men were getting closer.

'We're never going to make it,' she screamed.

There was the sudden judder of an outboard motor, just out to sea. A boat racing along in the shallows.

'Help!' Casey screamed, not caring who was steering it. 'Please help us.'

The little boat turned sharply, heading to the beach. Past thinking, she dragged herself towards it.

'Careful, Casey.' Ed grabbed at her arm. 'We don't know . . .'

'Casey!' The yell reached out across the water. 'Come on!'

'It's Hessa,' shouted Casey. 'And the girls from the ship. Oh, thank God . . .'

52

Hessa grinned down at them.

'Guess you needed saving.' She was almost laughing, a triumphant gleam in her eye.

Romida and the two other girls were sitting in the front of the boat, huddled up in the cool night breeze, Romida's eyes shining with excitement. The little fishing boat was chugging north.

'All three girls wanted to come back for you,' said Hessa.

Ed and Casey had collapsed in the bottom of the boat, unable to sit up. Lying on her back, Casey stared up at the stars.

'Tell them thank you,' she managed.

They had come in under fire. The fishing boat was a big target for the men on the shore, and the bullets sent up explosions of water all around them.

Hessa had ignored it all, steering the boat straight to the beach. She and Romida had grabbed Casey's arm and hauled her on board with startling strength, almost capsizing the little boat in their urgency.

Ed had scrambled onto the boat, half-pushing it round in the rush before Hessa rammed the outboard motor to its full speed, the little boat juddering away over the waves, painfully slowly.

'Never again,' Casey's voice came out of the night.

'You always say that,' said Hessa.

Closer to the shore, Hessa could see a boat cruising to and fro. They had a huge spotlight hooked up to the bow, searing back and forth across the waves. There would probably be men waiting back at the pier, too. Veering from the beam of the spotlight, Hessa turned the little fishing boat further out to sea and headed south. Down this way, several huge ships lay anchored far out in the ocean, slowly swinging round with the currents. They were waiting for the highest tides, when they too would be rammed up onto the Bhatiari flats.

Other ships – newer vessels – were waiting to sail into the port of Chittagong. As she steered, Hessa kept a wary eye on the vast ships, in case the monsters started to move. She caught Romida's eye, and smiled.

Slowly, the fishing boat made its way down the shoreline. Eastward, the lights of Chittagong glowed orange.

Finally, as the sky began to lighten, Hessa steered closer to the shore. At last, she saw what she was looking for. Patenga beach, just south of Chittagong, close to where the sweep of the Karnaphuli river meets the sea.

It was a broad, ugly beach. Busy, even at this time of the day, with bright plastic chairs and pushy hustlers. Huge planes from the Shah Amanat airport roared past every few minutes. As Hessa grounded the little boat on the dirty sand, two boys on skinny horses cantered up.

'You ride?'

'Not now,' Hessa smiled.

They hurried up the beach, leaving the boat bobbing in the shallows. The boys on the horses would make the dinghy theirs within minutes.

They fell into two taxis, which crawled through traffic back to the hotel. Dropping with exhaustion, they stumbled into the hotel. As they banged on the hotel room door, it swung open as if the occupant had been waiting just the other side. And there was Miranda, gripping the baby with one arm, mobile phone in her hand.

'Thank God,' she said.

The three girls from the *Tephi* stood awkwardly just inside the hotel room as Casey told Miranda about the *Beauvallet* in half-sentences.

'You stink,' Miranda observed helpfully, at the end.

'Did the girls from the building get to the safe house OK?'

'Yes,' said Miranda. 'Despite my driving. I dropped off Layla too, and Savannah went over as soon as she'd handed over Poppy.'

Savannah had stayed in the hotel room with the tiny baby all night. 'I miss all the fun,' she had grumbled as they set off to the pier. 'But I wouldn't sleep anyway, waiting for you to get back.'

'Oh, thank God,' said Casey, feeling a flood of relief.

'How,' asked Ed, 'the hell are we going to get out of here? Dylan and his lot will have the whole of Chittagong sewn up by now. They'll be turning the city upside down.'

'Did they actually see your faces? With any luck, they won't have worked out who we are yet.'

'But how are we going to get Poppy back to England?' Ed asked. 'We can't possibly leave her.'

Miranda had handed the tiny girl over to him as soon as he walked in. She had cuddled into him, snug in a little pink blanket, tiny hands in fists.

'Don't worry,' said Miranda. She was looking at her watch. 'We're all flying out of Chittagong in a few hours.'

'But how can we get a passport for Poppy?' Ed's voice rose. 'We still don't know who's been handing out the passports since William Cavendish retired.'

'No,' agreed Miranda. 'But it's far too dangerous for us to stay out here. Raz didn't tell Casey how long it would take for him to bring a passport for Poppy, and waiting is too dangerous now. We're too compromised.'

Casey was looking stubborn. 'I could stay though. I might be able to . . .'

'No.' Miranda's voice was firm. 'We're going home.'

'But' – in her exhaustion, Casey was intractable – 'we may never be able to work it out properly. Raz had never heard of Greystone, and Dylan was contemptuous of him. There's someone else in control, and we might never find out who it is from the UK.'

'I don't care,' said Miranda.

'I need to go to the safe house,' said Casey. 'I want to talk to all the women.'

'It's dangerous,' said Miranda.

'I have to. We need to get Romida and the other girls over there anyway.'

'I'll come too,' added Hessa.

'I've been speaking to Dash,' Miranda went on. 'The *Post*'s Christmas appeal is going to fund a safe house for the girls from the *Beauvallet*.'

'I suppose that's something.' Casey was still looking mutinous.

Every year, the *Post* picked three charities, and the journalists spent a day drinking brandy and eating mince pies, while readers rang up to donate their winter fuel allowances. The editor inevitably ended up being harangued for twenty minutes by a Mrs Pegg from Harrogate about moving the crossword from page 22 to 23; Casey once got quite a good story out of a Mr Ball from Colchester about a dubious local planning officer.

As Ed stood up to head for the bathroom, there was a knock at the door. Ed tensed, eyes flickering around the room. 'Don't answer it,' he ordered.

But Miranda was untangling the locks and bolts, and then the door swung open.

Hessa grimaced as she looked up. 'What is he ...'

'I can't believe,' the man said, 'that I am doing this.'

It was Gabriel Bantham, stepping gingerly into the room.

'Hello, Gabriel.' Casey stepped forward, a cocktail-party smile on her face. 'How nice to see you.'

Bantham's mouth twisted into a smile as he looked at her. 'And how lovely it is to see you again too, Miss Benedict.'

His light brown hair was smoothly in place, the shoes glossily polished. Even in the heat of Chittagong, Bantham wore a cream linen suit, a square of blue silk peeping out of his breast pocket. In his left hand he held a passport.

'For a Pippa Lancaster,' he said. 'Who I gather will disappear soon after she gets back to the UK. Daughter of a Miranda Lancaster.'

'That's what my passport says,' Miranda shrugged.

They shook hands, Bantham holding on to Casey's for just a second too long.

'Her date of birth is backdated,' he said. 'Some airlines won't fly newborns, apparently.'

Casey had called him, as soon as Poppy was born. And he'd understood, without being told, that this would buy her silence for ever.

'They'll know though,' he had said. 'I can do it, but I can't do it without being caught.'

'But this way' – and there was almost a laugh in her voice – 'you will be the hero of the hour.'

'You can't do that,' he had said. 'You can't make that happen.'

'Every story needs a hero,' said Casey. 'And this one hasn't got one yet.'

'But it's illegal.'

'Not,' she said, 'until we say so.'

He could hear the icy arrogance in her voice. Bantham had been working in London when the *Telegraph* faced down the prosecution bosses, after brazenly sending tens of thousands of pounds to an anonymous Swiss bank account. *Go on*, they dared the politicians. *Arrest us. Just try it.* But the money was for the disc that contained evidence of the MPs' expenses scandal, and by then the public was deep in a raging fury over duckhouses and moats and tennis courts and swimming pools. Quietly, the police looked the other way.

'If I did help you, we'd have to have met somewhere before,' Bantham had bargained. 'Not in DC.'

'Never in DC.' Casey buried the Four Seasons smoothly. 'Somewhere else, many years ago.'

'You knew I would be able to get this baby out of Bangladesh.' He was thinking aloud.

'I'm turning to you because you're the only person who can possibly help us,' said Casey.

Bantham thought about it for a moment. 'What happens to the baby when you get home?' he asked.

Casey had asked Heather about the theoretical registration of a newborn in the UK. 'There is a system for women who insist on having babies outside of the hospital system,' the health editor had said thoughtfully. 'Free-birthing, they call it. Not my cup of tea, but each to their own. There is a way of registering births after that. I can find out.'

'We obviously can't rely on the clinic's systems any more,' said Casey. 'But we will manage, don't worry about that.'

'All right,' Bantham had agreed, in the end. 'All right.'

Now Casey looked at him straight. 'Thank you,' she said, 'for doing this.'

He shrugged. 'Maybe I needed ...' He stopped talking. 'Maybe you coming to Washington wasn't the worst thing that could have happened to me.'

There was a glimmer of a smile in her eyes, and a second later, it almost echoed in his.

'And you promise ...'

'I promise,' she said. 'It would hardly help me now, anyway.'

'No,' he agreed. 'That much is true.'

Bantham handed over the passport now. 'I'll come back in a few hours,' he promised. 'Get you to the airport.'

After he had gone, Casey stood up. 'I have to go.'

Hessa stood too. 'I'll go and find a couple of tuk-tuks.'

'Be careful,' was all that Miranda said. 'And shower first.'

Outside, a few minutes later, the blazing heat reached down into Casey's lungs, choking her. Dust rose from the road, whirling in the hot wind. She felt exhausted, bruised by the fear of the night.

Hessa and Casey sat in an tired silence as the tuk-tuk made its way along the crowded streets, past rows of sagging shacks. A second tuk-tuk, carrying the three girls, puttered behind.

Idle dogs watched as their tuk-tuk creaked past, its motor like an angry wasp in a jar. Garlands of black wires criss-crossed the narrow street. There were street peddlers everywhere, crouching beside makeshift market stalls. Bags of crisps were carefully lined up under a tattered tarpaulin, next to stacks of oranges, or skinny, fatalistic chickens. Here and there, Casey saw trophies swiped – or sold on – from the refugee camps. A UNHCR blanket here, a Save the Children rucksack there. The black market always thrives.

On one corner, a small gang of street children waited patiently, nowhere better to be. A small boy, hair cropped close, held his little brother's hand, swiping at his nose with the other. There was an adult slump to the older boy's shoulders as he stood there in his ragged, oversized T-shirt.

As Casey watched, the boy glanced up, and she saw his expression shift from childish interest to calculation in a split second. Then the tuk-tuk pulled away, leaving the boys far behind.

Finally, they pulled up next to an ugly, low-slung building, and the driver gestured. They climbed out, Romida's eyes wide and thoughtful.

A girl in a sari opened the door cautiously. She relaxed when she saw Casey.

'I messaged Savannah,' Casey explained to Hessa. 'They knew we were coming.'

The girl led them down a tiled corridor, cool after the scorch of the street. In a blur, Savannah burst through a door. 'They made it.' She dragged Casey into a hug. 'You made it. They got out. You found Romida!'

Casey couldn't help but smile in the face of Savannah's boisterous enthusiasm.

'Where are the other women?' Casey asked.

'This way.'

They followed Savannah to a large, patchily painted blue room, with high ceilings and a white-tiled floor.

The women from the shipyard were sitting in a rough circle in the middle of the room. Layla was sitting to one side, cross-legged, talking to one of them. They glanced up as Casey and Hessa walked in. Casey looked around the room, and spotted Khadija, head bowed, stitching two small pieces of fabric together. She looked very young. Thirteen probably, Casey remembered with a jolt.

A row of iron beds ran down each side of the room, the white sheets carefully folded. A whiff of disinfectant in the air hinted at hospitals, while a ceiling fan purred overhead. The room looked out onto a tiny garden, the green almost a shock to Casey's eyes.

Layla stood up. She nodded to Hessa and Casey. 'You made it then,' she smiled briefly.

'How are they?' asked Casey.

'So-so,' said Layla. 'Shocked, mostly.'

'How many of them are pregnant?' Hessa asked bluntly.

'All the women from the shipyard are pregnant,' Layla said carefully. 'Savannah is arranging for those girls to travel back to the camps and their families, if that is what they want. But first she wants to make sure they don't go straight back to where they used to live, because they might be targeted again. The charity is helping Shamshun – Romida's mother – move to a different sector of the camp, for example. It might help.' Layla shrugged. 'It might not.'

Moving cautiously, the three girls from the *Tephi* sat down on the edge of the circle. There was a murmur of welcome.

'They only operated on one of them – Tasmina – three weeks ago,' Layla said flatly. 'She wants to get back to the camp as soon as possible. And, well . . .'

'Abortion is mainly illegal in Bangladesh,' Savannah broke in. 'But they have other techniques, which work early on.' She shrugged.

'It's her choice,' said Hessa.

For a split second, Casey thought about the would-be parents, somewhere thousands of miles away. Desperate. Desperate for this, this end of a dream, this end of a nightmare. She pushed the thought away.

'Can I speak to Romida?' she asked. 'I know she may be exhausted . . .'

Layla tilted her head, instinctively protective. 'I'll ask her.'

Casey watched as Layla crossed the room to crouch down by Romida, introducing herself. They chatted, and Romida turned to stare at Casey, the briefest of smiles flickering across her face as she nodded.

'It's OK,' Layla called across. 'She'll talk.'

Casey kneeled down beside Romida, smiling. Romida grinned back with a quick, confident charm. Already she looked quite different to the haunted girl on the ship. There was a toughness in her eyes, and in the tilt of her jaw. Looking at her, Casey could see the girl who had fought the soldiers in Rakhine with all her strength. She could see the echo of Shamshun, too, the woman who had walked for miles through the forests, fighting for her daughter, fighting to survive.

You never know how you can run, until you run for your daughter.

'You said you had met my mother,' said Romida, as Layla translated smoothly.

'Shamshun,' said Casey. 'She will be so excited to see you, Romida.'

Romida's eyes lit up. 'I cannot wait to see her.' Her eyes clouded slightly. 'But she will be so angry with me ... I should never have gone ...'

'Of course she is not angry,' Hessa interrupted. 'And Jamalida will be so pleased to see you, too.'

'Jamalida.' The memories filled Romida's eyes. 'I told them to wait for her, back in the camp. I told them she wouldn't be long ... I was so stupid.'

'Do you know the name of the men who snatched you from the camp?' Casey asked.

Romida's head sagged. 'Jeetu,' she said. 'He said his name was Jeetu, but that might be a lie. I thought he was so nice. And then he hit me. He hit me hard. It hurt. It hurts.'

The bruises still showed on her face.

'Do you remember anyone else?'

'There was another man, but I never knew his name. He told me he had a gun, That he would shoot me if I made a sound. But I didn't care. I shouted, I tried to throw myself out of the car. I screamed. I said I didn't care what they did to me, that they could kill me if they wanted, but I would not go. I would not go.'

The will to live gleamed in Romida's eyes: the ruthless, absolute determination to survive. But then her shoulders slumped. 'Jeetu told me they would go to my mother's tent. They said they would go to her, and rape her … And kill her … And there was nothing I could … I knew they would … I stopped fighting then. I didn't know what to do.'

Romida paused, gazing at the whirl of the ceiling fan.

'They dragged me out of the car.' Romida's voice was empty when she spoke again. 'We were in some street, I don't know where. People were staring. And then they looked away. They knew not to get involved. They knew, and they looked away …' Her eyes filled with tears, but she rubbed them back, almost angry. 'They dragged me into a house. It smelled. It was disgusting. I didn't know what would happen, or where they were taking me, or where I was. I thought they were taking me to work in a brothel … And then Jeetu forced something over my mouth, and everything just … faded. When I woke up, I was on that ship. With two other girls.'

'I am so sorry,' Casey murmured. 'So sorry.'

Tasmina interrupted, gesturing angrily. Romida flinched as she listened.

'Tasmina is saying' – Layla spoke carefully – 'that they never saw the babies, that they didn't know what happened to them. And then Zohra … Zohra …'

Tasmina was crying, pushing away one of the other girls as she tried to hug her.

'How can people do this?' Layla translated impassively, as Romida blazed with a blistering rage. 'How dare they? How dare they do this to us? We are people.'

And Casey thought of the shrug from the world. Hundreds of thousands of people in a bleak refugee camp, and a casual 'that will do'. And soon, so soon, they would be trying to send the refugees back to Bangladesh, where the murders and the gang rapes could start all over again. Casey felt that burn of anger, for Romida, for all the girls with no future. *It's not fair*: a childish whine for such an injustice.

'But I am free now,' Layla translated as Romida straightened up. 'I have survived. And now I will go back to the camp' – a wry smile spread across her face – 'and I will see my mother, and Jamalida, and everyone. And one day, Jamalida and I will be tailors together, as we always said.'

Khadija leaned forward and handed Romida two pieces of fabric. Her eyes met Casey's defiantly. 'I am not afraid,' she said.

Casey spoke to all the women, one by one, taking careful notes. Some of them described being taken off the ship, to a clinic with basic medical facilities. Driven in the back of what might have been an old truck, they thought. Khadija – the brightest, the angriest – swore about the men, using words that Layla refused to translate.

'They could have been taken to anywhere in Chittagong,' Casey said in an aside to Hessa. 'And the surrounding area.'

'The thing is,' Hessa stumbled, 'many of these women might not even know what IVF is. You know what Savannah said about that footballer. It's hard to get information in those camps, with those rates of illiteracy.'

Casey dug out a photograph of Dr Greystone without much hope, but the women shook their heads.

'Rich Bangladeshis typically travel to Singapore or Bangkok for IVF,' murmured Hessa. 'In fact, the wealthiest would travel abroad for most medical issues. They don't have much faith in Dhaka's hospitals.'

'All you needed here were the basic requirements for the frozen embryo transfers,' said Casey. 'Presumably Greystone could coordinate the egg extraction and fertilisation anywhere in the world. They just had to ensure the carrier woman was at the right point in her cycle.'

They said goodbye to the women, Romida giving Casey a sudden bright grin.

On the way back to the hotel, Casey leaned back in the tuk-tuk. 'We still don't know the scale of it,' she said. 'Were those women the only ones that Greystone's lot has seized? Or are there other sites, scattered around the country? How much is he pulling in from this scheme?'

'Emily would be able to tell us exact prices,' said Hessa. 'Surrogacy varies from country to country. In the US, it's about $150,000 all in. It's less in Kenya. In the Ukraine, it's more like $40,000. Some countries have more delays. The clinics vary too. Some clinics offer several rounds; others offer certain guarantees. Your money back if you don't get a baby. Then there are the legal costs for getting a baby back to the UK – or wherever. They vary dramatically too. Given that Greystone seems to be able to get the kids back to England fairly straightforwardly without any waiting lists, he's probably able to charge quite a premium even though he's operating under the radar. Let's say $25,000 per child.'

'God.' Casey put her head in her hands. 'The mathematics are barbaric.'

'And how many a year?' Hessa persisted. 'If there were fifteen women at the shipyard when we got there … There could be, say, twenty babies a year.'

'That's half a million dollars a year from the shipyard women alone,' calculated Casey. 'And Greystone has access to an endless stream of desperate women on Harley Street. There could be other sites in Bangladesh, or anywhere else, too.'

'There may even be word of mouth back in London,' said Hessa. 'Although, as the Burton-Smiths show, if you don't want to know, they certainly won't spell it out to you.'

'He would be making millions every year,' said Casey. 'How old was Vivienne Hargreaves's son? Three? It could have been running for years.'

'I wonder what happened to the Rohingya women after they gave birth,' said Hessa.

'I suppose they would just have another baby,' said Casey. 'Or …'

Hessa turned her face away.

'I wonder if one of the women from the shipyard ended up in the garment factory?' Casey speculated. 'And that's how she managed to get the message into the skirt Cressida found.'

'Maybe,' muttered Hessa. 'Maybe she wasn't able to get pregnant, so they shunted her out to the factories. I suppose we'll never be able to find out.'

'Probably not,' said Casey. 'Any attempt to find her would put her in such danger.'

'But she was so brave,' Hessa clenched her fists. 'She was so very brave.'

They were both silent with exhaustion by the time they got back to the hotel. Miranda was waiting, bags packed, with Bantham and Ed and the baby.

'Hurry,' she said.

Bantham had come in a diplomatic car. 'I told the High Commissioner I needed to meet up with a few old contacts,' he said. 'He's already suspicious.'

He gave them a lift to the airport all the same.

'This is the bit that they will really get me on,' Bantham almost laughed. 'Inappropriate use of a government car.'

'Get out of the country as soon as possible,' Miranda said to him briefly. 'The Commission may not be safe either.'

Miranda jiggled the baby in the sling almost instinctively, leaning away from the tiny weight. Casey watched the pair of them, a couple of places back in the queue. Casually bored, Miranda handed over the passport for a small Miss Pippa Lancaster, and the border guards shrugged them through.

53

They bounced through Dhaka, Qatar, and landed home. The English spring waited for them: the tulips red and gold in the parks, and the blossom blowing down the streets, confetti for a thousand brides.

As their car drew up at the *Post*, Dash and Ross hovered at the entrance. A stern young woman stood beside them.

'Got her from that nanny place.' Ross jerked his thumb. 'The one the Royals use.'

The woman's mouth tightened. 'I'm Nina Reynolds,' she said to Miranda.

'It would be very useful if you could take over with Poppy for a short while,' Dash said hastily. 'We need Miranda's help on a project ... Urgently.'

'Of course.' Nina Reynolds spoke with precision, neat in her uniform. 'I understand that a room has been booked in the hotel across the road.'

'I booked it.' Janet, the Editor's personal assistant, appeared. 'It's all done.'

'Marvellous.' Miranda deposited Poppy into Nina's arms like a parcel. 'I'll – um – pop round in a bit, Nina.'

'I'll show you to the hotel,' said Janet. 'This way.'

Hessa watched as the little group disappeared across the street. Poppy was crying. 'She'll be OK, won't she?'

'She'll be fine,' promised Casey. 'Much better than she would be with us, anyway. Come on.'

They all crowded into the investigations room, Dash dragging in chairs from the main room. Ross stood by the door, one eye on his newsroom.

'Where have you got to?' Dash asked briskly.

'Savannah is organising everything for the safe house back in Bangladesh,' said Casey. 'But whoever is in charge of operations in London will know that someone got to the *Beauvallet*, and brought the women out. So they'll either be seeking revenge, or panicking.'

'I'd assume these people were dangerous,' said Miranda. 'Not panicking.'

'We're sending funds out to Savannah's organisation.' Dash was tapping his pen on his notepad. 'The owners okayed that.'

Just as the Editor gets his definite article, so too in a newspaper do the owners.

'But we still don't know' – Casey was fiddling with some treasury tags – 'who is behind it all.'

'Greystone, surely?' Dash looked up, surprised.

'Raz had never heard his name,' said Casey. 'Dylan didn't behave as if Greystone was his boss. There is somebody else.'

'And did you find out who that might be while you were in Chittagong?' Dash asked briskly.

'No.' Casey was staring at the wall behind his head. 'We never got anywhere near him.'

'And can you think of any way of getting to that person?'

'No,' Casey admitted. 'Not immediately.'

'Well. There we go.' Dash turned to Miranda, trying to move the conversation forward.

'I wonder,' Miranda pondered, 'when Greystone's people will start telling the prospective parents that the women have gone missing in Bangladesh? Presumably, the parents whose surrogates were pregnant will all go into meltdown.'

'Honestly.' Hessa dropped her head into her hands. 'What a mess.'

'If this gang hold their nerve,' Casey persisted, 'they can get things back to normal in a few months' time. It's a setback, sure, but if we don't nail the key people now, they could just start up again. I imagine the parents don't know each other. So they could tell each set of parents, "Terribly sorry, tragic miscarriage. It can happen, we did warn you." And the parents won't know the difference.'

Casey imagined the pockets of grief all over the world. For all those lost children, who weren't lost at all, not really.

'And those kids just grow up in Bangladesh?' Dash asked. 'Abandoned children growing up in that little safe house? They'll never fit in.'

'I don't know.' Casey stared blankly at him. 'I don't know.'

'For fuck's sake.' Dash was angry, quite suddenly. 'How can we ever fix this, Casey? These are children. *Children*.'

The room fell into silence, startled by his anger. A glance flickered between Casey and Miranda.

'We could never just go in and fix it ...' Casey's words fell away. 'It's not how it works. We know that ...'

'We will think of a solution,' said Miranda. 'For the time being, those women need medical care and a decent place to live. They've got that. As things progress, we can see what the women want – for themselves and their children – and we can work that out.'

'It'll be a nightmare.'

'But for now' – Miranda spoke smoothly into the hush – 'the mastermind may think they can just get away with it. Carry on. Maybe even start up again, quite soon ...'

'So they won't necessarily panic,' Hessa chimed in evenly.

'We need to work as fast as possible.' Dash concentrated on the new problem. 'If they do work out that you're journalists, and who you are, you could be in serious danger, even in England.'

In the squash of the room, Hessa had her feet up on her suitcase. 'Why don't we start by getting Poppy to the Burton-Smiths? Then at least that is done.'

'I've already tried ringing,' said Casey. 'They didn't answer.'

Hessa gave her a quick glance. 'Isn't that a bit odd?'

'They'll call,' said Casey. 'We told them to get out of the house in Surrey, just in case.'

'Leaving everything else aside, we have to get on with publishing, Casey,' said Dash. 'Miranda's got the film of Greystone in his office. You've got info on the team out in Bangladesh. It's more than enough to be going on with.'

'No,' said Casey. 'You're going too fast. There's someone tying it all together.'

'This Dylan character.' Miranda spoke to Casey. 'He seemed to be in charge of operations in Bangladesh?'

'But what links Dylan and Greystone?' said Casey. 'How would they ever have come across each other? A Harley Street doctor and an Asia-based drug dealer. It doesn't make sense.'

'Maybe Greystone decided that he needed a contact in Bangladesh.' Dash thought it out. 'When his arrangements in Nepal – and wherever else he was operating before that – fell through. He put out feelers and came up with Dylan. We know that Vivienne Hargreaves had let it slip that her father was a diplomat out there, so Bangladesh became the obvious choice.'

'There's someone else.' Casey felt the certainty grow.

'You haven't even met Greystone,' said Dash. 'You don't know him.'

'Miranda?' said Casey. 'What did you make of him? From your memo, he didn't strike me as the sort of person who would be going out to these countries, to make these deals. He's far too urbane.'

Miranda shrugged. 'You can't tell from a few minutes.'

'You can tell a lot,' said Casey flatly. 'Especially you.'

'OK.' Miranda bit her lip. 'Probably not then. But Greystone could have any number of contacts who put him in touch with Dylan.'

'We have to start publishing as soon as possible,' Dash repeated. 'You know that, Casey. Especially with this story.'

Casey glowered at him. *Stay ahead of the story.* It was always crucial. Tell the story, own the story. Journalists got blindsided all the time. They climbed on the roller coaster, not knowing where it would end. Pandora's Box, wide open.

'We don't have it all yet,' Casey said again.

'You've got enough. Maybe it's not the whole story, but it's enough to publish. Get up to north London to see Greystone, and then we can get started.'

'I'll get the other reporters stuck in,' Ross joined in. 'Robert can pull together some of the articles we'll need. I'll tell Xav we need a column. Video can get going on the footage. All that stuff from Greystone's office and the Bangladesh filming needs to be edited too, with subtitles and the rest of it. Foreign can put together stuff on Bangladesh while Heather does a backgrounder on overseas surrogacy.'

Robert was the chief reporter, brilliant at pulling together dozens of complicated facts into a readable piece.

'All right.' Casey kicked at her suitcase. Fine.'

She stood up abruptly, her chin jutting out, and turned to Dash one more time.

'I need to check one thing. It's important. I need one day.'

Dash stared at Casey for a long time, tapping the desk with a biro.

'Please,' she managed. 'We've got to do this right. Otherwise, what was the point in it all?'

'All right,' Dash said slowly. 'You can have one more day, Casey. Then we publish what we know.'

He could see he had lost her already. Casey was checking her phone, thinking, before she looked up, eyes sharp.

'We've been looking at this the wrong way.'

54

It was almost midnight when Casey's flight landed at Nice airport, the darkness blotting out the rows of private jets lined up on the tarmac.

Past caring about the *Post*'s budget, she took a helicopter transfer down the coast, just a few miles to the tiny principality perched on the edge of France. The residents of Monaco treated the helicopter like a taxi service anyway, the ticket office tucked in next to the taxi counter.

Casey knew where she would find Maurice Delacroix. Folded into a booth at Teddy's, the little nightclub next to the harbour side.

Delacroix saw her as soon as she walked in, and was on his feet in a second.

'Cassandra.' His mouth curved as he raised her hand to his lips. 'It has been too long.'

Before Casey had sat down, a waiter rushed forwards with a fresh bottle of champagne. Delacroix spent more in Teddy's than almost anyone else, and it was one waiter's task to keep a watch on his table at all times.

'Would you give us a moment, Tiphaine, my love?' Maurice turned to the girl sitting on his right.

Tiphaine pouted, just for a beat. Then she stood and sashayed away across the club in her red feathered dress and Louboutin heels. Just before she reached the tiny dancefloor, she blew Delacroix a kiss over her shoulder.

'That' – Delacroix's eyes ran over Casey – 'is a beautiful dress.'

'Thank you, Maurice.' She caught his eye with a smile.

Casey disliked the skintight Hervé Léger dresses, but she had laughed about this one earlier with Miranda as she yanked open the cupboard in the corner of the investigations room.

'It never matters how long this dress lies in a crumpled heap.'

A quick shake and the sequined black dress was ready. Casey had done her make-up as her flight descended towards Nice.

'Now, how may I assist you, Miss Benedict?'

Casey had met Maurice Delacroix a few years earlier. She had been in the Vandals club, on the opposite side of the port from Teddy's, circling one of the richest Russians in the world. All week long, the Russian had been watching her, dark eyes flickering in a still face.

Casey had been in a different Hervé Léger dress then. Imperial purple, her mouth a curve of scarlet. Simpering on a bar stool, and kicking her heels carelessly.

In the end, Kuznetsov had sent one of his bodyguards across to her. 'You join us, yes?' and it wasn't a question.

Casey had sat across the table from the Russian, while his eyes flicked from her to the dancefloor and back, unspeaking. She had tried all her wiles: the half-questions, the flirtation, even the clowning. Nothing worked.

All around them, eighteen-year-old girls flirted relentlessly with men three times their age. They were professional, the Monaco girls.

Later, much later, the Russian stood. 'You. Come with me.'

Casey knew Kuznetsov's enormous yacht waited out in the Mediterranean. Too large to dock in the Monaco harbour, so the tenders raced back and forwards to the coast, like bees to honey.

Every instinct screamed no, but Casey hesitated. *The story, the story, the story.*

She stood up, smile glimmering. And just then, a man stopped in front of the table. Brazilian, from his accent.

'One moment,' Kuznetsov told Casey, over the Brazilian's shoulder.

As she was standing by the table, another man – so casual, just passing – stopped and turned to her, and spoke so quietly that she almost missed the words in the roar of the club: 'Who are you with?'

Casey turned with a jolt. He was tall, this man, with a tanned face that would have been unremarkable but for the intensity of the black-eyed stare. Beautifully dressed, in a dark suit, the jacket thrown over his shoulder. His voice was English public school, with the faintest of French inflections. Casey guessed he was in his early fifties.

'I don't' – Casey had almost stumbled over the words – 'know what you mean.'

'You don't have time to mess about,' said the man. 'Are you with an agency, or are you working alone?'

Casey tossed her head, and was moving away when he grabbed her elbow with a surprising strength.

'It's dangerous enough if you are an agent,' he said, sitting down on a bar stool, so offhand. 'But if you get on that ship without proper backup, that man will kill you.'

'I know how to look after myself.'

She jerked at her arm, but his fingers only tightened. The Brazilian was wandering off, Kuznetsov looking around for her.

'Tell him you're staying with me,' said the man. 'Tell him, or I will blow your cover.'

'You wouldn't.'

A whisper in her ear. 'I would.'

Kuznetsov had stepped towards her then. 'We go now.'

'I see you've met my little friend, Andrey.' The man stood up from his bar stool, limbs unfolding, all nonchalance. 'I'm sorry to do this, old boy, really I am. But I very much need this girl's company, just for a few minutes.'

'Maurice.' Kuznetsov's face moved into an approximation of a smile.

The two men shared the briefest of hugs, but Casey sensed the tension flaring between them. She almost stepped towards Kuznetsov, but the grip on her arm tightened again.

Then the Russian shrugged, stepped back. 'If you insist, Delacroix.'

Kuznetsov turned on his heel, ignoring Casey. He strode out of the door of the club, clicking his fingers at one of the girls sitting at a table outside. The girl stood up sharply, and shimmied after him, heels clacking on the pavement.

'You just blew weeks of work,' Casey stared after the Russian. 'I only needed one fact. You …'

'I saved your life,' Delacroix shrugged. 'That man likes girls to scream as he fucks them. And his bodyguards are chosen to be deaf.'

'Well, what about her?' Casey gestured at the girl tottering towards the tender, precarious in her heels.

'You can't,' Delacroix said thoughtfully, 'save everyone.'

The Brazilian reappeared beside them. 'He wasn't up for the Kazakhstan deal, Maurice.'

'No,' Delacroix murmured after the man had moved on. 'He wouldn't be. But thank you for asking anyway. Drink, my dear?'

Delacroix was a fixer, Casey learned later. One of the small group of men around the world who put together deals worth billions, taking a slice every time. By the time Casey met him in Monaco, he had his own vast fortune, taking cut after cut after cut.

He was charming, amoral. Made her laugh that evening, and every evening after.

'You owe me,' he said, hours later that night, as he kissed her hand goodbye. And he was a man who called in his promises, she thought. Honour among thieves, or something close to it.

They met, now and again. His tentacles reached everywhere.

'Never write about me,' he had ordered that night. 'That's the deal, for saving your life.'

'I don't know that you did.'

'I did, my girl. I did.'

She had kept her promise, half-believing him. Now and again, he rang her – from strange time zones, never the same number – with a clue or a tip. They always offered up gold.

Like many of the very richest, he liked having a journalist to call. Not quite a pet, but tame. More or less.

She didn't know how he had peered through her veil that night, but he was the only one who ever had.

'Delacroix.'

'Miss Benedict.'

'Are you well?'

'Very.'

'And are you working on anything special at the moment?'

Delacroix inclined his head thoughtfully. 'I suppose I'm selling an oil refinery.'

'An oil refinery?'

'Well, the machinery inside the refinery. It's old, so it will fail the strict new regulations where it is at the moment. Red tape, you know. So tedious. But we can dismantle it, ship it, and then put it back together again. So I have to find a country where they don't care so much about these petty rules. Nigeria, maybe. Angola, possibly. Lebanon, probably.' His teeth gleamed for a second. 'Yes, Lebanon.'

'You're impossible.'

'If I don't do it . . .' he shrugged. 'I saw you got Kuznetsov, in the end.'

'Yes.'

'I knew it was you.'

She had waited for a week, in a small café close to where the tender docked in Monaco. Sat there, quite invisible, in her plaid shirt and rolled-up jeans.

She had followed the girls the morning after, as they staggered off the tender, tottering away up the narrow Monaco streets.

The first three wouldn't talk. The fourth would, trailing behind her to the police like a deflated helium balloon. When the police shrugged, she brought in the fifth the next day. Kuznetsov was arrested two days later.

'But you never wrote about it.'

‘The women I spoke to didn’t want anything in the *Post*.’ Casey tilted her head to one side. ‘And he’s in jail anyway now, so it doesn’t matter. Our Paris correspondent wrote up the basic trial stuff. Not the story I wanted, but you wrecked that one …’

She didn’t tell Delacroix that she had come down to Monaco to find the girls on her holiday. *South of France*, they said in the office. *Very nice.*

‘Kuznetsov had it coming.’

‘Who,’ Casey asked, ‘took over his businesses?’

‘Who,’ Delacroix grinned, ‘do you think?’

‘You’re a disgrace,’ she said, and he half-winked at her in the hot twilight of the club.

‘So.’ Delacroix waved away a waiter trying to top up her glass, and poured the champagne himself. ‘What do you need, Cassandra?’

‘I want to know who bought a ship for scrapping in Bangladesh. It was sold a few weeks ago, the *Tephi*,’ Casey spelled it out. ‘And another one called the *Beauvallet*. They were probably bought by the same person or company.’

Delacroix narrowed his eyes as he stared across the club. ‘It should be possible to find out. This ship is in Bangladesh at the moment?’

‘Yes. It’s being taken apart right now. The *Tephi* used to belong to the Alexakis family.’ Casey named one of the Greek shipping dynasties. ‘But it was sold to a cash buyer in Hong Kong a few weeks ago, and I can’t track it any further. The *Beauvallet* belonged to a BVI shell company, and it operated under the Liberian flag.’

‘And you need to know soon?’

'Tomorrow.'

'Tomorrow?' He raised his eyebrows with pretended surprise. 'It is impossible.'

'It is important.'

'All right,' Delacroix sighed. 'I am sure it will be achievable. For you, Cassandra.'

'Thank you.'

'You know the rule.'

'I know,' Casey exhaled. 'I owe you.'

'One day,' he murmured. 'One day.'

55

Delacroix called her a few hours later, in the breaking dawn. Casey answered the phone as she was sitting up in bed, blinking at beige curtains.

'Portunus Marine,' Delacroix said in her ear.

'Who?' Casey pushed back her hair. 'Have you ever heard of them?'

'Never,' he said. 'But there is no mistake. Portunus Marine bought both the *Tephi* and the *Beauvallet* out of Hong Kong. They were bought from the original owners by cash buyers, who sold them on to Portunus Marine. Portunus are still holding those ships now. Even if they are in bits all over a beach in Bangladesh.'

'Thank you, Delacroix,' Casey said, meaning it.

'It took hours.' He put a grumble into his voice.

'There haven't been hours.' Casey looked at her watch.

They had left the club together at the end of the night, after a few more rounds of idle gossip. Delacroix added the drinks to his vast bill with a gesture as they left.

'They'll just be getting started in Hong Kong now,' he had said, as he waved her goodnight. 'It's a good time to make calls.'

Delacroix barely slept, she knew. The long nights in Teddy's were a way of filling time, as much as anything else.

'And you've never heard of Portunus,' said Casey, scowling at the curtains. Nice airport was waking up beyond her window.

'No,' he said. 'I can make some more calls, if you like. But they seem to be some wreckers in Bangladesh. Nothing more. There's no name behind them that people know.'

'Damn.'

He didn't ask why she wanted to know. He never did.

'Thank you,' said Casey, after a pause.

'Any time,' he said, and the phone went dead.

Casey scrambled onto the first flight to London. 'I'll be in the office by nine,' she messaged Miranda.

She tried the Burton-Smiths again. No answer. She felt her worries deepen. Emily should be waiting by the phone, high-wire tense. Casey stared at the blank screen, and bit her nails.

The Heathrow flight was almost empty apart from a few expats on their commute. As the plane curved over London, Casey peered down at the silver ribbon of the Thames. Hyde Park, Regent's Park and bridges like stitches. She tried to spy the *Post* building, in the grey of the morning.

'Nearly there,' she texted Miranda, as the plane trundled towards the gate.

Messages were already bleeping in. Gabriel Bantham: *Call me.*

She rang him as soon as she was off the plane.

Bantham answered at the first ring, his voice ragged with nerves, an echo of that panicked diplomat in Georgetown.

'Erica Whiddon,' he said. 'Erica Whiddon.'

'Yes?'

'Erica Whiddon.' It was as if his mind was stuck on the words. 'Erica Whiddon,' he said again.

'What?' Casey interrupted him. 'Who is she?'

'She's a friend of mine,' Bantham managed. 'At the Commission. We got on well, always did.'

'Is she the person?' Casey asked. 'The person who fixed the passports?'

There was a long pause.

'I think so.' His voice was faint, reeling with shock. 'Yes.'

'Why?'

Her brisk questions chipped away at his shock. 'She worked closely for me and Sir William out there,' he said. 'A sort of deputy. And she stayed on in Dhaka.'

'Have you spoken to her about the passports?'

'Spoken to her?' There was a long dull silence.

'Yes, Gabriel. Have you spoken to her about it?'

'I can't.'

'Well, I'll call her then. Take me through why you think—'

'You can't.'

'Of course I can, Gabriel. We've got to hurry.'

'You can't.'

'I can.'

'She's dead.' Casey stopped, staring at the adverts for banks and scent and duty-free whisky, travellers flowing around her like a rock in a river.

'What happened?' Her mouth moved eventually. 'I'm sorry, Gabriel. So sorry to hear that.'

'They found her' – his voice was unsteady – 'in her flat this morning. In Gulshan. She'd been attacked. Beaten about the head. Blood everywhere, they said.'

'Do they know who did it?'

'No,' he said. 'They have no idea.'

The phone line was silent for a beat.

'Can you leave the country?' Casey asked. 'I think you should get out of Dhaka as soon as possible.'

'She was such a nice woman,' Bantham said. 'Never married or anything. But she was so thoughtful. Remembered birthdays. She was always pleased to see you.'

'She sounds lovely, Gabriel.' Casey fought for patience. 'But why do you think it was her?'

'She had access to the emergency passports.' Gabriel sounded almost dreamy. 'She's who Sir William would have turned to for help. And she had a sister, back in England, who had serious problems. I'm not sure what, but supporting her cost a lot, I know. Erica helped out. It was a big pressure. When I saw Erica yesterday, I asked after her sister, and you could just see that tension had gone. And I just suddenly realised.'

'Sounds plausible,' said Casey. 'You need to get out of Bangladesh, Gabriel. It could be very dangerous. Would it look odd, you leaving today?'

'No.' His voice was still hazy. 'I told everyone I would only be here for a couple of days.'

'Get to the airport,' Casey ordered. 'Go there right away, Gabriel. I'll look at flights.'

'Poor Erica.' It was as if he was talking to himself. 'Poor Erica.'

'Yes,' Casey agreed. 'Poor Erica.'

After she hung up, Casey stood, processing her thoughts. Then she hurried through the airport, almost running. She raced through passport control, ignoring the still luggage belts, burst out on to the concourse and raced towards the train station. And almost fell as a hand grabbed hard at her shoulder.

56

'Ed,' Casey gasped.

'Be quiet,' he muttered. He had her firm at the elbow, towing her smoothly across the huge hall.

'Ed, what are you *doing*?'

He paused behind one of the big pillars, pushing her close to the concrete. 'Stay there.'

'What . . .'

Ed was scanning the concourse, eyes narrowed.

'There. Grey jacket, blue jeans, white sign with red writing.'

'Doesn't,' Casey was over her shock, grumbling slightly, 'narrow it down much.'

'Just look.'

She saw the man almost at once, among the crowd of bored chauffeurs and happy families. *Casey Benedict* read his sign.

'Who the hell . . .'

'I don't know.' Ed was searching the rest of the airport now, eyes casual, but focusing in on every person.

'How did he . . .'

'I don't know,' Ed said again. 'Miranda texted me to say you were flying in. I thought I would come and meet you. Find out what was happening with the story.'

‘Oh,’ said Casey. ‘That’s …’ Then she sharpened her voice. ‘But how did he know? Whoever he is.’

‘I was waiting for you,’ said Ed. ‘Your flight was a few minutes late. I just saw him there, in the corner of my eye. I’ve checked with Miranda. She didn’t send anyone.’

‘Who is he?’ Casey was watching the man.

He was deliberately anonymous. The sort of person who would be near-impossible to describe for a photofit. Medium height, medium brown hair, medium brown eyes. Hard muscles though, and a toughness in his movements. There was a menace about him too, the crowd keeping a step back even in the crush.

‘I don’t think I’ve ever seen him before,’ said Ed.

‘Me neither,’ said Casey. ‘But surely he wouldn’t expect me to just get into a car with him?’

‘You might.’

Exhausted, in a Heathrow so familiar, where she thought she was safe. Assuming the newsroom had sent out a car for her. A shudder went down her spine. ‘They might think I would,’ she corrected him.

‘Well then.’

They watched the man waiting for her. ‘Are you sure he is working alone?’ asked Casey.

‘No.’

‘We should follow him,’ she murmured. ‘Or maybe … Maybe I should just walk up to him, see what happens.’

‘Casey.’ Ed turned to her, the anger flaring. ‘He could be waiting to kill you, for God’s sake. You have no idea. You just don’t know.’

‘Not just like that in an airport. Surely?’

‘You’re not doing it,’ he said. ‘Absolutely not.’

'Well, what then?' Casey stared across the airport. 'We need to find out where he is going. Who he is working for.'

The man was watching the exit gate, cat at a mouse hole.

'He doesn't know what you look like,' said Ed. 'He didn't react when you walked out.'

'You grabbed me pretty fast.'

'Even so. He missed you. He was expecting you to walk up to him.'

They watched him for a few more minutes. Briefly, keeping her voice steady, she told him about Erica Whiddon.

'You have to be careful,' Ed breathed out. 'Promise me.'

Their eyes met. Around them, the crowd ebbed and flowed. She could sense him standing very close, his body tense.

You promised.

'I need to get to the office,' Casey said briskly. 'I need to keep working, and find out who is behind all this.'

'It would be tricky to follow him from here anyway,' said Ed, equally efficient. 'He'll probably have a car.'

For all the filmic car chases, it was hard tracking a car, especially without being spotted, especially one driven by someone who checked, always watchful.

'He could be here for hours,' said Casey, 'before giving up. There are flights from Nice all day.'

'Call Dash,' said Ed. 'Tell him to send two reporters to keep an eye on him, and try to work out where he goes.'

'All right,' said Casey. 'All right.'

Ed and Casey arrived in the office at the same time as Miranda.

'Shit,' Miranda had said, when Casey rang from Ed's car. 'And we have no idea how many other people may be on our case too. Shit.'

Staring out of the car window, Casey told Miranda about the murder of Erica Whiddon.

'They probably,' Miranda said flatly, 'have similar plans for you.'

'Drive straight into the underground car park,' Dash messaged Casey two minutes later. 'I'll tell them to have it open as you arrive.'

Dash was waiting for her as she walked into the office, cutting her off at the doorway to the investigations room.

'Are you OK?' His eyes were on Casey's.

'I'm fine.' She pushed away his concerns.

'We need to publish now,' said Dash. 'As long as we don't publish, they'll think the story can be stopped by offing you.'

'I know,' Casey said. 'But I need more time, Dash. We're not there yet. We haven't—'

'We're close enough,' said Dash. 'And I can't take the risk …'

'Give me one more day,' said Casey.

'You've already had that.'

'I can't … not yet.'

He glowered at her. 'You can have a few more hours,' he said reluctantly. 'Then that's it. And I'm getting more security into the building. Operate out of that central conference room. Janet can order in some sandwiches. You stay here.'

Casey sighed. The bleak little conference room looked out into a small internal light well. The only view was broken blinds, and 15 feet to a blank brick wall. They had started using that room for investigations after one of the early leaks. After a big information dump especially annoyed the government, and the men in grey suits had turned up.

'The Chinese can work with a direct line of sight,' they'd said, peering disapprovingly out of the smeary windows in the main office. 'They can track everything you type from the other side of the road. And what you say, mind. They shine lasers on the windows, and transcribe that. It's a total pain, to be honest.'

'Fine,' Casey snapped at Dash.

The head of news walked away from her, across the newsroom, swatting the air with his notebook.

Hessa and Miranda looked at Casey, crumpled, still carrying her small suitcase, the sequined black dress crushed inside.

'Are you all right?' asked Miranda. 'You look like hell.'

'Thank you.' Casey felt her mouth twist into a grin. 'I'm fine. But we have to work out who is behind all this.'

'Poor Erica Whiddon,' said Hessa quietly.

'I don't suppose they'll get very far on tracking her killers either,' said Miranda, as Casey collapsed at her desk. 'It sounds like a professional job.'

Talking quickly, Casey explained her meeting with Delacroix. 'I thought if we could find out who is running that shipping yard, we might be a step closer to working out who is in charge of the whole thing,' she finished. 'But ...'

'Portunus Marine?' Miranda shook her head as she stopped speaking. 'Don't know them.'

'I'll look for everything available about Portunus Marine.' Hessa turned to her computer. 'But there may not be much.'

'And I'll try the name on a few shipping people I know,' said Miranda. 'We might get lucky.'

'We're running out of time.' For a second, Casey felt the despair clutch at her. 'What if Portunus is just another dead end? Whoever is behind this will just disappear ...'

The room fell into silence. Casey scowled at her notes. She had pages of them now, spread out across her desk. She moved them around, matching facts to each other, one at a time.

'Portunus Marine,' she murmured. 'Portunus.'

'Poppy's fine,' Miranda said, when she returned a few minutes later. 'She's still in the hotel, with Nina Reynolds.'

'I can't get through to the Burton-Smiths,' said Casey. 'I don't understand it.'

Miranda bit her lip. She stood, and walked to the door. 'Tillie,' she shouted across the newsroom.

The young reporter was at the door to the investigations room in seconds, like a puppy to the rattle of a lead. 'Can I help?'

'Can you go to this address in Surrey.' Miranda tore out a page from her notepad. 'And see if there is anyone around. There's a neighbour at number thirty-eight, ask her. She's got a terrier called Choccy. Talk about the dog, not the *Post*, OK?'

Tillie bounded off, glowing. Hessa scowled at her retreating back, with the gleam of competition, and Casey laughed out loud.

The day wore on, the precious hours rushing past. They had moved into the gloomy conference room, Robert joining them neat in his suit. Ross sent across other reporters to bolster the team, all carefully briefed, all hiding their excitement.

As they worked, Casey crawled all over Portunus Marine, and got nowhere. Portunus. Portunus. Portunus. The words stopped making sense.

After a few hours, Miranda looked up, arms spread hopelessly.

'No one knows a bloody thing about Portunus Marine. Sorry, babe. But we've got enough for this story, you know. You've nailed Greystone.'

Hessa was keeping an eye on the coverage of the death of Erica Whiddon. The story of the murdered diplomat was breaking on the wires, just a small story for now. There were no clues, no arrests. The Foreign Office had put out a short, sad statement.

Casey felt the walls of the conference room close in. Picking up her coffee, she prowled around the office, searching for inspiration, and willing the clues to fall into place. She paced past Sport. She fidgeted with piles of newspapers. She hesitated by the newsdesk, half-listening as Ross dealt with today's crisis. A stringer in Venezuela snatched, and Ross spitting down the phone: 'He's been kidnapped in fucking South America. Frankly I'd leave him there, but the branding people say I can't.' Ross waited a beat. 'Well, I've told the branding lot that his ransom can come out of their fucking budget. That shut them right up, let me tell you.'

He peered up at Casey. 'Don't look at me like that, you. That lot'll let him go in a few days anyway. They always do. As he'd fucking know if he'd done any sodding research on those jokers in the first place.'

Casey threw a pencil at her news editor and walked on, knowing there was no querying Ross in this mood. Some days he reminded her of a schoolboy with his magnifying glass, burning ants one by one.

Casey paused by the Comment desk. 'We've got such an insightful piece coming in from the shadow deputy PM,' Sophie, one of the editors, was saying. 'Really exploring the ancient Greeks' understanding of democracy … Demos and kratia. That delicate balance. Just so meaningful.'

Behind her back, Casey could feel Ross rolling his eyes. Ross took a lot of joy in winding up the Comment desk.

But the day was wearing away. Casey read through Robert's piece: a careful dissection of what they knew about Greystone's activities. Gabriel Bantham's role had been carefully sculpted. The daring diplomat who bent the rules to save a baby: a sort of truth. The words bounced off Casey's brain like hailstones.

Arthur, the *Post*'s crime correspondent, had hammered out a short article on the mysterious death of Erica Whiddon. Hinting, only. Sir William Cavendish's name appeared nowhere in any article, the spotlight delicately angled away.

Tess Dulverton, who could concoct features in a few effortless minutes, had put together a story on Vivienne Hargreaves. On the second day, Tess's article would focus on Dominic and Emily. They were all carefully anonymised as promised, glued together from fragments of Casey's notes.

'Have you heard of phantom limb syndrome?' Zoe says, as tears fill her eyes. 'Your mind sends back those flashes, bursts of pointless pain.'

And at the bottom of the article, the careful warning: *All names have been changed.*

And Laura, the *Post*'s chief opinion writer, had written a searing evisceration of the surrogacy industry, scalpel-clinical and burning with rage.

Casey peered at Laura's words, forcing them into her mind.

'Casey.' Dash appeared beside her. 'We need to move on this.'

'Dash ...' But his jaw was fixed.

'Go and front up Greystone.' It was an order. 'Get it done. Get him.'

57

Casey hesitated outside the opulent house. The gold sterile mansions stretched away on both sides of the avenue. The house next door to the Greystones' was still empty, windows boarded. Someone had graffitied the garage, in an angry flash of red. Turning away, Casey pondered the Greystone house, safe behind its tall black gates. The Porsche Cayenne she'd seen on her last visit was parked next to a silver Aston Martin.

A pickup, private security, cruised down the street. As it passed Casey it slowed, just fractionally, just for a second. Almost unnoticeable, but that most discreet of warnings: *We've noticed you.*

Casey's eyes followed the pickup as it grumbled along the street, past where Ed was waiting in his car. He had insisted on driving her up to north London, with one of Dash's new security people tense in the passenger seat.

'But you're not coming in with me,' she said. 'I need to go in alone.'

'It's not safe,' he had insisted. 'The Dhaka team may have warned him about the raid on the *Beauvallet*. You can't.'

Casey thought about Ed waiting patiently in the airport. The kindness, the concern: so unfamiliar.

'Thank you,' she said quietly. 'But I have to go.'

Now Casey glanced at the intercom, and discounted it. There was an art to getting people to talk, but there was often a simple luck in getting to them in the first place. A phone could be put down in a second, the fragile connection cut so easily. Face to face was easier to assess, calculate, rush. Even if she hated it.

But how to get to him? Casey had tailgated dozens of people through apartment doors; it was the sort of illegality that rarely bothered the police. She had approached targets with any number of excuses. They all had, everywhere. Right the way up to the new Prime Minister's wife, once, blinking on her doorstep in the dawn after an election. She had blearily signed for a big bunch of flowers, tugging her nightie to decency, glancing up too late at the wall of photographers. It had been worth a whip-round for that bouquet.

It was a beautiful day, the sky a scrubbed bright blue, spring rustling in the new green leaves.

Just then, Casey stiffened, hound to a scent. A blonde woman had walked out of the house, the slam of the door loud in the silent street. Her car keys in her hand, it was just a few steps to the Porsche, but the woman paused, glancing up at the sky.

Clio Greystone, Casey thought. The wife.

Casey assessed her dispassionately. Tall, with the same blonde hair Casey saw everywhere. A golden shimmer, with just enough expensive chestnut lowlights to avoid that hint of brass. Clio had an aquiline nose that a woman with slightly less confidence might have had tailored by some Harley Street artist. But it gave her face an elegance that was set off by a curving mouth.

She wore a beautifully cut blue dress, a leather jacket thrown over the top for the spring chill. Long legs ended in studded ankle boots, and Casey had seen Cressida carrying that bag last week. Balenciaga, at a guess.

A nice little trophy, she thought.

As Casey watched, Clio threw the keys back into her handbag and strode towards the gate. There was a bounce in her step, and the builders on the scaffolding opposite watched her appreciatively. A side gate purred open.

The Greystones' road ended on a pretty high street, with several boutiques and a picture-perfect café that served cupcakes in a rainbow of colour. Casey followed Clio down the street, her mind racing. She walked past Ed and the security man, parked up, without a flicker.

At the café, Clio peered through a window, and a bell jangled as she pushed the door open.

Casey tapped at her phone. 'Keep talking.'

'Sure,' said Miranda, and Casey stayed chatting on her phone as she walked into the café. It was a small space, just a few tables. Mismatched teacups, riotous geraniums and curling rococo chairs. The cupcakes were a burst of colours, decoration in their own right: lemon meringue or blueberry, chocolate mocha or red velvet.

Clio, restrained, had ordered only a coffee, and was moving to one of two empty tables. They were next to each other, Casey was relieved to see.

Casey made her way to the counter, only glancing at the display. 'Lemon raspberry,' she said randomly. 'And fresh mint tea.'

'I'll bring it over,' the waitress smiled, and Casey sat down, almost next to Clio.

As she sat, Casey was talking quietly on the phone. 'I don't know what to do next … You don't know what it's like … They don't know why it won't work. I can get pregnant', a gleam of a tear in her eye. 'I just can't stay pregnant.'

Clio was flicking through a pile of magazines stacked on the windowsill, but Casey knew she was listening.

Casey spoke for a few more minutes, then hung up the phone. She dug through her handbag, failed to find a tissue and smudged away mascara with a fingertip.

'Here.' Clio was holding out a tissue.

'Thank you,' Casey choked.

'Sounds like you're having a difficult time.' Clio was all wide-eyed sympathy.

'Oh,' Casey managed. 'I'm sorry. I didn't meant to bother anyone …'

'Gosh, don't worry,' Clio smiled at her.

Sweet-natured, Casey diagnosed. Mother of two: lunches and charity balls and PTA. Regular tennis, and a lot of Pilates. Four holidays a year, at least, and welcomed by name – and a wide smile – at every shop on Bond Street. Casey smiled back weakly.

'In fact,' Clio went on, 'I know someone who might be able to help.'

They talked for a long time over the lemon raspberry cake, Clio telling Casey about various friends who'd had, 'Well, you'd call them miracles, honestly.' Until finally they were leaving the little café, with a glowing smile at the waitress behind the counter.

Clio led the way back down the road – 'I'll take you to meet my husband; it's less than five minutes away, so convenient.'

Just a few steps from the gate to the house, and then Clio was throwing her keys onto the hall table, shouting, 'Darling, I'm home.'

The hall was large, double height, with a white marble floor leading away to a distant kitchen. Stairs edged with black wrought-iron banisters swept towards a glittering chandelier.

'I wonder where he is.' Clio looked around. 'He's usually absolutely flat out at work, but he's at home today for some reason.'

As Casey peered up the stairs, Greystone appeared at the banisters, urbane in chinos and a smart blue shirt. He didn't look dangerous, Casey thought. But then, neither did she.

'Darling, this is Cassandra,' Clio sang out. 'I've told her all about you.' Clio finished the introductions, and then grabbed her car keys. 'I've just remembered. Got to pick up Tamara. Back soon.'

The daughter, Casey remembered. Just thirteen. She would be ensconced in the expensive London day school just around the corner. Or bunking off to the shopping mall, more likely.

Greystone and Casey stood awkwardly as Clio's boots clattered down the stairs.

Still smiling, Casey started to speak, sympathetically at first, because she often tried sympathy first. 'Sorry to bother you. I'm Casey Benedict from the *Post*. Just a few questions ...'

It rocked him.

I'd like to ask you about your clients ... I'm sorry, I know this is difficult ...

He couldn't speak for a moment, but then his face tautened, the anger surging.

'Dr Greystone?'

'I don't know what you're talking about . . .' The words were strangled. 'Who did you say you . . . Go away . . .' He paused, then almost a shout. 'Get out of my house.'

Casey held her ground.

'You do know, Dr Greystone, I'm afraid.' Harder now. 'The *Post* has been investigating your activities for several weeks . . .'

'Get out of my house, or I will call the police.'

Familiar as a dance.

'We've spoken to two different women who say you coordinated their illegal surrogacy programme in Bangladesh,' said Casey. 'I personally visited one of the sites where women are being held against their will in Chittagong.'

'I'm calling my lawyers. I'm calling the police.'

Greystone was walking towards the door with the jerky movements of extreme shock. He was thin under the blue shirt, Casey noticed, almost scrawny. The unctuous charm was quite gone.

'Just so I am clear with you, Dr Greystone. The *Post* is planning to publish several articles about your activities in both Harley Street and Bangladesh. The articles are due to appear in tomorrow's paper.'

Greystone yanked open the front door.

'Get out. *Get out.*'

'There's one last thing,' said Casey. 'Were you working alone, Dr Greystone? Was it you doing all this by yourself?'

She stepped out of the door, turned back to look at him.

Knowing he could slam the door, he calmed down very slightly.

'I will be writing about the ownership of Portunus Marine,' Casey tried again. 'The company that bought the *Tephi* and the

Beauvallet, where the women were being held. Do you have any comment to make about Portunus?'

Greystone froze, his eyes gleaming, the gold-rimmed glasses askew. Then he snapped back to the moment. 'Leave me alone,' he snarled, and the door slammed shut behind him.

It was rarely dignified.

Casey opened her satchel, and pulled out a long, detailed letter. An R-2-R – a right to reply – giving the target every opportunity to respond. All the allegations, in careful legalese. It was hard to fight when it was all on tape, but people still gave it a go sometimes, their lawyers rubbing their hands in glee.

I knew she was a journalist. Every time.

Almost casual now, Casey posted the letter through the door and turned away.

'Did you get him?' Dash was waiting as she walked through the door.

'No denial.'

'He's had every opportunity to respond?'

'I'd say so. Give him a few more hours.'

Dash stood there, eyes narrowed. Then he pushed back his hair with a sharp gesture. 'Let's get him.'

58

The *Post* swung into action, Ross lashing his team along. He crouched over a desk in the conference room, red pen in hand.

'Xav, I'm going to need another hundred and fifty words for the leader,' he shouted across the room. 'We've been given more space. And Graphics, where the fuck are you on that Bangladesh image?'

Anthony, the *Post*'s head lawyer, was reading through Tess's piece in despair. 'We're admitting we know the identity of some of Greystone's clients,' he protested. 'What if the authorities demand to know who they are? I can't keep up with how many laws they've broken. They could all end up in jail.'

'They're sources,' Ross growled. 'We protect our sources.' As he spoke, Ross was proofreading a map of Bangladesh. 'Why the fuck' – he crossed out a word with a red slash – 'can't any of these morons spell Chittagong?'

'Archie.' Dash rang his political editor, based over in the *Post*'s scruffy office in the heart of Parliament. 'We need some strong words from the Opposition about the dangers of surrogacy. Inquiries, questions in Parliament, you know the sort of thing. Paul Heyworth should be up for raising it in Parli. He's always useful.'

As he put the phone down, Dash shouted across the office. 'Sadie.' Another of the feature writers appeared at the door of the conference room. 'Can you pull together eight hundred words on slebs who've opted for the surrogacy route? There are loads of them, aren't there? Lots of pics for that one please. Talk to Stan.'

'That' – Ross rubbed his hands as Stan, the picture editor, scuttled to find the photographs – 'will really do the numbers online.'

'But for the love of Satan,' Anthony howled, 'don't imply they've all been off to Bangladesh with Greystone!'

They all gathered round Ross's computer to send the story live, faces lit up by the screen. Dash stood a step away from the desk, almost laughing at Anthony's despair. Just one click of a button, genie from the bottle, and they watched the story sweep around the newsroom.

The story would dominate the paper tomorrow, with all the power of a gathering wave, the big, bold, angry headlines demanding a strange sort of justice.

Casey imagined people peering at their screens like doctors in a laboratory, the heads shaking, the eyes narrowing. She imagined the politicians later on television. Lips compressed, eyes concerned, so carefully outraged. She thought about the ire on daytime television, the shudder down Harley Street and the flickers of terror in homes across the country.

Not a secret, any more. A big, awkward mirror to the world.

'Fucking great stuff,' emailed Jessie Miller within seconds.

'Bastard,' wrote another rival, and she didn't know if he meant her or Greystone.

At her desk, Casey stared at the photographs of the house in Hampstead, the tall building in Harley Street and the long-range snap of the doctor leaving his rooms. That photographer would have sat in his car, halfway down the street, and Greystone would never even have known he was there. They could photograph people in near-darkness now. She traced Greystone's face on her proof, staring down at him.

And for a second, she felt almost content.

59

Dash ordered them to spend the night in the hotel next door. Casey failed to sleep, listening to the growl of traffic outside. *Ed had waited for her at the airport. He had come to see her.*

'Be careful,' he had messaged her earlier. 'Please take care of yourself.'

'I will.'

'You won't.'

'I'll try.'

She smiled at the memory. Then she thought of Poppy, just a couple of floors away, and the grin faded.

'Poppy's fine,' Miranda had insisted. 'The only problem is that the nanny thinks I am a terrible mother. We have to track down the Burton-Smiths.'

Casey had called Emily and Dominic again and again, the phone ringing out impotently. Tillie had reappeared in the office late in the evening: the neighbour hadn't seen the Burton-Smiths for days. *The dog was nice, though. I got special dog chocs.*

The *Post*'s security guards paced the corridor outside Casey's room all night, and she was back in the office before dawn, hurrying down the street, glancing over her shoulder. Dash was already there, skimming through the pile of rival newspapers delivered as soon as they were printed.

'You all right?' He didn't look up. 'Good follow-up from the other papers.'

'Fine.' Casey fiddled awkwardly with a stack of books, sent in for review.

'Keep going on it then,' he said. 'I know what you're thinking. We've got a second tranche of stories to publish today, anyway. I read your piece about that girl, Romida. It's very good, Casey.'

Dash rarely handed out compliments. Casey stared at him blankly. Savannah had sent her a photograph that morning. Romida and Shamshun, wrapped around each other, Shamshun crying with joy. In a new tent, tiny, barely high enough to stand upright. Back where they started, but with a strange sort of happiness.

'There is more to the story,' Casey said stonily, trailing off towards the conference room. 'Much more. But everyone involved will dive for cover now.'

Hessa ricocheted in a few minutes later, Miranda just behind her.

'Tom is barely speaking to me,' Miranda said, almost to herself. 'I don't know how this is supposed to work.'

'What's going on with Greystone this morning?' Hessa asked, not listening.

'Greystone's being investigated by various authorities,' said Casey. 'Tillie's outside the house in Hampstead, with a crowd of hacks. I imagine Greystone will be arrested at some point.'

'Are the wife and kids there?' Miranda asked.

'Not as far as anyone knows. Certainly no photographs of them going in or out.'

'The thing is,' said Miranda thoughtfully, 'that we can promise anonymity to Vivienne Hargreaves and so on. But Greystone can take the whole pack of cards down with him. He'll have all the names.'

'I know.' Casey had been worrying about it. 'But surely it would just make things even worse? And Vivienne said he's been careful with documentation at the clinic if nothing else.'

'So what now?' Hessa was electric with energy this morning, bouncing from one foot to the next.

'Now,' Casey said thoughtfully, 'we try and work out what the hell has happened to the Burton-Smiths. We try and figure out if there is anyone else behind Greystone. And we find out who is hunting us.'

Miranda waited until Hessa was out of the room. 'When should we call the police? About Dominic and Emily?'

'I don't know,' said Casey despondently. 'If we call the police, they could lose Poppy for ever. We don't actually know anything has happened to them yet.'

She stood up, and began to roam around the big newsroom. The room was filling up slowly, reporters scuttling to their desks as Ross glowered at them.

'I liked how that democracy piece turned out, Sophie,' the Comment editor was saying, all joviality. 'Or Sophia, should I say? Demos, kratia ...'

Casey spun around, striding back towards the investigation room.

'Hessa.' Casey hurried to her desk. 'What is the name of the company that owns the Harley Street building?'

'Aceso Incorporated.' Hessa didn't have to glance down at her notes.

'Aceso,' Casey said. 'Portunus. Arachne.'

'Arachne?' Miranda asked. 'Where did Arachne come from?'

'Could Arachne have been the name of that garment factory in Chittagong?' asked Casey. 'Hessa, you said that the name on the sign didn't make any sense in Bengali. That it wasn't a normal Chittagonian word.'

As she spoke, Casey was scrolling through her phone to the photograph snapped from the tuk-tuk in Sagorika.

'Ar-ack-ny,' Hessa tried out the Bengali syllables in her mouth again. 'Yes,' she said carefully. 'Arachne could be right.'

'Arachne was a weaver,' said Casey. 'In Greek myth.'

'Arachnid,' said Miranda. 'Spiders.'

'Exactly,' said Casey, tapping at her computer. 'So Arachne Incorporated could be the vehicle for the weaving interests. Garments, in this case. And then Portunus was the ancient Greeks' god of ports, so that could be the company he uses for buying and selling ships. And Aceso is the goddess of the healing process. So that makes sense for the Harley Street building.'

'One second.' Miranda stood up. 'Peregrine,' she shouted across the office.

Peregrine Courtenay wrote the *Post*'s crossword every morning, before lunching with the paper's astrologer. They often spent lunch hastily cobbling together a horoscope for Aries, because the astrologer had forgotten it on the Tube. Today, Peregrine wore a maroon smoking jacket, mustard trousers and alarmingly bright red socks. His eyebrows bristled severely. Cressida occasionally begged to be allowed to make him over for the fashion pages.

'He's a perfect Before shot,' she would wail.

'My *dear* girl,' Peregrine would respond, outraged.

'Peregrine,' Miranda coaxed him now. 'Could you possibly read through this list of companies, and see if any of them have ancient Greek links?'

The eyebrows looked approving. 'Of course.'

Miranda handed him a list of companies put together by Hessa. They sat in an impatient silence as Peregrine read through them, humming gently to himself.

'I'm afraid not that I can see.' He handed back the list. 'I am sorry that I am unable to help, Miranda.'

'That's all right,' said Miranda.

'I'll be off then.'

Peregrine pushed himself out of his chair.

'Rhapso,' he said, almost to himself.

'I'm sorry, Peregrine?' said Miranda.

He pointed to the black bag leaning against the wall, the smart carrier bag Cressida had shoved at Casey all those days ago, with the long silky ribbons. 'Rhapso,' Peregrine said again. 'She was a nymph worshipped in Athens. Her name comes from the Greek word "to sew" or "to stitch".'

'Really?'

'And that gives us the word rhapsody.' Peregrine didn't appear to have heard Miranda. 'From *rhaptein* and *ōidē*, meaning song or ode. Sewing songs together; rather lovely really.'

'Are you sure?' said Casey.

'Of course.' Peregrine looked stern. 'It's just odd that they've used a thunderbolt as a logo. The thunderbolt represents Zeus, of course.'

Casey pushed her hair back from her face, thinking carefully. 'There was an oak-leaf image on the garment factory in Bangladesh,' she said slowly. 'What would that represent?'

'Zeus,' said Peregrine promptly. 'He and Hera were the oak god and oak goddess, of course.'

'There's an eagle on the Aceso paperwork.' Hessa was looking through her notes.

'The eagle is one of his symbols too,' Peregrine agreed.

They contemplated it for a moment.

'So maybe,' Miranda said, 'the parent company of all these different operations is Zeus. The king of the gods. Almost an inside joke.'

'Indeed. Perhaps.' Nodding, Peregrine ambled out of the office.

'That means it definitely can't be Dylan behind it all,' said Casey after he had left. 'I never thought it was him anyway, but he said all his businesses were run out of Bangladesh. So why would he bother with a building in Harley Street?'

'Fine,' said Miranda. 'It's not Dylan. But who is it? That man you just saw in the airport?'

Casey shook her head. 'I don't think so. He looked like someone who fixed problems.'

'Could Greystone himself have been Zeus?' asked Hessa.

'That receptionist in Harley Street,' Miranda remembered. 'She said that Dr Greystone worked all hours. Could he possibly be operating these different businesses, right the way around the world, while also running a fertility clinic? It was a serious operation, that Harley Street place. There's no doubt about that.'

Casey was shaking her head. 'It can't be Greystone,' she said. 'There has to be someone else.'

'I'll ask Cressida if anyone on the fashion team has any idea who is behind Rhapso,' said Miranda. 'There's a chance they may know.'

'Declan Bentley might know too,' said Casey. 'He has excellent spies.'

He had texted her earlier: 'Rhapso still seem to be in business. Sort it out, love.'

'All these companies are registered in the British Virgin Islands,' said Hessa. 'Which means it's the same problem we always have. No shareholder info.'

Casey dropped her head into her hands. 'Bloody hell.'

They sat there in silence for a moment.

'I'm going for a run,' said Casey. 'I can't think.'

She always ran when she was struggling with a story. Breaking down the battle into stride after stride after stride.

'Go to the gym,' Miranda's head jerked up. 'Don't go outside.'

Casey hated the *Post*'s tiny gym, and its warm, grimy air. She climbed on the treadmill, unenthusiastically. In her head, she ran the big loops around Hyde Park. Past the shouts of Speaker's Corner. Past the Serpentine, swans serene. Past the Round Pond, Emily crying. Thoughts of Emily jolted her back to the gym.

Casey pushed buttons and accelerated, feet pounding. There was a seam of an idea in her mind, buried deep. A miner digging along a thin vein of hope.

Who are you? Tell me who you are.

Portunus. Rhapso. Arachne. Aceso.

Zeus.

Everything hurt. Lungs screaming, legs burning.

Who are you? Who are you? Who are you?

She almost fell off the treadmill when her phone rang. She scrambled across to her bag and snatched it up. 'Hello? Casey?' A voice, wavering. 'It's Emily.'

60

'Emily?' Casey jumped up. 'Oh, I'm so glad to hear from you. Are you all right?'

'I'm fine.' Emily sounded awkward, almost abrupt. 'I'm sorry not to have called you earlier, Casey. We're away from London. I didn't have any phone reception …'

'Oh,' Casey hesitated. 'Are you …'

'I'm fine.'

There was a silence.

'Poppy's here in London,' Casey went on. 'And she's beautiful, Emily. She's absolutely perfect.'

'Thank God.' Emily's voice changed, immediately tearful. 'Thank God.'

'Where are you?' Casey asked. 'Shall we bring her to you?'

All at once, the sobs burst out of Emily, hard, rasping sounds. 'Oh, Casey …'

Casey could hear Dominic's voice in the background, harsh with tension.

'Can you bring her to me, Casey?' Emily managed. 'I need to see her. I've been waiting …'

'Of course,' Casey grinned. For the first time in days, she felt an emotion close to happiness. 'As soon as I can.'

'Promise me you'll bring her?'

'I will, Emily. I promise.'

'I've got to . . .' Emily fought for air. 'I need to . . .'

'I'll be there as soon as I can.'

Through gulps, Emily read out the address.

'Just outside Guildford,' Casey visualised the map. 'I won't be long.'

'I can't wait to see her,' whispered Emily. 'Little Poppy Naomi Burton-Smith. Keep her safe, Casey. Promise me? Keep her safe.'

'Emily . . .'

'Casey.' For a second, Emily sounded quite cold. 'Please get her here as soon as you can.'

Miranda drove, weaving impatiently through the London traffic. Casey sat in silence, staring into space.

Portunus. Rhapso. Arachne. Aceso.

'Have you ever thought about it?' Miranda interrupted her thoughts.

'Thought about what?' Casey rubbed her eyes.

'Kids. And all that.'

'Not really. Not yet. Have you?' A pause. 'Has Tom?'

'A bit. Yes.' A long pause. 'It all just seems so unfair, doesn't it?' Miranda gripped the steering wheel. 'That these women will do anything – *anything* – to have children. And I'm ambivalent, at best.'

'Everything's unfair.' Casey turned towards Miranda. 'So Tom wants kids.'

'Yes.' Miranda let out a long breath. 'And it's going to be the thing that finishes us, after all that.'

'I had wondered,' said Casey carefully.

'Becky, and all that.' Miranda pulled a face. 'Me. Doesn't seem like a good basis for anything, does it?'

'No.' Casey softened it. 'Sorry. But it might just be that she flirts with him, and all the things we ...'

The windscreen wipers swept back and forwards.

Unless we're working, Miranda didn't say. 'Don't. Yes.'

'Well, what do you want?' asked Casey.

'It's all the bits of my life that I don't enjoy ...' Miranda was almost speaking to herself. 'The cooking, the cleaning, the knowing where I'll be at three thirty exactly on Thursday afternoon – it's all those things that would become my everything. They would submerge everything else. And all the things I love, those are the things that would disappear.'

'But we'd make it work, you and I. No matter what.'

'Maybe.' Miranda's eyes were on the darkness of the road. 'But I wouldn't be running to Heathrow for the next flight to Dhaka.'

'No.'

'There's something so primitive about the whole thing,' Miranda said.

'Has he offered to look after this theoretical child?'

'Tom? No.'

'Ask him? At least he would realise what he is asking you to give up.'

'Maybe. How about you?'

'Oh, I don't know,' Casey waved. 'I suppose if I want one at some point, I'll have one. I've never understood men being smug about it all. That tick-tock crap. If I wanted a child – really wanted one, above all else – I'd probably be able to have one within a year. And where would they be?'

'Quite.'

'Although I suppose it's that sort of confidence that leads all the way to Chittagong.'

Miranda almost laughed, and Casey smiled across at her.

Tilney Cottage was to the south of Guildford, just outside one of the pretty little villages that were slowly sprawling into each other along the main road.

Casey stopped the car next to an empty cricket green, the jangle of an ice-cream van in the distance. Miranda looked across at her.

'Are you sure about this?'

'No,' said Casey. 'But it won't take long to check, and there was something in Emily's voice.'

They stepped out of the car.

Tilney Cottage sat at the end of a long, potholed drive, surrounded by fields, just out of sight of the road. Woods reached around the house, thick as a winter coat.

'Why on earth do they call these houses cottages?' Miranda had asked, as she stared at an old printout of the agent's brochure. 'It's hardly a bloody cottage.'

Casey flicked through the brochure. The kitchen was country-perfect: a navy blue Aga, a row of copper saucepans. 'We'll go across the fields,' she said.

They had dressed for it, in walking boots and coats, safe from the chill. A bridle path ran along the shelter of a hedgerow, taking them a few hundred yards from the cottage.

Close up, Tilney Cottage was a big, tile-hung house, surrounded by yew hedges. It had the air of a house that had been rented out for too many years. Shabby, and not quite cared for, the swimming pool a leaf-filled hole.

Casey had checked with the agent. A nice couple had hired it for a month, and then it would be available for rent again. 'They're charming, the current tenants,' the girl had trilled. 'I'm sure I could show you around, say, this Friday?'

Clouds were gathering overhead now. In the gathering gloom, lights showed downstairs. 'Let's get a bit nearer,' Casey murmured.

They crept closer, to where the shape of the topiary was blurring slowly along the boundary of the garden.

Casey dropped to the ground, edging through the hedge. Twigs tore at her hair. Now she was just a few yards from the back of the house, flat against the ground. She could see two figures at a big kitchen table. Then she froze at a sudden movement by the window: a man jerking the curtains closed. She caught the taut cheekbones, the sharp eyes.

The man from the airport.

The curtains snapped shut.

Here.

61

Miranda and Casey sat in the car, staring across the rainswept fields.

'He was going to kill us, wasn't he?' Casey spoke quietly. 'If we had walked into that house with Poppy, he would have ...'

'And you didn't see Dominic and Emily?'

'No,' said Casey. 'But they could be upstairs somewhere if they're in the house. It's impossible to tell.'

Cellars below the kitchen, she had read in the particulars. *Attics.*

'Damn.' Miranda thumped the steering wheel.

'They must have worked it out when we checked out of the hotel in Chittagong,' said Casey. 'When the people they thought were Dominic and Emily disappeared at the same time as the raid on the ship ... It must all have been too suspicious. We were so stupid.' Casey slammed her fist into the dashboard. 'Naive.' Her worst criticism.

'Why is he here?' Miranda scrubbed her hand across her face. 'What does he want?'

'I don't know.'

'That man waiting at the airport, he could have been meaning to bring you back here too. We hadn't published anything then. I suppose they might have thought they could stop it all. But now …'

An elderly man squeezed past the car, tugging an old black cocker spaniel along in the pouring rain. He peered disapprovingly at the two women.

'We need to move,' said Casey.

'But where?' Miranda sounded almost despairing as she rattled the car keys. 'We have to call the police now … This is a kidnap, Casey. It's too serious for us. We need to get Dominic and Emily out of there right now.'

'If we call the police, whoever is behind Greystone will get away with it,' said Casey. 'The police won't know what to do with all this. Not in the timeframe. They'll catch the man down in Tilney Cottage, probably. Possibly. But then what? They won't have seen any of the evidence we saw in Bangladesh. They'll never catch up.'

'But we can't leave Emily and Dominic just trapped in that house,' said Miranda. 'Not like that. Not with him.'

There was a pause. 'We have to,' said Casey reluctantly. 'Poppy Naomi, that's what Emily said. She was trying to warn me that something had gone wrong. Naomi was the name of the surrogate who kept the Burton-Smith baby a few years ago. Emily would never have named this baby Naomi. She was warning me.'

They sat there in silence for a minute, car headlights flashing past hypnotically. Then Casey sat forward.

'Emily said, "Keep her safe." That's her priority. Not the police. Poppy is all that she wants.'

'It might be,' said Miranda. 'It's what you want to believe, Casey.'

'The police will cause chaos,' said Casey. 'The Burton-Smiths could lose Poppy for ever over this. You know that. They know that.'

'Maybe.'

'No one outside that gang knows the Burton-Smiths are involved yet. If we keep their secrets, they could just quietly re-register Poppy over here, and get on with their lives. Heather worked out a way they might do it. Poppy Lancaster just disappears for ever.'

'The police won't like it,' said Miranda. 'They'll want to know who the families are.'

'We'd never tell them.'

'That would be hard. They'd go for our computers, not that they'd find much.'

'We have to work out who Zeus is,' said Casey. 'Finding him is the only way of getting Dominic and Emily out safely.'

'How?' Miranda raised her palms to the sky. 'How are you going to find him?'

'I don't know,' said Casey. 'But we need to get back to the office.'

Shaking her head, Miranda put the car into gear.

'Portunus,' Casey was murmuring to herself as she dialled. 'Arachne. Aceso.' She swiped at her phone. 'Toby? I need a hand with something.'

Toby had worked with Casey and Miranda in the past. At the *Post*, he was a data journalist, in anarchic T-shirts and torn jeans. He was pale, his head almost shaved, and he rolled his eyes behind Ross's back a lot. In the office, he was a brilliant coder, a magician delving into a dark parallel world of pythons and rubies and perls. The *Post* averted its thoughts from what he got up to outside the office. Casey, occasionally, sidled up to him.

Now, she spoke fast. 'Toby, can you get a list of every company set up around the world in the last – say – five years, and cross-reference them against the names of all the Greek gods and goddesses? And any other mythical names.' She paused. 'Yes, all of them. Thousands, yes. I know it's a bit odd … But it might just throw something up … ASAP please. You're a star.'

Casey ended the call, and turned with a grin to Miranda. 'It might work,' she said again.

As she spoke, Casey was scrolling through her phone. 'Aristaeus,' she murmured. '"Minor god of cheese-making, bee-keeping, and other rustic skills." God, some of these are obscure. Asclepius … Atlas … Attis …'

The car raced along, the rain spattering against the windscreen as the miles rolled past.

Casey sat up sharply in her seat. 'Tartarus,' she read out. 'Both a deity and place in the Underworld. They had that bull logo – that's another Zeus symbol. Tartarus Energy, the company Bantham mentioned out in DC. They're another one.'

62

'Tomorrow,' Miranda said, as they pulled into the car park under the *Post*. 'You need to sleep, Casey.'

Casey stared at her in bewilderment. 'We can't sleep while Dominic and Emily are … And Poppy …'

'Just for a few hours,' said Miranda. 'You have to.'

'I've got a couple of calls to make.' Casey was edging towards the escalator. 'At the very least, I've got to give Emily a reason why we didn't turn up at Tilney Cottage. You go home.'

'Who are Tartarus Energy anyway?' Miranda called after her.

'Bantham mentioned them by mistake.' Casey turned back briefly. 'They own the rights to drill oil in a big chunk of central Africa. But there is a rival company that claims to hold the same rights as well, because they were awarded by an early government. A mess. The MPs were due to make quiet representations to their president on behalf of Tartarus.'

'Typical.'

'Go home, Miranda,' said Casey. 'I won't be long.'

As soon as she was at her desk, Casey pulled up the MPs' register of interests. It was a huge list, regularly updated, of all the people or companies who had funded parliamentarians' fact-finding trips or campaigns. It also showed some of the

MPs' own financial interests. In theory, an MP couldn't own 20 per cent of a company and then stand up in the Commons to make long speeches about its brilliant products. In theory, an MP couldn't be sent on a five-star junket to Antigua by a pharmaceutical company, and then vote for amendments that gave the company a huge tax break. In practice, loopholes had been found, time and time again.

Now, Casey read through the register carefully. She searched for the six MPs she had seen in Washington DC, hunting for the name of the company that had funded the trip.

'Chrysos Finance,' Casey read to herself a few minutes later. 'Someone's got a sense of humour, at least.'

She pulled up the threadbare information available for Chrysos Finance. Superficially, it was a small company offering wealth management for optimistic retirees. A basic website provided an address in the heart of the city, superimposed over glossy photographs of skyscrapers and smiling men grouped round a polished boardroom table. Just enough detail to avert the attention of a busy political correspondent. Deliberately mundane, thought Casey, and not even a phone number.

The Chrysos logo was a golden raindrop.

Zeus transformed into a shower of gold to seduce Danaë, Casey read in one of the books on Xavier's desk.

Googling, Casey found that forty-seven other companies operated from the same office at Chrysos. Casey looked up Chrysos's accountants. The same as Tartarus Energy. She sighed to herself.

Leaning back in her chair, she called Gabriel Bantham.

Bantham sounded furtive as he answered the phone.

'Have you heard anything more about Erica Whiddon?' he asked, rushing on before Casey could get out a word. 'I've decided to resign from the Foreign Office, I thought you should know. Time to do something else. I'll find something. The FCO has been in touch about ... Well. They're not thrilled. But they didn't threaten anything. And if I'm leaving anyway ... I don't know ... I hope ...'

'I haven't heard anything else about Erica.' Casey tried to sound reassuring. 'I will let you know as soon as I find out anything. But Gabriel, there's something else ... When those MPs came out to Washington, do you know who organised it all? I think the trip was funded by a company called Chrysos Finance. Can you remember if they were involved in the planning?'

'Chrysos,' Bantham said hesitatingly. 'I don't remember ...'

He paused, thinking. 'There was a blonde woman who travelled out with the MPs. She seemed to be organising them. Knew about hotels, pick-ups, that sort of thing.'

'What did she look like?'

'Elegant,' Bantham was definite. 'Blonde hair, smart suits. Good legs,' he excused the comment with a half-laugh. 'Well, you did ask.'

'None of them mentioned Chrysos at all?' she said. 'While they were out there?'

'I don't think so.' Casey could imagine Bantham furrowing his brow as he spoke. 'They were just enjoying the jaunt.'

'Did they end up meeting the African president?' asked Casey.

'They did,' Bantham said slowly. 'At the Washington Ballet. There was a cocktail party. Several of the MPs went.'

'Including Alicia Dalgleish?'

'Yes,' Bantham said confidently. 'She definitely went along. She told me how much she enjoyed the ballet.'

'And did the blonde woman go too?'

'Yes,' Bantham said. 'She seemed to be good friends with Alicia. Chummy.'

'Did you think' – Casey made the question sound casual – 'that the blonde woman might have had anything to do with Tartarus Energy?'

'Tartarus . . .' Bantham did the calculation fast. 'Christ. No. I don't think . . .'

'Tartarus was never mentioned?' asked Casey.

'No,' said Bantham. 'I don't . . .'

'How did the MPs come to be going to the Washington Ballet? Who organised it?'

'I can't remember,' Bantham said after a pause. 'It was the MPs themselves who had made those plans. It wasn't the embassy who sorted that visit . . .'

'Do you think that Alicia might have been involved in planning that meeting? Or this blonde woman?'

'She could well have been,' said Bantham. 'You think that Chrysos is linked to Tartarus?'

'It might be.'

'What does it mean, anyway? Chrysos?'

'Chrysos' – Casey felt her mouth stretch into a wry smile – 'is the spirit of gold.'

'So that would mean,' Bantham worked it out, 'that Chrysos funded the MPs' trip, so they could lobby for its sister company while they were in DC?'

'Something like that,' said Casey. 'Something like that.'

As she read Casey's messages about Bantham, Miranda was perching on the uncomfortable sofa in the sitting room. She had lit the wood-burner earlier, but the fire had petered out.

They never sat on the uncomfortable sofa, Tom and Miranda. Never just the two of them, companionable and cosy.

Miranda stared around the room, and for a moment, it glimmered with another life, a different life. A pile of toys in the corner: plastic, those bright primary colours. A toddler, pulling himself up to lean on the coffee table, on little sturdy legs. Herself, cooking, unseen in the kitchen, with the occasional irritable shout. Noise, warmth, colour: a different world superimposed.

She heard Tom's footsteps hurry up the garden path, the crunch of the key in the lock.

So familiar, unfamiliar.

He saw her as he walked in, nodding, still polite. The pile of toys evaporated, the child faded away.

'Tom ...'

He knew at once. She saw him try to keep his face steady, calm, but for once he couldn't hide the flood of hurt. The vulnerability made her heart twist, and she wanted to reach out, hold him, undo it all.

'You chose, then.'

You have to choose.

'I didn't want to, Tom. It didn't have to be a choice.'

'It did, Miranda.'

A pause, a nod. 'I know.'

For a moment, they reflected the same sadness: two mirrors, an infinity of sorrow.

'They tell you that all women …'

'Yes.'

The stage was struck. And Miranda saw it all so clearly. All at once, the bright backdrops of their lives were just paper, tattered, faded and torn. The props – the pretty tiles in a hallway, a sky-blue watering can and those lovely unseen blinds – neatly packed away. And the memories, which had been everything, would be wilfully abandoned. A forgotten memory, a forgotten life.

I tried.

Did you?

'Tom …' Her eyes filled with tears, a sudden burn in her throat. It seemed impossible that it could all be pulled apart by just a few words.

Anyone would.

Anyone wouldn't.

'What?'

'I'm sorry.'

'I know.'

63

When she had finished speaking to Bantham, Casey called Emily.

'Poppy's a bit ill, Emily. I want to take her for a quick check-up before I bring her down to you. I'm really sorry about the delay.'

'Why? What's wrong with her?' The terror was electric.

'There's nothing to worry about, Emily,' Casey said slowly, separating out each word. 'I just want to make sure that I am keeping little Poppy Naomi safe. I want to keep her safe.'

'All right.' The tension in Emily's voice dissipated slightly. 'Please do that. But hurry, Casey. I can't bear it much longer. Without her . . .'

'You could come up to London,' Casey suggested. 'Meet me at the hospital?'

There was a long pause. 'No,' said Emily wistfully. 'I'll wait for her here. But see you as soon as possible, Casey. Please. Keep her safe.'

After an awkward goodbye to Emily, Casey sat at her desk long into the night, researching Alicia Dalgleish. Alicia's face stared back at her, gazing confidently at the camera. Glowing skin, and dark blonde hair immaculately cut into a long, glossy bob with a sharp fringe. The bob was slightly longer at the front than the back, and looked like it was blow-dried everyday. Dark brown eyes glowed with a crisp intelligence. She was beautiful, Casey thought, without being pretty.

Alicia Dalgleish been in Parliament for seven years; one to watch before she was even elected at thirty-two. Two enchanting little girls and a good-looking husband. A doctor: brains and compassion, in a conveniently distinct field.

Two little girls, thought Casey. *Two little girls.*

She had ricocheted up the ranks in Parliament, making a below-average number of enemies. There were occasional rumours of ruthlessness all the same, but Casey was inclined to ignore those because those claims were made about most successful women. She wondered what the opposition had on Alicia. There was always something.

But she couldn't be Zeus, Casey thought. No busy MP could travel around the world running this operation.

Just in case, she might ask Archie to ring Alicia first thing tomorrow. The political editor could easily ask the chair of the Foreign Affairs select committee for a chat about Bangladesh without triggering suspicions. And then they could analyse every word of the conversation.

Meanwhile, Casey trawled around Alicia's known contacts, for anyone who might be the woman Bantham had seen in DC. There were no blonde women in Alicia's entourage. Her chief of staff was a man, grey-haired, nervous-looking. Her parliamentary secretary was Edith, efficient, with a dyed black crop. None of her known donors or supporters fitted the description.

Frustrated, Casey clawed through company documents for Tartarus, Aceso, Portunus; searching for shareholders. But they were all buried offshore, impermeable layers of paper between Casey and her goal.

She checked her phone.

Ed: *Don't get too tired.*

Ross: a long list of tasks.

And Miranda, baldly: *Tom's gone.*

Casey read the message again and again. She tapped her phone.

Are you all right?

No. Not yet. A pause. *I will be.* A long pause. *I had to choose.*

I'm so sorry.

A cough next to her desk, and Casey glanced up. Cory was standing next to her desk, shifting awkwardly from foot to foot. 'Casey,' the night editor smiled apologetically. 'Dash told me to physically throw you out of the building if you hadn't left by now.'

'It's all right.' Casey stretched to her feet. 'I'm off, Cory.'

64

Casey was back in the office as dawn was breaking, meandering sleepily between the empty desks, head full.

'Morning, Casey!' A bright chirp.

'Morning, Tillie.' Casey forced herself to focus, to joke. 'Anything more from Mrs Warman?'

'Oh God,' said Tillie. 'She rang yesterday morning. "Can I speak to Ross please?" she said, in a tone that made me physically drag Ross across the newsroom. When I got him to the phone, Mrs W had evidently passed the phone to one of their children. Ross was very brisk, "What did Mummy want you to tell me?" Pause. "Come on now, what did Mummy want you to tell me?" Another pause. "Oh, Christ, happy birthday!" Honestly, he is the worst.'

'Mrs Warman once brought in the kids to say goodnight to Ross,' said Casey. 'She lined them up beside the newsdesk. He's a disgrace.'

'I heard a rumour,' Tillie dropped her voice, 'that when Mrs Warman decided she wanted kids, and Ross was never home, she just drove to the office one day and ordered him down to the car park.'

'I don't think that' – Casey pulled a face – 'is a rumour.'

They were laughing together as Hessa walked in, the brittle insecurity showing on her face when she saw Casey talking to Tillie.

'Can you go to the Greystones' house in north London as soon as someone is in to cover the desk?' Casey said to Tillie.

'Of course!'

'It's OK, you know,' said Casey, as she and Hessa walked to the investigations room.

'What do you mean?'

'When Miranda arrived at the *Post*, I thought it might block me from doing investigations,' said Casey. 'It didn't, of course. Just made me better. You and Tillie might be a brilliant team one day.'

Hessa unlocked the room in silence. 'I suppose so. It's just . . .'

'You've worked so hard to get here. I know. It's OK,' said Casey. 'We know you're good.'

'OK.' Hessa's face broke into a smile. 'I will try.'

'Good.' Casey bent her head over her computer, pushed Ed out of her mind. 'Now get to work.'

Casey went to get more coffees from the machine. She was keeping an eye out for Miranda, and as she came through the entrance, crossed over to see her.

'Are you OK?'

'I'll be fine.' Miranda jerked her chin up, and Casey recognised the gesture. *Just let me get on with it.*

'We need to get Zeus's name out of Alicia Dalgleish,' Casey was saying as she passed a coffee to Hessa back in their office. 'It's the only way.'

'OK,' said Miranda. 'What else would we like to know?'

'Where Zeus is,' Hessa reeled off. 'How they know each other. What Zeus gets out of it. What Alicia gets out of it. Apart from all-expenses trips to DC, of course.'

Miranda sat down at her desk, and Casey saw her breathe in and out, and then focus.

'Dalgleish may not know,' Miranda said, 'the crisis she is walking into. She might just tell us everything to try and get her point of view across.'

'She'll know,' said Casey. 'She'd have to. It's just a case of how deep it all goes. If the Tartarus deal is a one-off thing, or if there's more.'

'She's tipped as the next party leader, you know,' said Miranda. 'And she's got a good chance.'

'Yes. Archie said that one of the big political consultancies was sounding things out for her,' agreed Casey. 'And doing some expensive polling.'

'She's got a lot to lose,' Hessa said thoughtfully.

'How can we do it?' Miranda was stirring her own coffee.

'We could email Alicia,' suggested Hessa. 'From an account that looks like a Tartarus account, asking her to come to a meeting this afternoon. And then follow Alicia from the House of Commons, and see where she goes.'

Casey chewed her nails. 'Not a bad idea,' she said. 'Although there are lots of exits from Parliament, so unless we waited in the corridor outside her office, it would be hard to follow her. And she might have something she really can't miss this afternoon, and just call Tartarus to change the meeting time.'

'Or,' Miranda added, 'if Zeus turns out to be based in the Bahamas, Alicia's going to be a bit surprised to be called in for a meeting this afternoon.'

Casey stabbed her notepad with her pen.

'How about the grandees on the board of Tartarus?' Miranda had read the notes. 'They might not be being paid enough to go down with the ship.'

'Lord Cornthwaite has Alzheimer's,' said Casey. 'I tried him this morning, but he doesn't seem to know anything about Tartarus at all. And as for Lord Matthews ...'

They all thought about it briefly. The year before, Lord Matthews had been caught out by one of the more ruthless tabloids with an eighteen-year-old dominatrix who certainly wasn't Lady Matthews. Previously chatty, he had refused to talk to a single journalist ever since.

'Well,' said Miranda, 'the simplest way is usually the best.'

'I know,' said Casey. 'I know. But we'll only get ...'

'Better than nothing.'

Casey pulled her phone towards her. She dialled the number for Alicia Dalgleish's parliamentary office, and when the secretary answered, Casey spoke in bored, upmarket tones.

'Ringing from Tartarus Energy. I've got a call for Ms Dalgleish. Urgent please.'

She was put through without a murmur.

The telephone purred for a second, and then the line was picked up.

'Clio.' It was Alicia Dalgleish's voice, clipped but friendly. 'How are you?'

And Casey cut the call.

65

'Clio Greystone.' Casey threw the phone back on her desk.

The same blonde hair Casey saw everywhere …

I've just remembered, I've got to run off …

'All along.' Miranda threw her notepad across the room.

'Damn it.' Casey thumped her hands down on the desk. 'The muse of history. How could we …'

Casey had grabbed her phone, was punching in a number. 'Tillie?'

Tillie interrupted her, voice high with excitement. 'He's just been arrested. Taken from the house … His lawyer was with him … He didn't say anything. What should I—'

'Tillie,' Casey interrupted her. 'Is there anyone else in the Hampstead house? Where are the wife and children?'

'I don't know.' Tillie sounded deflated. 'I can ask the guy from the *Mirror* …'

'OK. Thanks. Talk later.' Casey put down the phone. 'Arthur,' she called across the office.

The crime correspondent bounded over. 'Yup?'

'Can you find out whether Greystone's wife and children are at the Hampstead house? Discreetly? He's just been arrested.'

'Can ask.'

'Very subtly,' Casey repeated. 'Make it sound like we just want to buy up the wife's story, so we're trying to work out where she is, rather than anything else.'

'Sure.' Arthur was reaching for his phone as he turned away. He was a good crime correspondent, and had got drunk with almost every police officer in the country.

'We have to get to Clio.' Casey clenched her jaw. 'Not just to front her up, but to force her to release Emily and Dominic from Tilney Cottage.'

'We will,' said Miranda. 'We'll find her.'

But Arthur was back in the office in just a few minutes. 'There's no one else in the Hampstead house,' he said, palms lifted. 'The children are AWOL too. Off the record, the police wouldn't mind knowing where they all are.'

'Bugger,' said Miranda. 'How the hell are we going to find her?'

66

The day ticked on. Casey was bent over her notes, nose almost touching the paper. *Come on … Come on …* She sat bolt upright.

'I know what we can do.'

She had Hannah on the line within seconds. Hannah was the *Post*'s south-east Asia correspondent based in Bangkok, young and bright and still unjaded.

'Hannah,' she said. 'Can you write a quick piece about the Bangladeshi garment industry?'

'Course.' Hannah was chewing something. Probably dinner, in Thailand. 'D'you want any top line in particular? There'll be something to write about. There always is.'

'Doesn't matter,' said Casey. 'But I need it fast. Can you file it to me when you're done?'

'Sure,' Hannah sounded confused. 'I usually send stuff through to the Foreign desk though.'

'I've talked to them,' Casey lied. 'Just get the copy together, and then email it across.'

'No problem.' Hannah was always sunny. 'It'll be with you in an hour or so, OK?'

'Great.' Casey was already hurrying across to the Sport desk. It was a busy day, and all heads were down.

'Arne?' Casey pulled a chair up next to the Head of Sport, its wheels squealing.

'I am busy now, Casey.' The tall Norwegian pushed her chair away. 'Come back tomorrow.'

'Arne,' Casey said again. 'Please.'

'What is it?' He glanced up. 'Is it important?'

'Very.'

'All right.' Arne pushed away a fringe of dirty blond hair impatiently. 'What? You can have one minute, Casey.'

'Can I read through your tennis coverage? For tomorrow.'

'What?' Arne looked distracted. 'Why? For God's sake, Casey…'

'It won't take a second,' Casey said soothingly. Arne had occasional temper fits that awed even Ross. 'I'll go through the articles right now.'

Arne made a noise close to a growl, and a gesture that might have been consent. He stood up sharply, and disappeared in the direction of the back bench. Casey heard a roar.

'I'll send the articles over to you,' Arne's deputy said pacifically. 'There's only one clay court event going on at the moment and some Davis Cup stuff, so we're just doing a couple of stories and a nib.'

'Thanks,' Casey smiled at the deputy. 'Won't be a second.'

She bent her head over the screen, biting her thumbnail.

'The number three seed couldn't find any answer to the Argentine's aces,' Casey read to herself.

Reaching for the keyboard, she fiddled with the copy for a moment, standing up as Arne reappeared.

'Casey, we are really tight on time today,' he said.

'Sure,' she stepped away. 'One more thing. Can you not publish that article until I say so?'

'What?' Arne looked up at her. 'You're ridiculous, Casey. It's ready to go now. All the other papers are live on that story.'

'Give me a few minutes,' she begged. 'Please.'

'I don't have time for this,' Arne returned to his screen, and then snarled. 'Casey, you have put a spelling mistake in my copy!'

'Only a tiny one,' she soothed him. 'And it's really important, I promise you, Arne. I wouldn't ask . . .'

Arne growled again. 'If I get any grief from the bloody Editor, I am telling him you did it.'

'And I added one tiny sentence.' Casey fled across the newsroom. 'Promise me you won't take it out?'

The head of sport waved his fist at her. But she knew he would leave the copy as she asked.

Finally, Casey washed up next to the Business desk. 'Nicky?'

The business editor looked up. She was tough, Nicky, and fiercely glamorous. She flaunted her intelligence in the way another woman might twirl a dress. Casey couldn't imagine her with a chipped nail. Staunchly supportive of the women in the office, Nicky had fought several battles for Casey and Miranda in the past, as if loyalty were just another currency, along with the dollar or the yen or the lek.

'Yup?' Nicky had one eye on her list. 'James, I needed that piece on high street voids ten minutes ago.'

'Are you doing a story about shipping today? It doesn't have to be a big article. Smaller the better, really.'

'Shipping?' Nicky raised an eyebrow at Casey.

'It's important,' said Casey, although Nicky would already know that.

'Maybe.' Nicky peered down at her list. 'Yes, there's something about insurance in the mix. You know how' – a brief gleam of teeth – 'these old monster ships always conveniently limp out to the deepest point in the ocean before sinking like a stone. The insurers are getting a bit fed up.'

'Great,' said Casey. 'Could you insert a random list of shipping companies into that piece somewhere? And include the name Portunus Marine in it? And not publish until I say so?'

'Portunus Marine?' Nicky pursed her lips. 'Never heard of them. Should I have?'

'No,' said Casey. 'They're a minnow. But I want them in an article today.'

'You'll have to explain later.' Nicky turned away with a smile. 'And it had better be good. Craig gets very precious when we mess around with his copy.'

'It might be.' Casey spun away.

'What are you doing?' She almost collided with Dash. She knew he had been watching her patrols around the newsroom.

'I just need to talk to Toby.' Casey dodged round him. 'I'll explain in a moment.'

Toby was sitting near the data team, tapping at his laptop.

'Toby?' He looked up at her, although his eyes didn't really focus.

'Casey. Hi. I sent you that list of companies.'

'Thanks. But I need your help on something else.'

She explained what she needed quickly, Toby's attention sharpening.

'How long would it take you to build something like that?'

'Not long.' Toby's fingers were moving rapidly already. He looked up. 'It's probably illegal though. Data stuff.'

'Fine.'

'Give me a few minutes then.'

Casey hurried back towards Dash, spoke fast. Dash rolled his eyes, and nodded.

Casey reappeared beside Toby. 'He says get on with it.'

It took Toby a few hours to put together his system. The tennis article was published first.

'It's ugly, that sentence,' Arne protested. 'I don't like it. And we are hours behind everyone else.'

'It's fine,' Dash cut him off. 'Publish it.'

Then Hannah's story on trade union protests in Dhaka went live, Casey inserting a list of garment companies into the copy just before it was posted. A few minutes later, Nicky pressed the button on the shipping insurance story, sending it speeding around the world.

And then Casey and Toby sat by his desk, and its chaos of wires, waiting and watching and hoping.

67

Twenty minutes later, Toby looked up.

'Your toy's doing its thing.'

The *Post* published dozens of articles every day, and the data from each story ran into a sophisticated analytics tool. The tool calculated how many people read the article, how they located the article, and then how long they spent interacting with it. Ross glowered at the metrics all day, tweaking headlines and snarling when only a few bored commuters clicked through to an article about a lion escaping from the zoo.

The tool also showed where people were reading a story. An article about Montevideo might see a surge of interest from IP addresses in Uruguay. A story about bullfighting would light up in Madrid.

For the three articles just published, Toby had built an extra gadget that captured a list of IP addresses as they clicked onto the articles.

'That way,' Casey explained to Dash, 'we can see everyone who is interested in these precise three topics. Whoever it is might well be particularly vigilant about coverage if they are the sort of people who actively don't want publicity.'

'Bait over a trap,' said Dash. 'Electronically. But the IP addresses might not give you enough.'

The IP addresses – Internet Protocol addresses – could be linked back to a geographical area, but they might also mislead.

'If we can find one IP address that's interested in all three of these articles,' explained Casey, 'Toby will be able to make a pretty good guess at where that person is right now.'

'OK,' Dash shrugged. 'But how can you be sure the person will know the articles have been published?'

'Hopefully, they've got news alerts set up for their companies,' said Casey. 'And those alerts will be triggered by the *Post* publishing any reference to those companies.'

Dash read through the three articles. 'Arachne Incorporated. Portunus Marine. And what's the third?'

'I added one letter to "aces",' said Casey. 'And then started the next sentence, "Limited crowd enthusiasm ..."'

Dash winced. 'No wonder Arne wasn't thrilled. Aceso Limited,' Dash spelled it out. He laughed. 'Honestly, Casey.'

'It might work,' she protested. 'And we haven't got many options.'

'Don't you think you might just end up with a whole load of addresses that read everything on the *Post* website?' said Dash.

'Toby's analysing a few other *Post* articles,' said Casey. 'So we can eliminate the bots.'

'Might work.' Dash turned to her. 'And then what?'

'And then ...' Casey stared across the newsroom. 'Then I don't know.'

It was very late when Toby came into the investigations room. Hessa and Miranda were working. Casey was curled up on the tatty sofa, half-asleep. Emily and Dominic were prowling round her mind; Zohra screaming in the dark.

'I think I've found it,' Toby said, and Casey sat up abruptly, rubbing her eyes.

'Show me?' she asked.

Toby kneeled down on the floor beside her with his laptop.

'There are about twenty addresses that have read all three articles,' he said. 'Addresses that aren't routine *Post* readers or from some automated system.'

'And then you ...?'

'Cross-referenced the ownership against that list of companies named after Greek deities.'

'And?'

Toby turned the laptop towards her. A huge house filled the screen. Jacobean, Casey guessed. Rows of stone-mullioned windows gazed out over rolling parkland and an exquisite lake.

'Christ,' said Casey.

'That IP address has only ever visited the *Post* site a few times,' said Toby. 'But the moment the three different news alerts went out on those stories, that address clicked on.'

Hessa was behind Toby. 'It's called Tawton Court,' she said. 'It's down in the New Forest. Owned through a company called Hestia Limited.'

'Goddess of the hearth,' recited Casey. 'It would be. Any guesses about who really owns it?'

'Nothing in cuts,' said Hessa. 'Although the locals might know. They almost always do.'

'They won't welcome calls right now though.' Casey glanced up at the big clocks on the wall, showing the time in London, Sydney, Delhi, New York.

'We could ask Carlos?' Carlos ran the property pages for the *Post*. His children's godparents were all estate agents.

'I don't think the agents would be thrilled to hear from him at this time of night either.'

'Stay in this office,' Dash had ordered. 'Promise me, Casey?'

'Probably.' With her fingers crossed, and they both knew it.

Casey was calculating rapidly, thoughts whirling. 'Hessa,' she said. 'What do we know about Clio now?'

Clio, muse of history.

There was a brief rustle of papers. 'Clio's mother comes from one of the Greek shipping families,' said Hessa gingerly. 'The Mantzaris family.'

'Bugger,' said Miranda. 'How the hell did we miss that when we were checking Greystone?'

The Mantzaris family had the same stratospheric wealth as the Alexakis dynasty. Houses all around the world, and careless millions splashed for fun.

'There's very little available on Clio. Slightly more on her parents. Clio's mother married the Hon Rupert Eyre.' Hessa sounded apologetic. 'So when we did a check, Clio showed up as growing up in the Home Counties, the daughter of Rupert and Helena Eyre. It all looked quite ordinary.'

There was a brief silence.

'Never mind,' said Casey. 'The Mantzaris connection explains how Clio knew about the shipping industry, and shipbreaking.'

'Yes,' agreed Hessa.

'And the Eyres had money either way?' asked Miranda.

'Some,' said Hessa. 'I mean, a lot by almost any standards. A nice house in Wiltshire. Mansion flat in London. Clio went to all the right schools, and I found a snap of the mother in *Tatler*.'

'But not by Mantzaris standards?'

'Exactly,' said Hessa. 'The mother was the youngest of four, and the only daughter.'

'And the Greeks believe in keeping their fortunes intact,' Miranda thought aloud. 'A bit of the cash would have splashed out to Clio's mother, but they don't like to dilute things too much. The women were expected to marry well, anyway.'

'So Clio grew up within touching distance of unimaginable wealth,' Miranda said slowly. 'But not quite there.'

'Well.' Casey peered at the photographs of Tawton Court. 'She's certainly made up for it since.'

'Rupert Eyre was a sort of man-about-town. Good-looking when he was younger, if you like that sort of thing.' Hessa's voice made it clear that she didn't. 'But probably spent money rather than made it. He wrote poetry,' she finished darkly.

'What are you thinking?' Miranda was behind Hessa and Toby, stretching languidly.

Casey met her eye. 'That it's probably worth a visit.'

Her phone rang.

68

It was Emily, voice twisted tight. 'Casey?'

'Emily!' Casey struggled for the words for a second. 'You … Where are you?'

'I'm in a hotel near Guildford.' Emily sounded as if every word was a struggle. 'Dominic and I decided to come here for the night. There was a flood at the cottage – all the electrics blew …'

Casey listened to the careful lie, the truth a guess.

'It was just easier than staying at Tilney, and we thought …'

'Are you all right?' Casey spoke calmly, slicing through the babble. She wished they had organised a duress code, a distress signal. Too late, too late. 'Is everything OK?'

'I'm fine.' There was an irritation in Emily's voice. 'But I am desperate to see Poppy. Right now. If she's ill, I'll drive up to London. I'll …'

Casey thought of Tawton Court, sixty miles beyond Guildford.

'I'll come to you,' she said hastily. 'I can bring Poppy Naomi.'

'I have to see Poppy,' Emily said again. 'We're in the Easton Hotel. Please come now.'

Emily spelled out the name of the hotel, gabbled the room number.

'I'll be there as soon as I can.'

'I need to see her.'

'I know.'

Miranda was by Casey's side as she ended the call. 'Emily and Dominic have somehow got out of Tilney Cottage,' said Casey. 'They're at a hotel near Guildford.'

'And you've said we'll go?' said Miranda.

'Yes. But Emily's made up some odd excuse for leaving the cottage. I don't know what is going on.'

'How did she sound?'

'Stressed. But she's been stressed for weeks. She didn't respond to Naomi, but I don't know if she even picked up on it.'

They sat there for a moment, contemplating the risks.

'We can't take the baby,' Miranda said eventually.

'No,' said Hessa quietly.

'But Emily's frantic to see her,' said Casey. 'She'll lose it if we don't take Poppy. She sounds on the brink.'

'It's too dangerous,' Miranda objected. 'You have no idea what is going on there. Look at the airport, and Tilney Cottage. This could be the third attempt to trap you.'

'Emily offered to come to London,' said Casey. 'It didn't sound like she was trying to manoeuvre us to the hotel. She's warned us before, and I didn't get a signal this time. And there will be other people in the hotel. It's not in the middle of nowhere, like the house. We can ask at reception if they're alone. We can—'

'Not the baby.' Miranda was firm. 'We just can't.'

'Fine,' Casey threw up her hands. 'But we need to go now.'

'OK,' Miranda conceded. 'We'll go.'

69

Miranda drove through the night. 'Try and sleep, Casey. You're exhausted.'

'So are you.'

Casey couldn't sleep. She stayed awake, all the way down the motorway towards Hampshire, blinded by the necklace of lights blurring back into the capital. She leaned back on her headrest, and thought of nothing much. She half-listened to the radio, some woman talking about rivers, poisoned from the source, and the Rio Tinto in Spain, which runs blood-red, so acidic that almost nothing can survive, trickling through the mountains like a leaking venom.

Wriggling in her seat, Casey tugged fretfully at her top. One of her favourites, soft grey. *Made in Bangladesh*, she had noticed as she put it on this morning. Sorrow here, joy there. The usual pattern. The morning seemed days away.

Now Casey watched the moon, floating far above the motorway. *Not long, Emily. I promise.* And her mind twisted and turned as she thought about what she would find at the Easton Hotel.

The gravel crunched as they turned into the hotel drive. It was a rambling Victorian building, with an ugly newbuild wing tacked on to the left. The concrete and the rows of identical windows clashed awkwardly with the bay casements and random turrets of the old building. The place looked shabby, unloved, a long way from the expensive gloss of Dominic and Emily's home.

Miranda strolled into the 24-hour reception, manned by a sleepy teenager.

'Hello.' Miranda gave a glowing smile. 'We've got a room booked. Twin beds. Thank you so much.'

Miranda stood on the faded lino, adding almost as an afterthought, 'Can I just check if our friends have arrived? The Burton-Smiths. Room 209.'

The receptionist broke off from her tapping for a second, squinted at her screen.

'They've checked in,' she said perfunctorily.

'Did they arrive with anyone else?' Miranda pushed. 'They said they might be bringing some friends.'

The teenager glanced up. 'Don't think so,' she mumbled. 'I saw Mrs Burton-Smith arriving. Nice lady. Didn't see anyone with her.'

Casey felt her body relax, very slightly.

The receptionist handed them a key, nodded towards a lift. She was fiddling with her phone before the lift creaked closed.

They hurried to the twin room Hessa had booked just a few minutes earlier. The carpet was worn, the twin beds half-covered in red nylon throws. The matching cushions were rubbed shiny, and plastic curtains dangled tiredly. The TV was slightly skewed on the wall.

'I'll go and talk to them,' said Casey.

'On your own?'

They like me, Casey didn't say. *You threatened them.*

'It means you can call the cavalry if something happens,' she said firmly.

They walked past the room once though, the briefest of recces. Room 209 was at the end of a corridor in the newbuild section, separated from the main stairs by a fire door, wire in the glass.

'I don't like it,' said Miranda. But the corridor was silent, still.

'We don't have time to wait,' said Casey. 'I have to speak to them now.'

70

Casey knocked quietly on the door. The door banged open, and Emily stood there, shivering with nerves. She took in Casey with a glance, and her panic boiled over.

'Where is she?' It was almost a scream. 'Where the hell is Poppy? What's happened to her?'

'I left her in London.' Casey tried to peer around the room.

'Why?' For a second, Casey thought Emily might attack her. 'Why would you do that?'

'I didn't know what was going on,' Casey said gently. 'I was concerned, Emily.'

The room looked empty. There was a leather holdall thrown on the bed, and a thin plywood wardrobe, with its doors slightly ajar. A cheap mirror was fixed to the wall, and the door to the bathroom was half open. No one else there, and Casey felt the adrenalin tick down.

Emily made a despairing gesture. Moving calmly, Casey closed the room door. Emily was glued to the floor, her arms falling to her sides.

'Where is Dominic?' Casey asked.

'He had to drive back to Tilney Cottage' – the words rattled out of Emily. 'We'd forgotten Poppy's cot, and we needed it ...'

She sank onto the bed, tears bursting to the surface. 'And now you haven't even brought her.'

'I didn't know what was happening.' Casey made her voice soothing. 'We came to Tilney Cottage and we saw …'

She stood awkwardly next to the bed, waiting for Emily to stop crying.

Emily looked up sharply.

'This is all your fault.' Rage burned from Emily's delicate features. 'All of it. You took our passports, you blackmailed us. You told us we would never see our baby.'

'I'm sorry,' said Casey. 'I really am. It was never meant to be …'

'You blackmailed us,' Emily shouted again. 'Dominic warned me, and I didn't listen. It was blackmail.'

'I know,' said Casey. 'But we can fix this.'

'You bloody journalists think you can do whatever you want. You just walk into people's lives and ruin them. How can you live with yourself? How can you do this?'

'It's not …'

'I believed Dr Greystone when he told me we were helping people.' Emily's voice rose higher. 'He's a respectable doctor. And then you … You …'

'I am sorry,' Casey repeated. 'But you have to tell me what is going on, Emily. Why is Dominic back at Tilney Cottage?'

Emily swallowed. 'I told you.'

'No,' said Casey. 'We don't have any more time for lies, Emily. What is happening at the cottage?'

Emily stared at her.

'I can help you,' said Casey. 'But I have to know what is going on.'

Casey waited, staring at the scuffed magnolia walls. At last, Emily stood up. She walked to the bathroom, splashed water on her face. Then she came to the bathroom door, calmer now.

'A man came to the house.' Emily swallowed. 'He broke in while we were asleep. When we woke up he was in our bedroom, his torch in our faces. It was terrifying. Completely and utterly terrifying. You don't understand … You couldn't. And now he's at the house with Dominic, while I … He said I could leave the cottage. I could go and get the baby. But Dominic had to stay, so I had to do whatever they told me. Dominic …'

'What does he want?' asked Casey. 'Who is he working for?'

'I don't know.' Emily sagged. She was wearing a black top, buttoned to the neck, and old jeans. She looked exhausted, bruised. Casey felt a twist of pity, almost protective.

'Did you get his name?'

'No.' A quiet syllable. 'Why couldn't you just leave us alone? Why did it have to be us?'

'I think I might know who is behind it all,' said Casey carefully. 'We think we have an address.'

Emily glanced up, eyes dull. 'I don't know,' she said. 'I don't know anything at all.'

'Look,' said Casey. 'You're safe. Go to London. Go straight to the *Post* offices. I'll tell my colleague Hessa that you're coming in. We will get Poppy to you as soon as possible, I promise.'

For a second, they stared at each other.

'It'll be OK,' said Casey, trying to smile at her.

'But … Dominic …'

'I'm going to get him out,' said Casey. 'I've got to hurry, Emily. I'll give you the address of the *Post*. I am sorry. But I promise it will all be OK.'

Casey turned, made for the door, and she didn't even know if she was lying.

71

It was still dark when Casey and Miranda reached the grand old forest where the poachers once hid, the shadowy ponies blinking blind in the headlights.

As they made their way down winding lanes, Casey was staring at satellite images of Tawton Court. It was huge. From her bird's-eye view, she could see a swimming pool and a lake, a tennis court and green swathes of lawn. In the middle of formal gardens, a maze had been etched out of yew. Casey traced it with her finger. To the south of the Court lay the home farm, and what looked like stables. Beyond the farm, a long strip of grass had been carved out of the woodland.

'Hestia Limited bought this house five years ago,' Casey said. 'Clio's fortunes must go back further than the recent projects.'

They parked the car in a layby, a quarter of a mile from Tawton's pillared gates. A pretty little gatehouse sat in darkness, the gates lying open.

'Come on,' whispered Casey.

A long drive wound its way towards the house, meandering through parkland. The grass was studded by ancient oaks, ghost sentries. To the east, the dawn was a grey splinter in the night, the house an inky bulk in the distance.

Quietly, they crept along the grass verge. Two hundred yards from the house, Casey stopped and peered upwards. The rows of stone-mullioned windows were dark. In front of the house, the drive opened up into a sweep of gravel punctuated by a tall marble sundial. Banks of rhododendrons circled the house, with a haha beyond. Casey and Miranda huddled among the plants.

'Do you think we just knock at the front door?' There was almost a laugh in Miranda's whisper.

'We don't have time to wait,' Casey muttered.

The sky was lightening now, the birds beginning to sing.

'There could be any number of guards,' whispered Miranda. 'There could be . . .'

'I know,' said Casey. 'But we have to. Stay here.'

'No, Casey.' Miranda's whisper was urgent. 'It's deliberately putting yourself in danger.'

'How else are we going to find out? How else do we get Dominic out?'

Casey stepped onto the gravel, the scrunch deafening in her ears. A step, a step, and another. She felt the fear ripple up her spine, and clutch around her skull. Now she was almost at the sundial, idle in the night. Daring the trap to spring. Wanting it, almost.

Come on. *Come on.*

Another step.

All at once, the floodlights blazed on, ripping the night into day. Casey was caught in the brilliance, a lamped rabbit.

The huge oak door swung open, and a figure stood there, the hall lit up behind her, a rifle in her hands.

'Hello,' said a woman's voice. 'Hello, Casey Benedict.'

72

'Run,' someone had told her once. 'Move faster than they expect. At twenty feet, you're an easy target. At forty – dodging about, sprinting – you're harder. Most people won't land that shot.'

But this woman was holding the gun with an easy confidence, the barrel aiming straight at Casey.

'I will shoot,' the woman said, and Casey believed her.

The woman walked forward, down the wide steps. A few paces away from the sundial, she stopped.

'Go into the house.' An order. 'Walk slowly.'

There was nothing else to do.

'All right.'

Casey began to move towards the building. The woman watched her, the rifle moving smoothly with Casey.

As she passed the woman, Casey glanced across. *That golden shimmer . . .*

'Keep going.' A voice like ice.

Casey walked up the wide limestone steps, through the oak door, into the brightness of the hall.

'On your left.'

The hall was baronial, a grand staircase sweeping away, and a vast carved fireplace dominating the space. A deer's head stared blankly above. Two huge bloodhounds sprawled beneath. As Casey crossed the hall, one of them looked up, yawning and stretching.

At the threshold of the drawing room, Casey hesitated.

'Do sit down,' behind her, the woman said mockingly.

Casey sat down on a huge white sofa. Straightening her shoulders, she looked at the woman.

'Good evening, Mrs Greystone.'

The woman smiled. 'Welcome to Tawton Court.'

They contemplated each other for a moment. A fire burned in the hearth, sending shadows dancing round the room.

'Phone,' said Clio, and as Casey handed it over, 'are you recording this?'

'No,' said Casey. Clio's eyes raked her. She stood, picked up Casey's satchel and slung it on the fire. Casey's eyes followed it, and then hardened on Clio.

'They know I am here,' said Casey. 'The *Post* knows.'

'Maybe,' Clio Greystone said thoughtfully. She folded herself into a white armchair.

Clio looked the same, and yet she was almost unrecognisable. The superficial glamour had been stripped away, along with the pretty dress, the studded boots, the Balenciaga bag. Clio wore a simple dark top and black cropped trousers. This woman enjoyed dropping the camouflage, Casey thought. She revelled in the act first, and then smirked in the mirror as she stripped off the layers.

The gun pointed squarely at Casey.

'I know what you've done,' said Casey.

'I should have guessed,' Clio almost smiled, 'when I found myself reading an article about a tennis match, of all things.

It was clever, that. Arachne and Aceso and Portunus. And I suppose you'll find the rest, in the end.'

A nice little trophy, Casey thought, raging inside. She stayed silent.

'But then you triggered an alarm as soon as you stepped on the drive,' said Clio. 'I imagine you expected something like that.'

Open gilded gates.

'Maybe.' Casey waited. 'You need to let Dominic Burton-Smith go, Clio. My colleagues will call the police. Please.'

'You have been busy.' Clio ignored her. 'Blackmailing William Cavendish. Running off to Dhaka. Searching that ship. You've been very persistent, Casey.'

A closed terrarium sat on the table beside Casey. Casey gazed at it now, at the cut glass, the moss, the delicate ferns. An elegantly perfect ecosystem, in its own discrete world.

'It wasn't blackmail,' Casey said.

'Maybe.'

'So why did you do it all, Clio?' Casey tried.

'You really are,' Clio sighed, 'most inconvenient.'

Casey turned back towards Clio. The gun was a jolt in this flawless room, sharp-cut black and ugly. Shadows flickered across Clio's face.

'I'll make you an offer,' Clio said into the silence.

'I'm not interested. When did you guess?' Casey asked, not wanting to know the answer. 'About me, back in Hampstead.'

'You walked past the house twice,' Clio said. 'I thought I would see what you wanted.'

And then you led me right to him, thought Casey. Abandoned your husband without a backwards glance. A pawn sacrifice, all ready.

'What do you want?' said Casey.

'I want to make you an offer,' Clio said. 'To forget all about me.'

Casey's head jolted up. 'But you can't. There's nothing I want from you. There's nothing you can give me.'

'Are you sure?' Clio stretched, cat-like. 'How about, say, this house? And a few million pounds? Everyone wants something.'

'No,' said Casey, and it was easy. 'You can't escape this, Clio. Even if you kill me, they'll know what you did. And they will get you in the end.'

Casey thought about Miranda, hiding outside, flat to the ground in the dark.

'You'll never see your children again either,' Casey went on, the oldest of threats, although she didn't know if it would work.

'My children left the country hours ago.' The ice was back in Clio's voice. Then she lightened again: 'You must have expected that, Casey. And you won't be able to stop me, if I decide to leave.'

A runway carved out of the forest, thought Casey. So close to the south coast of England. Clio had her escape route planned all along.

Clio was gazing up at the chandelier. 'But you make deals, Casey. Or so I gather.'

Casey was watching Clio's face, and knew she had expected the first offer to be rejected. There was a bottle of champagne beside Clio, cork popped, half a glass poured. Casey wondered if Clio had opened it as she waited for the enemy at the gate.

'Sometimes,' said Casey. 'Not now. Not for something like this.'

'Always, I think. Because even in that grim old house in Guildford, the Burton-Smiths still thought they would get their baby back, nice and safe. Go and live a happy little life in their pretty Surrey house. They really believed it, you know. They trusted you, Casey.'

Casey stared at Clio, across the beautiful room. Clio waited.

'I believe that you're a brutal sort of pragmatist, Casey.'

'The Burton-Smiths are sources,' Casey said automatically. 'And the *Post* always protect its sources.'

'That is a fig leaf,' Clio mocked her. 'And you know it.'

'We have to protect our sources.' Robotic.

'If they'll play your game to your rules, you'll protect them? It's no better than a protection racket, Casey. Secrets for silence. While you promise the world it's the precise opposite.'

Casey was watching the flames. Out in the hall, one of the bloodhounds yawned in a long whine.

'You buy stories,' Clio sneered. 'Just to bury them.'

'Some maybe. Not us.'

Clio stood up, walked over to the fireplace. She peered at herself in the mirror, smiling at her own reflection.

'That girl out in Bangladesh,' said Clio. 'On the ship. She died, Casey. Died for Emily and Dominic's fantasy. But you'll protect them all the same.' Clio paused, fiddling with a tiny ornament. 'You knew that already, didn't you, Casey? That the girl died.'

Casey clenched her jaw. 'Zohra. Her name was Zohra. And, yes, I knew that.'

'You'll cover it up.' Clio separated out each word.

'I'll tell her story.'

They stared at each other in the mirror.

'The parasite that kills its host,' Clio said thoughtfully. 'Such a grim thought. Wasn't it Charles Darwin who said he couldn't believe in religion because no god would design a parasitic wasp that ate its host from inside?'

'And no god could have put Zohra on that ship.'

'Something like that. We're all part of it,' Clio said, almost to herself. 'You know that perfectly well, Casey. And at least, this system made a few people very happy. And they're doing it for a child, not a cheap top.'

'It ruined lives.'

'So.' Clio's voice changed as she turned away from the mirror. 'You always protect your sources.' She paused. 'And you always keep your promises, Casey?'

'I try to.'

The sky was slowly brightening to grey outside. 'Well,' Clio went on, almost mocking. 'In any case, maybe I can be a source?'

Clio was watching Casey's face intently.

'You must be mad,' Casey said, without thinking. 'You? No. Never.'

But even as she spoke, she felt the curiosity spark.

'You don't know what I'm offering yet.'

'Tell me then.'

Clio almost smiled. 'Not without your promise.'

Casey stared across the room, the headlines flickering.

'No.' Casey forced the word out.

Clio sighed.

'I can't.' Casey was shaking her head, feeling the tug like a magnet.

'Are you quite sure?' Clio's voice was low.

'You're not my source,' said Casey more firmly. 'I won't protect you.'

'Fine,' Clio shrugged, as if she were bored. 'Then I'll tell my friend that we don't need Dominic Burton-Smith any more.'

Picking up her phone, Clio was watching Casey for her reaction. Casey tried to keep her face steady.

Emily, shivering in the wind . . .

Promising each other again and again that this time it would be all right . . .

Casey kept her face expressionless.

'You'd let him die?' Clio said wonderingly. 'Really, Casey? You'd protect his reputation, but not his life?'

'What do you gain by killing him?' said Casey.

'Fine,' Clio murmured. 'Have it your way.'

She threw herself back into the armchair and reached for a laptop, typing in a long password. A hidden projector whirred into operation, beaming a huge image onto the wall. It was Dominic and Emily, Casey realised, side by side. They were in a kitchen. Tilney Cottage: Casey recognised the blue Aga.

'The thing is,' said Clio thoughtfully, 'that it's always a matter of perspective.'

She pushed a button, and Dominic began to move.

'They came out of nowhere,' he was saying, his voice oddly deep. 'We had no idea what to do. They threatened us. We were completely terrified. They told us we would never see our baby ever again.'

Casey felt her stomach twist, her throat tighten.

There was a pause. 'Emily?' a voice asked.

Emily swallowed. 'Dr Greystone told me that we would be helping women in Bangladesh. He's a proper doctor. We had no idea . . . We didn't know . . .'

Her voice trailed into tears, a delicate shape hiding her face against her husband. Emily's shoulders shook.

'Live by the sword,' murmured Clio.

'They blackmailed us,' Dominic gritted his teeth on screen. 'We had no choice. They were absolutely ruthless. They stole our passports, they impersonated us. It was blackmail, all of it. The reporters from the *Post* blackmailed us.'

Casey felt a surge of fear.

Clio stilled the picture with a click. 'They go on for quite a long time in that vein,' she said. 'These are serious allegations, Casey. Against both you and Miranda Darcey.'

'They're acting under duress.' Casey forced the words out. 'You've kidnapped them, and of course they're saying whatever you want them to say.'

Kidnap, blackmail; the invisible threat was all. The murder of the soul: just words.

'Your problem is' – Clio gestured at the screen – 'that if you go to the police, they will have to stick to this truth to keep their baby. And they will, Casey. Dominic will happily destroy you to bring that child home.'

'That's not why . . .' Casey's voice faded away.

'Not why you did it?' Clio asked smoothly.

'No one will believe anything the Burton-Smiths say under those conditions.'

'Really?'

'No. And Emily wouldn't . . .'

'Emily?' Clio smiled. 'Emily wouldn't what?'

Clio clicked another button, her eyes never leaving Casey's face. Casey felt her stomach turn.

The kitchen at Tilney Cottage disappeared, a new image flashed up on the wall. And Casey glanced up, and heard herself choke.

73

It was Casey herself, standing in a shabby hotel room. The plywood wardrobe, the scuffed magnolia walls, the mirror on the wall. The Easton Hotel. Clio pressed play, and the words echoed round the room.

You took our passports, you blackmailed us. You told us we would never see our baby.

I'm sorry. I really am. It was never meant to be ...

You blackmailed us ... It was blackmail.

I know.

I know. The words were spikes in Casey's mind.

I know. I know. *I know.*

Trapped in the pixels, by her own truth. *In her own words.* Casey's palms were wet, and she felt the shiver in her spine. It was as if there were hundreds of eyes in the room all at once.

Blackmail. Up to fourteen years in prison. *Fourteen.*

'I thought I'd send this to Jessica Miller at the *Argus*.' Clio turned back to the screen. 'Or just publish it on the internet.'

No escape. Followed everywhere, for ever.

Casey felt herself begin to shake.

'You say it yourself, Casey.'

'It's edited,' Casey managed.

'Only slightly,' Clio shrugged. 'Not enough to help you.'

'You can't.'

'I can.'

Casey felt the futility of it all sweeping over her like a wave. Nowhere to hide. Scrabbling against the sides, no foothold, no hope. *This is how it must feel.* The runaway train, unstoppable. The blaze of the searchlight, blinding.

For a split second, she thought of Emily, going to the bathroom to splash water on her face. She'd got the shot by then, could relax very slightly. Still wired up like a suicide bomber, but she had done it. Casey wondered if Emily had felt that moment of quiet triumph. Got it. Got *you*.

I liked you; I thought you liked me.

Emily, in her black top, carefully buttoned to the neck. One button, just a tiny bit different. Turning to face Casey, just as the camera required. Probably another camera in that leather bag, so casual on the bed. Another in the open wardrobe. As many angles as possible, every time, just in case. Emily must have sent the footage as soon as Casey walked out of the hotel. Almost impressive, that speed, that ruthlessness.

'I think we've reached a stalemate,' Clio said calmly. 'Walk away, Casey.'

Casey was staring at the screen, back to Dominic and Emily frozen in their kitchen prison.

'No,' she said very quietly.

'They say you should fight fire with fire,' said Clio. 'But I think I prefer mirrors. And you don't like this one.'

Mirrors reflect the soul, she'd read once.

No. They only reflect the mask.

'You've ruined my husband,' Clio went on, 'but no one wins if you don't drop this right now.'

'No,' Casey said again. She thought of all those approaches, time and time again. *The straw hat ripped away, the half-smile frozen.*

Clio stood up from her armchair, impatient, the gun slotting smoothly into position.

'You're running out of time, Casey,' said Clio, almost sympathetic. 'You're out of cards to play.'

'No,' said Casey. She stared up at Clio, and into the black heart of the gun. And as she looked up, Tawton Court plunged into darkness.

74

Casey reacted faster. She threw herself over the back of the sofa, diving for cover. The gun fired, and the terrarium exploded by her ear, shards of glass ripping through the air. She scrambled frantically for the door, bullets blasting into the wall inches from her head.

Somehow Casey made it to the door. A frantic scrabble at the handle, and she was racing across the hall to the oak door and out into the air. Down the stairs she bolted, and across the gravel. In the slow dawn, the gardens spread out before her, the acres of Tawton's park beyond. In the far distance was the deep safety of the New Forest. There was no sign of Miranda.

Casey didn't hesitate. She raced across the lawn, past the darkness of the rhododendrons, leaped down the haha and sprinted across the park.

There was silence behind her. Casey was running faster than she ever had, making for the cover of the woods. The grass seemed to sprawl out for ever, but finally, finally, she reached the shadow of the woodland.

Casey slammed into the first oak, using the tree to swing round and check whether Clio was following.

The parkland was empty, the silence eerie.

Gasping, she scanned the house, the gardens, the park. Nothing.

She turned. Trying to remember the map, she sprinted off through the trees.

It was very dark in the forest, the grey of the morning only just piercing the gloom. Casey slipped on last year's beech leaves, and struggled over fallen branches. Legs burning, lungs heaving, she ran and ran, blundering into animal burrows, hair catching on twigs. It felt as if the wood was trying to grasp her. Grab her, trap her, keep her for ever. Witch brambles tangled her feet, and she almost screamed at the scuttle of some animal.

Behind her, the silence was almost unbearable.

Clio would never let her escape. Never.

Casey scrambled on and on. Surely there should be a road here? Surely ... But there was nothing. The wood seemed endless, with its spiking enemy branches. And slowly, so slowly, Casey realised she was lost.

She ran on, desperate now. Glanced over her shoulder one more time. The ground dipped away sharply beneath her feet, and she sprawled forward, slamming hard into the dirt.

And there, slumped on the earth, she heard it: far in the distance, the sorrowful bay of the bloodhounds.

Clio was riding the big horse with careless ease, cantering smoothly.

Casey ran, the whole world blurring as every fibre of her being fought to get away. She raced down a slope, feet slapping the ground with the burning panic of a hunted animal. Branches ripped at her clothes, and the dark closed in.

The snarls and whimpers of the hounds were drawing nearer. She could sense their excitement as they raced effortlessly across the ground. This was their element, they were born to hunt, and Casey felt the exhaustion claw at her limbs. She thumped into the ground again, her fingers tearing at the earth. Scrambled to her feet, sprinting off again.

Never give up.

Casey imagined the teeth ripping into her. Struggling desperately, as the dogs ripped at her throat, her stomach. Animals, gutting her. It was primitive, this terror, shuddering across her skin, burning in her throat.

The hounds were so close now, wailing their frenzy.

Making the kill.

She would be torn to pieces, left for dead.

The gun fired, wood splintering as the bullet hit an oak just ahead of Casey. She screamed with all the breath she had left.

'Stop now!' Clio was close. Casey could hear the pounding of the horse's feet just behind her. 'Stop or the dogs will take you down.'

Still, Casey ran. The gun fired again, and Casey felt the hot burn as the bullet seared past.

'The third time, I will be aiming for you,' Clio shouted.

And Casey was falling, crashing to the ground.

75

She sensed rather than heard Clio call off the dogs, shouting at them urgently, and shoving them away. Then she was lying there, sprawled among the dead leaves, staring up to the grey of the sky.

'Get up,' said Clio.

Still holding the gun, Clio pulled out a pair of handcuffs from a rucksack.

'Put them on.' She nodded briskly at Casey. 'Don't mess about. I'll check.'

There was nothing else to do. Casey clicked on the cuffs, one at a time. Clio reached across, tugging briefly at the handcuffs.

'Good,' she said.

From her bag, Clio produced a long chain, clipping one end to her saddle and the other to the handcuffs.

'Now,' said Clio, 'we go.'

She vaulted back onto her big black thoroughbred, and rode forwards. The chain jerked at Casey's hands, and she was hauled into a walk.

'Don't fall behind,' Clio spoke over her shoulder. 'I won't stop.'

It was surreal, walking through the peaceful beauty of the forest, a prisoner. Casey watched Clio's back, straight in the saddle. The two hounds were exploring the woods now, quite playful. Casey could hear them crashing through the damp scrub of the bracken, giving chase to a squirrel. Clio's horse broke into a jog, dragging Casey forward.

'Wait,' Casey pleaded. 'I can't …'

Clio glanced back, tugging slightly on a rein.

'Hurry up.' There was no softness in her voice now.

Casey scrambled forward again.

They walked on, Casey's legs heavy with tiredness.

Where is Miranda? Where is she?

Try. Keep trying.

'This isn't going to work, Clio,' Casey shouted abruptly. 'You can destroy me, but that won't be enough.'

Clio looked back, with a smile. 'Maybe.'

'You won't get away,' Casey said.

Clio glanced back at Casey. 'No?' she raised an eyebrow. 'I'm the one who won't get away?'

'It doesn't matter what you do to me,' said Casey. 'They'll get you.'

'We'll see.'

Clio kicked the horse, urging it into a trot. Casey was hauled along, fish on a line, battling to keep up as her wrists bruised on the cuffs.

'Let me go,' she screamed.

The horse trotted faster, yanking Casey along. Any moment, she would slip and fall, and be dragged helpless over the rocks and the branches.

'Please,' Casey heard herself beg. 'Please don't do this.'

'Take my deal, Casey.'

Casey struggled through the leaves. 'I can't.'

They had reached the edge of the woods now. Casey stared around and realised that they were on the edge of the airstrip. The narrow strip of grass – clipped short and rolled – disappeared into the distance. To the left, Casey could see the collection of buildings that made up the home farm, and a few hundred yards away a small plane.

'Last chance,' said Clio. 'Last chance, Casey.'

'No,' Casey said.

Clio glanced around at Casey, her mouth a thin line, and kicked her horse hard.

The horse half-reared and leapt forward. For a split second, Casey saw the chain whip through the air, before the jolt hit her, almost yanking her shoulders out of their sockets. Casey was torn through the air, crashing face-first down onto the grass.

The horse galloped along the runway, whiplashing Casey in its wake. Casey screamed as a blazing pain flashed down her arms. She tried to roll onto her side, in a hopeless effort to save her face, her teeth, her eyes. The world skidded past, a blur of grass and sky. She couldn't breathe, couldn't see, couldn't think. The pain swallowed her. She hit a clump of grass, bounced in the air, slammed back down.

'Stop,' screamed Casey. 'Please stop.'

'Will you?' shouted Clio.

Casey couldn't answer, was battling to stay alive.

'Will you?' The witch's scream.

'No,' Casey gasped.

Clio jerked the horse, pulling him to a halt.

Casey lay on the ground, her arms contorted, her clothes torn. Her limbs were covered with cuts and bruises, and blood poured from her forehead.

Clio shrugged. 'At least I waited until we reached the grass.'

Almost meditatively, Clio slid off the horse, unclipping the chain from the saddle. Casey was gasping for breath, trying to move her arms.

'So you won't do it,' Clio said, almost to herself.

There was a long pause.

'No,' Casey muttered. 'No, I won't.'

'But why not?' There was frustration in Clio's voice. 'How do you decide, Casey? You? What gives you the right to make these decisions?' She jerked at the chain.

'I don't know,' Casey whispered, almost to herself.

Clio stared at her a long time.

'Fine,' she said. 'Stand up.'

The gun centred on Casey's forehead. Casey moved her arms, legs, somehow nothing was broken. Wearily, she dragged herself to her knees, then foot by foot, she stood.

'Come on.' Clio jerked the chain, sending a spasm of pain down Casey's arms.

Slowly, they started walking towards the plane.

76

Just as they reached the little plane, there came a roar from the farm buildings behind them. Clio's head whipped round.

Exhausted, Casey peered over her shoulder.

In the far distance, a huge tractor was rolling out of one of the farm buildings.

'What ...' Clio's voice died away.

'Miranda,' Casey whispered. Relief flooded through her. Miranda, still here. Fighting for their survival.

'Who?' Clio spun round to Casey.

The tractor was dragging a huge steel trailer behind it, almost thirty feet long and twenty feet high. As Casey watched, the tractor ground its way down the side of the airstrip, crunching through gears.

'Hurry.' Clio yanked Casey towards the plane.

The plane was a little Cirrus, Casey registered, almost unconsciously. Able to fly five people hundreds of miles without refuelling. There was no way of knowing where Clio might go in this plane.

The morning mist was burning off now, the sun breaking through in patches. Behind her, Casey heard the blare of the huge engine. Halfway down the strip of grass, the tractor was turning, labouring across the runway. As Casey glanced back, it came to a juddering halt, bisecting the airstrip.

'Fuck it.' Clio's eyes were wide. 'What is he doing?'

'She,' said Casey flatly. 'And she's stopping you from getting away.'

Panic flickered in Clio's eyes. 'What do you mean?'

'Miranda will have sabotaged every other way of escaping,' said Casey, almost singsong, as if she were reciting a poem. 'I wondered where she was, all this time. But she'll have made sure that there is no escape for you, Clio.'

Clio was vibrating with alarm, eyes stretched wide. 'Fucking bitch,' she exploded. She spun round and pointed the gun at Casey. 'Get on that fucking plane,' she spat.

'You'll never make it, Clio,' Casey pulled back against the chain. 'You've only got half a runway to take off. Maybe a thousand feet. Less. It's impossible. Even if you try, every pound will matter if you're going to get over that trailer. Take me, and you'll definitely crash.'

Clio stared up the runway. She was shaking, Casey saw.

A tiny figure jumped out of the tractor, and stood gazing in their direction.

Clio made a gesture of wild frustration, almost clawing at the air.

'Give up, Clio.' There was no emotion in Casey's voice. Her shoulders sagged, the blood trickling down her wrists.

'I can still shoot you before I go.' Clio swung round. 'You fucking ... journalist.'

She turned on Casey like a lioness. The adrenalin flooded back, the pain in Casey's arms disappearing.

'Please.' Casey's eyes were on the gun. 'Don't do this.'

'Take the bargain,' Clio screamed, all control gone. 'I'll give you everything. I can't …'

'No.' Casey gritted her teeth. 'Never.'

Abruptly, Clio threw down the chain. She ran towards the Cirrus, clambering aboard.

'Don't do this,' Casey shouted after her. 'Please. You'll never make it. This plane can't take off down that short a runway.'

Clio's eyes blazed. 'Get away from me, you bitch. Get away or I'll kill you for the fucking sake of it.'

The engines roared, slicing through Casey's words. Clio was throwing anything heavy out of the little plane, lightening the load as much as possible. As Casey watched, Clio hurled her own rucksack away.

'Please don't,' Casey screamed.

Clio turned the little plane in a tight circle. Casey could just make her out in the cockpit, leaning forward, urging on the little plane as it if were her black thoroughbred. She taxied the plane as far down the runway as possible, until the wings almost scraped the trees as it turned. The engines were screaming now, the noise deafening Casey as she scrambled to the side of the runway. The horse galloped away into the forest, tail bannering in the sun.

'Please …' Casey shouted.

But the little plane was moving forward now. Slow at first, and then accelerating as fast as possible, racing over the grass, into the morning sun.

Clio almost made it. The landing gear clipped the huge trailer, and the Cirrus plunged like a swift shot from the skies. The nose of the plane dived into the ground with astonishing violence, burying itself in the grass as the Cirrus cartwheeled, all its speed gone in a shattering whirl and a final stomach-turning crunch.

'Clio,' Casey muttered.

She found that she was running up the field, snatching up the chain and sprinting towards the stillness of the plane, the handcuffs jolting her wrists.

As she ran, Miranda appeared, almost a surprise. She had dived to the side of the airstrip as the Cirrus raced towards the trailer.

'My God, Casey,' and Casey knew her face was bad from Miranda's horror. 'What did she do to you?'

There wasn't time to stop, wasn't time to explain. Casey dashed on, racing to the splintered wreckage.

Clio was dying, Casey could see that at once. 'Call an ambulance,' she screamed to Miranda.

'But—'

'Call one,' Casey shouted. 'Right now.'

The cockpit had ended up on its side, quite separate from the airplane's wings. The windscreen was smashed away, and Clio was suspended by her harness, the blood pouring from her head. Below her waist, the plane had crushed her, the heavy machinery crumpled like paper.

'Clio.' Casey scrambled towards her. 'Clio.'

For a second, Clio smiled up at her, her teeth red with blood.

'Hello, Miss Benedict.'

'Stay still, Clio. Help is coming, I promise.'

Clio was looking round the cockpit, eyes vacant. With an immense effort, her eyes found Casey's face again.

'I should have surrendered.' Clio tried to focus on Casey. 'But we never give up, do we?'

'Clio ...'

'I'm dying, aren't I?' Clio tried to smile, almost matter-of-fact.

'An ambulance is coming,' Casey whispered. 'Hold on. It's coming.'

Casey tore at the shreds of her jersey, trying to make it into a pad for Clio's head, the handcuffs impeding every movement.

'It'll be here in just a second, Clio. Just hang on.'

But Clio's eyes were looking past her, and it was as if the whole field were filled with old friends.

'To life,' she whispered.

And Clio died then, her face tipped up to the sky, the light going out of her eyes.

77

'Come away, Casey.' Miranda was tugging at her arm, pulling her away from the ruins of the airplane. 'You can't help her any more.'

Slowly, Casey let Miranda lead her away, tears spilling from her eyes.

'We have to go.' As Miranda spoke Casey tried to concentrate on her words. 'We have to get out of here, Casey.'

'But' – Casey was hazy, eyes wavering around the field – 'I can't . . .'

'We have to get back to Dominic Burton-Smith,' Miranda said evenly. 'The ambulance is coming. The police won't be far behind. And the air-accidents people, too. We can't stay here.'

But Casey was staring at Miranda, her eyes haunted. 'How did we end up here, Miranda? How?'

Miranda looked at her. 'What do you mean?'

'All this.' Casey gestured. 'Sir William Cavendish, Gabriel Bantham, the Burton-Smiths. This whole trail of destruction . . .'

'You know why we did it,' Miranda said carefully. 'To stop Greystone. To stop Clio.'

'But . . .' Casey's head hurt. 'All this . . .'

'The end justifies the means,' said Miranda briskly. 'You know that.'

'But does it?' said Casey. 'Always? We go from life to life, hurling grenades. And then we just walk away.'

'It's our job to walk away,' Miranda said, and Casey stared at her.

'But how?'

Miranda put her hand on Casey's arm. 'Come on. We can talk later. We need to go . . .'

'What gives us the right?' Casey heard Clio's echo.

'What gives anyone the right?' said Miranda.

The birds were singing in the trees, louder now.

'There's a video back at the house,' said Casey. 'The Burton-Smiths accusing us both of blackmail. You and me. And Emily filmed me. In the hotel.'

Miranda hesitated. 'The police may never find it,' she said. 'And even if they do, the only way to fight blackmail is to be bold. Face the threat. Then it loses all its power.'

'Maybe. Not always.'

'We have to go,' Miranda said again.

'But we can't just go.' Casey pulled away. 'We can't leave her . . .'

She stepped away, stood staring at the wreckage.

'We'll wait for the first emergency services,' said Miranda. 'But we have to get to Dominic, Casey.'

Casey ignored her.

'Casey?' Miranda's voice sounded like it was coming from a long way away. Now there was a siren, far in the distance.

'Casey,' Miranda said, more urgently. At last Casey shook herself.

'All right,' Casey stood up straight. 'All right.'

'What did she do to you?' Miranda was staring at her. 'I saw you talking in her sitting room. I saw you smiling ... I thought if I knocked out the lights, you'd be able to get away. And then you ran out of the house, and she didn't follow you, so I thought you were safe, and I went to take out the cars ...'

'She had a gun, Miranda.' Casey almost laughed, on the edge of hysteria. 'A gun.'

Energy was flowing back through Casey's veins now. She forced herself to think clearly, staring at the destroyed cockpit. Shrugging, Miranda turned away from her, walking close to the wreckage, peering at it thoughtfully.

Casey blundered towards the rucksack Clio had thrown away at the last minute. Dropping to her knees, she searched it.

Her own phone. A key that unlocked the handcuffs. A gun. Casey stood, rubbing her red raw wrists. She stared down at the rucksack.

A safe distance from the debris, a helicopter landed with a busy clatter, the paramedics running towards the mangled plane. But they stood back after a few seconds, nothing to be done.

'I'm going to take my friend home,' Miranda said loudly, as the medics glanced towards them. 'She had an accident with a horse, and she's in shock. She needs to lie down.'

Miranda walked Casey down the road, to where they had parked the car. Only a few hours ago, but it felt like a different life. The sky was bright now. Two little girls trotted past on ponies, red jumpers bright against the woods.

They climbed into the car. 'Right,' said Miranda. 'Do you need a doctor?'

'Later.'

'OK. Tilney Cottage.'

Miranda braked to a halt beside the cricket pitch. The pub landlord was watering his gaudy hanging baskets in the weak sunlight. It seemed impossible that the Burton-Smiths had been just a few hundred yards away, imprisoned in their pretty cottage.

Casey moved to open the car door.

'No,' said Miranda. 'You've done enough.'

'But . . .'

'And he might have been briefed about you,' said Miranda. 'He won't know who I am, not exactly.'

In her black trousers and black top, Miranda could be an undercover police officer, a Jehovah's Witness, a hostage negotiator. Or a journalist.

'Plus,' said Miranda, 'you look terrible.'

Casey touched the cut above her eye. 'I know.'

'Call the police if anything goes wrong,' Miranda said briefly, and Casey thought of the long list of disasters those few words might mean.

'I will.'

Casey followed Miranda, all the same. Creeping up Tilney Cottage's long potholed drive, and ducking behind the sprawling laurels. The black Porsche Cayenne stood in front of the house, sleek and menacing.

Casey held her breath as Miranda – shoulders square, moving purposefully – marched towards the house.

The man came to the door. Casey watched as Miranda absorbed his initial rage, and then addressed him fluently, assuredly.

Casey looked away as Miranda went for her phone. Scrolling through the photographs, one by one. Showing him. She knew what they would be. Clio. Trapped in the wreckage, broken, desperate.

And dying.

This is what we did to a kidnapper. Look. See.

She saw the man's body language shift, his eyes go to the Porsche.

Your freedom for his, a cruel sort of trade.

But as Miranda stepped back, the man's chin lifted. Faster than Casey could see, his hand whipped to his side.

And a gun, black and lethal, pointed straight at Miranda.

78

Miranda put her hands up. She was still talking smoothly, not giving away her fear. She was trying to convince him, Casey could see, her hands making hushing gestures even as she held them up.

But he was angry, blazingly furious. He stepped out of the house, the gun still pointed at Miranda as she backed away.

'Shut the fuck up,' he was shouting at Miranda. 'Don't you fucking move.'

Before she knew what she was doing, Casey was moving quietly across the drive.

Miranda's eyes never flickered towards her, and in her hand Casey held Clio's gun. She had grabbed it from the abandoned rucksack back at the airstrip, ramming it into her pocket almost without thinking.

On the Apollo, all those years ago, clowning around with the Marines. Paper humans, and bullets splashing into the sea.

The grip was smooth beneath her fingers, almost seductive, and now she was just a few feet away.

'Get the fuck out of here,' Casey said quietly.

He froze, then started to turn, but Casey snarled. 'Don't you fucking dare. I've got a gun, and I will fucking kill you.'

The man made to turn again, and Casey fired the gun, just the tiniest shift of her finger, almost nothing. The bullet grazed his shoulder, blasting through the yew hedge. The man winced, just slightly.

'Next time,' said Casey, 'it'll be your head.'

He stood there for a moment, the crows cawing into the sky, agitated by the gunshot.

'Clio's dead,' said Casey. 'It's over, and I'm giving you a chance to get away.'

Another beat. And then – haltingly, sullenly – the man began to lower his hands.

'Put down the gun,' said Casey. 'And walk towards the car, very slowly.'

Casey saw Miranda stand back as the man crouched down, placing the gun on the ground.

'Don't look at me,' said Casey. 'Get in that car and get the fuck out of here.'

Casey held Clio's gun as the Porsche engine roared, sending the crows shrieking into the air again. And then Casey and Miranda watched together as the car stormed off up the drive, turning onto the road with a furious jerk.

'Thank you.' Miranda turned to Casey with a twisted smile. 'Thank you very much indeed.'

79

By the time Casey had limped to the house, Miranda was unlocking a door in the kitchen.

'Where is she?' Dominic exploded out of the cellar. 'I heard a gun. Where is Emily? Where is Poppy?'

'We'll take you to them,' said Miranda. 'Both of them.'

'But where the hell are they?'

'Poppy is in London,' said Casey. 'Emily's on her way up there now. We'll drive you up straight away.'

She fought away the memory of Dominic speaking to the camera, his arm around Emily's shoulder. *The end justifies the means . . .*

'Are they all right?' Dominic's voice was hoarse. 'Has anything happened to them? Who is looking after Poppy?'

'We hired a nanny.' Casey tried to sound soothing. 'The best. Poppy is being very well cared for, Dominic.'

'I didn't know what was happening. I've got to . . . I've got to . . . Oh God.' He put his hands to his face.

He'd been beaten badly, Casey could see. One eye swollen closed, blood in his hairline. *Not friends, no.*

'You could have got us killed,' he spat at Casey, as he looked at her. 'You stupid, unthinking . . .'

'I am sorry,' Casey said, knowing it could never be enough, knowing he would have let her die. 'We came here as fast as we could.'

'We were trapped in that fucking cellar,' he shouted at her. 'For days. My wife … We thought we were going to die.'

'I know. And I am very sorry …'

Dominic slumped into a kitchen chair. He looked grey under the bruising.

'We're just fucking collateral damage, aren't we? Emily and I. For your stupid fucking story … We couldn't get out. I thought he was going to kill us both …'

'It's a bit' – Miranda's words sliced across the room – 'like Zohra, out in Bangladesh. The woman who gave birth to your baby. Except she was held for months and months, before dying in agony.'

'Is this what this was to you?' Dominic was on his feet again. 'Some sort of revenge?'

'No.' Casey stepped between them. 'Of course not. We came as soon as we could, Dominic. And we are very sorry about what has happened to you and Emily. It must have been terrible. But it's over now. And Poppy is safe. You're all safe.'

They stood there, in the cosy kitchen, stunned to silence.

They're very nice, the current tenants.

'What's been going on?' Dominic asked tiredly. 'While we were in the cellar. Have they been caught? What happened to your face?'

Casey told him as briefly as she could, watching his face harden at Clio's death.

'Good,' he spat.

'So you see,' Casey finished, 'we have to get up to London now. We have to hurry.'

'Yes,' he nodded. 'I do see.'

80

There was electricity in the air as Casey and Miranda walked into the office.

'You're here at last.' Dash surged across the room.

Dash's words blurred as Casey listened.

Rob's finished the backgrounder. Graphics working on the maps. The lawyers aren't happy, but then they never bloody are.

'What happened to Clio Greystone?' Dash ended, his voice dropping a notch. 'There's a story on the wires. Light airplane crashed in the New Forest. The pack are assuming she was trying to get out of the country, away from the media scrum after her husband's arrest.'

'We fronted her up, she crashed her plane,' said Miranda.

'That it?'

'Yes. I was driving a tractor. It was a bit complicated.'

Dash's eyes flickered over Casey's face.

'Fine. The police have been in touch, though. They'll have to interview you.'

'OK.'

For a second, Casey felt shaky. She sat down on the sofa, forcing the walls to stop spinning. Dash watched her, almost pityingly, and then he stood up, and walked back towards the newsdesk.

Casey and Miranda sat on the sofa for a moment, side by side.

Cressida paused beside them for a second. 'I've seen that video. Think we're probably losing the Rhapso ad spend.'

'Sorry,' Casey sighed.

'Worth it,' Cressida flicked her hair, moved on.

'You did it.' said Miranda.

'Only just.' Casey breathed a sigh. 'Because of you. Thank you. I don't know what would have happened if you hadn't showed up when you did.'

'Any time,' Miranda said cheerfully, the bounce irrepressible. 'And we've still got to get Alicia Dalgleish.'

'We will,' said Casey. 'Somehow.'

'I know.' Miranda smiled widely. 'Coffee?'

'Please.'

Casey watched Miranda stride off across the office, then she walked back towards Dash.

'The Burton-Smiths are next door, in the hotel. I need to take them to Poppy.'

'Oh.' Dash hesitated for only a second. 'Of course.'

Janice, the editor's secretary, had booked a second room at the London Grand, a cosy little cocoon for Pippa Lancaster to become Poppy Burton-Smith.

A couple of floors up, the nanny's mouth pursed as Casey picked up her tiny charge.

Thank you so much for your time, Nina, sorry we needed you longer than we thought, I hope it wasn't too much of an inconvenience.

Casey left Miss Reynolds packing her clothes in tissue paper. Very carefully, she carried the little baby down the corridors of the London Grand, past the heavy golden mirrors. There was a gurgle and a small hand waving, a sweet baby smell and a memory that wasn't quite real.

She was so tiny. It was quite impossible to imagine this small bundle as a whole human being. *Is this all that we fight for?*

As Casey walked, thoughts flickered through her mind.

Romida, and a dress of red roses.

Zohra, screaming in the dark.

Clio, teeth red with blood.

The lift, all gilt, slid open. In the lift, a woman in a neat business suit smiled longingly at the tiny baby. 'Isn't she a darling?'

You never know how you can run, until you run for your daughter.

Like a dream, Casey was at the door to the hotel room. She didn't have to knock. The door was torn open, and Emily erupted into the corridor.

Later, they sat in the hotel room, Casey perched awkwardly on the edge of the bed. On a sofa by the window, Emily's head was bent over Poppy. Dominic was beside them, and for a moment, they looked photogenic, perfect, despite Dominic's bruises. *Come as a couple, leave as a family.*

Emily looked up at Casey, meeting her eye squarely. She looked older. Tougher. She'd lost weight since those spring days in Bath. Barely eating, Casey thought. Barely sleeping. There was a new determination in her eyes.

'You saw the footage?' There was no embarrassment.

'Yes,' said Casey unemotionally.

‘I managed to warn you the first time. But then …’

‘I know.’

‘I had to do it.’

‘I know. I can hardly blame you. It’s what I …’ Casey’s voice trailed off. ‘You do what you have to do.’

Emily nodded, shifting Poppy’s weight. Her face darkened. ‘They’ll investigate Clio now,’ she said. ‘The police might find that footage, and then …’

Casey shrugged, exhaustion settling like snow. ‘They might. They may not even look. If they do look, they may not be able to get past Clio’s passwords.’

‘But …’

‘Go and look after Poppy,’ said Casey. ‘If something happens, we will work it out.’

Emily looked down at Poppy, her finger tracing a cheek, a tiny nose.

‘Dominic told me about Zohra,’ said Emily. ‘I’ll always think about her.’

Her voice was light, blithe.

They sat there in silence. Casey remembered Emily, standing in the cold breeze of Kensington Gardens, clutching the photograph of a young, smiling girl. *Zohra*. Zohra, beside the kindly stern poster, of a nurse with a needle.

The photograph that let Emily believe it was all a kindness; or was it a photograph that let her pretend it was all a kindness?

We always expected the men to fight, Casey realised suddenly. And now …

‘You got your story,’ said Emily, after a minute.

'Yes.'

Casey stood stiffly, shards of pain everywhere.

'I must go,' she said.

'You don't understand, do you?' Emily said.

'No,' Casey said flatly. 'I don't.'

'But you do.' Emily's voice was calm. 'You – of all people – know what it is like to want something beyond all reason. So that you'll risk jail. You'll risk lives. You'll risk everything. You know exactly what that feels like, you just want something different.'

'I don't—' Casey stopped, the room filling with silence.

For a second, Emily smiled up at her, that easy charm surfacing again. All at once, she was the beautiful girl, strolling arm in arm with her husband.

The perfect family.

'Goodbye, Casey,' she said. 'Goodbye.'

81

Outside the hotel, the storm was breaking. The wind chased paper cups down the street with a hollow rattle, and commuters scuttled for cover. There was thunder in the air.

You have to choose.

The sky darkened. Casey stood in the growl of the traffic.

You have to choose.

A taxi clattered down the street, breaking the spell. *Go.* Casey ran forward, arms windmilling. The taxi veered towards her and she was gone.

'Where to, love?'

Casey's mind whirled, and there was only one thought.

I always climb hills in a thunderstorm …

'Primrose Hill,' she said instinctively.

'Course.' The taxi spun on a sixpence.

He won't be there, Casey insisted to herself. *He won't, he won't, he won't.*

The storm roared. By the time she was paying the driver, the excitement was twirling round her. Face slick with rain, she couldn't make out the top of the hill, the cast-iron lamp posts gargoyles in the gloom. *You have to try.* And Casey raced up the hill.

She made for the benches, up where *Liv loves Charlie*, so that it almost made her laugh aloud. And then she caught her breath. There was a figure, sitting, staring out over the city.

'Ed,' she shouted, her voice cracking. 'Ed.'

The man turned. She could make out the silhouette of his shoulders against the darkened sky, the angle of his head. *Him.*

'Ed!' she called again.

Now he was moving towards her, hurrying down the path.

'Ed.' The shock hit her, and she skidded to a halt.

He hesitated. 'Are you all right? What are you doing here, Casey?'

She couldn't breathe, lungs heaving, almost turned away and ran. 'I just ... What you said up here ... You made me promise not to ask you again ...'

He almost laughed, his face creasing in the ugly glow of the storm. 'You haven't come up here to ask me to come on the next story?'

'No.' Almost a shout. 'But I don't want to choose.'

'I don't understand.'

'I don't want to choose ...'

He moved nearer. 'What do you mean, Casey?'

'I've been stupid.' Casey pushed her hair back. 'I've been stupid, and thoughtless, and careless.'

'Casey ...' For a second, the sun gleamed through a break in the clouds.

'But I just realised,' said Casey. 'I realised that if I never asked you ... Never told you ... You might not know.'

So no one can say ...

'Know what?'

She looked up. He was smiling at her now, and there was an expression she hadn't seen in his eyes before.

'Casey, you're an idiot.'

'I know.' She couldn't look at him suddenly, stared down at her shoes. 'I promised I would choose, and walk away. That I wouldn't ask you . . .'

He stepped towards her, almost clumsily.

'I see who you are, you know,' he said. 'I know who you are. For all that you hide it, and fake it, and pretend, I know who you are. You don't have to choose.'

He kissed her then, pulling her to him. The storm was passing, the sky beginning to lighten.

'We'll find a way,' he whispered. 'There will be a way.'

'I know,' Casey said. 'And we will.'

ACKNOWLEDGEMENTS

As a child, when I was feeling blue, my mother used to say, 'Why don't you make a list of your friends? And then ask yourself, "Would that group of people be friends with someone who wasn't quite nice?"'

I had forgotten about that until I came to write these acknowledgements, but there is something rather lovely about writing down a list of friends, and thinking how lucky I am to have you all in my life.

Once again, a huge thank you to Collette Lyons and Paul Vlitos. I am sorry that I have stayed on your floor so often that you have been reduced to building the Holly Watt Memorial Loft Extension, but I am sure other people will enjoy it too. I can't wait for Ellery Lloyd to take over the world.

Amelia Hill, David Pegg, Alice Ross – thank you for reading *The Dead Line* almost before I had finished it. Encouragement and advice at just the right time!

Felicity Fitzgerald, Alex Marrache, Laura Roberts, Rosie Lough, Jasmine Miller, Harry Wardill, Clara Barby, Jessica Sheehan, Toby Darbyshire, Justine Moxham, Robert Winnett and Claire Newell – you're all just great.

Thank you Richard Fitzgerald for advising me on crashing planes, and Presiley Baxendale for just being wonderful. Thank you Vidiya Khan for having me to stay – and answering every question about Bangladesh. Thank you Sarah Mahmud for being Sarah Mahmud – and also translating bits of Swiss German.

Francesca Hornak and Kate Kingsley – the Authors' Support Group keeps me going at times! To the VHS – Eve Williams, Linda

Zell, Rosie Tomkins, Laura Hamm and Antonia WIlliams – it's been a journey…

None of this would have happened without my wonderful agent, Andrew Gordon at David Higham. Team Raven at Bloomsbury literally changed my life. Thank you to the Queen of the Ravens, Alison Hennessey – and Lilidh Kendrick, Philippa Cotton, Amy Donegan, Sara Helen Binney and Glen Holmes.

Thank you also to Val McDermid for picking *To The Lions* for the New Blood panel at Harrogate. It made a huge difference.

My family – especially Cressy and James and Nicky and Simon – have been rock stars.

And, darling Jonny, thank you for everything, especially our little peach pip Izzie.

NOTE ON THE AUTHOR

Holly Watt is an award-winning investigative journalist who worked at the *Sunday Times*, the *Daily Telegraph* and the *Guardian*. Her first novel, *To The Lions*, won the CWA Ian Fleming Steel Dagger. *The Dead Line* is her second novel.

NOTE ON THE TYPE

The text of this book is set in Minion, a digital typeface designed by Robert Slimbach in 1990 for Adobe Systems. The name comes from the traditional naming system for type sizes, in which minion is between nonpareil and brevier. It is inspired by late Renaissance-era type.